SONG OF SLUMS

It's 1846, in the middle of the Age of Steam. As well as locomotives and factories, there are steam-powered airships and strange velocipedes, all drowning in an endless sea of smog. King George IV is on the throne, the wealthy factory-owners are itching to seize power, and vicious bands of ex-soldiers can't wait to start another world war.

In this period, young women are supposed to be ladylike, and 17-year-old Astor expects a life of quiet luxury after she marries the handsome magnate Lorrain Swale. Instead, she finds herself abandoned in the Swale household and treated with contempt by the whole family.

Help arrives in the form of the enigmatic Verrol. Together they escape and plunge into the murky slums of Brumming-ham, where they fall in with Granny's Gang. Granny Rouse has a vision of a new kind of music taking the world by storm, and enlists them in her band, the Rowdies.

Suddenly it's all coming true . . . the irresistible gang-music rhythm is catching on, and fame is at their fingertips. However, the Swale family hasn't finished with them yet. Arriving in London Town for their greatest-ever performance, the Rowdies get caught up in a diabolical plot to overthrow the government.

Astor has come to a turning-point in history that is also a turning-point in her own life.

Also by Richard Harland

Steampunk novels, the 'Juggernaut' duology:
Worldshaker
Liberator

The 'Heaven and Earth' fantasy trilogy:
Ferren and the Angel
Ferren and the White Doctor
Ferren and the Invasion of Heaven

The 'Eddon and Vail' SF series:
The Dark Edge
Taken By Force
Hidden From View

Other fantasies:
Sassycat: the Night of the Dead
The Wolf Kingdom quartet

Richard Harland

SONG OF THE SLUMS

ALLEN&UNWIN

SYDNEY • MELBOURNE • AUCKLAND • LONDON

First published in 2013

Copyright © Richard Harland, 2013

All rights reserved. No part of this book may be reproduced or transmitted in any form or by any means, electronic or mechanical, including photocopying, recording or by any information storage and retrieval system, without prior permission in writing from the publisher. The Australian Copyright Act 1968 (the Act) allows a maximum of one chapter or ten per cent of this book, whichever is the greater, to be photocopied by any educational institution for its educational purposes provided that the educational institution (or body that administers it) has given a remuneration notice to Copyright Agency Limited (CAL) under the Act.

Allen & Unwin
83 Alexander Street
Crows Nest NSW 2065
Australia
Phone: (61 2) 8425 0100
Email: info@allenandunwin.com
Web: www.allenandunwin.com

A Cataloguing-in-Publication entry is available from the National Library of Australia
www.trove.nla.gov.au

ISBN 978 1 74331 005 2

Teachers' notes available from www.allenandunwin.com
Richard's website is at www.richardharland.net

Cover design by Cathy Larsen
Cover photo of laneway by Pippa Wischer
Cover photo of characters by Tim deNeefe
Text design by Cathy Larsen
Set in 10/15 pt ITC New Baskerville by Midland Typesetters, Australia

Printed in Australia by McPherson's Printing Group

1 3 5 7 9 10 8 6 4 2

MIX
Paper from
responsible sources
FSC® C001695
www.fsc.org

The paper in this book is FSC® certified.
FSC® promotes environmentally responsible,
socially beneficial and economically viable
management of the world's forests.

To Terry and Chris
in memory of great times making music

PROLOGUE

<hr />

'Come on down!' called Verrol. There was an urgency in his voice that Astor hadn't heard before.

She joined the musicians down below, but when the young buzz guitarist offered her his instrument, she shook her head.

'I can't play that.'

'Like a harp,' said Verrol.

How could he be so absurd? 'It's nothing like a harp.'

He lowered his voice. 'I thought you could play all sorts of instruments.'

'Proper instruments. That thing doesn't even have the right number of strings.'

'Drums, then.' He turned and announced it to the gang. 'She plays the drums.'

The drummer was a spiky-haired boy of about ten wearing a green-striped jumper full of holes. He handed over his drumsticks, just springy metal rods with leather-bound tips.

'I can't do this,' she whispered to Verrol. 'They're not even proper drumsticks.'

'You can. You have to.' His handsome features were drawn and taut.

Astor took her seat on the upturned box, and stared at the kegs, cans and pots before her. It was impossible. She had

1

never played percussion in her life. But clearly Verrol thought this was their only chance to join the gang.

Verrol conferred with the other musicians, then counted them in.

'One, two, three, four.'

He tapped on the drums to start her off. It was the same rhythm as before, and she took it up, trying to reproduce the same pounding, driving quality. The other musicians came in with their savage, half-melodic guitar sounds. Verrol danced in front of her, jumping and gyrating, long legs flexing to the beat.

Once she had the hang of the drums, she began to experiment with the timbre of different pots and pans. But there was something missing.

'Put more energy into it. Harder! Stronger!' Verrol was almost pleading. 'Play for your life!'

PART ONE

Swale House

1

'Which one?' Astor whispered to her mother, as they descended the steps from the airship.

'Which one would you prefer?' her mother whispered back.

The aerodock was the huge flat roof of Swale House, which rose above the smog like the deck of a boat. The gas-filled airship blotted out half the sky as it swung and creaked on its mooring ropes. Astor, her mother and stepfather approached the three Swale brothers and the reception party.

Astor had no doubt which brother she preferred. One was a heavy-set man with the neck of a bull, while the second was a skeletal creature who wore dark tinted glasses. But the third was as handsome as the others were ugly. Whereas they were in their forties, he was in his twenties; whereas they wore silk cravats and embroidered waistcoats, he wore a simple dark tailcoat and close-fitting breeches. He had raven-black hair, a pale complexion, straight nose and large, liquid eyes.

Astor's heart skipped a beat. 'Is it *him*?' she asked.

'Of course.' Astor's mother seemed as pleased as if she'd been getting engaged herself. 'Lorrain Swale. The other two are already married.'

'Why is he so much younger?'

'Child of a second marriage. How do you like him?'

Astor didn't want to admit how much she liked him. She knew that the Swales were the wealthiest family in mid-nineteenth-century Britain, and that marriage into such a family was a wonderful prospect for her. But she had never expected Lorrain to be so good-looking. She could fall in love with a face like that.

A sudden fanfare rang out from a line of trumpeters, all dressed in the blue-and-gold livery of the Swales. Other liveried retainers held up a banner emblazoned with the word DORRIN, which was the surname of Astor's stepfather. Astor was a little puzzled, since she was the one getting engaged, but perhaps the Swales weren't aware that she'd kept her own father's surname of Vance.

Marshal Dorrin called Astor and Mrs Dorrin to attention with a sound somewhere between a cough and a bark. Then he clicked his heels and strode across to the reception party. He was a hero of the Fifty Years War, and still looked the part with his ramrod-straight back and magnificent mane of silvery hair.

He shook hands with the bull-necked brother – 'That's Bartizan Swale,' Mrs Dorrin murmured to Astor – and with the brother who wore dark glasses – 'That's Phillidas Swale.' He nodded to Lorrain without shaking hands, then bowed in the direction of two mousy-looking women who stood further back. 'Their wives,' Mrs Dorrin explained. The wives seemed embarrassed even to be noticed, and kept their eyes on the ground as they dropped half-hearted curtsies.

The Marshal and two older brothers talked for a while, but Astor couldn't hear what was said. Lorrain seemed hardly involved in the conversation . . . was he looking at her? Perhaps he was too shy or polite to stare, but she sensed hidden glances under lowered eyelashes.

He would like what he saw, she was sure. She had always been told she was pretty as a child, and now, at seventeen years old, she was equally admired as a young woman. She didn't need to be vain to know the effect of her slender figure and copper-coloured curls. For this special day, she had chosen a small-waisted dress with a large bustle, white lace collar and cuffs, and her favourite dove-grey boots.

Meanwhile, their servant began unloading baggage from the airship. Astor wished he would wait; a single servant seemed so meagre compared to the Swales' army of retainers. Travelling in one of the Swales' airships, they could hardly have brought a large retinue, but still . . . the man wasn't even wearing a proper uniform, just everyday black.

Mrs Dorrin reclaimed Astor's attention with a whisper behind her hand. 'I think there's someone who can't stop looking at you.' She meant Lorrain, of course. 'He's head over heels already.'

Astor grimaced at her mother's overheated imagination. Mrs Dorrin was a great believer in romantic love, as shown by her taste in clothes: pink bonnet, pink dress and countless ribbons and bows. She was a dainty five feet tall, half a head shorter than Astor, with a middle-aged figure that had plumped out into soft curves. Astor felt a great affection for her mother, though perhaps not quite the respect that a dutiful daughter ought to feel.

Astor didn't care so much about romantic love. Her step-father had arranged this engagement without ever consulting her feelings. No doubt he wanted her out of his household just as much as she wanted to be gone. He had never been fond of her, and his cold, grey, military influence made Dorrin Estate into a cold, grey, unwelcoming place. For Astor, marriage was simply a means of escape . . . or had been, until she set eyes on Lorrain.

He was still glancing at her sideways while Bartizan, Philli-das and the Marshal talked on. Astor wished he would come

7

across and claim her . . . speak to her as his future bride . . . kiss her hand . . . something, anything. She wanted him to be forceful, decisive, impetuous. But perhaps these new pluto-cratic families were even more formal than the old landed gentry?

Things would be different afterwards, she promised herself. She pictured the scene when they were alone together. Being taller, he would have to swoop down to kiss her, but she'd be no little bird to his eagle. He'd get a surprise when she cast formalities aside. Oh yes, a very big surprise . . .

A second fanfare of trumpets broke in upon her thoughts. The conversation had ended, and Bartizan and Phillidas turned to lead the way down from the roof. On one side of the aerodock was a block-like structure with huge metal doors and 'SWALE BROS INC: 1808–1846' painted in red letters on its walls. A retainer entered a glass booth, pulled a lever and started up a *chug-chug-chug* of hidden machinery. Puffs of steam appeared from vents above the doors, while the doors them-selves rolled slowly back to reveal the upper entry into Swale House.

Astor and her mother followed the Marshal across to the entry. The sky had grown darker in the last few minutes as the late-afternoon sun sank towards the surrounding sea of smog. They had begun their flight from Dorrin Estate in the Pennines, where the air was fresh and clear, but here in the industrial Midlands, the city of Brummingham lay permanently blanketed by pollution. Astor knew that families like the Swales made their wealth from factories belching out soot and smoke.

Mrs Dorrin must have misinterpreted Astor's frown because she spoke in a bright, encouraging tone. 'Don't worry, dear. You'll win him.'

That made no sense to Astor. Why should she have to win Lorrain? Win his love *after* they were married? But her mother thought he was already head over heels in love.

She shrugged, and dismissed the phrase from her mind as they passed in through the doors.

2

The interior of Swale House was like nothing Astor had ever seen before. They descended two floors down a grand spiral staircase and came to an even grander hall. Gaslights mounted in crystal chandeliers shed their brilliance over embossed wallpaper, while the rich red carpet felt like velvet under her feet.

More flunkeys were lined up along the hall, and bowed as they went past. When they entered a reception room, Astor's head whirled at the sight of so much gilt and marble, so many portraits and ornaments. It was showy rather than tasteful, but it took her breath away.

'This can all be yours,' her mother whispered. 'Just think of it!'

In the centre of the room was a table on which several sheets of paper had been neatly laid out, along with an inkstand and quill. Mrs Dorrin drew Astor off to one side, while the Swale wives retreated to the other side. Marshal Dorrin and the Swale brothers advanced to the table. The Marshal produced a lorgnette and leaned forward to examine the papers.

'You'll be happy, my dear, I know you will,' Mrs Dorrin prattled on. She wasn't watching Lorrain but her own husband.

'Look at me. I nearly broke my heart after your father's death. You were my only consolation. I never hoped to find love again – until Marshal Dorrin came into my life. Such an admirable man.'

Astor bit back her personal views on Marshal Dorrin. Admirable he might be, but not very loving in her opinion. Even towards his wife, he made few visible displays of affection. Astor would certainly expect a lot more from *her* husband.

A muffled jangle of musical strings made her spin in alarm. Her harp, her precious harp! She glowered at the young man carrying it – their own servant from the Dorrin household. Why was he trying to carry it on his own? The Swale retainers had brought down all the other items of baggage, which they were now stacking inside the door.

'You knocked the strings,' she said accusingly.

He lowered the harp to the floor and ran his hand over the doeskin cover. 'Sorry, Miss.'

'What's your name?'

'My name? Verrol, Miss.'

'Then listen to me, Verrol. You don't understand, but a harp goes out of tune very easily. Ask someone else to help you carry it.'

'Ask someone to help me carry it,' he repeated slowly, almost sarcastically. He had the face of a man in his early twenties, yet older at the same time. It was a strong face, a saturnine face, a far from unattractive face . . . but the faint twist on his mouth displeased Astor, suggesting hidden insolence.

She was about to snap at him when she realised something about the baggage piling up inside the door. It was all hers! What about her mother and stepfather? Where were their belongings?

Before she could question her mother, the Marshal, who had been signing papers, laid down his quill and turned from the table. 'Time to leave, Mrs Dorrin,' he said.

Astor gaped at him. 'You're going?'

Marshal Dorrin kept his eyes fixed on his wife. 'I've done what I came to do.'

'It's all right, dear.' Mrs Dorrin gave her daughter a placatory smile. 'You'll manage very well on your own.'

Astor shook her head. 'No! You *can't*! Don't go, Mother.'

For a moment she was a little girl again. Mrs Dorrin appeared uncomfortable. Marshal Dorrin held out an arm for his wife to take.

'The airship is ready to depart,' he said in a frosty voice.

Mrs Dorrin clutched at the explanation. 'Yes, you see, dear, we have to travel when the airship can take us. It doesn't belong to us.'

'But you must stay for the ceremony,' Astor insisted. 'I need you here!'

'Ceremony?' Mrs Dorrin's eyes flitted helplessly this way and that. 'I don't know about a ceremony.'

'What?' Astor swelled with indignation. 'You mean, that signing was it?' She gestured towards the papers on the table. 'That was *all*?'

Marshal Dorrin frowned and winced. Astor could almost hear him muttering 'insubordination' under his breath.

'Shush, dear,' Astor's mother said in a whisper. 'You're upsetting your stepfather.'

Upsetting her stepfather was exactly what Astor intended to do. She let fly with a passion. 'You can't do this to me! I won't be abandoned! I won't stand for it!'

Bartizan seemed amused, Lorrain concerned, Phillidas blankly indifferent. The Marshal gazed around the room, baffled and fuming. Astor's only power over him was that he hated any kind of scene. His military training hadn't equipped him to deal with the emotions of women.

A ripple of harp strings broke the silence. Their servant – Verrol – had brushed against the cover of the harp again. Marshal Dorrin glared . . . until his face lit up with sudden relief.

'*He* can stay with her,' he said.

Astor looked from her stepfather to Verrol and back again. 'What?'

The Marshal turned to Bartizan and Phillidas. 'If that is acceptable to you, of course. Only for a few weeks while she settles in.'

Bartizan shrugged. 'I'm sure we'll find work for him.'

'Munnock can take care of it,' said Phillidas.

Marshal Dorrin addressed his servant in a brusque military bark. 'You remain at Swale House until further orders. Understood?'

'Yes, sir.' Verrol's formal response didn't quite match his raised eyebrow or the hint of a grin at the corners of his mouth.

'It's not the same,' Astor protested. 'I don't need a male servant. I need—'

'Mrs Dorrin, *if you please.*' Again the Marshal held out an arm for his wife to take.

'No!' Astor caught her mother by the elbow as she started to move off. 'I need you!'

Mrs Dorrin gave her a pleading look. 'Please don't make me choose,' she murmured.

That knocked all the wind out of Astor. 'Please don't make

me choose' meant she'd had already chosen. Her mother's loyalty was to the Marshal not to Astor. The battle was over before it had begun.

Mrs Dorrin saw she'd conceded. 'You're going to be such a lucky girl,' she said, and gave her daughter a quick hug and a peck on the cheek. 'And now I really must go.'

Astor watched her hurry off arm-in-arm with Marshal Dorrin. *You can hardly wait to get away*, she thought bitterly.

The room emptied in an instant. She heard Bartizan and Phillidas talking to the Marshal as they walked back along the hall. The liveried retainers and Swale wives followed behind. Only Verrol and Lorrain remained, along with a single Swale servant.

3 Astor studied Lorrain out of the corner of her eye. She suspected he was studying her out of the corner of *his* eye too. If her stepfather had just signed the papers for their engagement, then presumably they were now a betrothed couple. They didn't seem very betrothed, however. Was this the Swale way of doing things? Was this the kind of business-like arrangement favoured by entrepreneurs and industrialists?

She waited for Lorrain to say something. With her mother and stepfather gone, he was the closest she had to family. He would be closer than anyone when they were married. But at present he seemed awkward and distant.

She wondered if the presence of servants constrained

him – especially Verrol. Her newly acquired servant still stood by the harp like a guard on duty. She could dismiss him, of course, but she didn't want to cast off her only small link to the past. In a world of strangers, she needed all the support she could get.

She decided to take the initiative with Lorrain. 'So here we are. The two of us.'

'Pleased to make your acquaintance, Miss Vance,' he said.

His words were bland, but his looks more than made up for them. As his deep, dark eyes met hers, Astor felt butterflies in her stomach.

'I'm sorry for my over-reaction just now,' she went on. 'I didn't know they were leaving so soon.'

'It must be very difficult for you, to be suddenly thrown into an unfamiliar situation.' His tone remained polite and courteous, but she thought she detected a gleam of real sympathy in his eye. 'If there's anything I can do to help . . .'

A sound like a snort came from over by the harp. Verrol looked down at the floor as though he'd been merely clearing his throat.

Lorrain clicked his tongue and turned to Astor again. 'I see you're a musician, Miss Vance,' he said.

Astor nodded. 'Like my father before me. Mr Jacob Vance. Principal violinist for the Royal Symphony Orchestra.'

'Really? You've inherited his talent then?'

'I hope so.'

'But the harp rather than the violin?'

'I play all sorts of instruments. The harp is the most ladylike.'

Astor didn't feel particularly ladylike right now. Why was Lorrain so distant? Why didn't he behave as a fiancé and a lover? *Talk about us!* she wanted to say. *Talk about your feelings!*

The sound of engines came to their ears: a rising thrum of power, faint yet unmistakable. Verrol strode across to a window on the far side of the room.

'The airship's taking off,' he announced.

Could he actually see it from there? Astor wondered. He was craning his neck looking upwards. She wanted to run across and look up too . . . but no, that would appear childish in front of her fiancé.

The sound grew louder, like a roll of distant thunder. Vibrations resonated in the floor beneath their feet.

'Up it goes,' said Verrol.

From where she stood, Astor could see only grey sky and tendrils of yellowish vapour outside. But she sensed the darkening of the light as some great shadow passed across overhead. A similar gloom passed across her heart, a feeling of isolation and abandonment . . .

She bit her lip and drove the feeling away. She had wanted to escape from her stepfather, and she'd achieved what she wanted. *I'm not afraid of being on my own*, she told herself sternly.

'Goodbye, Marshal; goodbye, Mrs Dorrin,' said Verrol.

Really, he was a *most* impertinent servant. 'Enough of that,' Astor snapped.

She turned to Lorrain – and discovered he was no longer there. She stared at his retreating back as he walked from the room. What—? She was too stunned even to call out.

Verrol and the Swale servant noticed Lorrain's departure too. Astor prayed she wouldn't flush under their inquiring glances.

'He'll be back,' she said in a hard, tight voice.

'We wait, then?' Verrol asked.

'Yes. Address me as "Miss" when you speak.'

'Then we wait, Miss.'

They waited for fifteen minutes. Astor couldn't work out what was happening. Had Lorrain gone off to fetch his brothers? Would they all come back to the reception room together? There was a bustle of voices and footsteps moving up and down stairs or along corridors, and various servants went past the open door. But there was no sign of Lorrain, Bartizan or Phillidas.

How could Lorrain just forget her like this? He'd offered to do anything to help – the very least he could do was to save his fiancée from humiliation. What other business could he be caught up in? What other business could be more important than his future wife?

After a while, the bustle died down, and all that remained were the quiet sounds of a household going about its daily activities.

Astor was conscious that Verrol and the Swale servant were watching her, awaiting instructions. The Swale servant hovered over the bags by the door, while Verrol had returned to stand beside the harp. Astor had no instructions to give them. She put on a nonchalant air as though this impossible situation were the most natural thing in the world.

Verrol was scowling, though he wiped the scowl from his face when Astor looked in his direction. At the end of fifteen minutes, he snapped his fingers and swung round on the other servant. 'What are you doing here?'

'I'm supposed to carry her bags and things.'

'Where?'

'To her room.'

'What room?'

Astor cut the man off before he could respond. 'No, I'm staying right here. Until someone *proper* comes.'

The servant gave a perfunctory bow. 'As you wish. Your choice, Miss.'

Obviously he took it that his responsibilities were at an end, because he marched at once to the door.

Verrol turned to Astor. 'Let me go after him. I'll question him.'

'About what?' Astor still had to maintain appearances. 'No.'

Verrol shrugged and stayed where he was. They waited another fifteen minutes.

Astor tried to go back over everything her mother had said about the engagement. Even before the journey to Swale House, she had been vague on the details. All the arrangements had been made by Marshal Dorrin, who had never discussed it with Astor directly. That wasn't so strange because he often left the business of communication within the family to his wife. At least, it hadn't seemed strange at the time.

Now everything seemed strange. No ceremony . . . although she'd certainly seen the Marshal sign the papers with her own eyes. But what about the banner bearing the name DORRIN? And what about Lorrain's manner to her? Even his courtesy wasn't quite right. Was it natural to offer 'anything I can do to help' to one's *fiancée*?

Certain words in her mother's whispered comments didn't sound quite right either. 'You're going to be such a lucky girl' – as though it was something in the future. And 'This can all be yours' – why *can*? Wasn't it settled already? And even more mysterious, 'You'll win him.' Why was it up to her?

Astor fought off a growing sense of some dreadful mis-understanding. Was she making a mountain out of a molehill? Surely there had to be a simple, rational explanation to make these mysteries go away.

She made herself think of something soothing. Music was always her consolation in times of stress. In her mind, she ran over a sonata by Haydn that she'd been learning to play. Then some of her favourites from the past: a piece by Ravelli and a cantata by Bach.

It was no use; Verrol's scowling presence was too much of a distraction. It was as though the situation was a humiliation to him personally. Even though he veiled his expression whenever she looked at him, she could tell what he was thinking. A servant with pride! She felt mortified enough without him adding to it.

'I'm going to find someone to ask,' he said at last.

'No. I'll do the asking if anyone asks.'

'You can't stay here forever.'

'I forbid it.'

He had already dropped the 'Miss', but Astor didn't have the heart to force the issue. She knew she was only covering up to save face. What else could she do? Perhaps she *would* stay here forever, just waiting and waiting.

Verrol subsided again, but there was a dangerous, almost wolfish twist to his mouth.

Astor gave up on her mental music and turned her attention to the objects around her. She focused on the smallest details of the portraits, the chandeliers, the carved legs of the table, the folds of the drapes. By the end of half an hour, every feature of the furnishings was etched in her mind . . . and she loathed them all. Everything in this room was her personal enemy.

Still nobody came. Her legs tingled and ached from standing on the same spot for so long. She felt as though she might never move again. It was like standing on the edge of a precipice, and the tiniest move would send her plummeting. Nothing could happen so long as she stayed as she was.

Numbed into a kind of trance, she wasn't even aware that her legs were giving way. She must have been swaying, but her mind had gone to sleep.

Luckily Verrol was keeping an eye on her. He sprang forward and scooped her up in the second before she dropped to the floor.

'Are you all right?' she heard him ask. His voice sounded weirdly floating and remote.

 For a moment, Astor relaxed in his arms.

'Are you all right?' she heard him ask again.

The closeness of his face was disconcerting. No, this wouldn't do at all.

'Let me up,' she said.

He raised her upright. Her legs were shaky, but she could stand by herself. His hands were still around her waist, holding her in a way that was firm yet gentle – and strangely confident for a servant. Almost presumptuous, in fact.

She shook her head and backed away to a respectable distance.

'You fainted,' he told her.

She denied it automatically. 'No.'

'I have to find someone to ask. They can't keep us waiting like this.'

Astor frowned. The 'us' sounded odd in her ears, as though he included himself with her.

'If you don't forbid me, that is,' he added.

She let her dignity slip a little. 'I don't understand it. Yes, go and ask.'

He was gone in a flash, leaving Astor alone with her thoughts. She listened to his footsteps padding away down the hall.

She didn't know what to make of him. He could act the servant, but he didn't seem like a servant. The closeness of his face a moment ago had brought back a vague memory of seeing him before . . . and a suspicion that he'd eyed her inappropriately even then. No doubt he was an outdoors servant at Dorrin Estate, which was why she'd rarely encountered him in the two years since she and her mother had moved there from London Town.

A sudden screech interrupted her reverie. Not Verrol's voice – but he was surely the cause. She didn't pause to think, she just set off running. What on earth was he doing?

Astor ran back along the hall to the grand staircase. Now she could hear his voice, and he seemed to be threatening someone. She arrived at the staircase, where the spiralling steps went both up and down. Verrol was half a floor below her with one of the Swale flunkeys. He held the man by the throat while twisting his arm behind his back.

'Visitors, reception, engagement,' he growled. 'Tell me.'

There was something horribly practised and efficient about his actions. Astor saw that the wolfish look was back on his face. The other man could only wriggle and choke until Verrol released the pressure on his throat.

'Marshal Dorrin visited,' he managed to bring out. 'The war hero.'

'Why was he visiting?'

'I don't know. Nobody told me. Please!' The flunkey was almost blubbering with fear.

Astor flew down the stairs. 'Stop! You're hurting him!'

Verrol glanced round with eyebrows raised. 'Yes, I am. He wouldn't talk to me without it.' He took hold of the man's chin and swivelled his head to look at Astor. 'Do you know who this is?'

'No.'

'Have you heard about her engagement to Lorrain Swale?'

'No.'

Still in Verrol's grip, the man swivelled his eyes to look up . . . and a sudden relief came over his sweating face. Astor and Verrol turned to see what he'd seen. One and a half floors above them, a dozen people were staring down over a balustrade.

Astor's heart sank when she recognised the skull-like head and tinted glasses of Phillidas Swale. Perhaps he had heard the same screech that she had heard.

'Tell your servant to take his hands off my servant,' Phillidas ordered.

Verrol's mouth was a hard, thin line, and his eyes were narrowed.

'Do it,' Astor told him.

For a second, she thought he wouldn't obey. Then a veil seemed to fall over his face, which became detached and expressionless. He released the flunkey, who bounded away to a safe distance higher on the stairs.

'If you have any questions, you may ask me,' said Phillidas. His voice was a high-pitched monotone.

Astor spoke up. 'Why did you all leave me in the reception room? Where's Lorrain?'

21

'Lorrain has nothing to do with you.'

'He's my fiancé, isn't he?'

The sudden braying sound took Astor by surprise. Then she realised that Phillidas was laughing. The laugh continued for half a minute, before stopping as abruptly as it had begun.

'Is it likely?' Phillidas leaned his elbows on the balustrade and put his fingertips together. 'Is it plausible?'

'I thought—'

'Do the calculations. What are you worth?'

Astor shrugged. 'I don't know.'

'Suppose you were to inherit your stepfather's estate. Fifteen hundred acres? Given the location, I'd say £2.50 an acre. Buildings, stock and other assets, at most another £1200. Total, £4950. Correct?'

He didn't wait for an answer, but continued on in his strangely mechanical voice. 'Now, how much is Swale Brothers Incorporated worth? I'll tell you. On the latest 1846 valuation, we're worth £2 458 750 000. Do you understand how that compares to your stepfather's worth?'

'I was never good at arithmetic,' Astor retorted tartly.

'It is . . .' Phillidas paused, and Astor could see his lips move as he performed the calculation in his head. 'It is 496 717 times the amount. Does that answer your question?'

'You could've just told me.'

'However.' Phillidas tapped his fingertips together. 'The calculation was based on an unreliable assumption. We have no reason to believe you'll inherit anything at all from your stepfather. I don't suppose he'd have left you here if he thought of you as his heir. Your only inheritance would have come from your father, and unfortunately he was a penniless musician.'

'My father played many times before King George himself. He was given an OBE.'

'Yes, and remained penniless.' Again Phillidas let loose his loud, braying laugh, which seemed to bear no relation to anything.

Astor had been beaten down about as far as she could go. 'So why did my stepfather leave me here?' she asked in a hollow voice.

'We're doing him a favour by taking you off his hands. We've hired you as a governess to teach our children.'

Astor was stunned. She did as she was told and followed where she was led. The world had fallen in on top of her, and she was too overwhelmed to try and fight back.

Verrol took charge, responding to instructions from the servants, guiding her along. He insisted on carrying the harp, while other servants carried her bags.

They descended by steam elevator: a platform enclosed inside a wire cage that chugged and chuffed its way down through floor after floor. The level on which they stepped out was very different to the luxurious upper levels. Here the lighting was less bright and the corridors much narrower, with bare boards underfoot instead of velvet carpets.

Finally someone threw open a door, and they trooped into Astor's new room. It was a quarter the size of her room at Dorrin Estate. She gazed around in despair at the plain wooden cupboard, chair and writing desk, at the iron-framed bed, coarse matting and dingy wallpaper. The light filtering in through the one poky window was a dim yellowy-brown.

'It's hideous,' Astor groaned. 'I *can't* stay here.'

Verrol set the harp down in a corner. The other servants deposited Astor's bags, then bowed themselves out.

'They still bow to you,' Verrol noted. 'Governess's rank. You're below the Swales but above an ordinary servant.'

She turned on him viciously. 'Is that supposed to be some kind of consolation?'

'Don't take it out on me.'

'It's easy enough for you. You're used to living like this.'

'I had to learn.'

'Well, I don't intend to learn. Never.'

'You think you have a choice?'

She scowled and sat down on the side of the bed. 'I can't believe she was in on it.'

'Who?'

'My mother, of course. She *couldn't* have been lying all along.'

'She could have been lying to herself.'

'To herself?'

'Perhaps she convinced herself first. I know she boasted about your engagement to other people too. I always had my doubts.'

'Phah! *You!*' Astor was aware she shouldn't be revealing family confidences to a servant, yet she couldn't hold back. 'She thinks Marshal Dorrin is the most wonderful man on God's earth.'

'She's married to him. He's only a stepfather to you.'

'What's that supposed to mean?'

'He doesn't feel about you as a real father would.'

24

'He doesn't feel anything at all. You heard Phillidas – he wants me off his hands. He doesn't like me and my mother being together.'

'It happens.'

'He wants her all to himself. I should've seen it coming.'

'Yes. You should have.'

Astor sniffed. 'You're quite the cynic, aren't you?'

'I have a lot of things to be cynical about.'

His face wore the same veiled look she'd seen before. If there was a story there, she didn't want to hear it. She jumped up from the bed and began pacing between cupboard and desk.

'I'll *make* him take me back,' she vowed. 'I'll turn up on his doorstep. I won't let him drive me away.'

'At Dorrin Estate?'

'Yes.'

'How do you plan to get there?'

'I can walk.'

'That may be harder than you think.'

Astor glanced towards the window, where the dwindling light was now a deep brown colour through the smog. 'Not tonight. I'll make preparations first.'

'Do you know how far it is?'

Astor didn't like being quizzed by a servant. 'I don't care.'

'It's not only the two hundred miles we came in the airship. You'd have to detour around industrial ruins and pits and poisoned wastelands. Three hundred miles at least.'

'So? You can lead me.'

'No, thank you.'

'What?'

'I won't lead you to your death. It's a dangerous world out there. You have no idea.'

'I'm stronger than I look.'

'You'd never survive. You've led a pampered life.'

Astor glared at him. 'How would you know?'

'I've watched you.'

'When?'

'For two years, in your stepfather's household.'

Astor tossed her head. 'Well, I never noticed you.' Which was almost true.

'Of course not. I'm only a servant.'

'Yes, you are. And now I'm giving you a direct order. You *will* lead me back to Dorrin Estate.'

He performed a mocking bow. 'I'm afraid I must respectfully decline to obey.'

Astor stopped pacing, brought up short by a sudden realisation. Yes, he *could* decline to obey, because there was no higher authority to whom she could appeal. She certainly couldn't reveal her plan to the Swales. It came down to her will against his – and the look in his steel-grey eyes told her she would never win.

A sense of her own helplessness rushed in upon her. She took in the oppressively cramped dimensions of the room, the bare walls and narrow little bed. Hateful, hateful, hateful!

And this was her future. Not for a day or a week or a month, but *forever*! She was condemned to live out her life as an insignificant, impoverished governess. Her future wasn't a future but endless, hopeless dreariness.

A tide of emotion heaved in her chest, and she knew she had to drive Verrol out in a hurry.

'Go!' she ordered. 'Leave!'

He stiffened visibly at the shrillness of her voice. He didn't understand, and she didn't want him to understand.

'Now! Get out of my room! Now! *Now!*'

She advanced upon him with sweeping gestures. She couldn't wait, she was ready to push him. But he turned and left of his own accord.

The moment he was out of the room, she slammed the door behind him. Then she took three paces to the bed, flung herself face down on the blanket and burst into a flood of bitter, uncontrollable tears.

Astor fell asleep fully dressed, still lying on top of the blanket. Later she woke in the dark, took off her shoes and crawled in between the sheets. Her fitful dreams harked back to her London childhood and number 28, Shoe Lane. The dining room and piano room . . . the back garden with its hanging ivy . . . the paved paths . . . the overgrown grass in the corners. In her dreams, the house was always filled with music and the warm, gentle presence of her father.

She slept through until morning, when she opened her eyes to wan, dismal light. She reached out for her bedside table but it wasn't there. And the window was on the wrong side, she was facing the wrong way, *everything* was back to front.

The cold, stark reality struck home again . . . as cold as the air around her, as stark as the room's meagre furnishings. It was all true. She retraced yesterday's events, desperate for something she'd failed to understand, some loophole. She didn't care about being engaged, or about Lorrain Swale, or about a life of wealth and luxury. She just wanted her life back the way it was before yesterday.

For hour after hour she lay there cudgelling her brains, sieving through her memories. There *had* to be a way out of this catastrophe . . . but she couldn't find it.

She was still in bed when someone knocked on her door.

'Go away,' she said.

'Your three pupils are waiting in the schoolroom.'

It was Verrol . . . the servant who wouldn't obey orders. He had refused to lead her back to Dorrin Estate, and now he was trying to make her act like a governess. Bile rose in her throat at the thought. No doubt he wanted to drag her down to *his* level.

Then she saw the doorknob start to turn. 'No!' she cried. 'Keep out!'

The doorknob stopped turning. 'Shall I say you're not well?'

'Do what you like,' she snapped.

Verrol went away and Astor stayed under the blankets. She began thinking about her mother, who would be back home by now. Would she be having second thoughts yet? No, she was probably consoling herself with thoughts of Astor falling in love with Lorrain and Lorrain falling in love with Astor. Ridiculous! It hadn't been true yesterday, and it was unthinkable today. Wealthy heirs only married governesses in the pages of romantic fiction. Mrs Dorrin was probably reading one of her favourite pink-and-mauve novels right now.

As for her stepfather, he was probably in his study, where he was supposed to be writing his memoirs or a history of the Fifty Years War or a book on the principles of military strategy. The exact nature of the work was never very clear, except that it was tremendously important, and nobody must ever interrupt him. Astor suspected he spent most of his time reading the newspaper.

Around noon, the door of Astor's room swung open, and a woman entered. She was dressed in the standard dark garb of a female servant, but her lace collar and smart bobbed hair suggested special status.

'I'm Mrs Munnock,' she announced. 'I've come to tell you how things work here. One of the skivvies will make your bed, but you're responsible for keeping your room tidy. Washroom and toilet facilities are two doors along the corridor to your left. You'll need to change out of your fancy clothes into something more appropriate. The last governess's clothes are still hanging up in the cupboard.'

She gestured towards bed, corridor and cupboard as she rattled out information. She seemed indifferent as to whether Astor was taking any of it in.

'Breakfast is at seven, lunch at twelve and dinner at six. As governess, you can choose to eat with the servants or have your food brought up to your room.'

'Eat with the servants?'

'Yes, the Swale servants. And your own servant too, of course.'

'Verrol.'

'Is that his name? Verrol. Yes, he's going to be trouble, that one.'

'He won't obey orders?' Astor suggested.

'No, he does what he's told. But he makes the maidservants act silly. Too good-looking by half. I've seen it already, as soon as they set eyes on him. Not that he encourages them, mind.' The woman frowned and folded her arms. 'Anyway, you've missed lunch. Dinner is in six hours.'

'Are you in charge of me?'

'Indirectly in charge.' Her stern features softened. 'Listen.

I hear you've come down in the world with a bump. I'll allow you the excuse of being sick for today, but don't push it further than that.'

She bustled out without another word.

Astor's stomach told her she was hungry, but it didn't matter. Nor did it matter that her hair was a mess and her clothes all rumpled. Let them work out what to do with her. She would just lie here and become someone else's problem.

Verrol reappeared an hour later. He knocked, then entered before she had time to respond. He was bearing a tray of food.

'Leftovers from lunch,' he told her.

Astor rolled over to face the other way. Verrol uttered a ho-hum sort of noise, and she heard the clatter as he deposited the tray on the writing desk.

'Up to you,' he said. 'It's there if you want it.'

She waited in silence until he was gone. She didn't intend to eat anyway.

The afternoon dragged slowly by. She watched the light moving across the wallpaper, then fading as the sun sank lower. Her resolve not to eat faded too, until eventually she got up out of bed and went over to the writing desk.

The tray was laden with unbuttered toast, sausage that had gone cold, a slice of beetroot and a wedge of cheese. Servants' food. She wolfed it all down without tasting a thing. Then she stepped across to the window.

Outside there was nothing but rolling, swirling smog. Down on this lower level of Swale House, she was submerged in it. She imagined factories, blast furnaces, canals, steam cars and traction engines – all the features of a major industrial centre like Brummingham. But what she saw was a yellowy-brown blankness.

She unhooked the latch and opened the window a few inches. Immediately, a revolting rotten-egg smell invaded her mouth and nostrils. She coughed, almost retching, and slammed the window shut in a hurry.

She went back to bed, and returned to bitter thoughts about her mother and stepfather, about Verrol, about the Swales. She was roused from her reverie by sounds of shuffling and rustling outside the door, then whispering and giggling. Children?

'Who are you?' she demanded. 'Go away!'

'Who are *you*?' a girl's voice called out through the door. 'Are you our new governess?'

'Go *away*!' Astor repeated.

But the doorknob turned, the door opened, and three children came trooping in.

Astor hated the way they looked at her. No civility, no pretence of respect – just blatantly examining her from top to toe.

The oldest of the three was a girl of about fourteen. She was hugely overweight, with rolls of fat that her green velvet dress could scarcely contain. Her dark hair grew in tight, crinkly waves, and her small black eyes were half-buried in the flesh of her face.

The youngest was a boy of about six, with blond hair, big blue eyes and cherubic features. His large, rounded head seemed out of proportion to his body, like the head of a baby.

The boy in the middle was the tallest, though clearly younger than the girl. He had a faint adolescent fuzz on his upper lip and a satisfied smirk on his mouth. Astor felt particularly uneasy at the way his eyes roamed all over her.

It was the six-year-old who piped up first. 'Why ith she drethed in bed?' His lisp only enhanced the impression of childish innocence.

'Perhaps they always go to bed in their clothes,' said the adolescent. 'Her kind of people.'

The girl cut him down. 'Of course they don't, dummy.'

She stepped up to the bed, moving lightly in spite of her bulk. Astor averted her gaze from so much bouncing, wobbling blubber.

'You can look at me, you know.' The girl's reaction was quick as a whip. 'There's plenty to look at. I'm Blanquette Swale.'

Astor said nothing. Blanquette swung a hand to indicate the adolescent. 'And this grinning fool is my brother, Prester Swale.'

The abuse had no effect on Prester. His smirk widened as he came up to stand beside his sister.

He studied Astor, then turned to his sister. 'She's pretty. Prettier than the last one. I like the colour of her hair.'

His effrontery took Astor's breath away. How dare he presume?

'How old are you?' she snapped.

Prester grinned and closed one eye. He was trying to wink at her!

Blanquette answered on his behalf. 'He's twelve, though he thinks he's twenty. Real mental age about six. The same as . . .' She swung round. '*Widdy*! Stop that!'

The younger boy was playing with the food tray on the

32

writing desk. He appeared to be pouring cold tea from cup to saucer, and back again.

'Leave it, Widdy,' Blanquette ordered. 'Before you break something.'

Widdy let the china drop, picked up a knife and fork, and came hurtling across the room like an avenging angel.

'Wheee-ee!' he cried as he ran up to the bed. He drove the blade of the knife, then the prongs of the fork, into Astor's mattress.

Astor jerked away. She gazed into the boy's wide blue eyes, but they held no expression that she could read. Neither Blanquette nor Prester appeared in the least surprised.

'Widdy is Uncle Phillidas's child,' said Blanquette, as though that explained everything. 'Our cousin.'

'Why did he stab my mattress?'

'Who knows? He doesn't act like a normal human.' Blanquette gripped Widdy by the shoulders and pulled him away from the bed. He flourished the knife and fork, then ran off.

'So, new governess.' Blanquette turned back to Astor and assumed a manner of exaggerated refinement. 'Pray tell us about yourself.'

Astor said nothing. She was at a disadvantage, lying tousled and dishevelled in an unmade bed.

'We'd *love* to hear.' Blanquette's smile was like cut glass. 'If you're not too *sick* to tell us.'

'You should've come to the schoolroom,' said Prester. 'We had to entertain ourselves all day.'

Obviously, they weren't going to go away. 'My name is Miss Vance,' Astor told them.

'Miss Vance.' Blanquette's tiny black eyes gleamed. 'Miss Governess Vance.'

'What's your first name?' asked Prester.

'That doesn't concern you.'

'*It doesn't concern us*,' Blanquette echoed sweetly. 'Even though we gave our first names.'

She sat down on the side of the bed. As the mattress creaked and sagged under the sudden weight, Astor found herself staring at a swelling expanse of green velvet.

Prester sat down too, very close to Astor's legs. Astor wriggled under the sheet to move further away.

There was a muffled thump from another part of the room.

'Come out of there, Widdy,' Blanquette ordered.

Widdy emerged from the cupboard. He still had the knife in one hand; in the other he held up some sort of belt.

'It won't cut,' he complained. 'Why won't it?'

Blanquette sighed. 'Why do you always have to cut things, Widdy?'

'Becauthe.' The lisp became even more babyish. 'I want it to be cut.'

'It's leather,' said Prester. 'Of course it won't cut. Find something else.'

'I want thith.' Widdy sawed one last time with the knife, then threw the belt away in anger. 'Thtupid garbage thing!'

He went after the belt and kicked it across the room.

'Isn't he adorable?' said Blanquette. 'So cute. He doesn't want to grow up ever. You'll find out when you try to teach him.'

'Will you be our teacher?' asked Prester.

'No,' said Astor. 'I'm not a teacher.'

'I don't need teaching anyway,' said Prester. 'I know everything already.'

Blanquette made a rude noise at him. 'Except history, geography, spelling, arithmetic and a few little things like that. My left buttock knows more than you do.'

'I can learn them if I want.' Prester preened. 'Easy as easy.'

Blanquette turned towards Astor. 'There you are, Miss Vance. Your star pupil. He'll be like putty in your hands. You're lucky you're prettier than Miss Minnifer.'

'Who's Miss Minnifer?'

'Our last governess. Poor Miss Minnifer.'

Prester sniggered. 'Poor, poor Miss Minnifer.'

'Her nerves got the better of her,' Blanquette explained. 'She locked herself in her room and wouldn't come out. *This* room. Until she was dragged out, of course.'

'She had funny ideas about teaching,' said Prester.

'Yes, she thought it was her duty to discipline us. Are you going to try to discipline us, Miss Vance?'

'I'm not going to do anything with you.'

'Except entertain us,' said Blanquette. 'You'll need to talk a lot more, though. You're much too quiet for us.'

Astor didn't know how to react. She'd had a nanny once, and a governess for a year before her father died – and she would never have dreamed of speaking to them in such a manner. The Swale children were so forward, so brazen, so vulgar! Lorrain's courteous manners seemed to be an exception in this family.

'Are you always so quiet?' Blanquette inquired. 'Can you raise your voice at all? Miss Minnifer used to shout more and more towards the end.'

'She used to go *wa-wa-wa-wa-wa!*' Prester uttered a high-pitched gabble like a frantic chicken. '*Wa-wa-wa-wa-wa!*'

Widdy picked up the sound and imitated it. '*Wa-wa-wa-wa-wa!*'

Astor looked across at him on the other side of the room. 'Tell him to move away from my harp,' she said.

35

'She wants you to move away from her harp, Widdy,' Blanquette repeated with a grin. 'He's not very obedient,' she added, for Astor's benefit.

Widdy was busy exploring the cover over the harp, feeling through the material for what lay underneath. Astor heard the muffled *plink!* of a harp string.

'He won't listen.' Blanquette's grin became more malicious. 'He doesn't like being told to stop doing anything. Can you imagine, he's not even properly toilet-trained. Won't that be fun for you, cleaning up his messes?'

Astor shuddered. 'I'm not your governess and never will be! I wouldn't be your governess if it was the last job in the world!'

'There, you're starting to raise your voice now. How loud can you go?'

'I don't—'

A ripping sound came from the other side of the room. Astor saw with horror that Widdy had made a great rent in the harp-cover with his knife. Now he was looking at the strings . . .

'*No!*'

She struggled to get up. With the weight of Blanquette and Prester sitting on the bed, the sheets were tight around her. She took precious seconds to fight free, to swing her legs to the floor, to come round from the wrong side of the bed—

Twang! Twang! Twang! Twang! Twang! Twang!

Widdy cut with the knife, severing half a dozen strings with a single slice.

'I'm making music!' he crowed.

Astor banged her shin against the corner of the bed-frame and almost fell to the floor.

Twang! Twang! Twang! Twang! Twang! Twang! More strings severed.

36

'That's enough, Widdy!' Blanquette lumbered into action, catching Widdy by the wrist before he could deliver another blow.

Astor wanted to howl. Her harp! Widdy had just destroyed her most precious possession!

'It's not so bad.' Blanquette had become conciliatory all of a sudden. 'Just a few strings. You can repair them, can't you?'

Astor let out a hysterical laugh. 'And where would I get replacements? You don't know what you're talking about!'

'We'll go,' said Blanquette. 'We'll leave you alone now.'

'Do what you like! I'm reporting you to your father!'

'You don't need to do that.'

Prester gestured towards Widdy. 'What about reporting him to *his* father?'

'All of you!' Astor strode towards the door. She couldn't even bear to look at her ruined harp. 'You'll all pay for this!'

Astor stormed up flight after flight of stairs. After her previous encounter with the cold, inhuman Phillidas, she felt she had a better chance with Bartizan. She demanded directions from servants she met along the way.

'He's probably in his office. Eight floors up, turn left at the top of the stairs.'

'Mr Bartizan's office? Keep left, take the corridor after the statue.'

'Go right at the end of the hall. Big foyer, you can't miss it.'

The foyer was bigger than big, with subdued lighting, green carpet and leather armchairs. A male receptionist glided forward to intercept Astor as she entered.

'May I have your name, Miss? Please take a seat.'

But Astor was already marching towards the frosted-glass doors at the far end of the foyer. Leaving the man spluttering in her wake, she pushed through the doors and found herself in an outer office area. There were massive, freestanding typewriters, filing cabinets, and pneumatic pipes encircling the walls. One clerk sat behind an adding machine the size of a grand piano, pushing in keys and working a treadle with his feet. Another was fitting a rolled-up message inside a brass message-cylinder.

'I'm here to see Mr Swale,' Astor announced.

The clerks frowned and shook their heads. The second one inserted the message-cylinder into the slot of a pneumatic pipe and sent it off with a whoosh of air.

'Through here, I presume?' Astor put on an air of assurance and headed towards an official-looking door that displayed the Swale family crest.

'Wait!'

'You can't!'

'Not without an appointment!'

Astor strode on into Bartizan Swale's office, closing the door behind her, shutting off the squawks of protest. The office was enormous and smelled of leather and cigars. Bartizan sat behind a polished mahogany desk, articulating orders into the horn of a speaking tube that went down through the desk and into the floor. He didn't have his daughter's rolls of fat, but he was equally immense, with thick, fleshy lips, a bulging nose and cavernous nostrils.

He pushed aside the speaking tube and swivelled in his chair to look at Astor. 'And you are?'

Did he really not remember? 'Astor Vance,' she said. 'Marshal Dorrin's stepdaughter.'

'Ah, of course. The new governess.'

Astor was still boiling with anger, but she had to speak to Bartizan as one adult to another, rationally and impersonally. 'I have an unpleasant incident to report. It's about Blanquette, Prester and Widdy. They came into my room and wouldn't leave. They behaved badly.'

'Behaved badly. Hmm.'

'Very badly. Widdy got hold of a knife and deliberately cut the strings of my harp.'

'Harp, you say? Musical instrument?'

'It's worth two hundred pounds. Or it used to be.'

'You want me to buy you another one?'

'I want you to punish the culprits.'

Bartizan spread his arms expansively. The width of his shoulders threatened to burst the seams of his jacket. 'Of course, I could buy you another one. Two hundred pounds is nothing to me.'

'It's more than just—'

'But I don't intend to.' He brought his fist crashing down on the desk. 'What does a governess want with a harp?'

'They should respect other people's property!' Astor protested.

'Should they indeed?' Bartizan leaned back in his chair and tucked his thumbs in his waistband. 'See here, Miss . . . Vance, was it? They're *Swales*. You understand what that means? They'll inherit the greatest fortune in all of Britain. Four times richer than the Royal Family. Swales is who they are.'

'They still need to be taught . . .'

She stammered to a halt, aware of the way his little piggy eyes were scrutinising her.

'You can teach them spelling and grammar and suchlike things, Miss Vance. But you don't teach them how to behave. You don't even think to judge how they behave. They behave as Swales. You behave as a governess.'

'I'm not a governess. I'm—'

'You are what I say you are!' His booming voice drowned her out. 'Don't you bring your snobby expectations here! Don't you try talking to me like an equal! You're not my equal and never will be!'

Astor felt the spray of his spittle on her skin. 'I expected you to support me,' she said.

'Support you? That's a joke.' He let out a great bellowing laugh in demonstration. 'Listen. I'm a plain-spoken man and I'll give it to you straight. The support you get from me is a roof over your head. Food and drink and a bed. That's all.'

Astor couldn't find the words for an answer. Still she refused to take a backward step.

'Do you believe you have a right to something more? Do you? Is that what you believe?'

He's browbeating me, thought Astor. *He wants to crush me completely.*

'You need to change with the times, little miss. Your old world doesn't exist any more. You la-di-dah aristocrats, with your genteel airs and breeding, looking down on everyone from a great height, telling everyone what to do. That sort of superiority doesn't count nowadays. It's what *I* have that counts.'

'Your money, I suppose,' Astor muttered under her breath.

Bartizan heard her. 'No! Not money but what generates

the money. Willpower, drive, force of personality. Mental toughness. You need a bit more of that, Miss Whatever-your-name-is. Don't come complaining and reporting to me because you can't keep control over your pupils. Don't whine and snivel because you don't have the force of personality to do it yourself. Look, you're going wet in the eyes right now!'

Astor willed herself not to blink. With every fibre of her body, she drove back the tears.

'Hnh! And you wonder why the entrepreneurs are taking over. It's because we act for ourselves, we seize the initiative, we don't ask for help from other people. We stand on our own two feet.'

Red blotches had appeared on the skin of his neck. Astor concentrated on the blotches and spoke in a quiet, level voice. 'Thank you for explaining that to me. I shall stand on my own two feet, then.'

'You have to make your own authority in this house,' he thundered on. 'No running off to Mummy and Daddy every time there's a problem. If you don't have the strength of character—'

'Thank you.' Astor cut him off. 'You told me that already.'

His mouth was still open, ready for the next boastful phrase. *He's enjoying this*, Astor realised. He could probably keep bullying and throwing his weight around all day.

She brushed a spot of spittle from her wrist, turned on her heel and headed for the door. Behind her, she could hear the sound of his breathing, heavy and aggressive like a bull about to charge. She hated him as she had never hated anyone in her life before.

When she passed out of Bartizan's office, she had to brave the stares of the two clerks in the outer room, then the gawping receptionist in the foyer. She was sure they all knew of her humiliation. But the intensity of her loathing bore her up, and she sailed right by them with her head held high. There were no longer any tears in her eyes.

She had reached a turning point. Some switch had clicked over inside her, and everything would be different from now on.

I shall stand on my own two feet. Astor kept repeating the phrase to herself like a mantra. No, she wouldn't be beaten down by Bartizan or any other Swale. She would show them! She might come from a genteel family, but she had as much strength of character as any jumped-up plutocrat.

All evening, she worked on possible strategies. She would have to play the governess, for a while at least. That meant she needed a plan for dealing with Blanquette, Prester and Widdy.

She went to bed, had a sound night's sleep, and awoke with her plan very clear in her mind. She sprang out of bed, ready to put the first part into practice.

The first part was her own appearance. She went to the bathroom and washed her face, neck and hands. Thankfully there was nobody else around. The cold water made her skin glow fresh and pink.

Back in her room, she put aside her rumpled travelling clothes and inspected the clothes in the cupboard. A black dress that must have belonged to Miss Minnifer suited her perfectly, and fitted perfectly too. She experimented for a while with a white fringed shawl, which she eventually draped and knotted round her waist. The effect was austere yet dramatic, setting off her rich copper hair as the only splash of colour.

She didn't care about impressing her pupils; it was enough that she felt good about herself. She certainly impressed Verrol when he came calling for her.

'Are you going to . . .' he began. Then his eyes went wide and he seemed to forget the rest of his sentence.

'Yes,' she said. 'I'm going to teach those brats today.'

As if with an effort, he turned away and went to stand looking out the window. Astor was still annoyed with him, but she definitely approved of that widening of the eyes.

She rummaged in her jewellery box and selected her simplest silver earrings. Prettiness was for fiancées and brides-to-be; she was something else this morning.

'Pity you can't help me with these,' she commented as she inserted one earring. 'I always had a lady's maid before.'

'I didn't volunteer for that,' he growled.

Astor glanced at him, and almost burst out laughing. The idea of Verrol helping her with her earrings was supremely incongruous. He might have the dexterity, but he was just too hard and lean . . . too unfeminine.

He turned back to the window and changed the subject. 'This smog,' he said. 'It's the same smog that covers half of England.'

Astor inserted the other earring. 'You're down in it too?'

'Five floors further down. But the smog doesn't bother me. My room doesn't have a window.'

'Oh. Right.' She felt that her question had been foolish.

'It's not so bad. And I know a place to get out above the smog.'

'You've learned your way around, then?'

'Yes, but this is a secret place. I can show you sometime, if you'd like.'

'Perhaps.' She wasn't yet ready to forgive his refusal to obey orders. 'Take me to the schoolroom now.'

The schoolroom turned out to be six floors above her own room. Verrol led her up flights of steps much narrower than the staircases she'd used yesterday.

'Remember the route for when you come back,' he said.

They were on the final floor when he pointed down a side passage. 'That's my place for climbing out above the smog. Any time you want a breath of fresh air, just ask.'

Astor had more important things on her mind than fresh air. 'I want to get to the schoolroom before the brats arrive.'

'It's not just a single room,' Verrol told her, striding on.

In fact, there were four interconnected rooms. One served as a storage space containing books, slates, boxes of chalk and assorted teaching paraphernalia. Another was bare except for a long table and two long benches, while a third looked like a miniature auditorium, with a low stage, chairs and an upright piano. Astor noted the piano with interest; although she preferred the harp, the piano was one of the other instruments she could play.

The fourth room was the brightest and most cheerful. Charts and diagrams covered the walls, floral chintz curtains adorned the window. There was a cast-iron radiator under the window, a row of three small desks facing a single larger desk, and a blackboard on a three-legged stand.

'Here's where you'll be teaching,' Verrol told her.

Astor began her preparations for the day as soon as he left. She was relying on memories of what her governess had taught her in the year before her father's death. She went to the store and began gathering materials: chalk, slates and a selection of books.

She had just finished loading everything into a box when she heard the creak of an opening door, then voices and footsteps. Her pupils had entered the teaching room.

She drew a deep breath. Time to act, time to make the first move! She balanced the box of books on her hip, turned the knob of the door and marched forward to the challenge.

10

'I have spoken to your father.' Astor addressed Blanquette and Prester. 'I have agreed to act as your governess, but *only* on condition that there is no bad behaviour. Absolutely no bad behaviour from anyone.'

Blanquette and Prester exchanged apprehensive glances. Obviously they hadn't heard the true story of what had happened in Bartizan's office. They really thought they could have been punished, and Astor didn't intend to tell them otherwise. Her lie was the only hold she had over them.

'Do you want him to apologise?' asked Blanquette, indicating Widdy.

Widdy stood behind his desk gazing at nothing in particular. Whether or not he understood the situation, he certainly sensed the atmosphere.

'Go on,' Prester prompted him.

'I'm thorry,' Widdy lisped. 'Thorry, thorry, thorry, thorry, thorry.'

Astor resisted the appeal of his childishness. 'We shall see,' she said. 'I'll be keeping an eye on your behaviour. Sit down all of you.'

She began teaching with a guess-the-word exercise, then a quiz, then a simple crossword puzzle. She soon discovered that Prester wasn't very bright and needed easy questions like Widdy. When Widdy shouted answers out of turn, she covered her ears and pretended not to hear.

·She shifted from lesson to lesson as soon as they showed signs of becoming bored. She gave them a period of drawing for half an hour, and fifteen minutes of silent reading. For one lesson, she entertained them with a game of Imaginary Journeys, where they had to make a list of places they wanted to visit, then decide on the things they would have to pack for the journey. She had played the same game with her father when she was five years old.

Her pupils were better at competition than co-operation. Blanquette liked to use her sharp tongue on Prester at every opportunity, while both older children treated Widdy as a relative outsider. That was fine with Astor; she could control them by playing them off against each other.

So, when Blanquette advised her on Widdy – 'Don't be too nice to him or you'll regret it' – Astor not only nodded agreement but worked to establish a kind of alliance with her. Blanquette was too smart to stay interested in simple games for long, but she could be drawn into the superior role of assistant teacher.

With Prester, Astor took a different angle. He was so used to his sister's scorn and mockery that he was eager for any praise. There wasn't much to praise about him, but Astor managed to massage his pride and convert every dim hint of intelligence into a major achievement.

Neither praise nor alliance had any effect on Widdy. In the drawing period, he attacked his slate with savage round-and-round scribbles. 'Killing the enemy!' he cried, and stabbed with his stick of chalk until he snapped it in two.

There was no limit to the amount of Astor's attention he could monopolise. It was useless trying to tell him, 'I need to spend time with the others now.' She couldn't reach him or reason with him in any way.

Luckily, Blanquette supplied the answer. 'He loves writing his own name.' Armed with that knowledge, Astor soon developed a technique to quieten him down. Whenever he threatened to run amok, she ordered him up to the blackboard. 'Write out your name, Widdy.'

It was senseless but it never failed. Widdy's sudden concentration as he formed the letters was wonderful to behold. By the time he went back to his seat, he'd completely forgotten what he'd been doing before.

Lunch was another ordeal, when a maidservant came to tell them that food was served. Astor had been looking forward to a break, but Blanquette soon crushed that hope. 'You have to eat with us,' she said.

They trooped into the room with the bench and tables. Tablecloths now covered the table, and there were five plates heaped high with sausages, bread, onions and tomatoes.

Astor was puzzled. 'Why five?'

'Two for Widdy,' said Prester. 'He always has double.'

He didn't eat double, however; he ate two lots of sausages and left everything else. Spattered bits of tomato and onion radiated around his plate on the tablecloth.

'Toilet, Widdy?' Blanquette suggested when they'd finished the meal.

Widdy shook his head.

'Go,' warned Prester. 'Or I'll rub your nose in it.'

Widdy went, and Astor breathed a sigh of relief. She remembered what Blanquette had said about Widdy not being properly toilet-trained.

Lunch over, they returned to the teaching room, and Astor went on with her lessons. Her pupils were harder to manage in the afternoon. One time, Blanquette let fly with a flash of vitriol: 'You don't know much for a governess, do you?' Another time, Widdy threw a stick of chalk across the room. But that was as bad as it got. Astor ignored Blanquette's comment as if she hadn't heard, and Widdy obeyed when she made him pick up the bits of chalk, even though it took him a full ten minutes.

She didn't trust any of them, not for a moment. Her one great advantage was that they had already done the worst they could ever do. Nothing could hurt as much as the destruction of her harp.

Prester kept glancing at the clock on the schoolroom wall. At five minutes to three, he put up a hand and announced, 'We finish at three.'

No one had told Astor a finishing time. She turned to Blanquette. 'Is that true? Your father will soon tell me if it isn't.'

'It's true,' Blanquette confirmed.

Astor grinned inwardly. She still had them bluffed with her pretence about Bartizan.

'Very well,' she said. 'Pack up your things.'

'I'll stay on if you like,' Prester offered. 'For extra teaching.'

Astor would have said no even if she hadn't observed the leer on his face. 'I think you've learned enough for one day.'

'We've been very good, haven't we?' Blanquette suggested.

Astor relaxed a little. 'Good enough.'

She watched as they filed out of the room. They *had* been good enough, but she didn't delude herself. Although she had won so far, it would be an ongoing struggle. Still, she had made an excellent start.

I'm stronger than I look, she thought with satisfaction. She had said that to Verrol, and today she had proved it.

11

Astor collected half a dozen books from the store. She was planning to go back to her own room and prepare for tomorrow's lessons. After today's experience, she knew that perpetual novelty was the only way to keep her pupils interested.

Retracing the morning's route, her good intentions faltered when she saw the side passage that Verrol had pointed out. The idea of returning to her own poky room submerged below the smog was suddenly very depressing. She deserved a reward for her effort and success, she deserved a breath of fresh air. Could she find Verrol's special place by herself?

The side passage was no more than fifteen yards in length, with three blank doors that she tested one by one. The first door was locked, while the second opened onto a room containing only boilers and pipes clad in lagging. Behind the third was a small circular space at the bottom of a vertical shaft. The shaft seemed to go up forever, as did the stone steps that encircled its walls.

Up to the open air! thought Astor. This had to be the way. She left her books in a stack behind the door and started the long ascent.

She had no idea how many floors she passed through. She climbed higher and higher, around and around until she was giddy. At the top, she pushed up out of a trapdoor and found herself in a chamber with narrow slotted windows, like the inside of a turret. A ladder mounted against the wall led to a sloping skylight.

The small glimpse of blue sky overhead gave her new inspiration. She scaled the ladder and found the skylight already open. It was a tricky manoeuvre to swing across from the topmost rung, but nothing was going to stop her now. She hauled herself up over the edge of the skylight and out into the open.

Glorious clean air! Dazzling sunshine! The skylight opened onto a curved slate roof, the cone-shaped cap of the turret. She revelled in the sensation of oxygen in her lungs and the sun's rays on her skin.

She was still inhaling and blinking when someone called out from the other side of the roof, 'Who's there?'

It was Verrol's voice. Of course – she should have worked it out from the ladder and the open skylight. A moment later he came into view around the slope of the roof.

'You!' he exclaimed.

Astor overlooked the lack of respect. 'Yes, me. I found the way by myself.'

She was still crouching on the roof, while Verrol stood in a kind of stone gutter at the base of the cone. She accepted his offer of a hand, and stepped down to stand beside him.

'Thank you,' she said.

Fortunately she had never suffered from vertigo, because the parapet that bounded the gutter was no more than a few inches high. She gazed out over the sea of smog, a dirty, billowing mass all around. By contrast, the sky was clear and serene, with a perfect, delicate blue that brought tears to her eyes.

'So that's Brummingham out there,' she said.

'*Under* there. Except for one chimney.' He pointed to something like a black stump sticking up above the yellowy-brown surface. 'That's the tallest chimney in Brummingham.'

'It's not making any smoke,' Astor observed.

'No, it's a munitions factory. Closed down since the end of the war. But you can hear other factories working.'

A low throbbing came to Astor's ears like a muffled heartbeat. She guessed that was the sound he meant.

'Come and join me,' he said, and suddenly turned to move off along the gutter.

Mystified, Astor followed behind, step by careful step. The mystery was soon resolved. On the other side of the cone, a rug had been laid out over the sloping roof in the sunshine. There was even a small basket containing food and drink.

'A picnic!' she exclaimed.

He grinned. 'I managed to wangle some food from the kitchenmaids.'

Astor remembered what Mrs Munnock had said about his effect on the maidservants. She could see what they found attractive. There was a loose-limbed ranginess about him that was most unusual in a male servant. Like a fox in a henhouse, she thought.

'So the cooks like you too?' she asked.

'What?'

'I heard you're very popular with the maidservants.'

'Am I? Not with the male servants. They've nicknamed me "lady's maid" because of my role with you.'

'Sorry about that.' Astor smiled to herself. Of course, the male servants resented any fox in *their* henhouse.

He shrugged. 'I can live with a nickname.'

Astor felt sure that none of the male servants would go beyond verbal mockery. Somehow he wasn't the sort of person to pick a fight with.

'Would you care to share my picnic?' he suggested.

She nodded, and sat on the rug. Verrol sat too, placing the basket between them. He stretched out his long legs and braced his feet against the parapet.

'Help yourself,' he said.

She dug into the basket and selected a cold beef sandwich. There was a relish on the beef so spicy that the first mouthful made her gasp. After another two mouthfuls, she was hungry for more. She followed up with a wedge of cheese, a jam tart and a patty cake.

Verrol pointed to the golden ball of the sun above the smog. 'An hour and a half to sunset,' he said. 'Then all the birds fly up.'

'Birds?'

'Every evening, in the last rays of the sun. The birds come out above the pollution and fly round in circles. Higher and higher, hundreds and hundreds of them.'

Astor shielded her eyes and looked out into the distance. 'Which way is Dorrin Estate?' she asked.

'That way.' He swung an arm. 'Due north. If we could see that far, we'd see the Pennines rising above the smog.'

'It was beautiful there, with the heaths and moors.'

'Mmm.'

'What about London Town?'

'South-east.' Again he indicated the direction.

'I was born there, you know.'

'No, I didn't know that.'

'Hah! So you don't know *everything* about me.'

They sat on in a comfortable sort of silence. After a while, Verrol lifted a stone jug from the basket, removed the stopper and held it out to her. 'Ginger beer, if you'd like.'

She accepted the jug and took several long swigs before handing it back.

'It's so peaceful up here,' she remarked.

Verrol pulled a sardonic face. 'Up here it is. Not down below.'

'What's down below?' Astor stared into the impenetrable pollution. 'You mean Brummingham?'

'Yes. Like all the cities in Britain. Ugly and brutal.'

'Why?'

'All the returned soldiers since the end of the war. There's no work for them, so they form militias and make trouble. They're bad news.'

'Why is there no work for them?'

'Because factories have shut down, and industrial production has dropped. There's no need to keep turning out weapons and military equipment now. The soldiers came home expecting to be heroes, and instead nobody wants to know about them. They're economically superfluous.'

'Oh.' Astor had never been interested in politics, and it didn't surprise her that Verrol was so much more knowledgeable. But there was one thing she knew about. 'What about the gangs from the slums?'

He paused a while before answering. 'Yes. They're at war with the militias.'

'They're evil.'

'Don't say *evil*. They're mostly kids who never had proper homes. They'll do anything to survive.'

'Including murder.'

He gave her a quizzical look – but she didn't want to say any more. She didn't even want to think about it. She reached for the jar of ginger beer and took another swig.

'You haven't asked about my first day as a governess,' she said.

'I was waiting to hear when you wanted to tell me.'

So she told him about her day. She described Blanquette, Prester and Widdy, and went through all the schoolroom activities she'd invented to keep them quiet. He grinned when he heard how she'd bluffed them over Bartizan. Having someone to recount it to made the day seem even more successful.

Meanwhile, the sun slid lower in the sky, and the air grew colder. She would have listened to him describe his day, but he merely shrugged. 'Just another day in the life of a servant.'

Eventually he put the stone jug back in the basket. 'Time to return to my duties before Mrs Munnock comes hunting for me,' he said. 'Are you coming?'

'No, I'll wait to see the birds. Can you leave the rug?'

'Yes. And the ladder too?'

Astor almost stuck her tongue out at him. 'Of course the ladder. Can you leave it there all the time?'

'Not a problem.' There was a silent question in the quirk of his eyebrow.

'I'll probably come up here again after school,' she said. 'What about you?'

'My work hours change from day to day. I'll come up when I have time off.'

In the next moment he was gone, disappearing around

the side of the roof. She listened to the *creak-creak-creak* of the ladder as he descended.

What a strange scene, she thought. Sitting on a roof . . . side by side with a servant . . . even sharing his food and drink! A week ago, she would never have believed such a thing could happen.

The sun touched the horizon twenty minutes later. As the last rays of light shone horizontally above the smog, one flight of birds flew up, then another, and another. Around and around they cycled, assembling into a wide, slow-turning wheel. Light glittered on their wings, and their cries were faint and faraway.

Astor felt like crying out herself . . . with triumph and sadness, with all the mixed emotions of the day.

12 Next morning, Astor went up to the classroom early. Her lessons were all prepared, but there was something else she wanted to do. She had remembered the piano in the adjoining room. Half an hour of music before the brats arrived! Her fingers were itching for the keyboard.

The miniature auditorium was in semi-darkness; the chairs were arranged in a half-circle as if for an invisible audience. Astor sat on the stool, raised the lid, and began to play. The piano wasn't in perfect tune, but close enough. As her hands swept over the keys, she heard the melody in her head exactly as it was meant to sound.

Music was her passion, as it had once been her father's.

Right now, it was her comfort and consolation too. When she played one of her father's favourite pieces, her memories of him came flooding back. He had played the piano as well as the violin, and often, when she was a little girl, he'd sat her on his lap and moved her hands and fingers to pick out a song on the keyboard. She recalled his neat beard, his light, brisk movements, his quiet smile and gentle eyes, and the sense of security that went with him like an aura. She'd been just six years old when he was killed . . .

She had been playing for ten minutes when she felt a draught of air from behind. Someone had opened a door – not the one that led to the other schoolrooms, but one that led out into the corridor.

She continued to play, without turning her head. It might be a curious servant, it might be her pupils arriving early. So let them listen! Let them appreciate something fine and beautiful for a change!

She played the piece through to the end, then glanced over her shoulder. It was Lorrain Swale! He stood just inside the doorway, listening as if transfixed. He looked away when she glanced at him, and his black hair flopped forward over his brow.

Her fingers chose the next piece as if of their own accord. Without even thinking about it, she began playing a love song by Schubert. She didn't need to look to be conscious of him now; she could feel his gaze on the back of her neck.

She thought of the way he'd looked at her when they first met, up on the roof of Swale House and then in the reception room. She hadn't been wrong about that. If it was up to him and not his brothers, he'd have already proposed by now. It could have been, *should* have been love at first sight.

She moved on from song to song, the sweetest, saddest

and most romantic songs she knew. It was like a dream, as if they were both caught up and enclosed in the flow of the music. Slower and slower she made it flow, softer and softer. Her fingers caressed the keys and produced only the faintest murmur of melody. She felt she had him at her fingertips, completely under her control.

It was a time outside of time, but eventually she brought it to an end, drawing out the last few notes, letting them hang suspended in the air. Then she swivelled round to look him in the eyes.

His eyes were brimming with tears, and his pale face was unusually flushed with emotion. The music had stirred him to the soul.

There was no need for words. Astor's look was an open challenge. *So what about it? What are you going to do now?*

Perhaps it was too much of a challenge. Lorrain blinked and shook his head as if to break the spell. Then he backed out through the door, moving slowly and vaguely like a man underwater.

As he closed the door behind him, Astor returned to reality . . . but a brighter and more hopeful reality than before. Could it all come true after all?

She didn't believe in romance, not in the way her mother did. Mrs Dorrin dreamed of Cinderella stories where a poor musician's daughter might win the love of a noble prince – or wealthy heir, in this case. Astor knew the real world didn't work like that. And yet . . . for a moment, she had held Lorrain Swale's heart in her hands, she was sure.

It wasn't enough for a happy ending, not by itself, but it was a start. There were huge obstacles in the way, but not insurmountable. Bartizan and Phillidas wouldn't be the first or last to underestimate her determination. It might take months or years, but she could make long-term plans and stick to them.

She sat on for a while, going over the scene in her mind. She now knew she could appeal to Lorrain with her music as well as her looks. If she could work on his feelings, if she could push him into a state of reckless defiance . . . She swung back to the piano and played a wild flurry of notes. It wasn't any particular tune, just an impromptu flourish of triumph.

She stopped when she heard sounds from the adjoining classroom. Her pupils had arrived. She closed the piano lid and marched to the store to collect the books for her lessons. She could deal with anything now!

13

Astor's second day of teaching went even better than her first. She perfected her divide-and-rule tactics, using Blanquette against Prester, Prester against Blanquette, and Blanquette and Prester against Widdy. She didn't much care whether they learned anything.

She was looking forward to the end of the day, when she could recount her successes to Verrol. She hardly considered the possibility that he might not be there on the roof of the turret . . . and in fact he was. As she climbed the ladder to the skylight, she could hear him singing to himself.

Such a strange sound! She paused to listen at the top of the ladder. If his ordinary speaking voice was a little rough and rasping, his singing voice was a hundred times more so. It hardly seemed to belong to him at all.

The sound stopped as soon as he heard her push up

through the skylight. By the time she circled round to the other side of the turret, he had already risen to his feet.

'Oh, it's you.' She grinned. 'I thought it was a flock of geese.'

He laughed, but he was embarrassed too. She had found out his weak spot! She felt oddly pleased about that. He was normally so detached and self-possessed, so untouchable in his cynicism.

'What's in the knapsack?' she asked. 'Another picnic?'

The same rug lay over the roof as yesterday, but a knapsack took the place of the basket. It turned out to contain pastries and sausage rolls neatly wrapped in greaseproof paper.

'Little presents from your admirers,' Astor chaffed.

She suspected he had been waiting for her; at least, none of the wrappings had been opened. They sat on the rug in the sunshine, eating and watching a few fluffy clouds trail across the sky. Between mouthfuls, she told him about her day – that is, her day with her pupils. Lorrain's visit was her own private secret that she kept to herself. It gave her a warm glow just hugging it close and *not* revealing it.

They were coming to the end of the meal when something silvery appeared in the sky. Verrol knew what it was at once. 'An airship. I expect it'll land on Swale House.'

'Will they see us?'

'Doesn't matter if they do. They won't care.'

The airship was a double-cigar shape, with the gondola mounted on a wing between the two cigars. Black lettering on the sides announced ORGEN & PORVIS INC.

'More plutocrats,' said Verrol. 'They're always travelling back and forth.'

Astor noted how his mouth twisted with distaste on the word *plutocrats*. 'You don't like them, do you?'

'Plutocrats? I hate them.'

'Why?'

'Because of what they've done to this country.'

Astor looked out over the sea of smog as the airship began to descend. Now they could see the coal-gas engines that spun four ducted fans and drove the great vessel forward.

'Pollution?'

'The industrialisation that causes the pollution. The war that caused the industrialisation.'

'But the plutocrats didn't start the war. The French did. They attacked us.'

'Actually, it was Britain that declared war on France.'

'They must've done something first.'

'Oh, everyone did something. France, Britain, Prussia, Austria, Russia, all the countries in the war. Everyone was responsible. But I didn't mean that the plutocrats started the war. I mean, they kept it going.'

Astor didn't understand. 'We couldn't stop until we won, could we?'

'You think we won?'

'I suppose.' Astor had been only thirteen when the war ended in 1842. She certainly remembered people celebrating as if for a victory.

'The Peace of Brussels should've been made thirty years earlier. They could have saved Europe from thirty years of rampant industrialisation and mass pollution. Not to mention two million dead and five million maimed.'

Astor was still struggling to come to terms with his previous revelation. 'So we didn't win?'

'Nobody won, except the plutocrats. Their factories made huge profits supplying war materials. It was only when they lost their grip on power that peace finally arrived.'

'I thought King George decided.'

'No, Parliament. He could only make peace when the Rural Party outnumbered the Progress Party in the Houses of Parliament.'

He had to shout the last words as the airship's engines thundered above them. Astor twisted her head to follow as the monstrous double-cigar shape passed over the turret and came in to land on the flat top of Swale House.

She turned back to Verrol. 'Are you a pacifist, then? Are you against all wars?'

'I don't know about *all*. Just wars that line the pockets of plutocrats while ordinary people sacrifice their lives.'

Astor was thinking of her stepfather and his ferocious attitude towards *pacifists*. 'Yet you work for Marshal Dorrin. You joined the household of a war hero.'

He shrugged. 'I didn't have much choice. Anyway, I have nothing against Marshal Dorrin. He was a very brave man, from all reports.'

'You admire bravery?'

'Yes.' His raised eyebrow made it into a question.

Astor had always been told pacifists were cowards, yet it was hard to think that of Verrol. 'You never considered volunteering to fight? You'd have been old enough before the end of the war.'

'No, I never volunteered, and I made sure I was never press-ganged either.'

'"Press-ganged"? What's that?'

'It's when you're kidnapped, hauled off to an army training camp and beaten until you obey orders.'

Astor frowned. 'I don't believe it. The British army would never do that.'

'Believe what you like. There weren't many genuine volunteers in any country's army by the end of the war.'

He seemed very sure of his facts. Indeed, he seemed far better informed than any servant had the right to be.

'How do you know all this?' she asked.

'I read. Newspapers come down to the servants' quarters after everyone else has finished with them.'

Astor was not entirely satisfied with that answer. There was some mystery in his past life, she was sure of it. Little by little, she was building up a theory about him.

They sat on in silence for a while, until he began packing up the remnants of the meal. Then she challenged him outright. 'Why do you never talk about yourself?'

'I'm not very interesting. Just a quiet, obedient servant.' His ironic smile belied his words. 'Nobody ever complains about my work.'

'You could do your work in your sleep.'

'True. A servant's duties don't take up much energy.'

'So what *do* you care about?'

'Why do I have to care about anything?'

'Because. You're smart, you know a lot. You ought to make something of yourself. Don't you have *any* ambition?'

'You think I should aim for the position of butler? Or do you see me more as the head footman type?'

Astor couldn't imagine him as either, yet she wouldn't be mocked out of her speech. 'Anything's better than just drifting and coasting. I think you're only living with a small part of your life. Everything you do, you leave most of yourself outside.'

'You want to motivate me?'

'We all need a long-term goal.'

'What's yours?'

Astor snorted. 'I won't be spending the rest of my life as a governess, anyway.'

The sardonic look in his eyes plainly told her that he knew she hadn't answered his question. Nor did she intend to. Lorrain Swale was her long-term goal, and this morning's scene was her own private secret.

'Ah well, no doubt you have something suitably ambitious in mind,' he said, and went back to packing up the picnic.

14

The weather turned drizzly over the next few days, and Astor didn't go back up to the turret. She saw Verrol only when he called on her in her room, usually with the excuse of passing on some item of information. However, their conversations never quite fell into the same easy flow as before.

She didn't see Lorrain at all, though she went early every day to the miniature auditorium. Sometimes she stayed on after the end of the school day too. Playing the piano soothed her soul, but she was disappointed to be making no progress towards her goal.

Meanwhile, her three pupils were becoming harder and harder to manage. Her original bluff was losing its power over them. They hadn't found out that there was no agreement between Bartizan and herself, but the lie had less impact every time she repeated it.

Widdy was her biggest problem. Blanquette and Prester had helped to restrain him for several days, but now, without exactly turning against her, they were more often amused by his madcap behaviour. She had to keep an eye on him the whole time.

She sensed that a crisis was approaching . . . and finally it arrived. It happened the first time she tried to teach them about music. She had prepared this lesson more carefully than any ordinary lesson, and she was looking forward to it. But it went badly from the start.

She led her pupils into the little auditorium and made them pull up chairs around the piano. Then she played a chord and asked for a volunteer to come forward and repeat it.

'Tinkle, tinkle, twangle, twangle,' said Prester, and guffawed at his own humour.

Blanquette applauded ironically. 'There,' she said. 'Who needs a piano?'

Astor felt her bile rising. With some cajoling, she persuaded Prester to come forward and sit on the piano stool. She pointed to the keys on which he should place his fingers, but he seemed unable to do it by himself. So she leaned forward from behind and placed his fingers for him . . . just as her father had done when teaching *her* to play.

Prester let out a vulgar whistle. Every time she managed to get one finger correctly placed, another slipped out of position. She was sure he was doing it deliberately.

'Try now!' she said.

He pressed down and produced a jangle of discordant notes.

'Wrong,' she said. 'Did you hear how wrong that sounded?'

'You set me up wrong,' he huffed.

'You only need to move two fingers and it'll sound right.'

'I liked it the way it was,' said Blanquette.

Widdy popped up suddenly at the far end of the keyboard. He raised a childish fist and thumped down on the keys. 'I make muthic!' he shrilled.

He banged on the piano again and again, hammering out a thunderous cacophony. Astor dropped the lid of the keyboard quickly, before he could cause permanent damage. A bit too quickly – because Prester's fingers were still on the keys.

'*Yow-ow-ow!*' howled Prester. He snatched his fingers out from under the lid and made a great show of blowing on them.

'Sorry,' Astor apologised. 'That was an accident.'

Blanquette heaved up from her chair. 'End of lesson,' she declared.

'Yes, we'll stop for today,' Astor agreed.

Prester shook his head and headed through the door to the teaching room. 'Stupid music! Stupid old piano!'

'Never again,' said Blanquette.

Astor wouldn't concede so much. 'We'll try again tomorrow,' she said as she followed them through.

She meant it too. She didn't really care about spelling or arithmetic or any other form of education, but she *did* care about music.

That night, she tossed and turned in her bed for hours. The episode with Prester kept coming back, and every time it made her more and more angry. *Stupid music! Stupid old piano!* His words burned like a personal insult.

She couldn't settle, she couldn't calm down. She recalled her childhood, when she'd played the piano sitting on her father's lap. Such a happy period! Such fond memories! And now the Swale brats were ruining it all for her.

Stupid music! Stupid old piano!

Everything that had gone wrong with her life rose up before

her. The betrayal that had tricked her into the role of governess at Swale House . . . the move from their cosy London home to her stepfather's home . . . and the original disaster that was the start of it all. Behind everything else lurked the grief and shock and sheer impossibility of her father's death.

Just thinking about it sent a pain through her chest and made the breath catch in her throat. It was like a door flung open in her mind. They had *killed* him!

The memory of that day flooded through her once again. An ordinary Saturday afternoon . . . out strolling with her father . . . and they were already heading for home along Fetter Lane. They lived in Holborn, outside the traditional territory of the gangs, but the feud between the two great crime families, the Mauls and the Starks, had spread its unpredictable violence everywhere. When the shooting started, the street emptied in a flash.

'Run!' her father shouted. 'Dean Street!'

She ran as fast as her six-year-old legs would carry her . . . and he was with her at least as far as the turn into Dean Street, when he'd urged her on again. 'Keep going! All the way home!'

More pistol shots rang out behind her. Only when she came into Great New Street did she discover she was on her own.

It was evening when they brought his dead body back into the house. Then everything got swept up into the adult world . . . conversations back and forth over her head . . . questions and recriminations . . . people in the house she'd never seen before . . . and that one phrase she would never forget: 'took a stray shot in the side of the head'.

She still couldn't accept it, she never would. She had been so sure he would walk back in through the front door. Even when her mother and governess started to panic, she had never understood what the fuss was about. It didn't make sense that something so big could have happened while her back was turned. *He can't have died without me knowing about it*, she told herself.

But he had . . . and the worst thought of all was that he'd been already dying when they came to Dean Street. He'd been hit in Fetter Lane, but he'd run with her to get her away. And she'd left him to die!

Tears sprang to her eyes, tears of frustration and loss. She gritted her teeth and pummelled her pillow. There was no escape . . .

The night went by in a feverish, restless blur. Always the same images mingling in a hundred combinations. Her father's death . . . her father at the piano . . . Prester at the piano. By morning, she still hadn't managed even a moment's sleep.

She was red-eyed and fraying at the edges, yet she hadn't changed her attitude towards her pupils. *Stupid music? Stupid old piano?* They might grow up rich and live for making money, but she would teach them that money wasn't the only thing that mattered. She was more than ever determined to give them a proper music lesson.

15

Astor made the announcement at the start of the day: 'We're going to have another music lesson after lunch.' Her pupils didn't respond with protests or groans, just a blank wall of silence. It didn't bode well.

From then on she couldn't give her full attention to other

lessons. The afternoon loomed like a great black rock up ahead. She was soon wishing she hadn't committed herself; by lunchtime, she would have been happy to forget the whole thing. But no, she had to show them who was in charge. She would lose all authority if she backed down now.

When they trooped back into the teaching room after lunch, she clapped her hands. 'Time for our music lesson. Into the piano room.'

Instead, they took their usual seats and sat there stony-eyed.

'Move,' she said in her sternest voice.

Blanquette gave a tiny shake of her head. Prester stared down at his desk. Widdy jumped to his feet and began running round and round the room. 'Wheee-ee!' he shrilled.

'Widdy! Go and write your name!' she ordered.

It worked – at first. Widdy took a stick of chalk and wrote out his name on the blackboard. But then he didn't stop. He wrote out his name again, and when he ran out of space on the blackboard, he continued scrawling letters on the wall.

'No, Widdy.'

Still he kept going. The next *Widdy* spread across onto a chart that was hanging on the wall. As the strokes of his handwriting grew wilder and wilder, the chalk ripped through the paper and left a great rip in the chart.

'Enough!' Astor sprang across and grabbed him by the shoulders. He let out a horrible, high, thin scream.

'Into the piano room!' she shouted. 'Now!'

When he tried to wriggle free, she gripped all the harder, pulled him away from the wall and pushed him towards the piano room.

Blanquette roared at Astor at the top of her voice. '*Don't you dare!*'

Astor stopped pushing but didn't relax her grip. Widdy's scream dropped in pitch and became a whine.

'Take your hands off him,' said Blanquette. She still sat behind her desk, yet she seemed somehow more massive. 'You don't touch any of us, ever. Understand?'

Astor released Widdy's shoulders, and he fell to the floor, writhing. She knew she hadn't really hurt him, yet he carried on as if he was in agony.

A moment later, the door from the corridor opened and a maidservant poked her head in. 'Is everything all right?'

'No.' Blanquette was first to respond. 'Go and fetch Tomlin, Royce and Barnaby. At once.'

The maid disappeared. Astor could only wait, frozen with indecision. The situation was out of her control.

It wasn't long before three male servants appeared, all big, burly men.

'Stand at the back,' Blanquette told them.

Astor struggled to reassert herself. 'No, that won't be necessary. The problem has been resolved. You may leave.'

'Stay,' said Blanquette.

The servants stayed. They formed a line across the back of the room, as if on guard duty.

'And you get up,' Blanquette ordered Widdy.

Widdy jumped up giggling, showing no signs of injury. He went across to the wall chart he'd damaged, knocked it to the floor and began trampling on it. The servants looked on impassively.

Astor returned to her teacher's desk at the front of the class. There was nothing else she could do.

'Take out your books,' she said. 'Silent reading.'

Blanquette and Prester didn't take out their books, but they remained silent. Astor caught the look of triumph in Blanquette's eyes and shuddered inwardly. After a while, Widdy grew bored with trampling on the chart and returned to his desk.

For the rest of the school day, the three servants stood motionless at the back of the room.

Astor had been beaten. She knew it and her pupils knew it. She had gambled and lost. Yet she was still their governess, she would still have to come here day after day, she would still have to pretend to teach them. She had dug her own grave, and there was no way out of the hole.

16

Astor had no desire to play the piano any more. Nor was she interested in going up to the roof of the turret, even when the drizzly weather came to an end. She dragged herself out of bed in the mornings and sank into bed early in the evenings. The thought of the schoolroom was a constant dull weight in the pit of her stomach.

Widdy was the same as he had always been, moved by his own inclinations regardless of anyone else in the world. Prester could still be manipulated through his male vanity. She had to put up with his showing off, but so long as he wanted to show off in front of *her*, she could play on that. Blanquette, however, was now an open enemy. The girl had enough empathy to understand how Astor was feeling, and enough malice to wound her feelings in the most vulnerable spots. The ridicule Blanquette had always directed against Prester was nothing compared to the ridicule she directed against her governess.

One day it was Astor's family. 'Ah, what a superior governess we have. The daughter of a famous general. Or wait a minute, was it a penniless musician?' Another day she picked on Astor's mannerisms and accent. 'From London Town, don't you know.' When Astor responded with a comment on her tormentor's Brummingham accent, Blanquette just curled her lips in the sweetest of smiles. 'Oh look, she's trying to bite back! Well done, well done! So terribly sharp and witty!'

Astor soon learned it was better to hold her tongue. She was no match for the Swale girl, who had an exceptional talent for spite and mockery.

The most hurtful mockery was when Blanquette made fun of her intelligence. 'Get ready, Prester! Pay attention, Widdy! The great mind is about to speak.'

It was no help when Prester tried to defend her. Blanquette could blow him away like a speck of dust. 'You think she's all right as a teacher, do you, Prester? But then you think that tying your own shoelaces is the height of intellectual achievement.'

Prester soon gave up trying to hold an opinion of his own. He went back to tittering and sniggering along with Blanquette, even when he didn't quite get the point of her jokes.

Blanquette was the spider in the centre of the web, controlling every thread. Astor grew to loathe the very sight of that bloated body, bulging out over her chair, squeezed in behind her desk. It seemed incongruous that she could make fun of others when she was so grotesque herself. But Blanquette was impervious to reflections on her size.

'No need to roll your eyes at *me*,' she told Astor over lunch one time. 'I like to eat. I'm a whale of a Swale.' She snorted with amusement. 'So what? I'm still a Swale. You have to

71

starve to keep your dainty little figure because you've got nothing else.'

Astor was helpless. Her existence grew even more miserable when Widdy discovered the fun of setting booby traps. He left marbles carefully placed on the floor, he balanced Astor's books in a tower that the slightest nudge would topple, he loosened the pegs that supported the blackboard on its three-legged stand. When the blackboard crashed to the floor, barely missing her toe, she wanted to scream. Instead, she had to pretend it had happened by accident, and calmly re-inserted the pegs and replaced the board.

She had to pretend to view a great many things as accidents: Widdy bumping into her, the disappearance of her pens and chalks, the bits of food thrown on the floor. She managed not to hear the giggles and guffaws, she managed not to be aware of paper darts and other flying objects. A good day was when she spent less than half an hour after school cleaning up.

Teaching was irrelevant. She tried to bribe her pupils with promises of an extended lunchbreak or an early end to lessons, yet even that was turned against her.

'How are you going to keep us quiet this afternoon?' asked Blanquette. 'You'll have to make us a better offer than this morning.'

Day by day, Astor had to concede a little more and stoop a little lower. She hated herself for doing it, and any reprieve she could buy was only temporary. There was no escape from the shame of her situation.

It was impossible to share it with Verrol. If she once started to tell him the truth, she'd never be able to stop. She foresaw herself dissolving into an abject, sobbing mess, until she ended up begging him to escort her back to her stepfather's

72

estate. But she'd already had her answer on *that* proposal.

She took to pretending she was asleep when he knocked on her door. One day, when he knocked repeatedly, she called out, 'Not now! I'm too tired.'

This time, though, he didn't just walk away, but threw open the door and strode in regardless. She had been sprawled out on her bed fully clothed, exhausted from yet another wretched school day. She struggled to sit up, straighten her clothes and make herself respectable.

'Sorry.' His brow creased with a look of concern. 'Were you . . .?'

'This had better be important,' she said. She didn't want to get into explanations with him.

'I think so. An airship just landed, a monster of a thing. I'm betting it comes from the Parliament in London Town. It has the opposition party's insignia on its side.'

'I don't care about politics.'

'I know. But something's going on, something unofficial. We can find out what.'

In spite of herself, Astor was curious. 'How?'

He grinned. 'I'll show you. We can spy on them.'

17

Seven floors up, they left the main staircases behind and turned off on one of Verrol's secret routes. He had obviously been doing a lot more exploring of Swale House. They slipped along a passage carpeted in dust and came to a room filled with pounding machinery.

'Pump room,' said Verrol tersely. 'Ventilation. Sucks clean air down from the roof.'

He skirted whirring belts and fast-spinning spindles, and led the way to a ladder. Climbing up, they entered a kind of chimney, squeezed in between a wall and a shiny metal duct. The duct wheezed and whistled with air passing through.

As ladder followed ladder, the main duct branched off into smaller ducts. At one branch, Verrol left the ladders behind and switched to a horizontal route. They crawled along a channel on hands and knees in absolute darkness. Part way along, Verrol opened a hatch at the side, and they scrambled back out into the light.

Now they were in a normal room – normal except for the dust-sheets covering all the furniture. Obviously no one had occupied this room for a very long time.

'More rooms than they know what to do with,' Verrol muttered.

On the other side of the room was a huge open fireplace. Logs lay neatly piled in the grate, but there was no fire. Verrol strode across, snatched up the tongs and ducked in under the hood of the chimney.

Astor ducked in behind him. 'What are we doing?'

'This is where they'll come for a private conversation. The retiring room.'

He seemed to be referring to the fire-blackened wall, and for a moment she thought he'd gone mad. Then she realised what he was doing with the tongs: working a loose brick out of the wall. He slid it free, then put his finger to his lips for hush.

She nodded, and together they peered through the hole in the wall.

On the other side was a bright, crackling fire. Back-to-back fireplaces! Astor was momentarily dazzled by the leaping flames; then she looked past the flames to the room beyond.

The retiring room was cosy and intimate, with wood-panelled walls that seemed to waver through the heat of the flames. Four leather armchairs made a half-circle around a low table, facing in towards the fire.

Bartizan and Phillidas had already entered the room, along with an important-looking personage in a high, shiny collar and pinstripe suit. He had slicked-back hair, heavy jowls and darting eyes. The three of them stood just inside the door while a bevy of servants poured drinks. The crackling fire masked their conversation, but they were evidently exchanging social pleasantries.

'That's the visitor,' Verrol whispered. 'Could be an MP.'

Then Bartizan made a peremptory gesture, and the servants left, closing the door behind them. Phillidas came forward to the fireplace and lowered himself into one of the armchairs. The visitor followed suit; Bartizan took up a position warming himself at the side of the fire. Astor found herself viewing more of Bartizan's posterior than she really wanted to see.

While Bartizan drank from an enormous brandy balloon, the visitor sipped from a slightly smaller one, and Phillidas toyed with what looked like a tumbler of plain soda water. When they spoke again, their voices carried above the noise of the fire.

'Well, to business,' said Bartizan. 'How are things moving along in Parliament, Chard?'

Astor heard the whistle of Verrol's sharply indrawn breath.

'Very promising,' answered the visitor. 'Stigwell is ready to come across if we offer him Foreign Affairs. Higgis has the Duchess well under his thumb, and she'll use her influence in the Upper House.'

Bartizan took a large swig of brandy. 'What about the Commons?'

'The balance is swinging our way. Looking better every day.'

'Don't soft-soap me, Chard, I'm not one of your politicians. Give a straightforward man a straightforward answer. Out with it.'

'Of course, of course.' Important as he might be, Chard still deferred to the Swales. 'On latest count, we have thirty-two definites. But the waverers are the key.'

'Thirty-two is barely a quarter of the Chamber,' said Phillidas in his high, flat tone.

'Yes, but as I said, the waverers are the key. Put them under enough pressure, and they'll vote with the Progress Party.'

'Number of waverers?' Phillidas demanded.

'We estimate thirty-five. Could be as many as forty.'

Phillidas tapped his fingertips against the side of his tumbler and appeared to be calculating.

'Pressure?' boomed Bartizan. 'We'll give them pressure!'

'Hassock thinks he's safe with his majority,' Chard went on. 'He'll play into our hands with his smugness.'

'And King George?'

'Difficult. But he doesn't have the power of his grandfather. The military don't love him the way they loved the old King.'

'Good.' Bartizan swirled his coat-tails. 'We'll settle him, then.'

He turned suddenly and reached down for the poker. Before Astor and Verrol could move, he began jabbing at the logs in the grate. The flames had been like a magical screen, but Bartizan's face was now so close, it seemed impossible for him not to see them. He didn't, though . . . and in the next moment, a cloud of sparks and smoke flew up from the logs, shielding them once again from view.

Verrol drew back in a hurry, but Astor was a fraction too slow. Smoke puffed through the hole and caught in her nose and throat.

Tears came to her eyes as she fought the urge to cough. Her throat seemed to have spikes in it. She staggered away while the cough kept rising, about to break forth . . . until suddenly a cloth clamped over her mouth.

It was Verrol, pressing his neckerchief into her face. Or pressing her face into his neckerchief, because his other hand held her by the back of her neck. She twisted instinctively, but he didn't let go.

She relaxed then . . . she made herself relax. She breathed in through the cloth, taking careful, shallow breaths. After half a minute, the cough reflex eased. She nodded her head, and Verrol accepted the signal. He dropped the neckerchief and his grip on her neck.

They were standing half in and half out of the unlit fireplace, under the edge of the hood. Astor looked back at the hole in the wall, but the smoke hadn't yet dissipated. She turned to Verrol and raised a quizzical eyebrow.

He explained in a whisper. 'The man they're talking to is Ephraim Chard, leader of the opposition and head of the Progress Party. The Progress Party is in league with the plutocrats against the Rural Party. The Rural Party represents old squires and landed gentry, while the Progress Party represents new urban industrialists and entrepreneurs.'

'Who represents ordinary people?'

'Nobody. Ordinary people don't get a vote. Don't you know anything about politics?'

Astor might have retorted angrily except for the need to keep her voice down. She waited a moment, then whispered, 'So what are they planning?'

'The Progress Party wants to get back into power. Chard wants to replace Hassock as Prime Minister. They talk about applying pressure, but I'm not sure how . . . Let's spy some more.'

By now, the smoke had cleared from the hole in the wall. They stooped, heads side by side, and peered through into the retiring room again. The fire had died down to its previous state, although Astor covered her mouth with her hand just in case.

The conversation had moved on. 'We have *our* men,' Bartizan was saying. 'All primed and ready to march. What about the rest?'

'Yorkshire and Lancashire are solid. Clydeside has been ready for weeks – they really hate the Rurals up there. Tyneport and Teesbank are coming along nicely.'

'Armed?' asked Phillidas.

'Many of them have kept their weapons from the war. Rifles and bayonets. The others have replicas.'

'*Replicas!*' Phillidas let out one of his strange braying laughs. He seemed unimpressed.

'What about the capital?' asked Bartizan.

'The London militias are prepared. We're still working to bring some of the small businessmen on board. But now that we have our figurehead . . .'

'Signed on the dotted line,' said Bartizan.

'Yes. It shouldn't take long to win them round now.'

'Give us a date.'

'Some time in November, perhaps?' Chard smiled his slightly oily smile. 'Unfortunately, not all our supporters are as bold as you.'

'That's why they'll stay *small* businessmen.' Bartizan snorted and straddled his legs further apart. 'The Swales reached the top by taking calculated risks. Am I right, brother?'

Phillidas didn't hear or didn't respond. Instead, he brought out a pencil and pocketbook.

'I'd like the figures,' he told Chard. 'How many militiamen? How many marchers?'

'Where shall I start?'

'Clydeside,' said Phillidas, as he wrote down the name. 'How many?'

'Five thousand. Jellett expects at least half of them to march.'

'Two thousand five hundred, then . . .'

For the next few minutes, the only conversation was about numbers, and the only activity was Phillidas writing in his pocketbook. Astor sensed a shrug from Verrol beside her. There was nothing further to learn.

They drew back together, and Verrol replaced the brick in the wall. When they stepped out from the fireplace, Astor had to laugh at the sight of him. Black stripes ran across his face where he had pressed against the soot-covered wall. He grinned and pointed back at her, so she guessed her face bore similar markings.

He wiped his face with the sleeve of his jacket, while she found a handkerchief to use. By the time their stripes were gone, they had both become serious.

'They're plotting a coup, aren't they?' said Astor. 'With those militias you were talking about?'

'Yes. I suspected something was going on, but I never imagined anything so big. This is bad.'

'Mmm.' An idea was beginning to form in Astor's mind. The plot might be bad for the country, but it could contain a glimmer of hope for *her*. 'Explain it all to me,' she said. 'Exactly what you think they're going to do.'

18

Dear Stepfather, she wrote,
I trust you are all well at Dorrin Estate. I am writing to communicate some vital information that has come to my attention during my residence at Swale House.

Astor had planned what to say last night, but had put off writing it out until this morning. It was the most difficult letter she had ever had to write. It was a struggle to say *my residence at Swale House,* as though she hadn't been betrayed into the role of governess, as though she were living in luxury rather than being reduced to this dingy little room. She gritted her teeth and went on.

The Progress Party is conspiring with the Swale brothers, Mr Bartizan and Mr Phillidas, and also other plutocrats in Clydeside, Yorkshire, Lancashire, Tyneport, Teesbank and London Town. They plan to force His Majesty to dismiss Prime Minister Hassock and the Rural Party by marching with many thousands of disaffected ex-soldiers.

Good, she thought, keep it dry and impersonal. Marshal Dorrin was always uncomfortable with expressions of personal feeling, especially women's feelings. He had lived too long in the army, that was his trouble. Women were a separate species to him, unknowable, irrational, unpredictable. And if there was one thing he liked, it was predictability.

Astor recalled the household at Dorrin Estate, where even the cooks were male. Everything ran to a timetable that had been set in stone long before she and her mother moved in. Astor always felt that the two of them were interlopers, too soft and indefinite to find a place in his rigid regime. No doubt he would have felt more favourably towards her if she'd been a boy.

She started a new paragraph.

Mr Ephraim Chard visited Swale House yesterday, and I personally overheard him discuss his involvement in the plot. He nominated November as a probable date. This isn't some wild plan; they've worked out all details and really mean to go through with it.

She considered the tone of her last sentence: was she trying a little too hard? It would have been so much easier to write to her mother! But no, that was impossible in this case. Mrs Dorrin understood politics even less than Astor, and she'd muddle everything up if she had to repeat it to her husband. What's more, the Marshal wouldn't take it seriously if it came through his wife; he'd be far more likely to dismiss it as – in his favourite phrase – 'womanish vapourings'.

In Mrs Dorrin's view, it was a proof of love that Britain's most famous living military leader had married someone who was a nobody in the eyes of the world. In Astor's view, he probably liked having a wife who was a nobody except insofar as he raised her up. Mrs Dorrin was soft, pretty and feminine – a perfect example of all the things he didn't understand. But perhaps he didn't need to understand them when she fitted his expectations so exactly. She was just a woman being 'womanish'.

None of that was relevant to this particular letter, however. Astor wrote on:

I do not presume to advise your course of action, but I am sure you will know how to act decisively against traitors. You would be shocked to hear how disrespectfully they speak of our beloved King George.

That was one thing she could count on: his patriotism. Her mother had told her countless tales of his brave exploits in the service of King and country. He had been wounded five times, and was renowned for leading his troops from the front. She was sure such a man wouldn't shrink from confronting the plotters.

There remained only the most important sentence to add.

I have additional information that I cannot risk setting down in a letter, but will be able to communicate to you face to face.

That should do it! She had no real additional information, but he would have to rescue her from Swale House if he thought she had. She signed off formally:

Your dutiful stepdaughter,
Astor Vance

and put down her quill with relief. She had done it! She had said all the things she needed to say while keeping back all the things she really wanted to say.

She folded the sheet of paper, then clicked her tongue.

Where to find an envelope? Were there any in the school store-room? Perhaps Verrol would be able to get hold of one.

Right now, it was time for her daily purgatory with Blanquette, Prester and Widdy. If they arrived at the schoolroom before her, heaven knows what damage Widdy might wreak. At least there was a possible end to her misery in sight.

19

Astor couldn't focus on teaching her pupils, or even entertaining them. Distracted by her hopes for the letter to her stepfather, she let them do whatever they wanted.

What Widdy wanted to do was gallop around the room like a racehorse. The others joined in the game by putting obstacles in his way: books and chairs and outstretched legs. Sometimes Widdy cleared the obstacles, and sometimes he didn't.

Astor closed her eyes and ears to the mayhem. She hadn't found an envelope in the storeroom, but she was sure Verrol could solve that problem. Sending it off was another matter; would he know where to find a postal service? She wondered if he had done any exploring outside as well as inside Swale House.

The horse-racing game amused Blanquette for a while, but her real interest lay in tormenting Astor. 'Good horsey,' she said, when Widdy performed a huge jump over a chair that Prester had flung in his path. 'You deserve a sugar lump. Why don't you go to our governess and collect your reward?'

Widdy trotted across and nudged against Astor's elbow. Then he nuzzled his head in her lap. He made a whickering sound and turned to look up at her with his big blue eyes.

In spite of herself, Astor had to admit he was cute. Widdy could be the most appealing of children when he wanted.

'Well done,' she said, and patted him on top of his head.

'Sugar lump, Widdy!' Blanquette egged him on. 'Where's your sugar lump?'

If she'd had a sweet or toffee, Astor would have played the game just to keep them all quiet. However, Widdy had an idea of his own. He nudged and probed over Astor's arm towards the diamante brooch she wore pinned to the front of her dress. He had decided to interpret the brooch as a sugar lump.

'No,' she said. 'Don't be silly.'

Widdy lowered his head, opened his mouth and snapped it shut over the brooch.

'Whoo!' cheered Blanquette.

It was a miracle the pin didn't stab him inside the mouth. He worried the brooch this way and that, trying to pull it off.

'Stop it!' Astor shouted. 'You'll hurt yourself.'

Hurt wasn't a word that meant much to Widdy. He kept pulling and worrying at the brooch, while Astor kept trying to push him away without actually manhandling him.

It was Prester who came to her aid. He jumped from his chair, grabbed Widdy from behind and yanked him backwards. With a sharp ripping sound, the brooch tore clean away from her dress. He spun the younger boy aside and flung him on all fours.

Widdy coughed out the brooch, which went skimming across the floor. It ended up next to Blanquette's chair.

'Well, well, what's this?' Blanquette bent to pick it up. 'A diamante brooch.'

'Thank you,' said Astor, holding out her hand.

'You mean "please",' said Blanquette. '"Thank you" is for when you get it.' She examined the brooch against the light. 'Cheap trinket!'

'Nevertheless.' Astor kept her hand extended. 'I'd like it back.'

'Why is a governess wearing jewellery anyway?' Blanquette asked of the world in general. 'A governess doesn't have the right to dress up. Jewellery's for masters, not servants.'

Astor chose to ignore her, and turned instead to Prester. 'You did well, thank you. You saved your cousin from a nasty injury.'

Prester preened. 'It wasn't for him. I did it for you.'

'Well, thank you for helping me, then.'

Blanquette blew a raspberry in Astor's direction. 'Go on!' she encouraged. 'Keep batting your eyelashes at him!'

Astor made the mistake of reacting. 'What?'

'That's what you do, isn't it? Bat your eyelashes. Flounce your pretty little curls.'

Astor flushed. Blanquette had a knack for knowing exactly where to twist the knife.

'I like her looking nice,' said Prester. 'Why not, if she can?'

Blanquette continued to address Astor. 'Go on, get those eyelashes working! Win him over! He doesn't have a brain, he should be easy.'

'Shut up, Blanquette,' said Prester.

He went across to his sister and, without warning, snatched the brooch from her. Then he carried it back to Astor like a trophy.

'Here's your brooch. Can I pin it back on for you?'

Astor pulled herself up straight and shook her head. She was very conscious of the revealing rip in her dress where the brooch had been torn away.

Blanquette was livid – and turned her rage on Astor. 'Typical! I know your sort! You think you're good-looking so you trade on it.'

'She *is* good-looking,' said Prester, in the very same moment that Astor snapped, 'You know nothing about me.'

Blanquette snorted. 'No? *No*? I bet you've been the same ever since you were a little girl. Charm the men and impress the women! You've never needed to talk sense or show one bit of intelligence. You rely on prettiness to get your way! Looking nice is all you are! You're nothing inside! All for show! That's what *you* are!'

Astor felt as if she'd been punched in the stomach. What had she done to deserve such abuse? How could Blanquette sum up her whole life like that? It was ridiculous, all guesswork and lies.

She could have hit back with 'You're only bitter because you're fat and ugly,' but she didn't. Partly because she wasn't quite sure that it was all lies. Of course she didn't deliberately trade on her looks . . . not *deliberately*.

Prester polished the brooch on his breeches. 'Let me pin it back on for you,' he said again.

He moved round behind her chair, and she sensed that he was standing very close. Much too close. Alarm bells rang in her head, but she didn't want to antagonise her only supporter.

'Shall I, then?'

'No, don't bother,' she said.

'It's no bother.'

'I'd rather you didn't.'

'Aren't I your favourite?'

His hands came down over her shoulders, down to the front of her dress. As she tried to shake him away, the brooch fell with a clatter to the floor.

'*Get off!*' she ordered.

Widdy produced a shriek of his own. '*Yii – yii – yii!*'

She jumped to her feet and swung to confront Prester. She found herself staring close up at the adolescent fuzz on his upper lip.

His smirk was as good as a statement: *You're no taller than me.*

'Don't you dare touch him!' Blanquette roared from the other side of the room.

Astor couldn't touch Prester, but he could touch her. And in the next moment, he did just that.

'I'm your favourite,' he said, taking a grip on her upper arms. 'You should do what I want.'

His grip tightened painfully. He was pressing against her, forcing her to arch backwards.

Enough! She went instantly from shock to rage. She lifted her knee high and caught him sharply between the legs.

The air came out of him in a great whooshing gasp. He sagged and clutched at his injured parts. His face was grey as he backed away.

'That's how much you're my favourite,' she snapped.

He propped himself up with his hand on a desk. She went after him and forced him to move further away. He was blubbering now, a mingled sound of humiliation, pain and resentment. Desk by desk he retreated, still unable to stand fully upright.

Astor dusted her hands as over a job well done. 'Now you see what happens,' she said.

Blanquette's voice rose threateningly. 'And now *you'll* see what happens.' She got up from her desk and crossed to the door. 'Come on, Prester. You too, Widdy. We're reporting this.'

A moment later, the three Swale children swept out into the corridor, slamming the door behind them.

20

Astor's chest was heaving, and the world seemed to sway in a haze around her. It was horrible and grotesque! A twelve-year-old boy who thought he could paw her just because she wasn't allowed to use physical force on him! The ugliness of the scene made her skin crawl.

She regretted what she'd done – and at the same time didn't regret it at all. It had been building up for weeks. The insolence of him! The insolence of them all! Bumptious little brats! For the sake of her own self-respect, she'd had to do it.

There would be consequences, though, she had no doubt of that. She needed to calm down. The idea of the piano next door flashed into her mind . . . and immediately she strode through the door into the miniature auditorium.

She sat on the stool and raised the lid of the keyboard. So soothing, the familiar arrangement of white and black keys! But when she began to play, there was no flow to her playing. Her hands were taut and clenched, and she couldn't concentrate on what her fingers were doing. Her father had always said you had to relax into music, yet how could she relax? The tune turned into a lumpy, jangling sound in her ears.

She thumped on the keyboard in anger and frustration.

Louder and louder, more and more violent! Then she shut the lid with a resounding crash. They had ruined that for her too! She kicked away the stool, stamped back into the other room and sat down in her teacher's chair. Gloomily she waited for someone to come and collect her.

It was a whole half-hour before they came. Five servants trooped in and ordered her to accompany them. They escorted her along corridors, into a steam elevator, up to the higher floors of Swale House.

She had no idea where she was being taken until she was actually inside the room. Then she realised: it was the same room where Bartizan and Phillidas had talked with the leader of the Progress Party yesterday. She had approached by way of a very different route today.

Her eyes flew at once to the fire burning merrily in the grate. She would have liked to think that Verrol was spying out from the back of the fireplace at this very moment. There wasn't much chance of that, however.

Bartizan and Phillidas stood in the centre of the room, with their wives and children lined up behind them. Astor remembered that Blanquette and Prester were Bartizan's children, while Widdy belonged to Phillidas. She held her head high as the servants brought her forward to face the two Swale brothers.

'Well?' Bartizan hooked his thumbs in his waistcoat pockets.

Astor swung a hand to indicate Prester. 'Did he tell you what he did to me?'

'Don't try to wriggle out of it,' Bartizan growled. 'You won't get far like that.'

'It was her fault,' Blanquette called out from behind. 'She led him on.'

Astor grimaced. 'A twelve-year-old boy? No, thank you!'

'A Swale.' Blanquette answered scorn with scorn. 'You should be so lucky.'

'Quiet.' Bartizan turned on Astor with an ominous smile. 'So you have nothing to say in your own defence?'

Astor tossed her head. 'My defence is what he did to me first.'

She knew they would punish her, but she refused to quail. The fire crackled and the room was quiet.

'There is one other thing,' said Phillidas, and brought out a folded sheet of paper he'd been holding behind his back.

Astor stared as he unfolded it. She recognised what it was even before he began reading selected phrases.

'The Progress Party is conspiring with the Swale brothers . . . marching with many thousands of disaffected ex-soldiers . . . Mr Ephraim Chard . . . act decisively against traitors.' Phillidas looked up and studied Astor through his tinted glasses. It was like being inspected by an insect. 'A letter written to Marshal Dorrin. Your stepfather, I believe?'

'I don't . . . how . . . where?'

'It was found in your room by your skivvy.' Phillidas's bony finger jabbed out at her in accusation. 'Incriminating evidence. Don't deny it. You know more than is good for you.'

'A vicious governess *and* a spy,' Bartizan rumbled. 'We have a nice little cell just right for you, Miss Whatever-your-name-is.'

'Miss Vance,' Astor replied automatically. She had nothing else to say.

Bartizan crooked a finger to summon the servants. 'Take her down to the basement and punish her.'

Before the servants could move, Widdy ran up to Phillidas. 'Can we, can *we*? Pleathe, Daddy!'

'It was me she hurt,' said Prester, appealing to *his* father too.

'Very well.' Bartizan nodded. 'You can each choose one punishment for her.'

Widdy let out a cheer.

'We can tell the servants what to do?' asked Blanquette.

'Yes.' For a moment, Bartizan looked like any other indulgent parent. 'Have you thought of something special?'

'Her hair,' Blanquette responded at once. 'She's so proud of it. I'll have it all cut off.'

'I'll do worse than that,' Prester promised.

'Me too!' Widdy piped up happily. 'Much worthe!'

Astor shuddered at the glint in their eyes.

'Well, think carefully before you choose.' Bartizan winked, then turned once more to the servants. 'A cell in the basement. The children will go with you.'

They descended by steam elevator: the three Swale children, Astor, and the servants guarding Astor. The platform of the elevator rattled and shook and picked up speed all the way down, until it seemed it must surely crash into the ground. But the brakes came on with a screech at the last moment, and clouds of white steam billowed in through the surrounding cage.

The servants didn't lay hands on Astor, but they penned her in on all sides. With Blanquette, Prester and Widdy leading the way, they stepped out from the steam into a huge, cavernous

91

hall with rows of massive piers and arches – massive enough to bear the weight of all the floors above. Straw lay scattered over the stone flags underfoot, putting Astor in mind of a stables. In the next moment, she heard snorting, snuffling sounds and the clink of harnesses and horseshoes.

'This way!' cried Prester, pointing.

As they passed between the piers, Astor discovered it was not so much a stables as an unloading dock. Lines of carts queued to pass under steel hoists that lifted out their cargoes enclosed in voluminous net bags. There were traction engines too, with black cylindrical boilers and striped canopies, pulling three, four or five trolleys. They queued to be unloaded by a pair of swivelling cranes.

While drivers and horses waited patiently for their turn, the hall all around was a hive of activity. Men in shirtsleeves and leather waistcoats bustled about emptying the net bags, piling up boxes, carrying sacks on their backs or rolling barrels over the ground. On the far side of the hall was a conveyor belt on rollers that carried away boxes, sacks and barrels through a hole in the wall.

Although Astor couldn't yet see any steps leading down to a basement, she knew every pace must be bringing her closer. She had to break free – but how? If only there was some way to distract her escort.

'What's that?' exclaimed one servant, swinging suddenly to the left.

'I smell smoke,' said Prester.

Cries of alarm rose from the other side of a row of piers.

'Look!' Widdy was wildly excited. 'Fire in the thtraw!'

In the next moment, the whole hall was in an uproar. The straw had caught alight in a long swathe of flickering yellow flames. The men in leather waistcoats ran in every direction for buckets and water, or to stamp out the fire with their boots. As yet the flames were only ankle-high, but they were spreading wide and fast.

It was the distraction for which Astor had prayed, and her escort of servants would have gone to help if not for Blanquette yelling at the top of her voice. 'No! Not our business! We go to the basement!'

Recalled to their task, the servants bunched even more closely around Astor. Someone pushed her in the back to hurry her along.

Then the horses panicked. The air was filled with neighing as the terrified animals reared up and kicked out, showing the whites of their eyes. Some broke free of their traces, others dragged their carts along behind. But there was no exit for them. Around and around they galloped, until the chaos became a single swirling circle.

Now or never! Astor picked a gap and darted out and away from her escort.

She was quick enough over the first ten paces, but her long governess's dress stopped her from running flat out. The servants shouted and gave chase. She was so focused on her pursuers that she barely noticed the horse and cart bearing down on her from the opposite direction. Just in time, she skidded to a halt.

There was no driver at the front of the cart. The horse flashed past at breakneck speed, the iron-rimmed wheels almost crushing her toes. All she could think was that her escape had failed, and the servants would seize her any second now.

Instead, someone leaned out over the tailboard, caught

her around the waist and scooped her up bodily into the back of the cart.

Verrol!

The cart slewed to the right, and she went sprawling. Verrol dived forward, recovered the reins and brought the horse under some degree of control.

'Can you drive a cart?' he yelled back at her.

'What?' She gripped the side of the cart and got up on her knees. 'Yes. Now?'

He was directing the horse towards a wall of blank arches. All solid stone except for the space under the middle arch, which was shuttered with wood. A door?

When she saw the wooden bar resting in its socket, she knew she'd guessed right. Here was an exit!

'Circle round and come back!' Verrol shouted in her ear.

He swung the cart parallel to the door, thrust the reins into Astor's hand and vaulted out over the side. The vehicle had barely slowed.

Astor concentrated on guiding the horse. She had driven traps and buggies on Dorrin Estate – how hard could this be? Out of the corner of her eye, she saw Verrol reach for the bar to open the door.

She veered to pass between the piers and around the cranes and traction engines. She didn't try to avoid the men in leather waistcoats, who were forced to jump out of the way. They added their yells and curses to the general hubbub. At least she'd drawn everyone's attention away from what Verrol was doing.

Coming full circle, she directed the cart once more towards the exit door. Verrol had slid the bar aside, and one wing of the door stood already open. He pushed the other wing wider as she approached.

But now warnings and orders rang out. Astor heard Blanquette's voice raised above all the others, she saw men turn and begin running towards the door. She aimed the cart towards the exit where Verrol was waiting.

Pulling back on the reins, she slowed the horse so that he could jump on again as they made their escape. But he didn't. He ran under the arch along by the cart . . . and Astor realised they hadn't made their escape at all. They had only entered a smaller chamber with a second arch and a second wooden door straight ahead. And *that* door was still barred shut.

She didn't need to use the reins; the horse stopped by itself and the cart jolted to a halt.

'What now?' she cried in despair.

Verrol gave no sign of having heard. He was busy closing the first door behind them. He swung the left-hand wing shut, dragged in the bar from the other side, then set his shoulder to the right-hand wing.

Astor could see Prester at the forefront of the horde rushing towards the smaller chamber. Verrol finished closing the right-hand wing just in time. He jammed the bar hard into place, wedging it in the middle of both wings.

Astor stared at the door as fists hammered on the wood from the other side. How long would it hold? She hardly noticed Verrol run forward to the second door.

Their pursuers stopped hammering and began jerking the first door back and forth. The wood bulged visibly, with ominous creaking sounds.

Meanwhile, Verrol was trying to open the second door. By the time Astor turned to watch, he had managed to push the wings a few inches apart. Dim yellowy light showed through the gap, and the smog rolled in. This was the outside door, no doubt of it.

He re-planted his feet, leaned in at a steeper angle and strained with all his might. He gave one last desperate heave, and the wings suddenly yielded, swinging wide on their own momentum.

In the next moment he was up beside Astor on the cart. He smacked the horse on the rump to start it moving forward. She prepared to use the reins, but he knocked them from her hand.

'No!'

'But—' The breath was squeezed from her body as he grabbed her round the waist.

'Jump!'

The horse sped out through the open door, but they didn't go with it. Verrol launched off in a tremendous leap, taking Astor with him. They cleared the side of the cart and slammed into the wall of the chamber.

Astor felt herself slipping down until her feet found a ledge in the stone.

'Up! Up!'

He had to shout above the grating, splintering sounds from the other door. The bar wedged against it was giving way.

She had no time to rage against his crazy choice to abandon the cart. There were beams of timber set higher in the wall, and already he was swarming up from beam to beam. She went up after him.

Higher again was a framework of rafters spanning the room from side to side. Verrol halted, knelt and reached down a hand to her. When she clasped his hand, he lifted her so fast she seemed to be flying.

In the same instant, the inside door burst open, and

servants and waistcoated men came surging through. When they saw the wings of the outside door gaping wide, they immediately rushed forward.

'After them!'

'Follow that cart!'

'Search the streets!'

'Listen for hooves and wheels!'

As Astor and Verrol watched from above, the pursuit streamed in one door and out the other, chasing after the empty cart.

Astor understood the trick of it now. Their pursuers automatically expected them to flee as far as possible from Swale House. No one even thought to look up into the shadows of the rafters.

Forty men streamed out through the chamber to search the streets, though not Blanquette, Prester or Widdy. The last men out closed both sets of doors behind them. Evidently this smaller chamber served to limit the smog flowing into the unloading dock.

But there was now smog in the chamber itself. Noxious yellow tendrils floated on the air and curled up through the rafters. The first whiff of rotten-egg smell made Astor want to gag.

She screwed up her nose and tried not to inhale. Verrol gave her a nudge, and she realised he had taken off his neckerchief. She let him tie it over her nose and mouth as a face mask. The fabric filtered out the worst of the smell, at least enough for her to breathe.

'You'll adjust to it by and by,' he whispered.

Twenty minutes later, another band of men came through. They were retainers in blue-and-gold livery, and they carried pistols, shotguns and other weapons.

'The Swale-men are hunting you down,' Verrol commented.

He called the retainers 'Swale-men', which sounded either derogatory or dismissive. The sight of their guns made Astor shiver.

'Why am I so important?' she asked.

'You could be a threat to them. You tried to write to your stepfather, so you might try again.'

'How do you know about that?'

'I was watching through the fireplace.'

'Ah, right. Lucky for me.'

'You were very careless leaving that letter where it could be found.'

Astor didn't like being criticised, though she supposed he had the right. He had sacrificed his position in the Swale household to rescue her – and no doubt his long-term future in the Dorrin household too. She didn't understand why he'd done it, but she was thankful he had.

After half an hour, the ordinary servants and waistcoated men came back in. Presumably they had their regular tasks to return to.

'When do we make a move?' asked Astor.

'When it's night,' Verrol replied.

Time passed. Astor shifted to take up a more comfortable position on the rafters. As Verrol had predicted, she had adjusted to the smell of the smog. It was as unpleasant as ever, but no longer made her want to throw up. She unfastened the neckerchief and handed it back to him.

Finally, the men in blue-and-gold livery came back in. As the door opened and closed, Astor could see that night had now fallen outside.

'They're calling off the search,' she suggested hopefully.

'Only because it's night,' said Verrol. 'They'll start again tomorrow morning.'

They waited another five minutes, then clambered down from the rafters. Verrol opened the door just wide enough to slip through. Outside, two gaslights flanked the door, casting a pool of sickly yellow light.

'Come away from the light!' hissed Verrol, and tugged her by the arm.

Astor's movements stirred the vapour and made it roll and eddy with a life of its own. It clung around her like a second skin, thicker and fouler than anything she had experienced so far. She clapped a hand over her nose and mouth.

Away from the light, the world dissolved into uncertain shapes and shadows. She couldn't even see to the other side of the street until they crossed over. Further along were more gaslights, which appeared to float suspended in the air.

They hurried along by the wall of another building. Then Verrol dropped her arm and plunged suddenly into a narrow alley.

'Follow me,' he called back over his shoulder.

They passed under bridges that arched across from building to building above their heads. It grew darker and darker the further they advanced, until it was like walking underground.

Astor held her arms stretched out in front of her, on guard against unseen obstacles.

Then she bumped into Verrol's back. A faint lightening in the murk announced the end of the alley, fifteen yards ahead.

'Where are we going?' she asked.

'Away from this area. These big houses are where the rich people live.'

'We're going to a poor area?'

'The poorest. Slumtown.'

Astor didn't like the sound of that. 'What's wrong with here?'

'No one in Slumtown will report back to the Swales. With luck we'll find a gang to join.'

'I don't want to join a gang.'

'Why not?'

'I don't like gangs from the slums.'

'No choice. We can hardly survive out here on our own.'

Astor had a dozen counter-arguments, but they all came down to one flaring objection: *those gangs killed my father.* However, Verrol strode off before she had time to object.

Emerging into another street, they passed more houses, keeping close to the walls. The walls were blank and forbidding, the houses were like fortresses. When there were any windows, they were mere slots set high above the ground, defended with iron bars.

Sounds came and went in the smog, mostly muffled but occasionally loud and clear. There was no way of telling what was close or far away. Everything seemed insubstantial, a world of ghostly rattles and clatters and clinks. It was a long while before they encountered anyone at all.

Astor didn't register the danger until Verrol suddenly

swung and flung her against the wall. Her shoulderblades and the back of her head made painful contact with the stone.

'Shh!'

She heard the footsteps then, all marching in step. It seemed an eternity before they came into view. They appeared in silhouette, at least a dozen of them.

Astor could only pray that she and Verrol were less visible against the darkness of the wall. The marchers passed so close she could hear their breathing and the swish of their clothes. But they continued on their way without missing a step.

'Who were *they*?' she asked, as they faded into the distance.

'Ex-soldiers. Ugly customers. You okay?'

She rubbed the back of her head and flexed her shoulderblades. 'Yes.'

They walked on. Astor tried to minimise the sound of her footsteps, while Verrol glided along like a ghost. She had the impression he'd done this sort of thing before.

They rounded a corner into another street. Here the gaslights were mounted not on poles but on wrought-iron brackets that projected from the house-fronts. Every house had a massive door set between pillars and studded with steel points; many boasted brass plaques announcing the name of the family within.

Verrol pointed to a vehicle that had pulled up a few doors further along. It was a tricycle with a huge wheel at the front, two smaller wheels at the back, and a box-like hutch between the back wheels. A man in a white apron reached in at the side of the hutch and came away bearing a tray.

'Pastryman,' Verrol muttered. 'Evening delivery. Must be some family putting on a banquet.'

Whistling to himself, the pastryman went up a flight of

stone steps and yanked on a bellpull. A moment later the door opened, and he vanished inside.

Verrol turned to Astor. 'Are you hungry?'

'What? Why?'

He nodded towards the pastryman's vehicle. 'Plenty more in there, I'm betting.'

Astor was shocked at the idea. 'You mean, just take things? Without paying?'

'Unless you've brought a purse with you.'

'But that's stealing.'

'Yes.' His grin was shameless. 'I'll steal some for you. Wait here.'

She watched as he ran forward, quick and lithe, checking in all directions. Even his manner was thievish!

A grating scrape of metal drew her attention to a house across the street. A man in a braided jacket was pulling back a barred gate that opened onto a courtyard. Inside, a magnificent coach with a pair of black horses waited to drive forth.

'Hurry up, Mr Tollamy!' cried a female voice.

'We don't want to be late!' echoed another.

There was laughter and refinement in those voices, which clearly belonged to gracious, cultivated ladies. Astor's mind flashed back to the kind of people who used to attend her father's concerts. *Her* kind of people.

Mr Tollamy finished opening the gate and sprang up onto the driver's bench. He flicked his whip, and the horses moved forward with a silvery tinkle of bells.

Astor came to an instant decision. Verrol was doing things his way, but she didn't have to sink to that level. She had been brought up as a gentlewoman, and she could still appeal to other gentlewomen. As the horses swerved to head back along the street she'd just come, she ran out from the pavement waving her arms.

'Help! Stop! Please!'

23

The driver didn't respond immediately, but something must have been said to him because after another thirty yards he pulled on the reins. As the coach came to a stop, the horses tossed their heads and jingled their bells again.

It was a coach in the most modern style, with inflated rubber tyres that swelled like circular balloons. The bodywork was of polished brass, the windows had the shape of large glass portholes. Two ladies looked out from a porthole as Astor ran up.

She slowed to a more ladylike walking pace. Since she couldn't do much about her dishevelled appearance, she would have to impress them with her manners.

'Come! Come closer!' cried one of the ladies.

They might have been on their way to an opera or concert, with their button-up collars, powdered cheeks and elaborate floral hair-decorations. Astor prepared a few well-bred phrases befitting the daughter of a musician who had received an OBE.

'I must apologise—' she began.

'Closer, closer!' exclaimed the same lady in a tone of light-hearted amusement. 'Don't worry about Mr Tollamy.'

Astor stepped closer again.

'Stand by the window, dear,' said the other lady. 'Where we can see you.'

Astor stood right beside the porthole. 'I must apologise for approaching you with no formal—'

'*Now*, Mr Tollamy!' both ladies shrieked together.

The slash of the whip cut through Astor's dress as though it wasn't there. Stroke after stroke! She sank to her knees, unable to defend herself, unable to think beyond the pain.

Lines of fire blossomed across her back and shoulders. When she managed to turn, there was Mr Tollamy leaning out from his bench on top of the coach. His arm rose and fell, curling the tip of the whip around her from left and right and left again. The ladies in the coach were howling with laughter.

Astor reached one hand up into the path of the whip, and the leather thong materialised out of thin air, wound suddenly around her wrist. She gripped and pulled, even though her hand felt as if it were being burned off. Mr Tollamy's arm jerked to a halt in mid-swing, and he almost fell from his bench.

He pulled back. The whip unwound, and she couldn't hang onto it. But he had lost momentum.

The ladies laughed till the tears ran down their faces.

'Good work, Mr Tollamy!'

'What fun!'

'I *did* enjoy that!'

Astor crawled away as they fell back in their seats, still giggling. Mr Tollamy faced forward again, shook the reins and clicked his tongue. 'Giddyup!' The horses moved off, and the coach trundled on down the street.

Verrol came running up, bearing an armful of assorted pastries. She struggled to her feet before he could offer assistance.

'What did you do?' he demanded. 'You weren't asking them for help, were you? Are you out of your head?'

He had seen at least the last part of what happened. Astor dusted herself down. She was furious with herself, with him, with the world. She was so furious that she hardly felt the pain of her welts.

'No, I'm not too badly hurt,' she said. 'Thank you so much for asking.'

'You little fool!' He was equally furious. 'You're a total innocent!'

'Am I? Then you're a thief and a bully.'

'Put up with it. You need me.'

His arrogance took her breath away. She was sick of being dominated and told what to do. 'Get lost! And take your thievery with you!'

She lashed out and knocked the pastries from his hands. A dozen tarts and cakes scattered over the roadway.

'You useless—'

Astor didn't wait to hear the rest of the insult. She swung on her heel and stalked off.

She felt triumphant in the moment. Would he follow? She walked on down the street, leaving him fuming. She couldn't and wouldn't go back to him now.

Twenty yards along, she heard his footsteps behind her. She had bluffed him! Good, let him follow her for a change. When the street ended in a T-junction, she made a turn to the left. *She* was choosing the route now.

Still she refused to look back over her shoulder. She kept on going until she came to an iron footbridge.

The smog, which had been lighter for a while, thickened up again here. Astor could see it coiling and wreathing over the surface of the water – if that stuff was water. It looked like thick green soup. She guessed she was crossing some kind of canal.

On the other side, she found herself in a park. At least, there were park benches and the trunks of trees, though the ground was mostly dirt with only a few scrubby patches of grass. Perhaps she hadn't chosen the best of routes. Seeing the glow of a gaslight ahead, she quickened her pace and headed towards it. It was like a welcoming beacon in the all-encompassing murk.

An iron railing marked the end of the park. Soon she found a gate and came out onto a street. It wasn't as wide as the streets before the canal, but it was a proper street with pavements on either side. She breathed a sigh of relief.

She didn't expect to hear Verrol's footsteps on the dirt and grass of the park behind her. But she made sure that her own footsteps rang out on the stone pavement. Twenty, forty, sixty yards . . . and still there was no sound from him.

When she finally looked back over her shoulder, the smog was an impenetrable wall. Her heart pounded painfully in her chest. What was delaying him?

Then a faint noise came to her ears. Footsteps, at last! She slowed down a little to narrow the gap between them. Perhaps she should stop until he caught up altogether?

The footsteps grew louder and louder, clearer and clearer. The sound on the pavement reminded her of hobnailed boots. With horror, she realised it wasn't Verrol's stealthy tread at all! And not one set of footsteps, but two!

She increased her pace. Instinct told her to run, but reason told her to walk calmly and confidently. Besides, if she ran for it now, how would Verrol ever find her again? Better to turn off somewhere, then retrace her route to the park afterwards.

Finding a place to turn off wasn't so easy, however. She had come to a different area of Brummingham here: not the mansions of the rich, but tall, grimy tenement blocks. At ground level, she saw only closed doors and shutters; higher up, lines of washing hung across from window to window. Rusty drainpipes and cables on pulleys ran up the sides of the walls, but they offered no means of escape to her. Everything seemed meaner and poorer than before.

After a while, the pavement came to an end, and she was forced to walk on uneven cobblestones. Iron gratings set into the cobbles shot up gusts of hot air and steamy vapour.

Still she hadn't found a place to turn aside. This one street seemed to go on forever. Sudden noises in the smog made her jump: clangs and screeches, an eerie wail, the savage bark of a dog. And always behind, that ominous tattoo of footsteps.

They were marching in step, she realised, just like the band of ex-soldiers who'd gone past before. Verrol had described that band as 'ugly customers'. No doubt these two were just as ugly.

She could have wept with gratitude when a laneway opened up to the left. She swung off into it at once, simultaneously hushing the sound of her own footsteps. She walked on tiptoe and moved further away from the street.

There was water underfoot, a drainage stream that ran down the middle of the lane. Before she realised, her shoes were filled with water, and the hem of her dress was sopping. The smell suggested sewage as well as water.

She stopped and waited to hear the hobnailed boots march past to wherever they were going. There was no reason to think they were coming after her, no reason at all.

She could have screamed when they turned and followed her into the lane.

Instead, she picked up her feet and ran. No point in keeping quiet now. She might have called for help if there had been a lighted window somewhere, but the windows that looked out on the lane were all dark or boarded up.

Fifty yards along, she discovered that the lane was a cul-de-sac. No way through! She ran round the ring of tenements at the end, and the walls were continuous, impassable.

She faced back the way she had come, trying to silence the rasp of her breathing. Still she saw nothing in the swirling vapour . . . but she had the impression that the two sets of footsteps had split up and spread out across the width of the lane. They were covering her escape on both sides.

Straight down the middle, then. She lunged forward – and two figures materialised out of the smog. They flung out their arms and closed the gap before Astor could dash through. In the grip of a nightmare, she faltered to a halt.

'Here's a pretty one, hey?'

'A real little sweetikins.'

The man on the left wore a red army jacket and a dog-eared military cap. When he opened his mouth, his gums were black and he had only one tooth.

The man on the right was younger and wore a leather bandolier and breeches with braces. A terrible scar seamed his face from forehead to chin, distorting his features. Half a beard grew on the unscarred side of his chin.

Astor struggled to speak in a level tone. 'I don't have money.'

Half-Beard's grin twisted his face even more hideously. 'We don't want yer money.'

'What, then?'

'Nothin'. Not for meself.'

'Nor me,' said One-Tooth. A length of gleaming metal appeared suddenly in his one good hand. 'But me blade now, that's a different story.'

'Same here,' said Half-Beard, and there was a blade in his hand too.

'Bayonets is the proper name for them.' One-Tooth turned his blade this way and that, as if examining it. 'Seen service overseas, this has. In all the King's wars.'

'And outside the wars too,' added Half-Beard.

'Must've stuck this into a dozen Fritzes and Froggies.'

'More.'

'Yeah, probably. But not since the war ended.'

'Mine too,' said Half-Beard. 'Mine hasn't had a chance to stick anyone for years.'

'They get thirsty, see,' One-Tooth continued. 'They need the blood.'

He reached out suddenly and tickled Astor's chin with the tip of his blade. Then her cheek. Then he flicked at a curl of her hair.

Her mind had frozen up, and her muscles had turned to jelly. She knew she was as good as dead already.

'Not goin' to scream, is she?' said Half-Beard.

'I reckon she'll stay mum,' said One-Tooth.

'Perhaps she's startin' to like us.'

A different voice cut across their gloating. 'But *I'm* not.'

Verrol!

Astor came back from the dead with a start.

24

The ex-soldiers spun round. Verrol stood observing from ten paces away, seemingly calm and casual. Yet there was a tautness about him like a spring wound back and primed.

'Push off,' snarled One-Tooth. 'We found her first.'

'This is *our* game,' Half-Beard warned. 'Go find yer own.'

'I have,' said Verrol. 'It's you.'

His voice carried a quiet menace, but the ex-soldiers weren't perturbed. When he slipped off his jacket, they laughed outright.

'He wants a fist fight!'

'Pity we don't do fist fights.'

'We do *this*!' Quick as a striking snake, One-Tooth swung and flung his bayonet at Verrol's throat.

Astor gasped. She could have sworn she saw the tip of the blade drive straight into the flesh – but she didn't. Verrol swayed to the side, reaching up simultaneously with the jacket he still held in his hands.

For a moment, neither Astor nor the ex-soldiers knew what had happened.

'Hey presto,' said Verrol as he unfolded the jacket to reveal the bayonet. He had caught it mid-flight.

'No!' One-Tooth gawped. 'Impossible!'

'He couldn't have!' echoed Half-Beard.

Verrol switched the blade across from his jacket to his hand.

'Stick him with yours!' One-Tooth urged his companion.

'Not me!' Half-Beard was already backing away. 'You saw what he did!'

'He's only a man,' snarled One-Tooth – though he was backing away too.

Half-Beard shook his head. 'He's the devil!'

In the next moment, they both broke and ran for their lives, ducking past Verrol on either side.

He didn't even turn to watch them go. He strode forward to Astor. 'Are you hurt?'

Astor couldn't answer, couldn't think. He still had the blade in his hand; she still stared at it in horror. Seeing her reaction, he shrugged and tossed the weapon aside.

She recovered her voice then. When she spoke, it was as though someone else uttered words through her mouth. 'Let's go and join a Slumtown gang,' she said.

So they set off. Astor concentrated on staying close beside or behind him. In her stunned state, it was the only thing she *could* concentrate on.

Time ceased to exist. They walked down countless streets, turned innumerable corners. The streets grew steadily narrower, and cobblestones gave way to grit and gravel. Flaking plaster covered the walls of the tenements, which were now only three or four storeys high. In many places, overhead pipes crossed from one side of the street to the other, dropping spatters of warm water or greasy liquid.

Astor brushed the spatters from her hair and shoulders, and trudged on. Her wet shoes squished softly with every step.

There were several strange sounds in the night, but one was constant: a dull *thump-thump-thump* of pounding and pumping and hammering. The ground seemed to throb under their feet like a living pulse.

'Industrial machinery,' Verrol explained. 'We're coming into the area of mills and factories. Most of them owned by the Swales.'

He was ready with another explanation when the blast of a

hooter cut through the smog, rising from a wail to a whistle. 'Foundry over there.' He pointed. 'Change of shift for the ironworkers.'

Astor thought she glimpsed a vast looming shape in the dark, but she couldn't be sure. As they continued on through the factory area, the walls grew blanker and blacker, no longer pierced by windows but louvred vents. Behind the vents, mighty machines rumbled and thrummed, sometimes building to a crescendo that ended in a thunderous belch. Astor soon learned to cover her face and jump aside when masses of noxious fumes puffed out from the vents after a belch.

She also learned to jump aside when mushroom-shaped hydrants in the streets disgorged periodic flows of liquid sludge. The industrial processes in the factory area evidently worked in cycles like the digestive processes of some great beast.

After what seemed like ages, they came to a rail marshalling yard. Astor had seen railway lines before, but never a maze of tracks like this. The endless intersections of gleaming metal baffled the mind.

'Slumtown's on the other side,' Verrol told her.

In the main part of the yard were freight trucks and locomotives, and men moving around through clouds of steam. The men were visible by the light of the carbide lamps that they wore on their heads. The locomotives looked like black, lumpish monsters, with their bulging funnels and dome-shaped boilers.

Verrol chose a spot further down the tracks, and they crossed over in the dark. On the other side, Slumtown announced itself with a row of giant slagheaps. There were no streets, only muddy paths.

'We won't see any ex-soldiers here, will we?' Astor asked.

'No. They don't come into the slums.'

He led the way past sheets of corrugated iron, planks, sacking, canvas, chicken wire and miscellaneous bits of furniture. Astor couldn't tell what was a human dwelling and what was discarded rubbish. Everything seemed piled higgledy-piggledy on top of everything else. The thought of living in such a place made her shudder.

'How do we find the gangs?' she asked. 'Are we going anywhere particular?'

'No. They stay hidden at night. We won't meet them till they want to be met.'

The only people they discovered were the most wretched of slum-dwellers: young boys who slept alone in forgotten corners; a girl in rags who jumped up and fled at their approach. The only sounds were the scutterings of rodents and, one time, the miaow of a cat. Smells of cooking wafted on the air, but Verrol refused to search for the source.

After ten minutes, he pricked up his ears. 'Hear that?'

Astor heard it. A regular rhythm, pounding like the rhythm of the factories.

'What is it?'

'Music, of course. Gang music.'

'Can we go there?'

'Let's try.'

They headed towards the music, detouring around pits full of scrap metal and mounds of vegetable refuse. It didn't sound much like music to Astor, though she heard hints of melody in it now.

They came out at the top of a stormwater channel, ten feet deep by twenty feet wide. There was no water at the bottom, just patches of sludge. Astor gazed down at a score of people congregated round a brazier made from a perforated metal bin.

In the flickering red firelight, they looked hardly human. Their clothes were an incongruous collection of scavenged oddments: moleskin tunics, woolly shawls, serge greatcoats, flannel jerkins, felt leggings. Astor was sure she recognised bits of bedspread, curtain and tablecloth incorporated. Many of the garments were held together only by woven string and knitting between the patches.

Even more bizarre were their trinkets and jewellery. They wore steel bolts as earrings, brass chains as necklaces, rubber belts as bangles, and cogs and springs as brooches and badges. The polished pieces of metal were the cleanest thing about them.

Verrol didn't share Astor's amazement; he was focused on the musicians who stood playing at the back of the crowd.

'See the instruments?' He pointed them out one by one. 'Brass guitar. Buzz guitar. Clapper and pealer. Drums.'

Astor followed the line of his pointing finger. The drums were mere kegs and cans and upturned cooking pots, while the guitars bore no resemblance to anything she'd ever seen. Their necks had been fashioned from long metal pipes, with copper plates attached to their fretboards. Instead of proper wooden bodies, one had what looked like a flattened steel bucket, the other a monstrous brass horn. They didn't even have the correct number of strings: five in one case, and eight in the other.

'Not *musical* instruments,' she exclaimed. 'No wonder they don't sound right.'

'They sound exactly the way they're meant to sound. It takes hundreds of hours to shape and tune the instruments for gang music.'

She was still digesting that information when the song came to an end. The musicians flung up their arms, the crowd whooped and cheered. Then the musicians laid aside their instruments, and the crowd milled around them, laughing and talking.

Astor turned to Verrol. 'So who do we see about joining?'

'It doesn't work like that. A gang lets you in if you have something to contribute. We have to win them over.'

She huffed with exasperation. 'Wonderful! How are we supposed to do that?'

He gestured towards the scene below. Now a different gang member had taken up the buzz guitar, while the drummer and brass guitarists were preparing to launch into a new song. Nobody had yet taken up the clapper and pealer.

'Here's our chance,' he said.

'Our chance?'

'My chance, then. I'll stake a claim for both of us.'

Before Astor knew what was happening, he had stepped forward and slid down the sloping side of the channel. He plunged in through the crowd and snatched up the clapper and pealer.

Astor gaped. How many more surprises? Was there anything he couldn't do?

The so-called music set Astor's nerves on edge, yet it was their only way of joining the gang. With all her might, she willed Verrol to be good at it – and he was. He was better than good.

Astor saw how he immediately picked up the timing and tune from the other musicians. He shook the clapper back and forth, and whirled the pealer around in the air. The clapper was a double-headed leather contraption that produced a thrumming pulse; the pealer was a set of metal discs in a frame that created a bell-like sound on three or four notes.

But the clapper and pealer weren't what he did best. He was a natural dancer. His limbs, which had always seemed so loose and casual, came startlingly alive, snapping back and forth on every beat. He didn't just keep to the rhythm, he expressed it.

The other musicians watched him and began to interact with him. Heads nodded approval in the surrounding crowd, hands and feet began twitching and tapping. It was as if everyone was catching the rhythm. Astor was amazed to realise her own foot was tapping too.

She switched her attention to the brass guitarist, who had a skill with which she was more familiar. In spite of the oddity of his eight-stringed instrument, his fingers flew like lightning over the fretboard. She knew her own fingering on the harp was nowhere near as nimble. Even her father on the violin could never have matched him.

If only you were in a proper orchestra, she thought. With a serious instrument and serious music, he could have created something beautiful. Such talent was wasted on this violent, jangling cacophony.

Whereas most of the gang members were in their teens, the brass guitarist was balding and middle-aged. Yet there was one person older again, a tiny woman in the crowd whom Astor hadn't noticed at first. Verrol seemed to be making a special effort to impress her.

116

Who was she? Unlike the younger girls who wore breeches and trews, she wore a kind of dress, a grey homespun smock. Sparse white tufts of hair grew on top of her head; a few longer hairs sprouted from her chin. Her small, wizened face put Astor in mind of a monkey. When the song drew to its end, everyone looked to her for a reaction.

She came forward to inspect Verrol at close quarters. 'You're good, dearie,' she said at last. 'Where are you from?'

He deflected the question. 'We've come to join a gang. Can we join yours?'

'Hmm.' She squinched up her face, adding creases between the creases. 'Granny's Gang *might* have room for a talented musician.'

'Are you Granny?'

'Granny Rouse. Who's "we"?'

'Me and my companion.' Verrol pointed. 'Astor Vance.'

'Vance? Sounds like a posh name. And you are?'

'Verrol.'

'Verrol what? Verrol Vance?'

'I don't use my family name. Nobody does. Just Verrol.'

'The two of you aren't married, then?'

'No.'

'So what are you? Lovers?'

Verrol and Astor exchanged glances. 'No,' said Verrol.

'Best friends?'

Astor would have settled for 'best friends' just to gain acceptance, but Verrol answered, 'Not exactly.'

Granny Rouse frowned at him. 'We'll give you a trial period with the gang,' she said at last. 'But not her.'

'I won't join unless she can too.'

'Suit yourself, dearie. I only said "trial period" anyway.' She stepped back to her previous position. 'Let's have another song. Tevvy, you take a turn on clapper and pealer.'

'No! Wait a minute.' Verrol was desperate. 'She's a talented musician too. Better than me.'

Granny Rouse obviously didn't believe it. 'Let's see.'

'Come on down!'

Astor had no choice, though she knew it wouldn't work. She might be talented, but not on *those* instruments.

She slid down the side of the channel to join the musicians. When the young buzz guitarist offered her his guitar, she shook her head.

'I can't play that.'

'Like a harp,' said Verrol.

How could he be so absurd? 'It's nothing like a harp.'

He lowered his voice. 'I thought you could play all sorts of instruments.'

'Proper instruments. That thing doesn't even have the right number of strings.'

'Drums, then.' He turned and announced it to Granny's Gang. 'She plays the drums.'

The drummer was a spiky-haired boy of about ten, wearing a green-striped jumper full of holes. He rose from his seat and handed his drumsticks to Astor. They weren't even proper drumsticks, just springy metal rods with leather-bound tips.

'I can't do this,' she whispered to Verrol.

'You can. You have to. It's our only chance.'

Astor took her seat, which was an upturned box, and stared at the kegs, cans and pots before her. It was impossible. Didn't Verrol understand that percussion was an entirely different skill? She had never played percussion in her life. But clearly Verrol thought this was their only chance to join the gang.

118

Verrol conferred with the other musicians, then nodded his head and counted them in.

'One, two, three, *four*.'

He tapped on her drums to start her off. She recognised the same beat as the first tune they'd heard.

She began using her drumsticks, experimenting with the timbre of the different pots and pans. She added clever variations and flourishes on top of the basic beat. Verrol danced in front of her, limbs gyrating this way and that.

'Put more drive into it!' he hissed out of the corner of his mouth. 'Gang-music style!'

Astor tried her best, but there was something lacking. What else could she do? The guitarists played mechanically; Granny Rouse was shaking her head.

'Harder! Stronger!' Verrol was almost pleading. 'Play for your life!'

What more could she do? She saw Granny Rouse shaking her head, and a rage swelled up inside her. Stupid drums! Stupid music! She would have shown them how she could really play if she'd had her harp! But the Swale brats had destroyed it! Stupid, stupid, stupid!

The frustration of this moment built on top of all the injustices of the day, on top of all the injustices of the last few weeks. Her pent-up feeling became a tidal wave. She might have thrown the drumsticks as far as she could throw . . . but instead she took out her frustration on the drums.

Beating them, battering them, hammering them! It turned into a delirium, a frenzy, as if every keg, pot and pan was the face of an oppressor! She just had to hit and hit and keep on hitting. Everything else disappeared into the distance.

Strangely, though, she never lost the beat. The musician in her still kept to the original rhythm – only a hundred times more fierce and savage. Sweat dripped off her face, and her hair fell forward over her eyes so that she could hardly see. But she didn't need to see. Sheer rage possessed her. She was scarcely conscious of the other musicians except as elements in the storm she created. All sense of time disappeared. She grimaced and grunted meaningless words to herself.

It seemed she had barely begun when Verrol danced in front of her drums and leaned in until she could no longer ignore him. She couldn't hear but she could read what he was mouthing: *Stop now! Stop!*

She didn't want to stop, yet her musician's instinct told her that the song had fulfilled its trajectory. Perhaps it was something the guitarists were doing. She built the sound up and up, bringing in every drum, then concluded with a tremendous final crash – so tremendous that the rebounding drumsticks leaped from her fingers and flew ten feet away.

She pushed aside damp strands of hair. Everyone was goggling at her.

The silence was unnerving. Astor saw the shock in their eyes and wished she could vanish down a hole in the ground. She had made a complete spectacle of herself.

She would have said 'Sorry', but the apology died in her throat. What she had revealed could never be recalled. She wiped the sweat from her forehead with the back of her hand. She felt utterly exhausted.

She rose from the upturned box with a gesture to the spiky-haired boy. He only shook his head and made no move to reclaim his seat.

'What did I do?' she asked Verrol in an undertone. 'Have I offended them?'

'Er, no.' He grinned. 'Stunned them, I think.'

Then two girls from the crowd stepped forward. They had caught the drumsticks that had flown from her hands – and now gave them back to her. Not to the spiky-haired boy, but *her*. Doubt and hope waged a confusing battle in her head.

'That was the best ever,' said the young buzz guitarist.

It still seemed a mistake to Astor. 'You *liked* it?'

'More than liked it,' said the older brass guitarist. 'Granny too. Look at her.'

Granny Rouse had her eyes closed and a blissful expression on her face. She swayed from side to side as though still hearing the beat in her head.

'Perhaps we should play another song?' Verrol suggested.

'No.' The spiky-haired boy held up a warning hand.

'Wait,' said someone else.

All at once, Granny had become the centre of attention. Everyone was watching her, clustering round with an air of expectation.

'What is it?' asked Astor.

'She might be going into a trance,' explained one of the two girls.

'It's a vision,' said the brass guitarist. 'She's having one of her visions.'

Gang members sprang forward to support her just before her legs gave way. Held up under the armpits, she sagged and lolled as if there wasn't a bone in her body.

'What is she, some kind of shaman?' Verrol asked.

'Shush now,' said the spiky-haired boy.

Suddenly Granny's eyelids flew open. Her eyes had rolled up inside her head, so that only the whites were visible.

Nobody spoke, nobody moved. For two minutes, it was a frozen tableau. Granny appeared to be breathing in short, shallow breaths, very fast. Then her eyelids descended, and the scene came unfrozen.

'That was a long one,' said the buzz guitarist.

'Bet it was about the music,' said the spiky-haired boy.

The chatter continued until Granny opened her eyes again. Her pupils and irises were back in place.

'What did you see, Granny?' The question came from a dozen throats simultaneously.

Granny was standing once more on her own two feet, and her breathing had returned to normal. When she spoke, her voice sounded a little raw and ragged.

'I saw gang music take over the world. I saw posters and newspaper headlines and people queuing for performances. *Gang music . . . gang music . . . gang music . . .* everyone was talking about it. Hundreds of millions of people. Even foreigners in foreign languages. It spread out beyond the slums and out beyond Britain. The whole world was going mad for gang music.'

There were whistles of amazement, and a few cheers.

'What does that mean for us?' asked one of the girls who'd caught the drumsticks.

'I don't know yet,' said Granny. 'But it means people won't be able to ignore the slums any more. Gang music will make them sit up and pay attention.'

Astor wanted to ask a more specific question: *What does it mean for me and Verrol?* But Verrol tapped her on the elbow.

'I think we're okay for now,' he said.

The spiky-haired boy took Granny by the arm. 'She's tired. Can't you see she needs rest?'

Granny nodded agreement. The trance had obviously drained her energy. 'Yes, I need to sleep on it. Back to the hide-out, and we'll have a meeting in the morning.'

That was the end of the night as far as Astor was concerned. The dramas of the day had taken their toll, and the effects all hit home at once. Granny wasn't the only one who was tired.

Astor had a dim impression of gang members emptying the makeshift brazier and gathering up the drums. She had an even dimmer impression of walking through Slumtown with Verrol beside her.

'This is the stacks area,' she heard someone say. 'All sorts of junk we can process and re-sell.'

They passed along aisles between stacks as big as houses. Every kind of scrap was collected here: crates, bottles, beams, tiles, bricks, ceramic pipes, paving stones and rusty metal wheels.

Then the journey came suddenly to an end. One minute they were trudging between stacks, the next they had burrowed right inside one particular stack. It was a stack of old timber – railway sleepers, in fact.

The interior was a long tunnel lit by a series of oil lamps. The ceiling came down so low that everyone had to crouch. Rugs and carpets covered the ground in a medley of colours and patterns; large padded bags had been spread out at intervals along the tunnel. The bags were for sleeping in, sewn together from strips of quilt and fleecy padding.

Her room in Swale House had been a palace compared to this!

After a brief period of discussion, sleeping-bags were found for the two newcomers. Apparently, girls slept at one end of the tunnel, and boys at the other.

Astor slipped into her bag, though she was quite sure she would never fall asleep. On hard ground . . . in an unfamiliar place . . . with strangers all around. But she dropped off the moment the oil lamps were doused.

PART TWO

—◆—

Slumtown

27

Astor slept deeply, peacefully. All her dreams were pleasant, and Verrol featured in many of them.

When she opened her eyes, thin shafts of light filtered in through cracks between the sleepers. Deliberately arranged cracks, because the stack of sleepers had to be at least thirty feet high and wide. After yesterday's terrors, she felt safe and protected under so much thickness of wood. She woke up happier than she'd been in a long time.

Rolling over, she looked at the sleeping-bags spread out along the ground – all empty. Either everyone had risen early, or she had slept in late. She couldn't see clearly to the other end of the tunnel, but she guessed Verrol was also up and about.

Verrol the mystery man! Yesterday had justified her original intuition that he was much more than a servant. She wasn't sure what else he was or had been, and even Granny Rouse hadn't extracted his family name from him. But the musical talent, the street cunning, the dancing and fighting . . . When she thought about it, his way of fighting was very similar to his way of dancing: a more deadly version of the same speed and co-ordination.

He's the devil, that ex-soldier had said. She pictured him as he had appeared to her yesterday, moving on the balls of his feet, gaze flicking ceaselessly in every direction. He was like some prowling predator, like a wolf. She had told him once that he was only living with a part of himself – but yesterday he had been in his element, no longer coasting or half engaged. Did he need danger to bring him fully alive?

A different Verrol . . . and perhaps a different Astor too. She sensed that she was entering a whole new phase of her life. Everything had changed when she and her mother had moved from London Town to her stepfather's country estate, and everything had changed again when she had moved to Brummingham and the miseries of Swale House. But this might be the biggest change of all.

Hopefully it would be an upward step. The young people of Granny's Gang *had* to be an improvement on the Swale children. And there was Verrol as well, to keep things interesting. She would work him out if it was the last thing she did.

She was still in her sleeping-bag when Verrol came looking for her. Because of his height, he advanced along the tunnel bent almost double. Yet even in that unnatural posture, there was poise and grace to the way he moved, and a minimal expenditure of energy.

'Ah, you're awake.' He grinned down at her. 'Granny's gathering the gang for a meeting, and she wants us there too.'

'Will she let us join, do you think?'

'More like a trial period. That's what she allowed me before.'

'Hmm. Are we going to tell her about the Swales coming after us?'

He shook his head. 'Better not.'

'Perhaps they've given up now, anyway?'

He shook his head again, decisively. 'No chance of that. They'll keep searching. You're still a danger to them.'

'Why?'

'Because of that letter to your stepfather. You could always write another one.'

'Do you think I should?'

He considered a while before answering. 'No, I think we should lie low and keep quiet right now. At least until we pass our trial period and become full gang members.'

Astor sniffed. 'We could just join another gang.'

'It'll be the same everywhere. We have to win their trust first.'

'Why don't they trust us?'

'Not us. *You*.'

Astor felt as if she'd been slapped in the face. 'What's wrong with *me*?'

'You're from a different social background. Posher. More genteel.'

'Because of my surname?'

'Because of your manners, the way you speak, everything about you. It stands out a mile.'

She digested the information in angry silence. 'And you're the same background as them, are you?' she said at last.

Verrol shrugged. 'You heard what I said last night. I won't join Granny's Gang unless you can too.'

Astor felt better about that, but she wasn't going to let the subject drop. She took pride in her family background. The Vances might have come down in the world, but they had been landowners in the past, and were still definitely gentry. As for the Dorrins – much as she detested her stepfather, they were her kind of people.

'You don't like us, do you?' she demanded. 'You don't like manners or polite speaking?'

'Not particularly.'

'When you went to work for my stepfather, you must have hated every minute of it.'

'Not for the reason you think.'

'You don't like the gentry and you don't like the plutocrats. You're against everyone.'

'Everyone except servants, slum kids, factory workers and rural labourers.' He grinned. 'I don't mind shopworkers, clerks, miners, sailors, schoolmarms, engineers . . .'

Astor cut him off with a snort. She had the impression he was laughing at her. 'Anyway, we have to see Granny now.'

'Yes.'

'And we won't tell her about the Swales.'

'No.'

'We won't even think about the Swales.'

He raised an eyebrow and made no answer to that.

'Turn around,' she ordered.

'What?'

'I have to get dressed, don't I?'

Verrol turned his back.

'Further away.'

Still in a crouch, he moved half a dozen paces towards the tunnel entrance. Astor wriggled out of her sleeping-bag and slipped on the outer garments she'd taken off last night.

She didn't want to lose the good mood she'd woken up with . . . and she definitely didn't want to think about the Swales. There might be a threat still hanging over her, but she didn't intend to live in fear. Today was a new day, a new start. She would banish the memory of Swale House completely from her mind.

The gang had assembled in a clearing between the stacks. All around, the ground was damp with morning dew. Although the sun wasn't directly visible, the brightness in the air made Astor blink.

'So *there* you are!' barked Granny Rouse.

There were more gang members than Astor remembered from last night. They stood in a semicircle facing Granny, dressed in their motley clothes and metal jewellery.

'You're in big trouble!' they shouted humorously at Astor and Verrol.

'You kept Granny waiting!'

'Shut up, you ninnies,' said Granny. 'This is serious.'

They laughed and shut up. Granny gestured for Astor and Verrol to take their place with the others.

'I'm going to tell you more about my vision,' she began. 'I told you I saw gang music conquer the world. I also heard the sound of the band that would do it.'

'Just one band?' someone called out.

'Just one band,' Granny confirmed. 'Better than anything anyone has ever heard. And a special sort of sound. I'm going to create the band to make that sound.'

There was instant hubbub.

'Can we be in it?'

'Me! Me! Me!'

'No, *me*!'

Granny shook her head. 'This has to be the best of the best. I'm only sure of one person so far.' She turned to last night's

131

brass guitarist. 'Purdy, there's nobody in Slumtown can play like you. You're in.'

Purdy scratched his balding head. Of all the members of Granny's Gang, he was the only one not bursting with enthusiasm. 'Gang music has never interested anyone outside the slums before,' he said. 'Why should it be different now?'

'Because there's never been a band like this before.'

'I can't believe—'

'You never believe anything, Purdy. It's not in your nature.'

'Just being realistic.'

'Time to stop being realistic. Time you started to dream. Don't you trust my visions?' Granny swung to appeal to the rest of the gang. 'Have my visions ever been wrong?'

They backed her up, with some qualification.

'Hardly ever.'

'Not often.'

'Mostly right.'

Granny took a new tack. 'Don't worry, Purdy. I've told you before: you have the fingers of an angel and the soul of an earthworm. It's not your fault. You don't have to believe, you only have to do what I tell you. And you'll do what I tell you, won't you?'

Purdy shrugged.

'Of course you will. You're a good boy.'

Purdy pulled a wry face. Though in his forties or fifties, he didn't seem to mind being called a good boy. It was probably better than being called an earthworm, thought Astor.

Granny addressed the semicircle again. 'Now for the rest. We need five musicians in a band. I'm going to give these two a go.' She pointed to Astor and Verrol.

The spiky-haired boy who'd played the drums last night exploded in disgust. 'She's a rubbish drummer! You ought to pick me!'

132

'Don't be silly, Hink,' Granny said, a little sadly. 'You know she's better than you. Whether she can be good enough . . .'

As Hink subsided, someone else spoke up. 'But they're not even in our gang.'

'They'll be in our gang if they're good enough for the band.' Granny confronted the objector crossly. 'Anyway, this isn't about our gang. Don't you understand? This band has to come from *all* the gangs.'

'What, even the Soapies?'

'Not the Twiners!'

'Not the Ratcatchers!'

'Not the East Side Hands!'

'Enough!' Granny stamped her foot at them. 'I don't want to hear that sort of talk! What have I been doing all these years except trying to get the gangs to live in harmony? Stopping feuds! Making common cause! And here's the best common cause of all – the triumph of gang music!'

The members of Granny's Gang hung their heads, abashed. She softened her tone.

'We didn't invent gang music. All the gangs play it, so they should all share in its triumph. We ought to draw some of the band from other gangs. Our singer, for example.'

There were cries of surprise. 'Singer? Why a singer? We never bothered with a singer before!'

'Unblock your ears!' Granny barked. 'I told you, this is a special sort of sound. I heard a singer in my vision.'

'Does it have to be five musicians?' Verrol asked.

'It's the usual number,' Granny answered with a scowl.

'But you didn't actually see five?'

'I didn't *see* anything at all. Why?'

'I could be your singer.'

'Sing as well as play clapper and pealer?'

'Yes.'

Astor fought back an impulse to giggle. She remembered the odd voice she'd overheard on the roof of the turret – when she'd compared his singing to a flock of geese.

'Hmm.' Granny considered, then nodded. 'Okay, let's audition you, then.'

'Now?'

'This very moment. A real singer doesn't need back-up.' She pointed to Astor. 'You can give him the beat.'

Somebody crossed to a nearby stack and brought back a barrel for a drum. Someone else found two rusty steel rods in another stack. Astor took up her makeshift drumsticks and knelt beside her makeshift drum.

'Same rhythm as last night?' she asked Verrol, keeping a very straight face.

'Right.'

She began drumming, and he came in after two bars. His voice was as weirdly rough and rasping as ever, only five times louder. Astor couldn't help it; the giggles exploded out of her.

He struggled on for another ten bars, and Astor struggled to maintain the rhythm. But as soon as she caught sight of his face, she burst out laughing again.

'What's wrong?' Granny Rouse demanded.

Verrol glared at Astor. 'Ask her.'

In all the time she'd known him, Astor had never seen him look so rattled. The fact that he took his singing seriously made it even funnier.

'I . . . er . . . can't stop thinking about geese,' she brought out in a stifled splutter.

'He's perfectly in tune, you know,' said Granny Rouse

severely. She turned to Verrol. 'Keep going. You can do without a beat.'

But Verrol shook his head. He had recovered his composure, and the usual cool, sardonic expression was back in place.

'No,' he said. 'My geese have all flown away. Sorry.'

There was a long moment's silence. Astor stared at the ground and managed to quell her giggles.

Then Purdy the brass guitarist spoke up. 'You know who has the best singing voice in Slumtown? Ollifer Prash.'

'He's a pain,' said Granny at once.

'Yes, also the biggest head in Slumtown. But if you want a singer . . .'

Granny pursed her lips. 'You're right,' she said at last. 'He could be the one.'

A long-faced, serious-looking girl spoke up – one of the two who'd caught Astor's drumsticks last night. 'Shall we go fetch him?'

'Do you know where to find him, Shannet?'

'He's in the market most mornings.'

'Good. Fetch him after breakfast, then. Our potential band members can go with you.'

It was the end of the meeting. Astor hoped she hadn't offended Verrol for life. She didn't mind at all that his singing was so ridiculous; actually, she liked him better for it.

Breakfast was a fry-up of mushrooms and onions, accompanied by a delicious kind of savoury bread that Astor had never tasted before. Afterwards, Shannet collected the three potential band members and led the way to the Slumtown market. Astor walked at the back of the group; she was wary of Verrol after the business over his singing, and preferred to let Shannet monopolise his conversation. The long-faced girl was far too serious to flirt, but she seemed to be enjoying a deeply serious discussion with him.

He's a bit old for you, though, thought Astor. *And that face of yours is definitely not an advantage.*

By daylight, Slumtown was almost as chaotic and ramshackle as it had appeared by night. Many of the canvas-and-board structures looked as though a strong breeze would flatten them. Shannet wove a route through one area where women sat knitting, another where mushrooms grew in boxes of earth, another where tar-like liquids bubbled in open pits, and another where people pounded some sort of grey pulp in vats. Astor guessed that Slumtown inhabitants eked out a living any way they could.

Finally, they arrived at the market. It wasn't much of a market by Astor's standards, just a dozen booths and trestle tables. They found Ollifer Prash sitting on a barrel in the very last booth while a sour-faced woman cut his hair with an enormous pair of scissors. He turned out to be everything Granny and Purdy had described.

'Hello, hello,' he said. 'Welcome to my toilette.'

He was a big man, with a smooth, shiny complexion. He pulled in his stomach when he realised he had visitors. His cream-coloured jacket was spangled with shiny metal studs, and he wore a very long scarf that looked like several scarves stitched together.

'You're the singer,' Shannet began.

'I am. Have you heard me sing?'

'*I* have,' said Purdy.

'Ah. So you've come to tell me . . . well, what have you come to tell me?'

'Tell him what a wonderful singer he is,' the sour-faced woman put in, snipping away. 'That's what he wants to hear.'

'No, no, no.' Ollifer spread his hands in a self-deprecating gesture. 'Only if they mean it.'

'You're good.' Purdy stated it as a simple matter of fact. 'We've come to offer you a job in Granny Rouse's new band.'

'It'll be the greatest band that ever was,' added Shannet.

Ollifer leaned back on the barrel and screwed up his eyes. 'How much do I get paid?'

'The same as the rest of us,' said Purdy.

'No, that won't do. The singer is the front man. I always get paid more.'

'Okay.' Purdy grinned. 'Five times as much as us. Ten times as much.'

'Which is still nothing,' Shannet explained. 'Nobody gets paid.'

'Like me, then,' sniffed the sour-faced woman. 'Do you think he'll pay me? Some hopes!'

'Hope springs eternal, Monia,' the singer murmured.

'Yes, and eternal is how long I'll have to wait. *Eyebrows!*'

Ollifer adjusted his head to the required angle, and Monia swooped down on him with her scissors.

'Did you ever see a man like this?' she grumbled. 'Has to have his eyebrows trimmed too.'

'The band will make money eventually,' Shannet went on. 'But what Granny really wants for you is fame.'

Astor noticed how Ollifer's eyes lit up at the word *fame.*

137

'Granny says the whole world will go mad for gang music,' she said. 'We'll be famous all over Britain.'

'All over—?'

'Stay still!' Monia warned.

'And other countries too,' added Shannet.

'Perhaps I—'

'*Still!*'

'Of course, if you don't want to be a part of it . . .' said Verrol.

'There!' Monia closed her scissors with a snap and stepped back, satisfied.

Ollifer ran a finger over his eyebrows and seemed satisfied too. He swivelled to face his visitors like a king receiving supplicants.

'I've come to a decision,' he announced. 'I can see this band of Granny's *needs* me. I'll try you out, and if I'm happy—'

'Feed him and he'll be happy,' snorted Monia. 'That's the only thing *he'll* be trying out.'

'Yes, thank you, Monia,' said Ollifer. 'My deepest gratitude to you. Until the next time, then.'

His deepest gratitude was the only payment he made for his haircut.

On the walk back to Granny and the gang, he regaled the others with stories of his singing career. The way he told it, his bad luck had been extraordinary, and the envy of others a constant obstacle. So many times he'd been on the verge of gaining a reputation beyond Slumtown, so many times something had gone wrong at the last minute.

'Thwarted, thwarted, thwarted!' he cried. 'But genuine talent can't be repressed forever!'

When they arrived at the stacks area, they found that a special shelter had been prepared for band practice. It was an open-sided lean-to, with a sheet of corrugated iron for a roof. The drums and other instruments had been set out ready.

Granny welcomed Ollifer with a no-nonsense lecture. 'Understand this. You're here to develop a new sound as a band. There's no room for individual egos.'

Perhaps Ollifer didn't fully absorb the message, because he soon started to lay down his own requirements. A smooth introduction . . . no unplanned guitar solos . . . watch for his hand signals . . .

'Enough!' Granny wagged her finger at him. 'If anyone gives orders, it'll be me, not you. I don't want the old Ollifer Prash. I want you to discover what you can be. Same goes for the lot of you. I want you all singing and playing as if you'd never sung or played before in your lives.'

So they began again. Purdy nominated some songs well known to everyone except Astor. But with Verrol's clapper providing secondary percussion, she soon picked up the rhythms. It was easy for her to play the drums as if she'd never played before in her life – because she never had. For this kind of music, there *was* no old Astor Vance.

As for Ollifer Prash, a strange thing happened to him when the real practice began. Not only did he have a huge voice, rich and resonant, but his voice was somehow bigger than his vanity. Once he started singing, he concentrated on the songs and forgot about himself. He was like a different man.

They played on through the morning until Ollifer remembered he was hungry. Then Granny organised a meal for them, allowing them half an hour's break.

Over dried fruit and oatcake, Ollifer soon returned to his usual state of ego. 'You're lucky I came to help you out. With my singing, this band can go far.'

'If the rest of us can come up to your level,' said Verrol with an ironic grin.

Irony was wasted on Ollifer. 'Or close to my level. Aim for that.'

'I know!' said Astor. 'We should all be like you and have our eyebrows trimmed!'

'It works for me.' Ollifer nodded. 'I need to feel good about myself when I perform. As I always say, how can I expect other people to love me if I don't love myself?'

Everyone burst out laughing. After a moment's surprise, Ollifer laughed along too.

Then Granny grew serious again. 'Don't kid yourself, Ollifer Prash. You're not there yet. None of you are.'

'We don't sound like the band in your vision?' Astor asked.

'No, dearie. Nowhere near.' Granny pointed to the instruments in the shelter. 'Back to your practising.'

Astor threw herself into the afternoon's practice session. Unlike Ollifer, she didn't care about fame, but she did want to be accepted into Granny's Gang. For Verrol and herself, the only sure way to acceptance was to live up to Granny's vision.

The band practised non-stop for the rest of that day . . . and all of the next, and the next. Although Ollifer belonged to the Trawlers gang, no one seemed to object when he walked across to the stacks area early every morning and returned to the Trawlers' area late in the afternoon.

140

Granny Rouse often came to watch, and so did other gang members when they had time off from their salvage-and-repair jobs. Still the band's sound didn't match up to the sound in Granny's vision.

'Something's missing,' she grumbled.

'A buzz guitar,' said Purdy. 'We need our fifth musician.'

Astor didn't enjoy gang music for its own sake, but more and more she enjoyed being good at it. She had an instinct for rhythms without even needing to think about them.

Best of all was the way the band members began to interact with each other. Purdy would throw off an impromptu riff, and Ollifer would take it up in a vocal echo; or Verrol would chime a deliberately wrong note on his pealer, and Purdy would incorporate it into a whole string of new notes. It was like a conversation.

As a beginner, Astor wouldn't have dreamed of adding ideas of her own. She was just happy to share in the general creativity. But then Verrol, in particular, started to draw her in. *Do something with this*, he challenged, switching his clapper to the off beat – and she did, she could, she always rose to meet the test. A thrill ran through her that was more than just the vibration from her drums. The music surrounded her like a cocoon, and she didn't even notice the ache in her wrists until the end of the day.

Potentially, she was a better musician than Verrol. She knew it, and she knew he knew it. His greatest talent wasn't for music but dance. Every now and then, he would break into movement, and she redoubled her efforts on the drums. There was something intoxicating about the way her rhythms controlled his limbs. From her – through drumsticks and drums – into him! His gyrations were taut and fluid, springy as elastic.

Purdy was the exact opposite. From the waist down, he never moved at all. Playing music was his skill, his expertise, and he took a professional attitude to it. His fingers flew over the strings as though the entire energy from the rest of his body had concentrated into his hands.

Where Purdy was self-sufficient, Ollifer craved an audience. Whenever gang members stopped by to watch, Ollifer immediately directed his singing to them. If there was no one else, he practised his audience appeal on Granny. She stood there with legs planted apart and let it wash over her.

Ollifer had been accepted by the gang as he had been accepted by the band – because Granny wanted it so. Everybody groaned or joked when Granny ordered them around, but nobody really rebelled. 'Why do you boss us about so much?' they complained; to which she replied, 'Because it's good for you.' They seemed to believe it too.

It was Granny who dealt with Hink, the spiky-haired boy who'd hoped to play the drums. He was always cheerful, always jaunty – and always finding fault with Astor. 'Call that drumming?' 'Is that the best you can do?' 'How do you like playing *my* drums?'

Astor didn't know how to react, but Granny did. 'They were never your drums, Hink. Go back to work. You're supposed to be reassembling stoves and heaters.'

'How come *she* doesn't have to work?'

'She's working for me.'

'That's not work, that's play. And she can't even do it properly.'

'Hush with the whingeing!' Exasperated, Granny raised a hand as if to cuff him. 'Do you want a whack?'

She was so tiny that even a ten-year-old like Hink towered

over her. Yet he dodged away with a grin and a cry. 'Ooo-er! I'm off!'

Granny was at her most dogmatic over the name of the band. The issue first came up among the band members when Granny wasn't there. They'd been practising a popular song titled 'Do or Die', about the legendary London gangster families, the Mauls and the Starks. In the song, the gangsters' deeds were daring and their street fights spectacular.

'That's what we ought to call ourselves,' said Purdy. 'The Starks.'

The others considered the suggestion.

'Why not the Mauls?' said Ollifer.

'I go for the Starks,' Purdy insisted.

Astor didn't go for either. 'I don't want to be named after a bunch of thugs.'

'Not thugs.' Purdy shook his head. 'They started out as gangs from the slums, just like us. They expanded their empires all across London Town.'

'Yes, criminal empires.'

'They were brave men willing to die for the honour of their gangs.' For someone usually so phlegmatic, Purdy had strong opinions on the subject.

'Legends get exaggerated,' Verrol pointed out. 'Especially in songs.'

'I think the Starks is good,' said Ollifer. 'Everyone knows the history, everyone would want to hear a band with a name like that.'

A different voice made them all jump. 'Aren't you forgetting something?' It was Granny Rouse appearing suddenly round the side of their practice shelter.

'Of course, we wouldn't decide anything without you,' said Ollifer graciously.

143

'No, you wouldn't. But that's not it. You're forgetting what happened to the Stark family.'

'They feuded with the Maul family,' said Purdy.

'Yes, and wiped each other out. You've heard of the Eden Street Massacre? You think that's something to name a band after?'

'But they're *famous*,' Ollifer protested.

'Famous imbeciles. How stupid can you be? Revenge and counter-revenge until they were all dead. Nobody else could have crushed them, but they did it for themselves. They might as well have put their pistols to their own brains.'

'We know you don't like gangs feuding,' said Purdy.

'They were *failures*!' Granny stamped her foot. 'If you name yourself after failures, you'll go the same way. You're asking for bad luck. I won't allow it. You have to be successes.'

That was the end of the discussion. Later the same day, Granny came back looking very pleased with herself.

'I have a name for you,' she announced. 'The Rowdies.'

'Rowdies?'

'*The* Rowdies,' Granny repeated.

'That's like your name. Granny Rouse and the Rowdies.'

'So what's wrong with my name?'

'I like it.' Astor nodded. Compared to the Starks, anything was an improvement.

'Good, because that's what I've chosen,' said Granny. 'From now on, you're the Rowdies.'

And so they were.

31

Next day, Granny had another announcement for the band. 'I've set up your first engagement. The North Side Stockies are having a party, and you'll provide the music.'

'When?'

'Three days time.'

'But we still haven't found our buzz guitarist.'

'I've put out feelers,' said Granny. 'Musicians will start coming to audition this afternoon.'

'We'll never have time to fit them into the band,' Astor objected.

Granny snapped her fingers. 'You don't have to sound right yet. It's only a Slumtown birthday party. If you can't do this, you can't do anything.'

The auditions didn't break into the band's practice time; instead, the hopefuls were asked to join in and play along. Most of them were buzz guitarists, with a couple of pitch guitarists and a girl who played the zither. They came from gangs all over Slumtown, with names like the Skimmers, the Brushies, the Crosscutters and the Downtown Dyers. Often their gang's particular form of work was reflected by their clothing, as in aprons or oilskins, high boots or clogs, tin hats or bucklewear.

They were all used to communal music-making, and joined in without a second thought. But none of them showed any talent above the ordinary level. Granny grew more and more irritable.

'No, that's not it at all.'

She was very certain about what she didn't want, very vague about what she did. As the night of their first performance approached, the Rowdies resigned themselves to performing as a foursome.

Although they didn't find their last musician, they did hear some news – very unwelcome news for Astor and Verrol. A buzz guitarist from the Marsh-end Tippers took one look at Astor's hair and exclaimed, 'A man was asking around for you.'

'Who? When? Where?'

'He came through our area yesterday. "A girl with copper-coloured curls," he said. He didn't say why.'

Verrol jumped in. 'Was he wearing blue-and-gold livery?'

'Not that I saw. He had a grey cape on. What's it all about?'

'Nothing,' said Astor. 'Don't let on where I am.'

The buzz guitarist grinned. 'Hey, this is Slumtown. Half of us have something to hide. We don't blab to outsiders.'

For Astor, it was like an old wound re-opening. She hadn't thought about the Swales for days. But this needed talking over with Verrol, and not in front of the others.

She hadn't had any serious personal conversations with him since she'd laughed at his singing. They related well in the band, but not quite so well outside of it. Now she waited to get him on his own, and found an opportunity after dinner.

The dinner tonight was a special treat: a whole chicken baked in clay, with a spicy pancake and the usual mushrooms. Since the weather was fine, the members of Granny's Gang ate in the open, then lounged around chatting. When Astor saw Verrol wander off by himself, she wandered off after him. He made a circuit round the gang's hide-out – and suddenly disappeared.

Astor called out in surprise. 'Verrol? Where are you?'

The reply came from up above. 'Here.'

She raised her eyes and saw that he had climbed the roof of the hide-out almost to the top of the wooden sleepers. His head and shoulders stood out against a haze of silver light, where a full moon showed dimly through the smog.

Astor clambered up after him. It was like ascending a flight of very steep steps. She sat beside him on one sleeper and rested her feet on the sleeper below. Verrol's long legs reached two sleepers below.

'So this is where you go?'

He nodded. 'Does it remind you of anything?'

She'd already had the same thought. 'The turret at Swale House. Picnicking on the roof.'

It was a pleasant memory, and seemed to bring them closer together. But there were less pleasant things to discuss first. 'The Swales are still searching for me,' she said.

'Yes. "Copper-coloured curls". Pity you're so distinctive.'

She took it as a compliment rather than a criticism. 'What can we do?'

'Apart from dyeing your hair or cutting it off?' He seemed amused at the idea, though Astor didn't find it funny. 'Only what we're doing already. We have to live up to Granny's vision and gain her protection.'

'She'd defend us against Swale-men?'

'To the death. *If* we become full gang members.'

'I wish we could hurry it up.'

'We're doing as well as we can.' He clicked his tongue. 'You're doing well on the drums. I think you like gang music after all.'

'No.'

'No? Not even a little?'

'It's all noise and jangle. I've been trained to enjoy a higher kind of music.'

'A higher kind? As in, a higher level of society?'

Astor didn't appreciate the sarcasm in his voice. 'At least my kind of music isn't primitive and repetitive. Gang music appeals to the body, not the mind.'

'Ah, well, your body seems to be enjoying it.'

There was a long silence – and not the comfortable kind of silence they had shared on the turret at Swale House. Their moment of drawing together had no sooner come than gone. After a while, Astor rose from her seat and made her way back down the side of the stack.

Why had it become so difficult between them? Was it because he was no longer a servant and she was no longer a mistress? He had been so easy to talk to once. Now it was all bristling and friction and taking offence . . .

32

The North Side Stockies' party took place in a shallow pit normally used for burning garbage. For tonight, it had been emptied out, cleaned up and turned into a wide, square space of fire-blackened cement. Brightly coloured graffiti spelled out HAPPY BIRTHDAY, KIFF! on the walls around the sides. Braziers flamed in the corners, while oil lamps dangled from overhead wires. There were guests from other gangs, but the majority wore the spotted red bandanas of the North Side Stockies.

The party was well under way by the time the band arrived. A man came hurrying up to them, talking at a million miles an hour. He had a goatee beard, a huge bugle of a nose and long, lank hair tied back in a ponytail. His left sleeve was folded and pinned up, where he was obviously missing an arm.

'I'm Reeth,' he announced. 'Master of ceremonies. We'll set up your drums, then call you when it's time to go on. Mingle with the crowd, have something to eat, whatever you like.'

'No, we won't mingle, thank you,' said Ollifer. 'Not a good idea.'

'Suit yourself.' Reeth flashed his white teeth a great deal, though his smiles barely touched his eyes. Clearly, he had other things on his mind, and rushed off as soon as he'd made arrangements.

Ollifer explained his reasons to the others. 'We have to keep ourselves apart or we lose our aura. Believe me, I've been through this a hundred times. We stay out of sight till it's time for the grand entrance.'

So, while Granny went off to talk to the Stockies, he led the way from the pit by a narrow ramp. Out beyond the lights, there were smells of animals and manure, and a constant low sound of clucking and snuffling. The Stockies gang specialised in stock- and poultry-raising.

The band found a quiet corner and a convenient loose sheet of tarpaulin. They spread the tarpaulin over the ground, and sat around talking about nothing in particular. Meanwhile, the noise from the party grew louder and louder.

'They seem happy,' Verrol commented.

'They'll be in a good mood for us,' said Ollifer.

But as the laughter and chatter continued to mount, Astor began to have misgivings. What if the Rowdies were only a very

149

small part of the night's proceedings? Did anyone even know or care that they were performing?

Her misgivings were confirmed when Reeth turned up to summon them. 'I found a spot for you,' he said apologetically, 'but it's got a bit packed in since we set up the drums.'

Their grand entrance proved to be no entrance at all. The only people who noticed were those forced to step aside as Reeth pushed a way through the crowd. The spot he had found for them wasn't marked off in any way, and Astor's drums were almost lost among the press of bodies.

Purdy strapped on his brass guitar, Astor took up position on her box seat. People grumbled in a good-natured way as Reeth and Verrol cleared a small space around the band.

'I'll do my best for you,' said Reeth.

He certainly tried. He waved his arms for hush and shouted at the top of his voice. He declared the Rowdies 'inspiring', 'amazing', and 'spectacular', but his voice scarcely cut through the hubbub. Even the people who heard were less than excited.

'We *have* listened to gang music before, you know,' someone said.

The band members looked at one another and shook their heads. This was an unexpected problem. Everyone here enjoyed gang music, but they were used to enjoying it, they'd heard it all their lives. They weren't going to break off talking for something so familiar.

'Let's change the order,' said Verrol. 'Start with "Made for Love".'

It made sense. 'Made for Love' was their loudest song with the heaviest beat. Verrol counted them in, Purdy hit the opening chords and Astor swung into the rhythm.

But the band was only there as a background for the crowd.

A few people turned and nodded, recognising the song. Then they went straight back to their conversations, voices raised against the music.

Astor tried to block off thinking about them. Her rhythms were what held the band together, and she had to avoid distraction. She closed her eyes and played by touch and feel. The audience would respond eventually.

But they didn't. There was no applause at the end of the first song. Had anyone even noticed the song had finished? When Astor looked up, she saw that Granny Rouse had come up to stand beside the band.

'What's the matter with you all?' Granny harangued the audience. 'Listen to this band! Pay attention!'

Among her own gang, Granny's commands carried absolute authority, but not here. Because she was so tiny, only those at the front of the crowd saw and heard her, and they merely shrugged as if to say, *We know what gang music is, thank you.*

'Move on,' said Purdy. 'Next number.'

Verrol counted them in, and they launched into 'Hair Hang Down'. Astor would have closed her eyes, but two girls just five paces away suddenly burst into convulsions of laughter over some private joke. The band didn't even exist for them.

A few moments later, they broke out in another cackle. One wore a spotted red bandana fastened with a brass clip, the other had straight blonde hair that hung to her waist. Astor wanted to strangle them. Their laughter snagged in her mind, and her eyes were drawn to them again and again.

She couldn't wait to reach the end of the song. But then there would be another, and another . . . How long could they keep going in the face of this indifference? Astor managed to maintain her rhythm all the way through, but Ollifer was starting to sound ragged. He needed an audience response more than anyone.

The two girls were still laughing on and off as the song concluded. Astor's spirits were at rock bottom, and she was sure the others felt the same. Ollifer turned round and spread his hands in despair.

It could hardly get any worse . . . but it did. Instead of counting them in for the next song, Verrol stood staring towards the wall at the side of the pit. Astor followed the line of his gaze, and discovered a new kind of problem. There, looking down from above, was a man in a grey cape.

The spy from the Swales! Astor's heart jumped into her mouth. A grey cape wasn't unusual in itself, but the man's attitude was. It was obvious he had no share in the festivities, and was quite detached from the crowd in the pit. Unlike them, he was giving his whole attention to the band – no doubt Astor and Verrol in particular.

'Count us in!' Purdy called out to Verrol.

'What's wrong with him?' Ollifer demanded.

Of course, the man in the grey cape meant nothing to the other band members. Only Astor and Verrol understood. A single spy couldn't do much by himself tonight, but next time he might not be on his own.

Astor turned to Granny, who had given up trying to win over the crowd. Astor remembered her words: 'If you can't do this, you can't do anything.' If they failed now, they'd never even get the chance to live up to her vision. They'd never be accepted into the gang or gain her protection against the Swales . . .

Verrol swung to Astor, his grim face a reflection of her own thoughts. 'I'll try something different.'

He snapped his fingers to the rhythm of the next song. '"Be with Me Soon",' he told Purdy and Ollifer. 'One ... two ... three ... four.'

Astor summoned every ounce of energy and threw herself into the rhythm of 'Be with Me Soon'. Purdy and Ollifer followed her lead. Verrol shook his clapper and pealer – then danced right out into the audience.

He danced in front of the two girls who'd been laughing. They wavered, half embarrassed and half fascinated. His fluid movements were directed exclusively to them, an invitation to dance. They kept on giggling, but it was a different sort of giggle now.

The girl with the waist-length hair consented first. She began swaying her hips, bobbing her shoulders, flicking out with her hands. Verrol caught her movements, mirrored them and amplified them. A moment later, the second girl joined in too. Verrol had his back to the band so Astor couldn't see his expression, but she could imagine it: smiling and dangerous and slightly predatory.

People turned to watch. After a few minutes, another girl joined in, then another. The plan was working – and Verrol wasn't finished yet. He called out to the band over his shoulder, 'Keep going, same song!' Then he set off dancing through the crowd, and the girls danced along behind him.

At the end of 'Be with Me Soon', without a pause, the band cycled round and started from the beginning again. Astor increased the tempo. She could see a line of people winding through the crowd, more and more of them all the time. They looped to the left and looped to the right, then around in a full circle and back towards the band.

'Kiff! Kiff! Kiff! Kiff!'

At first, Astor didn't grasp what they were chanting. Then she remembered: Kiff was the name of the birthday girl. Verrol had drawn her into the dancing! She came back with him at the head of the line and kept on dancing right in front of the band.

They had everyone's attention now. Adrenalin surged through Astor's veins. She shot a glance towards the side of the pit, and the ground above the top of the wall was empty. The spy had gone! She felt as though the power of her drumming had driven him away.

When they came to the end of 'Be with Me Soon' for the second time, she capped it off with a massive salvo of drums. Then she maintained a quiet *tap-tap-tap* on just one drum as the audience burst into whoops and whistles of applause. The dancers clapped with their arms raised high over their heads.

Verrol took up his place with the band again, still moving to the *tap-tap-tap* of the drum. The girls at the front of the crowd continued to dance with him. 'Give it everything!' he roared as the band launched into their next song.

Astor gave it everything. The audience was with them, they were going to be a success. They had done it!

33

That was the night when Astor fell in love with gang music. She'd previously liked the fact that she was good at playing it – but tonight it played her. Every chord rang through her bones and bloodstream. Her drums became as much a part of her as the hair on her head or the palms of her hands. She forgot about classical piano, harp and violin; *this* was her kind of music.

She lost her sense of self completely. The feeling that swept her away now wasn't rage and anger but joy and love. She wanted to hug every note to her breast like a lover.

The band played all the songs they'd planned, then went back over their opening songs again. The crowd hadn't paid attention before, but they paid attention now. The applause went on forever.

In the end, Granny called a halt. 'That's enough. You've given them an hour and a half. They'll keep you here all night if you let them.'

With Reeth's help, she ushered the band members away. The crowd watched them go, drinking in their every move. A clamour of conversation sprang up, as loud as before the band started playing. Only now it was the Rowdies that everyone was talking about.

Reeth brought them up out of the pit by a different ramp to the one they'd used before. They threaded their way between corrugated iron hutches and pens of wire netting, and arrived finally at a pen that was empty of animals but furnished with bales of straw. The bales made comfortable seats, and they all sank down except Reeth.

Astor was exhausted yet buzzing with adrenalin. Her clothes were wet with sweat, and her hair was dripping.

Reeth was buzzing with enthusiasm. 'I never guessed! Never!' The words rattled off his tongue as he paced up and down. 'Granny Rouse's Rowdies. I thought you'd be an ordinary gang-music band. Incredible! Just incredible!'

'Gang music is what they play,' Granny told him.

'But different! Better! Those driving rhythms!' Reeth was looking at Astor as he spoke.

155

'And the singing,' put in Ollifer. 'Don't forget the singing.'

'Of course! The complete package!' Reeth turned to Granny. 'I'd like to offer my assistance. I think they can be bigger than just Slumtown.'

'Perhaps.'

'That's where I come in. I have *contacts*.' On the word *contacts*, he sawed the air dramatically with his one good arm. 'I've been around a long time. As a performer, as a manager. I can get them into venues all around Brummingham.'

'I think Granny's our manager,' Purdy put in.

'But does she have contacts?' Reeth alternated his appeal between Granny and the band. He was never still for a moment, and his voice grew more insistent all the time. 'Okay, here's a proposal. Co-managers. Reeth and Rouse. Rouse and Reeth. What do you say?'

Granny nodded. 'Well, if you can get them into venues outside of Slumtown . . .'

'Oh, I can, I will. I *believe* in these people. You'll be amazed how much I can do. Once I start I'm unstoppable.'

'Yes, but not yet,' said Granny. 'Only if they can get the right sound.'

'They sound right to me.'

'Granny's had a vision of a band,' Astor explained. 'We have to live up to it.'

'Exactly,' Granny grumped. 'They're still missing something.'

And if we don't find it, Verrol and I don't get accepted, thought Astor. Bleak reality resurfaced as the adrenalin drained away.

Reeth rubbed his bugle of a nose and scanned the Rowdies. He must have realised they wouldn't go against Granny because his excitement dropped several notches. 'Hmm, well, if that's the way it is . . .'

He broke off and swung round at the sound of voices calling out. Girls' voices, somewhere on the other side of the hutches.

'Just a minute, this could be for me,' he said, and went off to investigate.

There was a long silence between Granny and the members of the band. 'You'll keep practising, of course,' was her only comment.

When Reeth came back a few moments later, it turned out that the girls hadn't been calling for him at all.

'They'd like to talk to you,' he told Verrol. 'They're very determined.'

'Who?'

'One's Avette from the North Side Stockies. I don't know the other, but she has blonde hair down to her waist.'

'Where are they?'

Reeth pointed. 'Just beyond the chicken shed. They say they'd prefer to talk to you in private.'

Verrol raised an eyebrow. 'I'd better go and see what they want.'

He rose and strode off with that impossibly loose-limbed gait of his. Astor retreated into her own thoughts. Of course, the girls must be the two that he'd first picked out to dance with. She had a very good idea what they wanted.

Next day, the two girls turned up to watch the band practise, and the day after as well. Avette was the brunette with the bandana, attractive in a dark, sultry way; Elvie was equally attractive in a bright, blonde way.

Since the band had always allowed onlookers, Astor could hardly object, though she fumed inwardly. The girls were only interested in Verrol, not in the band. They were forever trying to catch his eye. If he danced, they danced too, jiggling around at a distance. It was obvious they would have liked to jiggle much closer.

Of course, it was none of her business what he did outside the band. One time she commented, 'They're just like your little maidservants,' but his only response was a sardonic grin. She certainly didn't intend to question him further. Unfortunately, that also made it difficult to talk to him about other things, such as the man in the grey cape.

The two girls were a constant distraction. As far as Astor could tell, Verrol didn't play up to their interest, yet he didn't reject it either. He must be so accustomed to female attention that he took it for granted. *Arrogance*, she decided. It wasn't good for any male to receive so much blatant adoration.

She tried to keep Verrol's mind on the music by calling out comments and suggestions as they played. When Verrol danced and the girls danced along with his movements, she sometimes brought the playing to a complete stop in order to experiment with a new rhythm or different effects.

On the third day, she had a better idea. A boundary line! She took a piece of wood and scratched a line in the dirt, five feet out from their practice shelter.

'No one closer than that,' she announced.

But the line backfired when the girls turned it into a new form of entertainment. They danced up to it, dangled their toes over it, played at pushing each other across it. They

158

danced even when Verrol wasn't dancing, and their giggling was more distracting than ever.

Astor had had as much as she could take. In the middle of a song, she threw down her drumsticks and marched out to them.

'Further back!' she shouted. '*Back!*'

Elvie had just stepped across onto the wrong side of the line. Astor kicked at the offending foot.

'Ow!' Elvie kept her foot where it was. 'What's *your* problem?'

'You! You're a problem today and you were a problem yesterday! You're not wanted here!'

Elvie appealed to Verrol over Astor's shoulder. 'Is that what the rest of the band says?'

'Stay on the right side of the line!' Astor snapped, and raised her foot to stomp down hard.

This time Elvie was ready. Before the stomp could descend, the girl bent and caught hold of Astor's leg behind the knee. When she lifted, Astor was forced into an undignified hop.

Elvie laughed in triumph. 'Now you come across to *my* side!'

She turned and dragged Astor over the line. Astor hopped twice and lost her balance. She reached out and snatched at the only thing to hold on to – Elvie's waist-length blonde hair.

Elvie screamed, and they both went down in a heap.

Astor struggled up onto her knees. Elvie confronted her face to face.

'What are you trying to do? Rip my hair out?'

Astor realised she was still holding on to a handful of Elvie's hair. She opened her fist and tossed it aside.

159

'You shouldn't let it grow so long.'

'Oh? Jealous?'

'It's ridiculous. Nobody has hair like that.'

'No? Nobody has hair like yours either.'

She was staring down at the top of Astor's scalp as though there was something odd about it.

'There's nothing wrong with *my* hair.'

'What about the colour?'

Astor was taken aback. Of course, the girl was simply trying to insult her, but why aim an insult at what everyone else admired?

Elvie, who had been studying her expression, let out a whoop. 'She doesn't know!'

'What?' Astor patted her hair defensively.

Elvie was merciless. 'You're going white at the roots.'

'No!'

'Yes.' Elvie's hand flashed out and plucked a couple of strands of hair. Astor hardly registered the pain, though it brought tears to her eyes.

'See?'

Astor could hardly focus, yet she could see that something had happened to the colour. At one end, the strands were perfectly white.

'Why did nobody tell me?' She whirled around.

'I never noticed,' said Ollifer.

'Nor me,' said Purdy.

Verrol had come forward from the shelter, but now paused awkwardly, saying nothing.

'*You* did!' she accused.

'It won't be like that for long,' he said. 'When it grows through it'll be one colour again.'

'One colour?' She gaped at him. 'Yes, *white*!'

'You must have had some kind of shock,' said Elvie. She'd achieved her moment of victory, and now sounded halfway sympathetic. 'They say that's what does it.'

The tears in Astor's eyes weren't only from the pain. She rose to her feet and blundered away.

'Leave me alone,' she said to the world in general and Verrol in particular.

35

Astor asked the serious-looking girl with the long face, Shannet, if she owned a mirror. Shannet didn't, but knew someone who did. It was a piece of steel polished to a reflective sheen, and when Astor held it to her hair, she could see the new white growth appearing from every part of her scalp. There was no hope for her.

She could guess the shock that had turned it white. Her worst ever moment had been two weeks ago, trapped by the two ex-soldiers in the cul-de-sac, when she'd thought she was as good as dead. Now, although she'd survived, it seemed that her hair hadn't.

It wasn't just an ordinary white, but an intense and snowy silvery-white. When it grew through, her head would stand out like a beacon. People would think she was an old woman at the age of seventeen.

She cried herself to sleep that night. When she awoke next morning, her mind was fixed in a state of grim determination. She would *not* feel sorry for herself, and she would never talk about it with anyone. All in the past! If she was fated to live her life as a freak, she might as well get used to it.

That morning, she went to Monia's booth in the market area and asked the hairdresser to cut off all her curls. Monia inspected the new growth at the roots.

'We can dye it, you know,' she said. 'I can make up a paste.'

'It won't be *my* colour, though.'

'No, nothing could match that shade of copper.'

'Then I want it cut short. Really short. Let the white show through, I don't care.'

Monia cut it back to an inch all over, like a helmet. The hairdresser seemed almost sad as she gathered up the fallen curls.

'Burn them,' said Astor. 'Throw them away. Good riddance to them.'

She was aware of people staring at her all the way back to the stacks area. She returned their stares until they looked away. For the rest of her life, her looks would never matter again. She had come to a turning point, and from now on everything would be different.

She remembered the Swale girl's words: 'You rely on prettiness to get your own way.' Astor still hated Blanquette, but it was true her looks had given her an advantage . . . with adults when she was a little girl, with men as she grew older. But Blanquette's other barb was not true: 'You're nothing inside.' Astor now knew she possessed at least two strengths of her own – a survival drive and an instinct for rhythm.

And rhythm would be her future. Her one and only goal in life would be to make this band work. No men, no relationships, no getting engaged or married. Granny Rouse's vision for the Rowdies would be *her* vision too.

From that day on, she threw herself into band practice. The way she had once played harp music was no more than a light-hearted hobby compared to the way she now played gang music. Hour by hour, she drove them all on with inexhaustible energy. They had to get better and better and better!

Gradually, the balance within the band shifted as the others responded to the change in her. Her relentless commitment made her into their unspoken leader. Purdy had never been a dominant force, while Ollifer was too self-obsessed to take charge of anyone else. As for Verrol . . .

She glanced up occasionally from her drums and watched him. He had made no comment about her new hairstyle, but she'd seen him turn away with a hint of a grimace. Since then, his gaze skimmed over her as though he couldn't bear to look at what she'd done to herself. Good! She didn't want him to look.

Had she ever been interested in him as more than just a friend? Thinking back, she wondered about her own feelings. But that was all far behind her now, all in the past. So long as Verrol followed her lead musically, she didn't care what he did with Elvie and Avette.

All in the past, all in the past, all in the past! The phrase sang in her mind to the rhythm of her drums.

In fact, Elvie and Avette never came back to watch Verrol at practice. Obviously, it had been only a bit of fun for them. Astor almost pitied their shallow-mindedness.

They would hardly have distracted her anyway, as she went deeper and deeper into the music. She found herself drawn to the very harshness of gang music that had originally repelled her. Now she embraced the jagged, dissonant tunes, the strange chords from the brass guitar, the thrum of the clapper

163

and jangling chime of the pealer. She had moved on beyond all forms of prettiness.

However, the missing instrument was still a problem. Four more buzz guitarists and a pitch guitarist came to audition, but they were no better than the ones rejected before.

'How many times do we have to do this?' sighed Ollifer.

'How many more are left to try out?' asked Verrol.

After another three days, the supply of musicians dried up completely. The band decided it was time to talk to Granny Rouse.

They found her sitting beside a pile of broken clocks, supervising the work of a dozen young gang members. The work involved picking apart the mechanisms in order to separate out bits that could be re-used. Granny listened to the band's complaints, then shook her head.

'No,' she said. 'The Rowdies have to be the best of the best. Nothing less.'

Astor was ready to shriek at her stubbornness. 'Maybe there just aren't any buzz guitarists good enough.'

'So look for a different instrument.'

'We have. Pitch guitarists and zithers.'

'Something different again.'

The band members looked at one another in surprise.

'But you heard it,' said Purdy. 'Surely you'd have heard anything really different.'

Granny snorted. 'How many times do I have to tell you? A vision isn't definite like that. I'll only recognise it when the whole sound's right.'

There was a long silence, until one worker put down the clock he'd been picking apart. It was the spiky-haired boy, Hink.

164

'I heard the weirdest instrument today,' he said. 'If you want different.'

'What sort of instrument?' Verrol asked.

'Different.' Hink turned to Granny. 'When I took your message to the Soapies gang. It was near there.'

'What did it look like?' asked Astor.

'Didn't see it, only heard it.'

Granny flapped a hand at him. 'All right, you'd better take them there. I hope this isn't a trick to get off work.'

Hink grinned and hopped up immediately.

 The Soapies' territory had the only relatively clean water in Slumtown, and the gang specialised in washing and laundry. Hink led the way around tubs where gang members worked, ducking under endless lines of clothes hung out to dry. Astor wondered how anything could ever dry in this murky atmosphere.

Beyond the washing lines, the slagheaps that marked the end of Slumtown loomed like ghostly mountains. The intervening ground was a wasteland, empty except for four huge sections of metal pipe. Hink held up a hand and stopped to listen.

'Yes,' he nodded. 'She's still there.'

'Where?'

'Come and see.'

With exaggerated caution, he led them towards one of the pipes. They could all hear the music now: haunting and heavy

165

with overtones. The way the notes flowed into one another made the hairs stand up on the back of Astor's neck.

'Shh. Don't startle her,' Hink said over his shoulder.

'Shy, is she?' asked Ollifer.

Hink pulled a face. 'She hides away to play by herself. What do you think?'

The pipe was twenty feet long, and the music came out at either end. Following Hink, they gathered at one end and peeped in.

The girl's back was curved against one wall of the pipe, and her legs were doubled up against the other. Someone of Verrol's height could never have squeezed into so small a diameter. They couldn't get a clear view of her face or the instrument, only an impression of dark hair and dark clothes. She moved an arm back and forth as she played, and appeared to be blowing into some kind of tube.

Perhaps she liked the reverberations inside the pipe. The harmonies she produced were like an entire orchestra. And the tune rising and falling . . . catching oddly on the way down . . . so yearning and intense and impassioned. It tugged at Astor's heartstrings.

'What *is* that?' Purdy murmured.

He meant the instrument. Astor prodded him to silence. Now she could hear the girl crooning softly to herself as she played. The words of a song?

After a couple of minutes, the others backed off to compare opinions. Astor had to tear herself away. She had no hesitation about her opinion.

'We need that instrument in the band,' she said.

'Granny makes the final decision,' said Purdy.

'Granny will like it. She *must*.'

'It'll change everything,' mused Ollifer. 'Not like normal gang music.'

'So it changes everything.' Astor was adamant. 'If the girl doesn't fit in with us, we'll fit in with her. We can—'

She broke off, a moment too late, as the tune came to an end. The volume of sound inside the pipe had masked their voices, but now, in the sudden silence, her words rang out loud and clear.

'Who's that?' asked the girl in a small voice.

The band members froze – all except Hink, who ran off along the side of the pipe.

'It's only us,' said Verrol. 'We'd like to talk to you.'

Hink reached the other end of the pipe just as the girl sprang out of it. A strap over her shoulder supported the weight of her instrument, and he brought her to a halt by grabbing the strap.

'It's nothing bad,' he told her. 'Please don't go.'

The girl looked at his hand on the strap, looked into his cheery, cheeky face – and stayed put.

The others came forward to meet her. She had straight black hair and an elfin face, with a small mouth and tiny pointed chin. Her eyes were enormous, made even larger by the dark circles painted around them. The jacket she wore was waterproofed with shiny creosote, and there were metal pins in her eyebrows, spiral springs in her ears and rivets through the wings of her nose.

She's as much of a freak as me, thought Astor with a surge of fellow feeling.

'What's your name?' asked Verrol.

The girl stared at him as if startled to be addressed – or as if hypnotised.

'Mave,' she replied at last.

'Ah, Mave. Nice name. What's the instrument you're playing?'

'I call it a melodium. I invented it. Why?'

While Verrol took on the task of explaining about the Rowdies, Astor studied the melodium. It was an outlandish contraption, combining a bellows, a tiny keyboard of wooden keys, and a brass whistle on the end of a tube. Astor guessed that the keyboard and bellows somehow transformed the notes blown in through the tube.

It turned out that Mave had already heard of the Rowdies and their performance for the North Side Stockies. She obviously approved of what she'd heard. But when Verrol talked of needing an extra member in the band, she shook her head.

'I don't like playing with other people,' she said

'Have you tried?' Verrol's tone was gentle and persuasive, but it didn't persuade Mave.

'I don't need to.'

'Don't you want to be famous?' Ollifer asked.

It was the wrong question. 'I play for myself. I don't care about anyone listening.'

Astor tried a different approach. 'Our band won't be complete without you in it.'

'I can't. Sorry.'

Was she a fraction less absolute? Astor tried again. 'That tune you were playing was so beautiful. We'd love to include it in our repertoire.'

'You would?' She was definitely more receptive now. 'I composed it.'

'Does it have words too?'

'Of course. I'm a songwriter.'

Astor turned to the others, hoping they'd play along. 'Our lucky day! We've been looking for a songwriter, haven't we?' She swung back to Mave. 'You *have* to join us now!'

Astor had struck the right chord, and Mave's resistance melted away. 'I'll join if we can play some of my songs.'

'We will. Promise.'

'Come with us now,' Verrol suggested. 'We'll see how it sounds.'

'Band practice?'

'Yes. Are you with the Soapies?'

'Sort of.' Mave glanced towards the lines of washing. 'I've finished all my jobs for today.'

'Granny will be able to organise a more permanent arrangement,' said Astor. 'Same as she did for Ollifer.'

They started back at once. Already the afternoon sun was sinking low, a huge, dull ball of orange blurred and magnified through the murk. Verrol walked with Mave, and his conversation seemed to be putting her more at ease. Purdy came up alongside Astor.

'I don't know about this,' he said. 'You went out on your own, back there.'

'Oh?'

'Making promises. Talking about permanent arrangements. What if it doesn't work out?'

'It will. I can hear our new sound in my head. It'll be wonderful.'

'Maybe. But will it be what Granny wants?'

'Well, it's what *I* want,' Astor snapped. 'And it ought to be what you want.'

Purdy merely shrugged, and fell back when she lengthened her stride. She walked the rest of the way wrapped up in her

169

own thoughts . . . which became less and less positive as they approached the stacks area. What if Purdy was right? What if she'd overstepped the mark? She couldn't afford to fall out with Granny Rouse . . .

The setting sun shed a reddish glow through the smog, but it wasn't yet time for the evening meal. When they came back to the place with the broken clocks, Granny and her young workers were still there, still sitting on the ground. But they were no longer working, and they weren't alone. Standing behind them were three dozen menacing figures in the blue-and-gold livery of Swale-men.

37

'This is bad trouble you've brought my way.' Granny Rouse turned to glare at Astor and Verrol. 'So when were you going to tell me the Swales were after you?'

'We thought . . .' Astor began, then ran out of words.

'We hoped it wouldn't matter,' said Verrol.

'Well, you hoped wrong, didn't you?' Granny huffed.

The Swale-men looked on impassively. They carried pistols or shotguns, and many of them controlled dogs on leashes. The dogs were huge mastiffs with bodies and heads encased in armour, showing only their eyes and teeth.

Then one man took a pace forward. He appeared to be the leader, balancing a blunderbuss in one hand and a leather purse in the other. He held up the purse and jingled the contents.

'There's a reward here for anyone that helps recover the fugitives,' he told Granny. 'Could be you and your gang.'

Granny glanced at the purse, then focused again on Astor and Verrol. 'Well? Is there anything you can say? Any reason why I shouldn't just hand you over?'

Astor could have said that the Swales would lock her up, that they were conspirators and bullies, that they were afraid of their plot being exposed. But Verrol spoke first.

'One reason,' he said. 'We've found our fifth musician for the band.'

He gestured towards Mave, who had been hanging back out of sight. Now Purdy and Ollifer drew away to leave her in Granny's full view. The old woman squinted at the strange girl, apparently not impressed.

'What does she play? What's that thing on her hip?'

Astor answered on Mave's behalf before she could break and run. 'It's her special instrument. A melodium. Don't judge till you hear it.'

Granny shook her head. 'When I said "different", I didn't mean *that* different.'

Another Swale-man broke in, a red-faced man with a bristling moustache. 'We're wasting time. Let's just take our two and go.'

He waved a flintlock pistol towards Astor and Verrol, and shook the leash of his dog. The animal uttered a deep-throated growl.

'Wait!' Granny held up a hand. 'I haven't said yes to anything yet.'

'They're Swale servants, Swale property.' The man's attitude was almost as aggressive as his dog's.

'Don't do anything you'll regret,' warned Granny, and snapped her fingers.

The rest of the gang materialised from behind the surrounding stacks. They must have crept up unnoticed, another fifty of them. They outnumbered the Swale-men, even though their weapons were only poles and iron bars.

Granny turned to the leader. 'I don't think you want to start a fight, do you? I'm sure you can indulge an old woman for a few more minutes. Perhaps some music to calm us down?'

'All we want—'

'All *I* want is to listen to this five-person band.' Granny levered herself up off the ground. 'Let's hear how they sound playing together. Probably not an improvement, by the look of that new instrument.'

As though everyone had already agreed, she shooed the musicians ahead of her in the direction of the practice shelter. The leader wavered for a moment, then decided to accept the situation. At his signal, the Swale-men and their dogs fell into line behind Granny and the band. The rest of the gang followed after the Swale-men or slipped along parallel aisles between the stacks.

The red sunset haze was fading to grey by the time they reached the shelter. Astor took her place behind the drums, Purdy picked up his brass guitar, and Verrol his clapper and pealer. Mave just stood looking awkward.

'Do you know "Jump Up and Dance"?' Ollifer asked her. 'Or "Mercy Me"?'

'I only play my own songs.'

'But you do *know* gang-music songs?'

Mave merely patted her melodium. 'I'll fit in if I can.'

It didn't sound promising. Verrol counted them in, and the band swung into the opening bars of 'Mercy Me'. Astor found it hard to concentrate, watching Mave out of the corner of her eye.

The girl's only movement was a slight nodding of her head in time to the beat. She seemed transfixed. Was it the unfamiliarity of the song or the presence of an audience?

At last, she put the brass whistle to her lips and flexed her fingers over the keyboard part of her instrument. But – still nothing. Wasn't she even going to try?

They were halfway through the song before she joined in. Then suddenly the wait was all worthwhile. Mave didn't just tag along but played as if she'd made the song her own . . . as if she'd been with the band through every practice session.

They sailed through the fourth verse and soared into the fifth. Then a roar from Granny cut them short. 'Stop! Enough!'

The band members dropped their instruments.

'That's unfair,' Ollifer protested. 'You have to give us a proper trial.'

'No, I don't.'

'We were *good*,' claimed Astor. 'It was a great sound.'

Granny swung towards the leader of the Swale-men. 'What did you think?'

'Why me?'

'You were tapping your foot to the beat. I saw you.'

The leader said nothing. Instead, it was the red-faced man who spoke out angrily. 'It changes nothing.'

Granny was grinning from ear to ear. 'Look, even the dogs liked it,' she said, pointing.

It was true: the armoured dogs were sitting back on their haunches as if the aggression had gone out of them. The red-faced man prodded his dog with his boot to make it bark.

173

'We still have our orders,' he said. 'Maybe we should take all five of them.'

'Phah! As if I'd let you take my Rowdies.' Granny clapped her hands and turned to the band. 'You've got it at last! That was the sound I heard in my vision! Exactly right!'

The leader shook his head. 'Those two are still fugitives. We can't go back without them.'

'Not fugitives,' said Granny. 'They're full members of Granny's Gang. They've passed their trial period, and now they're under my protection.'

'We have the guns,' growled the red-faced man, and raised his flintlock pistol to aim at Granny's head.

'Yes, shoot me first,' said Granny calmly.

'No!' cried Astor.

Granny turned her back on the red-faced man and marched up to the leader. She took a grip on the end of his blunderbuss and directed the barrel straight at her own chest.

'Shoot me first,' she repeated. 'But be aware of the consequences. You can't kill all of us. What happens next?'

The leader chewed his lip and looked uncomfortable.

'I'll tell you,' Granny went on. 'You kill me, and my gang spreads out to tell all the other gangs. You think you can make it out of Slumtown then? Not a single one of you will escape alive – and that's a promise.'

The leader believed her. 'Okay, okay. Keep your musicians.' He pulled the barrel of his gun away, and let it drop. 'Lower your weapons,' he ordered the Swale-men.

There were no objections, not even from the red-faced man. Instead, there was an outburst of barking from his dog, and a kind of gurgle from the man himself.

Nobody had seen Verrol move, yet there he was –

standing over the red-faced man, who had suddenly fallen to his knees. The gurgle was due to the man's own dog-leash wrapped round his throat. The dog was barking and tightening the leash as it struggled to break free; the flintlock pistol had somehow transferred across into Verrol's right hand.

As everyone watched, the dog made another leap and dragged the man over full-length on the ground. He was too busy trying to unwrap the leash from his throat to bother about his pistol, even when Verrol tossed it on the ground beside him. Two other Swale-men came across to help.

'Better leave fast,' Granny advised the leader. 'You wouldn't want to be still in Slumtown when the news gets around. As from tonight, every gang will know about you, and they'll all be on the alert. You wouldn't want to come back for a second try either.'

The Swale-men trooped off with their heads down, muttering among themselves. The red-faced man could barely walk, held up only by his two helpers. Purdy played a triumphant riff on his brass guitar.

Granny turned to Astor and Verrol. 'Of course, I'd never have let them take you anyway.'

Astor's ironic expression was a match for Verrol's. 'Oh, now you tell us,' she said.

Mave was the magic ingredient for the Rowdies. Quiet and shy as she was in ordinary life, she was free and fearless as a musician. She brought a new creative spark that set everyone else on fire.

Astor enjoyed her drumming more than ever. She added new metal pots to her drum kit, and a suspended brass bowl that she used as a gong. Not having to worry about acceptance into the gang was a huge weight off her shoulders.

Naturally, Granny demanded to know the full history of their involvement with the Swales. She didn't get very excited when she heard about the plutocrats' planned coup.

'Old lot or new lot, they're all as bad as each other,' she sniffed.

'The plutocrats are worse than the old lot,' said Verrol.

'Maybe, but we can't do anything from here. Gang music is *our* way to conquer the world. I'm going to tell Reeth to look for outside venues from now on.'

They hardly needed extra encouragement. The experience of playing together as a full band was intoxicating, and they kept at it for hour after hour, day after day. Everyone watched everyone else's moves, and built on them. Mave would turn to Purdy and throw in a variation; Purdy would nod and elaborate in a higher key; and Verrol would come in and insert deep notes on the off beat.

'Love it!' shouted Astor – and from then on, it would be included in their repertoire. Or at least, it would be included until they invented something even better.

Not all their inventions were serious. Often someone would toss in a ridiculous sound effect or a few bars from a nursery tune, and the whole band would go into fits of helpless laughter. Once, though, when Purdy struck a chord and stretched it out to an impossible length, they laughed at first – then grew gradually thoughtful. 'We could actually do something with that,' Verrol said.

The creativity didn't stop even when they took a break. Mave could never bear to be separated from her melodium and kept it always at her side. Then she would pick out a few notes . . . or Purdy would hum . . . or Verrol would whistle . . . or Astor would start tapping her fingers.

'What do you reckon?'

'Hey, do that again!'

'Take it up at the end.'

'I'm thinking "Hair Hang Down".'

'We could use it for the bridge.'

'Let's try it out!'

A moment later they were all scrambling for their instruments. Somehow, every break kept sliding back into another practice session.

They worked on incorporating two of Mave's songs immediately: the one they'd heard her play inside the pipe, and another that Astor particularly loved. All of Mave's songs had a dark, gritty quality, more melodic but also more unsettling than the band's other songs. The lyrics were equally dark, about loss and doom and suffering.

Astor liked the contrast with their usual material. 'It gives us variety,' she explained. 'That's what we lacked before.' She slowed the two songs down until the rhythm became very powerful and heavy, while Ollifer sang the lyrics with feeling as if he really meant them, even though he complained that he didn't understand a single word.

Astor's first impression of Mave didn't go away on closer acquaintance. The girl was as odd as her appearance, and so reserved that she could appear sullen. Her personality came out in her music; at other times, she had a way of becoming absent even when she was sitting right next to you.

Astor gained a new insight into Mave's oddity one night after dinner. Band practice had finished two hours ago, but Astor had found a tin basin that she wanted to try out with her drums. She returned to the practice shelter in the dark – and made an unexpected discovery.

There, behind the drums at the back of the shelter, lay Mave, fast asleep. The girl had only pretended to go off home to her own gang. She was curled up against her melodium like a lover.

Astor didn't know whether to feel sad or annoyed or what. As she stood looking down, Mave opened her eyes – huge, round eyes, which seemed to possess their own luminosity in the dark.

'I need time alone,' the girl said in answer to Astor's unspoken question. 'The Soapies get on my nerves.'

'How long have you been doing this?'

'Since I joined the band.'

'Doesn't it get cold?'

'I can stand a little cold.'

'You'll be stiff and sore lying on hard ground like that.'

'Then I'll be stiff and sore.'

You seem to like suffering, Astor thought but didn't say. 'I'm sure you could sleep in our hide-out,' she offered.

'I don't get on well with other people.'

'It would be safer than sleeping here.'

'I have nightmares. I cry out in my sleep.'

'We can find a private sleeping spot for you. Nobody will disturb you, and you won't disturb anybody.'

Mave was wavering, but not won over. Astor came up with another reason. 'If you sleep with us, we'll have more time for band practice. We'll bring Ollifer in too.'

Mave's tone changed. 'We could keep going as long as we liked . . .'

'Makes sense, doesn't it?'

'I don't *need* other people . . .'

'No, but in this case . . .'

'Okay. I'll give it a try.'

Astor waited as Mave rose to her feet and strapped the melodium over her shoulder. 'Actually, you do get on well with *some* other people. Me and Verrol and Purdy and Ollifer. Don't you think so?'

A small smile crept unwillingly over Mave's face. 'Yes, I suppose I do.'

Smiling, she was beautiful. Her chin was too tiny, the shape of her face was all wrong, the dark circles painted round her eyes were downright bizarre. Yet she had her own uncanny kind of beauty, like a wild animal. Astor had hardly noticed before. It was a pity that probably no one else would ever notice.

Finding a private spot for Mave was easy; there were several small separate nooks under the railway sleepers. Next morning, Astor persuaded Ollifer to try the same arrangement. And that very afternoon, there was even more reason for maximising their practice time, when Reeth turned up looking mightily pleased with himself.

'I've been working hard for you,' he told the band, gesturing grandly with his one arm. 'Talking to everyone. I've landed your first engagement at an outside venue.'

'Where? When?'

'Be ready by six tomorrow evening. I'll come and collect you.'

When Reeth came to collect the band for their performance, half of the gang came too. Carrying Astor's drum kit, they marched across Slumtown and out into the streets of Brummingham.

The venue was in an area of tenements where factory workers lived. It turned out to be a tiled space roofed over by a canvas canopy and closed off by buildings on either side. In front of the buildings were counters serving drinks and snacks. A crowd of a hundred or more people sat on parallel wooden benches facing a stage.

'This is a drinking shop,' said Granny.

'Yes,' agreed Reeth, 'but they put on musical acts every weekend.'

A woman bustled up to him flourishing bare, brawny arms. She had a proprietorial air, and rattled off a barrage of instructions. Reeth nodded.

'She wants you to start at once,' he told the band. 'The crowd needs settling down.'

They made their way forward to the stage. Astor was keyed up and mentally prepared for the performance of her life. But her heart sank when she saw groups of militiamen among the crowd. They were ex-soldiers like the pair who'd attacked her in the cul-de-sac, and wore red jackets or other remnants of military uniform. The sight of Granny's Gang seemed to stir them up.

'Hey, where did that lot come from?'

'They look like Slumtown kids.'

'We don't want those vermin here.'

'This is our territory!'

The hostile shouts continued as Astor supervised the setting up of her drum kit. The gaslight illumination was especially bright over the stage, and she kept her head down while secretly surveying the crowd. It would have been amazing bad luck if the same pair of soldiers had been present – and they weren't. She was thankful for that, at least.

The band didn't wait for an introduction from Reeth. Verrol counted them in, and Astor struck up the rhythm of their first song.

The ex-soldiers focused their heckling on the musicians.

'That's a Slumtown band!'

'Scum of the earth!'

'Losers!'

'Go back to where you came from!'

Mave's naturally pale face turned an unnatural white, and she retreated to the rear of the stage alongside Astor.

'Don't worry,' Verrol called back to her. 'It's only the militiamen. The others are okay.'

Astor wasn't so optimistic. The majority of the audience seemed to be siding more and more with the troublemakers. When the band reached the end of their first number, the ex-soldiers booed. Members of Granny's Gang cheered, but that only made the boos all the louder.

Granny herself stood silent and frowning. She hadn't anticipated this. Everyone knew it would be a struggle to spread gang music beyond Slumtown, but right now the band was being condemned before anyone had even listened to their music.

Watching the audience through the next song, Astor was sure she saw shoulders swaying and heads nodding in time.

The beat was working on them. At the same time, the heckling grew more and more strident . . . and it was Mave who now became their particular target.

'What's googly-eyes playing?'

'Something out of the garbage tip!'

'Sounds like she's strangling the cat!'

'Meow! Meow! Meow! Meow!'

When someone called out, 'Leave that poor puss alone!', the whole audience erupted in laughter.

By the end of the song, Mave was at the corner of the stage and looking ready to jump off at any moment. Ollifer's normally smooth, shiny face appeared almost haggard.

'I can't sing like this!' He turned to the band, eyes wide with distress. 'I can't make them like me!'

'Keep singing!' Astor ordered, and kicked off with a *boom-boom-boom* on her gong. '"Made for Love"!'

It was make-or-break time. If they lost the audience on this song, there would be no coming back. The ex-soldiers responded by raising the volume of their abuse.

'Go home to your slum!'

'Get a job!'

'You call *that* music?'

Astor had no plan in view – she just shouted at the top of her voice, '*Yes, we call it music!*'

Verrol echoed her shout, and chanted it to the beat of the song.

> *Yes, we call it music!*
> *Yes, we call it music!*

Now it was becoming a plan – to turn the hecklers' own

words back on them. Astor sang along with Verrol.

> *'Oh yes, we call it music!*
> *That's right, we call it music!*
> *Music, music, music!*
> *We do, we call it music!'*

Their response tickled the audience's sense of humour, and there was a ripple of laughter. Astor flourished her drumsticks, and Ollifer and Purdy joined in, hollering the line in a dozen variations. Then Mave made a contribution on her melodium, producing a sound like blowing a raspberry. The raspberry was directed at the hecklers, who had fallen silent under the laughter.

The mood was shifting. Verrol stepped forward at the end of the song, and seized the moment. 'And now a little number we'd like to dedicate to all our militiamen friends out there. It's called "Shut Up and Dance!"'

Astor guessed at once, and launched into the rhythm of 'Jump Up and Dance'. Ollifer guessed too, and sang the usual lyrics apart from the chorus. For the chorus, the whole band came in to roar, 'Shut up, you slackers, shut up and dance!'

The audience laughed. Some of the militiamen still tried to interrupt, but most people were now paying attention to the band. Verrol cracked another joke before the start of the next song, but it was hardly needed. The rhythms of gang music took over from where the humour left off.

With every new song, the band went from strength to strength. Ollifer regained his confidence and reached out to the audience with his voice and his arms. Astor's drumming became the beat of her heart and the pulse of her blood.

By the fifth song, the heckling had stopped completely. The militiamen gathered in a disgruntled group at the back behind the benches. We've won, Astor exulted. *They've given up!*

By the eighth song, everyone was tapping their toes and snapping their fingers. This was one of Mave's two songs, and Verrol encouraged her to step forward to the front of the stage. No shrinking now! Swept away by the music, Mave had become a different person. Even her face was flushed.

Astor was wrong about the militiamen giving up, however. On the very next song, when the band was in full flight, suddenly the gaslights popped and sputtered – then went out one by one. The entire area under the canopy was plunged in darkness.

The band ground to a halt. There were cries of surprise from the audience, followed by more particular shouts of annoyance.

'Ouch!'

'Watch where you're going!'

'Who did that?'

Nothing was clear, just shadows and running footsteps. Astor had an impression of bodies surging forward from all sides, but she still wasn't prepared for the blow that came suddenly at her out of the dark. It knocked her clean off her seat behind the drums and sent her sprawling across the stage.

There was a cry from Mave and a squawk of protest from Ollifer. Astor's head was muzzy, and her eyes still adjusting to the dark. She heard the crash of a falling body and Verrol's voice cursing, then grunted orders and feet thumping across the stage. When she reached out to snare a foot, a boot kicked her hand away.

It was all over in half a minute. There were more angry exclamations from the audience, followed by a jangle of guitar strings. The attackers were surging out as they had surged in.

A moment later, the yellow glow of an oil lamp appeared in the darkness, held aloft by the drinking shop's brawny proprietress. The militiamen had vanished, all except one who stood by the exit at the back.

'This show is terminated,' he declared in a loud, belligerent voice. 'We have confiscated the instruments.'

Astor levered herself upright and looked around. Ollifer was sitting with his head in his hands, Purdy lay spread-eagled on the side of the stage, and Mave was bleeding from a cut above her eye. The melodium was gone, and so was Purdy's brass guitar. Astor let out a cry of rage when she saw that half her drum kit was also missing.

Even Verrol had been taken by surprise. The militiamen hadn't taken his clapper or pealer, they'd just pushed him right off the stage. Now he rose into view in front of the first row of benches.

'This is a warning!' bellowed the ex-soldier at the back. 'No more gangs in our territory!'

As he turned to go, a tiny body came hurtling straight at him. Granny Rouse! She crash-tackled him around the legs.

She couldn't drag him to the ground, but she hung on like a terrier. Unable to shake her loose, he seized her by the waist, lifted her up then flung her down. Astor couldn't see, but she heard the thud of old flesh and bones hitting the tiles.

185

There was no cry from Granny herself, but the audience booed and hissed.

'That's not right!'

'No way to treat an old woman!'

But the ex-soldier had freed himself from Granny's grasp. He swung away and set off running.

'Get him!' yelled Hink. 'After him!'

The spiky-haired boy gave chase, followed by twenty other gang members including Verrol. Astor jumped down from the stage and ran forward to check on Granny first. Someone was taking the old woman's pulse, someone else held her head propped up off the ground. Her face was grey, but she opened her eyes and saw Astor.

'Go get your instruments back,' she ordered. 'I'll be fine.'

Astor nodded and ran on to join the pursuit.

The ex-soldier was soon hunted down. Two streets away from the drinking-shop, a commotion of shouting and brawling broke out. Astor turned a corner and came upon the gang members holding him down on the cobblestones. Hink sat astride the man's waist and was trying to throttle him.

'You hit our Granny! You hit our Granny!'

Verrol seized Hink by the collar and hauled him off. The ex-soldier twisted furiously, but the others still held him pinned.

'Rabble! Rats! Parasites!' The man burst into a flood of abuse. His smooth, pink complexion made him appear no older than Astor, yet the glass ball in his left eye socket presumably came from a wartime injury.

Verrol bent down over him. 'Where have you taken our instruments?'

The ex-soldier glowered. 'To our headquarters, of course. You'll never get them back.'

'Perhaps if we ask nicely.' Verrol's smile was shark-like. 'When you take us there.'

'We'll kill the lot of you first. Scarrow knows how to deal with filth like you.'

'Scarrow's your leader?'

'Yes. You don't stand a chance against trained fighting men.'

'I suppose we'll just have to ask very, very nicely. What's your name?'

'Corporal Tyke to you.'

'Let's go, then, Corporal Tyke.'

For a moment, Astor thought the ex-soldier was going to resist.

'Or I can break your arm,' said Verrol pleasantly.

Tyke sat up as the gang members released him. 'Oh, I'll take you. You'll soon wish I hadn't.'

Verrol yanked the man's military jacket down off his shoulders so that the sleeves became manacles trapping his wrists behind his back. Then he gripped him under the armpits and hoisted him to his feet.

'Forward march, Corporal.'

They set off. Verrol and Astor marched on either side of Tyke, while the rest of the gang followed behind. Tyke led them along streets like canyons, between factories and warehouses. There were few windows, and none of them showed a light.

'How many of you are there?' Astor asked Tyke.

'That's for you to find out.'

Verrol spoke across from Tyke's other side. 'They organise themselves in regular army units. Ten in a section, thirty in a platoon, a hundred in a company. This lot's probably a platoon or two.'

Astor shook her head. 'What's the point of it all? I don't see the sense.'

Again Verrol answered. 'They like being soldiers. There's nothing else for them now.'

Tyke sneered. 'We don't need anything else. We were proud to serve our country. We still are. You wouldn't understand.'

'You were conscripted,' said Verrol. 'What's to be proud of?'

'Wrong. I joined up by my own choice. I lied about my age to get in.'

Even Astor was surprised. 'You didn't care about getting killed?'

'It's not about that. It's about facing up to danger as a team. You have to learn not to put yourself first. You depend on your mates, and they depend on you. It's about discipline and following orders.'

'The way you follow Scarrow's orders,' said Verrol drily.

'And Scarrow follows the orders of leaders above him. Chain of command.'

He sounds like my stepfather, thought Astor. Marshal Dorrin always seemed to prefer a kind of iron necessity ruling his life.

'Scarrow fought overseas for twenty years,' Tyke continued. 'I fought for four, and lost an eye in the Battle of Bratislava. But we did our bit. We served and fought. Much thanks we got for it when we came home.'

'There were no jobs for them,' Verrol explained to Astor. 'Factories were already starting to lay off workers.'

'We never got a chance.' Tyke sucked in air, then erupted in an explosion of bile. 'It's a *pigsty* of a world. A stupid, dirty, senseless *pigsty*!'

188

Astor was amazed at the depth of his resentment. Her life had contained plenty of injustices lately, but she hoped she would never shrivel up inside with that much bitterness.

They passed along an alley and arrived at an open area of bare ground. The smog lay heavier here, dense and foul-smelling. Directly ahead, on an old train line, stood three railway carriages. Flags draped the sides of the carriages and hung suspended from nearby poles.

Union Jacks, thought Astor. *This must be their* –

Tyke sprang forward. He was about to yell a warning to his comrades when Verrol hooked a foot round his ankle and brought him crashing down. In the next moment, Verrol's knee was planted between his shoulderblades.

'Something to tie him up.' Verrol snapped his fingers at the gang members rushing forward. With his free hand, he unloosed the neckerchief from his own neck and wadded it into Tyke's mouth. When Shannet handed him a belt, he fastened it round the corporal's head to keep the gag in place.

'You expected him to do that,' said Astor. 'You were waiting for it.'

'He was far too willing to lead us here,' Verrol agreed.

He hauled Corporal Tyke back up on his feet. Other gang members held out more belts, straps and cords.

'Just tie his hands for now,' Verrol ordered. 'Then walk him back to the alley and truss him like a chicken.'

'Where will you be?' Astor asked.

Verrol turned to survey the three railway carriages. 'I need to spy out their headquarters.'

'Are we going to fight them?'

'Not trained soldiers, not if we can help it. We use strategy.' He grinned. 'Be back in a few moments.'

Ten minutes later, the strategy was in place. Verrol reported fifty-odd militia-men in the first and second railway carriages, but only half a dozen in the third, which was where the band's 'confiscated' instruments had been stowed. He divided the gang members into different teams for different tasks.

Strange how he's become our leader, Astor thought to herself. Nothing had been proposed or discussed or agreed. For some reason, everyone just seemed to accept that Verrol was the best person to take charge.

They moved forward under cover of smog and darkness, across ground littered with scraps of paper and broken glass. Sounds of singing and raucous laughter came from the first and second carriages. One team separated off and made for the surrounding flagpoles – to cut down a selection of the largest flags and accompanying ropes. Another team veered towards the back of the second carriage – to undo the coupling that linked it to the third.

Astor and Verrol were in the third team, along with Hink and Shannet. They made straight for the third carriage. The blinds were down over the carriage windows, but didn't completely cover them. Astor and the others hoisted them-selves up to peer in.

The interior appeared to be both living quarters and sleeping quarters. Bunks lined the walls; military uniforms, underwear and weapons hung from hooks on the upper berths. Six men sat on stools playing cards.

Verrol directed attention to the goal of their mission.

Mave's melodium, Purdy's brass guitar and four drums from Astor's drum kit lay on top of a mattress in one of the lower berths.

So far so good. The team stepped down and filed along to the back of the carriage. Here, above the buffers, was a metal ladder leading up to the roof.

Hink went first, and the others followed. The roof was almost flat on top, but curving down at the sides towards an inch-wide rim of guttering. Verrol set off at once to the opposite end of the carriage, stepping gingerly. His next task was to check when it had been uncoupled from the second carriage.

Astor stayed with the others at the back. She knelt and held her ear close to the roof. Inside, the militiamen had started to shout at one another, apparently arguing over their cards. Excellent!

Meanwhile, the team that had been cutting down flags now approached the third carriage. With the flags rolled up in bundles under their arms, they climbed the metal ladder and joined Astor and the others on the roof.

No sooner was everyone up than Verrol began signalling. It was time for the next stage of the operation. The team with the flags moved into position above the carriage doors on either side. For the moment, Astor, Shannet and Hink had nothing to do except keep out of their way.

Verrol was looking down into the gap between the second and third carriages. Astor couldn't see but she could imagine – how the team that had done the uncoupling now set their shoulders against the buffers of the third carriage.

Push, Astor willed them on. *Push, push, push!*

For a long while, nothing happened. Then, with the tiniest

creak, the carriage moved. One inch, then another, then another. Verrol had already started back along the roof, arms outstretched for balance as he walked.

By the time he rejoined his team, the carriage was in slow, steady motion. The militiamen inside were still having a shouting match . . . perhaps someone had been exposed as a cheat in their game. Whatever the cause, the timing couldn't have been better!

Little by little, the carriage built up speed. Soon it was travelling at a slow walking pace, then a fast walking pace. The track seemed to have a fractional downhill gradient. The other two carriages disappeared gradually into the smog.

It couldn't last. Listening through the roof, Astor heard the shouting peter out . . . followed by puzzled exclamations, curses and questions. But now they were almost at the end of the track.

They crouched on all fours, bracing for the impact. With a dull thump, the buffers of the carriage met the buffer stop at the end of the track.

There were shouts of rage from the militiamen. The impact had obviously taken them by surprise. The team with the flags rose silently to their feet, unfurled their flags and held them out wide. In the next moment, the carriage doors opened, and heads appeared.

'What was that?'

'Where are we?'

'Why have we moved?'

Astor counted as they jumped down to the ground. One, two, three, four, five of them. They scanned all around in every direction – except upwards.

When the sixth man jumped down, the team with the flags launched into action. They flung themselves out into the air like great silent birds. With their Union Jacks spread out for wings, each one sailed down on top of a chosen target.

The militiamen hardly knew what hit them, before the flags enveloped their heads. With muffled cries and helpless flailing, they were knocked down, then rolled over and over on the ground. Their attackers wrapped them up in the flags and wound the flag-ropes round them. The team that had pushed the carriage ran forward to help finish the job.

Meanwhile, Astor's job was just beginning. She followed Verrol as he slid down the roof and swung himself in through the open doorway. But she misjudged the width and smashed her knee against the side of the door. For just a moment, she could go no further.

She gestured for Hink, Shannet and the others to pass her by, and they rushed on through a sliding door into the interior beyond the vestibule. She rubbed at her knee until the pain diminished, then hobbled after them.

The air beyond the sliding door was stale with smells of tobacco and unwashed clothing. Overturned stools bore witness to the sudden end of the militiamen's card game. The team stood facing the lower-berth mattress where the instruments lay.

'I'll take the brass guitar.' Shannet pointed.

'I can carry two of the drums,' offered Hink.

'Good.' Verrol leaned forward and gathered up the melodium. 'I'll take this, then.'

Astor was about to say, 'I can carry the other two drums,' but the words never left her mouth. As Verrol straightened and stepped away, a tattooed arm appeared from the upper bunk on the other side, aiming a pistol at the back of his head.

'Don't move a muscle,' said a harsh, grating voice.

Verrol stayed frozen in place, the others whirled and gaped. Astor moved to the same side of the carriage as the man who held the pistol, and dived quietly onto a lower-berth mattress. He couldn't see her as she couldn't see him.

'Turn around slow,' the voice ordered.

Verrol turned slowly around. 'Ah, Scarrow,' he said. 'I didn't see you before.'

'Yeah, spoiled your little plan, didn't I? I was having a kip.' The pistol prodded Verrol's forehead, jolting his head back. 'No one to move.'

Astor began to creep forward from mattress to mattress. Scarrow was three bunks away, and she felt certain he didn't know she was there. Even Verrol and the others hadn't realised.

'What now?' asked Verrol.

'Maybe I should just blow your brains out,' said Scarrow.

'Then you die too. You can't shoot us all with one pistol.'

'I got other weapons.'

The bunks butted right up against each other, and Astor crossed easily from one to the next. Uniforms and underwear dangling from hooks made a partial curtain at the side.

'Filth like you don't deserve to exist,' Scarrow went on.

194

'Begging and stealing is all you're good for. This country would be better off without you.'

Astor hadn't decided exactly what to do until she saw a glint of steel among the uniforms and underwear. A military sword! If she could only unhook it . . .

Very carefully, she gripped the blade between her fingers, avoiding the razor-sharp edges; very cautiously, she raised it upwards. She couldn't see where the guard of the hilt hung over the hook, but she could feel when it came free.

Perhaps Verrol had glimpsed the movement out of the corner of his eye, because his next words to Scarrow were louder and deliberately provocative. 'If we don't deserve to exist, what about you? What's the use of soldiers without a war?'

Astor lowered the sword down on the mattress beside her. It was almost a yard long and curving towards the point. She carried it with her over onto the next mattress, directly below Scarrow.

He was snarling at Verrol now. 'You got no idea what's coming. We'll be needed again, soon enough. And you'll be blown away like the scum you are.'

He jabbed the pistol viciously into Verrol's forehead. Although he hadn't yet pulled the trigger, he was surely building up to it. Astor extended the sword along the side of the bed, took a two-handed grip and lined up on the tattooed arm overhead.

'What's coming, then?' Verrol asked.

'For you, a pistol ball in the—'

Astor swung. In a glittering arc, the sword swept up and smashed into Scarrow's wrist.

The impact jarred her hands, the pistol went flying through

the air, and Scarrow let out a howl of pain. She hadn't caught him full-on with the edge of the blade, but she'd dealt him a very deep gash.

A moment later, Scarrow leaned out over the edge of his mattress and bent down to gape at his attacker. Verrol grabbed him by the neck, pulled him off the mattress and brought him crashing to the floor. Meanwhile, Shannet darted down the carriage to recover the pistol. By the time Scarrow had disentangled himself and sat up, she was pointing the barrel straight between his eyes.

He had been sleeping in his singlet and underpants. His entire body was covered with tattooed designs in black, red, green and purple ink. The name Scarrow appeared in many places, while the skin across his chest was reserved for tattooed rows of tiny coffins – dozens and dozens of them.

He raised his arm, and the hand that had held the pistol hung limply dangling. Blood dripped from his wrist to the floor.

He turned to Astor with an ugly expression. 'Slut.'

'Manners,' cautioned Verrol.

Scarrow twisted suddenly on the ground and bit him on the ankle like a rabid dog. He must have bitten deeply, because Verrol's face spasmed with pain as he hopped back a pace.

'Shoot him,' Astor told Shannet. She swung her legs out from the bunk and stood up. Her heart was thumping, and she was charged with adrenalin.

Shannet looked at Verrol, who shook his head.

Scarrow laughed and snapped his jaws once more in the direction of Verrol's ankles. Verrol only stepped back another pace.

'Coward,' the militiaman sneered. 'Come on, fight me man to man. I'll whip you good.'

Verrol's calm was almost supernatural. 'I don't think so.'

'One useless hand, and I'll still whip you. What odds do you want? You want my arms tied behind my back? Would that make it easy enough for you?'

'He could beat you with *his* arms tied behind his back,' said Astor.

'No he couldn't. Because he doesn't have the guts. He's a spineless, snivelling, lily-livered coward.' Scarrow whirled his injured hand and spat at the same time. Drops of blood and globules of mucus spattered over Verrol's breeches.

'You shouldn't have done that,' said Astor. 'Now you'll be sorry.'

Verrol shook his head. 'We only want what we came for. Our instruments.'

Astor didn't understand Verrol at all. She was just itching to give Scarrow a kick. Instead, she helped with gathering up the band's instruments.

Then Shannet kept the pistol trained on Scarrow while the others tore off strips of sheet and bound his legs. The militia-man would be immobilised long enough for them to make their escape. He was still jeering at Verrol as they left the carriage.

The teams regrouped and headed back to the venue. They expected the other gang members to be waiting for them, but only a score of drinking-shop patrons remained. The arrival of Astor and Verrol caused a flurry of comments.

'It's the drummer and the dancer.'

'Loved your music! What a performance!'

'You got your instruments back, then?'

'When are you doing your next show?'

Astor brushed aside the praise and enthusiasm. 'Where's Granny and the rest?'

'Ah, the old woman.' The patrons shook their heads and their expressions clouded over.

Astor's heart missed a beat. 'What's wrong with her?'

'She was in a bad way after she got knocked about.'

'Took a turn for the worse.'

'They carried her off on a stretcher.'

Hink uttered a sound that was half sob and half yelp. 'But she's going to be okay?' he insisted.

The patrons shrugged noncommittally. The proprietress of the drinking-shop came up to join the discussion.

'They were taking her back home to your hide-out,' she explained. 'We made a stretcher for her out of an old door.'

'Let's go,' said Verrol.

They jogged through the streets of Brummingham, retracing their route to Slumtown. Then across Slumtown, past shacks and shelters, garbage pits and mounds of scrap. Seized by a growing fear, they hurried faster and faster all the way.

The night was almost over by the time they reached the hide-out, with just a hint of pearly dawn light filtering through. The stretcher had arrived before them, but not long before. A throng of gang members clustered in the clearing outside the stack of sleepers, talking in low, anxious voices. Purdy, Ollifer and Reeth were there too, and Mave with a bandage over her forehead.

'How is she?' cried Astor, running up.

The throng parted to let them come forward. The stretcher had been lowered to the ground, and Granny was still there on it. Her complexion had turned a ghastly shade of grey.

'She's not good,' said Reeth. 'We think it's her heart.'

Astor remembered Granny calling out that she'd be fine, and to go recover the instruments. She felt dreadful.

Then Granny opened her eyes. She seemed to have difficulty focusing.

'Who's that there?' she quavered.

Purdy bent over her. 'It's Astor, Verrol and the others, Granny. They just got back.'

'Did they recover their instruments?' the old woman asked at once.

Astor spoke out in a loud voice. 'Yes.'

'Good.' Granny's wizened face creased in a smile. 'That's our drummer girl, isn't it? The audience loved you, you know.'

'Yes. How are you feeling?'

'I'll be right.'

'You don't look it.'

'Then I won't be right. It's not important. I'm ninety-five years old. I can't go on forever.'

Hink shook his head in violent protest. 'You can! You must! You're our leader!'

'Don't be silly. You'll have another leader after me.'

Hink clamped his hands over his ears. '*No!* Don't say that!'

Granny looked at him, and her expression softened. 'Okay, I'll stay around a bit yet. Now I think I'd like to stand up.'

She lifted an arm, but nobody moved to take it.

'Be sensible, Granny,' said Purdy. 'You're not well enough yet.'

Granny snorted. 'I didn't get to the age of ninety-five

by being sensible. Do you want to finish me off with your disobedience?'

In the end, she gave them no choice. She dragged herself up on one elbow and obviously intended to keep struggling until she was back on her feet. Several gang members raised her gently upright.

'That's better. Always listen to your Granny.' She turned her face towards the entrance of the hide-out. 'Now you can all help me to my bed. Except the Rowdies. They have to go practise.'

'What, *now*?'

'Yes. Non-stop practice. You have to be perfect.'

Everyone except the Rowdies assisted Granny into the hide-out. At one point, her legs collapsed, and she would have gone down in a heap but for the arms supporting her. Astor looked away before the tears could spring to her eyes.

Granny continued to go downhill. Each day, she spent more time sleeping than the day before. When she was awake, she soon grew irritable and told people to stop hovering over her all the time.

The only thing that perked her up was when Reeth arrived to announce that he'd set up another engagement for the band. 'It's a festival they're putting on eight days from now. The organisers are using an empty warehouse in the east industrial district. I made them give us top billing. You'll have an audience twenty times the size of anything yet.'

Granny brought her hands together in a soundless clap. 'What did I say? Your last audience loved you. The militiamen couldn't prevent that.'

'Even better.' Reeth turned to the band members gathered around. 'The attack on you and your instruments created extra interest. Now everyone's curious about the Rowdies. It worked in our favour.'

Astor noticed how he had taken to speaking of 'we' and 'our', as though he included himself with the band. He also turned up more and more often to watch the band practise. Was he positioning himself to take over as sole manager when Granny was gone? Astor didn't much like that thought coming into her mind – and she didn't much like Reeth either.

'They're all talking about you,' he said one time. 'Sholdo Felp and the other organisers. They can't wait to meet you.'

And another time: 'I'm building you up and up. I don't mention gang music so much as a new sound with incredible rhythms. Your reputation's spreading like you wouldn't believe.'

And then again: 'I told them you're working on some amazing new songs. Sounding better than ever.'

He was almost embarrassing. *Why does he have to try so hard?* Astor wondered. Even when he watched the band practise, he could never simply relax and enjoy the music.

The new songs they were working on were two more of Mave's. Original material was becoming a large part of their repertoire. As the next engagement approached, they worked on bringing every song up to performance standard.

It was at the end of one late-night practice session that Verrol touched Astor on the elbow and said, 'Can we talk?'

'Okay,' she said with a shrug. The band had been playing

by the light of three oil lamps, one of which Astor carried. She turned back and put it down on the flat top of a metal drum. 'So, talk.'

'Do you think I'm a coward?'

'I don't know what you are.'

'You wanted me to fight an injured man.'

'It was his choice. He wanted to fight you.'

'Did I need to prove I could beat him?'

'Not for me. You don't have to prove anything for me. I don't understand you, that's all.'

The habitual sardonic expression was entirely absent from his face. He frowned and chewed his lip. 'There's nothing to understand.'

Astor frowned back. 'You were already a servant at Dorrin Estate when my mother and I came there, weren't you?'

'Yes. I remember the day you arrived.'

Astor chose not to mention that she had no similar memory of *him*. 'How long had you been there?'

'Four years.'

'My stepfather took you on?'

'No, his head steward. Marshal Dorrin was still with the Army General Staff.'

'And before then, were you a servant in some other household?'

'No.'

'Hah. I thought as much.'

He stared into the glow of the oil lamp and said nothing.

'What were you then?'

'Does it matter?'

'No. Except I told you all about my past. If you don't think that deserves some return . . .'

'I didn't ask you to share your secrets.'

Astor waited him out. After a long pause, he resumed. 'I prefer the present. I'm a better man now than I was in the past.'

'You're trying to leave something behind, aren't you? Something that stopped you from fighting Scarrow. Something that turns you against war and violence.'

'Not fighting Scarrow was just common sense. If I'd done anything to him, he'd have come after us. He'd have had to take revenge.'

'Not if we shot him. Same as he was ready to shoot you.'

'Then his platoon would've had to take revenge. By letting him off, I let him keep his pride.'

'He spat on you.'

'I can put up with a little bit of spit. It made us more equal in his mind.'

'What about *your* pride?'

'Me? I don't have any.'

She studied him closely. The light of the oil lamp hollowed out his cheeks and sharpened his cheekbones.

'I don't believe you,' she said. 'I think you're one of the proudest people I've ever met.'

His eyes flashed towards her, then away. She had taken him by surprise, yet instinct told her it was true.

'Oh well, you know all about me then.' He tried to laugh it off. 'I admit I'm very proud to play in the Rowdies.'

She let it pass. Whatever his big secret was, she could see he wasn't going to reveal it. She collected the oil lamp, and they walked back to the hide-out, side by side but apart. In fact, she had never felt more distant from him.

How could he be so proud and yet so willing to be

humiliated? He was a mass of contradictions. So fast and yet so languorous . . . so dangerous and yet so passive . . . so sharp and yet so muffled . . . No, he was *impossible*. She couldn't work him out at all.

'Come quick!' Hink burst forth from the hide-out, shouting and waving his arms. 'It's our Granny!'

Gang members turned to him in dismay. In the last three days, Granny Rouse had grown so weak that she could barely lift her arms. For the last twelve hours, Hink had refused to leave her side, crouching by her sleeping-bag in the tunnel under the sleepers. Astor feared the worst – until Hink explained.

'She's had one of her visions! You have to come and hear!'

With a sigh of relief, everyone dropped what they were doing and rushed into the hide-out. Bodies packed in so tight that there was hardly room to breathe. They kept absolutely still and strained their ears for Granny's faint, quavering voice.

'I saw the band. Clearest vision I ever had.' She spoke very slowly with drawn-out pauses. 'I saw every face and every instrument. Mave was there with her melodium. We got everything right. The Rowdies were playing to an audience of thousands.'

Purdy spoke up from somewhere along the tunnel. 'Could be our next engagement.'

'No.' Granny had heard him. 'This wasn't Brummingham, this was London. The biggest auditorium in the biggest city. Thousands and thousands sitting in rows. Such clothes, such finery. They kept clapping as if they'd never stop. Even the toffs loved gang music.'

She broke off to cough. No one dared interrupt. When she resumed, her voice was fainter than ever.

'I've seen the future. I watched the whole scene looking down from above. The future of the Rowdies. They only have to seize it. Seize it for the rest of us. Are they all here?'

'Yes!' 'Yes!' 'Yes!' Responses came from different parts of the tunnel.

'Good. I'd like to hear them perform.'

'What?' 'Now?' 'Where?'

'Of course *now*. At the practice shelter. Take me there.'

They took her out to the practice shelter by lifting the corners of her sleeping-bag and carrying her in it like a hammock. Astor had a funny feeling about this performance, a foreboding that caught in her throat and brought a dampness to her eyes.

At the shelter, she sat behind her drums, while Purdy, Mave and Verrol took up their instruments. Granny was lowered to the ground right in front of them, and the rest of the gang formed a semicircle further back.

The band struck up 'Muddy Boy Beat', one of their old standards. Astor kept glancing at Granny, and found it hard to throw herself heart and soul into the music. The old woman's eyelids drooped, and she lay very still.

When the song finished, Astor called out in the silence, 'Is she all right?'

Granny's eyes flew open. 'I'm okay, but your music isn't. What's wrong with you? All technique and no feeling.' She scowled at Astor in particular. 'Put some life into it! Hit those drums!'

Astor didn't know why, but she felt more like crying than ever. '"Take Me Home",' said Verrol, and counted them in for the start of the next number.

They must have played better this time, because Granny tapped her fingers to the beat. Little by little, though, her tapping grew more intermittent, and she'd stopped altogether by the end of the song.

Astor was almost afraid to call out. 'Granny?'

'I'm still here.' Granny sucked in air and seemed to be making a supreme effort. 'I want you to remember something, you band members.'

'What?'

'This around you. This dirt, this corrugated iron, these stacks of scrap. This is where you began. Never forget it. Never forget us. Look at every face.'

The band members looked at the faces in the semicircle. The rest of the gang looked back at them, utterly serious, utterly solemn.

'You'll travel far away from Slumtown,' Granny continued. 'You'll probably live a glamorous, exciting life. This won't be your home much longer. But you must always, always carry it inside you.'

'Because this is the place the music comes from,' said Verrol slowly.

'This is the place the music comes from,' she confirmed with a nod. 'Now I'm ready for your next song. The most powerful beat you can do.'

'"Made for Love"?' suggested Ollifer.

'Yes.' Granny let her eyelids droop. But before the song could begin, she looked up at the band again. Her hand lifted in a tiny flutter of movement that barely left the ground.

'Wait. I still need a promise from you.'

'Anything.'

'Just name it.'

'You have to promise that you'll never lose faith in the Rowdies.'

'You won't let us,' said Purdy.

'You have to promise to do it for yourselves. When I'm not around any more.'

Purdy shook his head. 'We want you to share it with us.'

'Ah, Purdy, you have the soul of an angel after all.' A smile creased the corners of Granny's mouth. 'No, I don't have to be there. Not if you promise.'

'I promise,' said Astor. 'I promise to make your vision come true.'

Verrol made the same promise, then Mave, then Ollifer, then Purdy. Granny waited until she had heard from each of them individually.

'There, you see?' she said. 'It can't go wrong now. It's as certain as if it had already happened.'

She lay back exhausted, chest heaving. The band looked uncertainly at one another – until she roused up again.

'What are you waiting for? Play! Loud, loud, loud! And everyone clapping along.'

'One. Two. Three. Four,' Verrol counted, and the band launched into the opening bars of 'Made for Love'.

It was the loudest they had ever played. First the band dominated, then the clapping, then the band again. Hink ran up and began banging away on one of Astor's drums; Verrol bellowed along with Ollifer in his rough singing voice; others filled in the backbeat with cries and yells like a chorus. The words hardly mattered, only the volume.

The song built up and up and up to a deafening crescendo, then crashed and fell away like a tumbling wave.

In the hush that followed, everyone turned to look at Granny Rouse. She had tried to join in the clapping at the start, but now she was motionless, her eyes wide open and fixed in the stillness of death. Her final expression was a smile of immense satisfaction.

46

Granny's funeral took place at dawn. There was a particular place for funerals in Slumtown, and a particular family, the Worrels, who looked after the cremation rituals. Two hundred people from many gangs attended the ceremony.

The place was the site of an old mill, where a stream poured down over a lip of stone into a circular pool below. Rock walls twelve feet high surrounded the pool, except at one point where the water flowed out under an arch into a tunnel.

In the first dim glow of dawn, the mourners gazing down from above saw only darkness. There were splashing sounds from the pool, and the quiet voices of the Worrel family exchanging instructions. Little by little, the light crept down towards the surface of the water.

Now three boats became visible, bobbing on the blackness. The Worrels rode in the two larger boats, while the canoe in the middle contained the body of Granny Rouse. She looked even tinier in death than in life, wrapped head to foot in tar-soaked rags.

Suddenly, a tremendous gout of yellow flame shot up from the canoe. The Worrels began a deep bass chant that echoed around the rock walls. Up above, the mourners shielded their eyes against the dazzle and joined in the chant.

While the two larger boats stayed at the edge of the pool, the canoe floated out to the centre. There the current caught it and rotated it. The flames consumed Granny's body with a continuous roaring crackle, as the burning vessel drifted on towards the tunnel.

The chant came to an end. In the silence that followed, a long, quivering note rang out. Not a normal part of the ceremony, Astor guessed, judging by the way people turned their heads to look. The source of the music was Mave, who stood five yards along from Astor in the circle of mourners. She was playing a dirge for Granny on her melodium.

Slowly, slowly, the note slid up the scale, semitone by semitone, then plummeted a full octave. Mave pumped the bellows with her elbow and blew into the tube, entirely concentrated on the sound of her lament.

Meanwhile, the canoe had reached the entrance to the tunnel. As it passed in under the arch, the flame diminished. Now it was like a candle that illuminated the subterranean brick walls.

Mave's music grew quieter, trembling between notes, and the unearthly tune sent a chill down everyone's spine. It was the essence of all grief, infinitely sad and sweet . . . and something more as well, some indefinable emotion that seemed to hover beyond the physical world altogether.

Time seemed to stand still as the burning canoe passed out of sight. Now only the light on the walls remained, drawn-out and dwindling. Mave's music followed it into the darkness, rising and falling between just two notes.

The mourners were so rapt, they had almost forgotten to breathe. When light and music finally ceased together, two hundred throats let out a long sigh. Astor realised with surprise that she wasn't even crying. She was beyond tears, beyond everything.

'That was amazing,' Reeth murmured to no one in particular. He had come along to the ceremony perhaps out of respect for Granny, certainly to show support for the band.

The final ritual was the handing out of small seedcakes. Every mourner took a cake to carry home and eat later.

Granny's Gang walked back to their hide-out in silence. Decisions would need to be made, life would have to go on, but for the moment they were absorbed in their memories. Only Reeth wanted to talk.

He came up to walk beside Mave, directly in front of Astor. Astor was still hearing the music in her mind, and paid no heed to their conversation until Mave raised her voice. Mave was the kind of person who *never* raised her voice.

Astor stepped up to join them. 'What is it?'

Reeth sawed the air with his single arm. 'I was talking about that tune she just played. Why not incorporate it into the band's performance? A total contrast in the middle of your other songs. What do you think?'

Astor didn't want to think, but Reeth kept going. 'You're the one always pushing for more variety. This could be the ultimate switch of pace and mood. Tremendous dramatic effect!'

Astor noted the tightly clenched expression on Mave's face. Reeth probably wasn't sensitive to such things, but she saw at once that Mave would never agree.

'It's not for me to decide what the band plays,' Reeth rattled on. 'But—'

'It was *her* song.' Mave cut him off with a hiss. 'Granny's song. I made it for her, not anyone else. Not for dramatic effect. I shall never play it again.'

Reeth still didn't understand. 'Seems such a waste . . .'

Astor stepped in. 'I agree about variety. But not that particular song.'

'I don't see—'

'No.' Astor shut him up. 'It's a matter of Mave's feelings.'

They walked on for a while. Reeth appeared to be rehearsing further arguments in his mind. Mave dropped back, but then came forward on Astor's other side.

'I do have another song that's just as sad,' she told Astor.

'Could we try it?'

'Yes. I've put words to it too.'

'Even better.' Astor swung towards Reeth. 'There you go. Problem solved.'

Reeth flashed his teeth in a smile. 'Good. Excellent. So long as it gives us that dramatic effect.'

Mave's new song turned out to be a love song. It was as sad as her dirge for Granny, but also filled with yearning, like the essence of all hopeless passion. Looking at Mave's elfin face and quiet demeanour, Astor could only wonder where such intensity came from.

> *'If I could reach for you*
> *Draw you in close*

211

Love would cry out from me
Deepest of notes
Love that's too big for my
Poor eggshell heart
Caged in this body
And locked behind bars.

I'm just a ghost of love
That you can't feel
Never be, never be, never be real.

Ghost words of love for you
You'll never hear
Ghost touches in the night
Still I'm not here
Ghost tears that fall for you
Dry on your skin
Ghost wishes want you so
Never let in.

I'm just a ghost of love
That you can't feel
Never be, never be, never be real.'

The band concentrated all their practice time on that one song, to have it ready for their next performance. At least they had a purpose to throw themselves into; the other gang members were aimless and disoriented since Granny's death. No one could fill Granny's shoes as leader, and no one wanted to put themselves forward in her place.

Astor was hardly involved in discussions about the leadership, so she was surprised when Hink came up to her one time after dinner. 'Why can't you use your influence?' he demanded.

'Uh?' She stared blankly at the boy.

'Persuade *him*. Verrol. He ought to be our leader.'

'Oh, right.'

'He says he hasn't been in the gang long enough. But we'd follow him.'

'Would you?'

'Of course. Anywhere. He's *meant* to be a leader.'

Astor remembered how Verrol had come forward to take charge of the raid on Scarrow's headquarters, but she'd also noticed how he had slipped back into being an ordinary gang member since. He was a born leader who didn't want to lead. Another of his contradictions?

'I don't have any influence with him,' she told Hink.

'You're his best friend, aren't you?'

'We're just in a band together.'

Astor didn't plan on trying to change Verrol's mind. Still, she couldn't help wondering if this was another element in his mysterious past. Had he once been a leader who had chosen to leave the role behind?

Within the band, she remained the one who drove the decisions. They worked out where to include Mave's new songs, and new ways of linking from song to song. At Purdy's suggestion, they selected two songs to leave for possible encores.

On the day before the performance, Reeth came up flourishing a scroll of paper. Unfurled, it turned out to be a printed poster for the festival. The names of the other acts were featured, but the biggest name was THE ROWDIES in block capitals. A third of the poster was taken up with portraits of Astor, Verrol, Ollifer, Mave and Purdy.

'Not bad, eh?' said Reeth. 'I used to have a bit of talent as an artist.'

Purdy whistled. 'You did the portraits?'

'Yes. Extra promotion for you. I wanted you to stand out above the support acts.'

What stood out for Astor was the bright red colour of her hair – a fair approximation of the original copper. The portrait was instantly recognisable.

'Have these gone out already?' she demanded.

'All over Brummingham,' said Reeth with satisfaction. 'Three hundred of them.'

'They'll guess it's me,' Astor groaned.

Reeth's satisfaction faded. 'Who?'

'The Swales. You should've done my hair white. It's half white already.'

'Not *half*,' Reeth protested.

Verrol looked thoughtful. 'Maybe they'll never see the poster in their posh part of town.'

'The militiamen will,' said Mave.

Reeth had an answer for that. 'Rumour has it the militiamen are leaving.'

'What, leaving Brummingham?'

'I heard some of them started marching out yesterday afternoon. Nobody knows where.'

'So there won't be any at tomorrow's performance?' Mave persisted.

Reeth rubbed at his great bugle of a nose. 'Maybe not.'

Mave and Astor exchanged glances. They weren't happy with the 'maybes', but it was too late to recall the poster now.

When the band arrived at the warehouse for their performance, a crowd of well-wishers was waiting outside to greet them. Although the festival was already under way, many people were more interested in catching their first glimpse of the new band than in watching the support acts. They pointed and gawped.

'There's the drummer!'

'Isn't he the dancer?'

'Look at that weird instrument!'

Reeth hurried the band through the crowd, muttering, 'Don't stop, keep moving.'

One of the organisers was waiting at a side door. He mopped his forehead and beamed all over his face. 'Never seen anything like it,' he said.

He ushered them in and closed the door behind them. They found themselves in a triangular room that had two sides of solid wall and a third of hanging green curtains. Obviously a corner of the warehouse interior had been screened off for the use of performers between acts.

Reeth performed introductions. 'This is Mr Felp, our stage manager. And these are the Rowdies. Ollifer. Astor. Purdy. Mave. Verrol.'

'Sholdo Felp,' said the man. 'Call me Sholdo. So you're the band that's creating so much buzz? I never thought I'd see the day when gang music spread beyond the slums!'

He shook hands all around with great enthusiasm, then called out to the others in the room. 'Come and meet the new sensation! They're here!'

215

People converged from all sides: stagehands, organisers, assistants and other performers. Astor was flattered and embarrassed to be the centre of so much interest. Everyone wanted to talk to them, question them, or just stand close to them. Ollifer naturally basked in all the attention. Reeth joined in too, answering questions on behalf of the band's more reticent members like Mave and Purdy.

In the end, Sholdo had to shoo the admirers away. 'Give them some quiet now, they're on next.' He turned to address the band. 'Seems like the audience is in a good mood. They should be nicely warmed up for you.'

They could hear a very different kind of band playing on the other side of the green curtain – comedy numbers, by the sound of it. Every now and then, the audience erupted into laughter.

Astor had the usual butterflies in her stomach, but her nerves were nothing compared to Mave's.

'They expect too much,' the strange girl whispered when the band was alone. There was a hunted look in her dark-ringed eyes, like some wild beast brought to bay. 'We can never live up to it.'

Verrol gave her one of his lopsided smiles. 'We'll do better than live up to it.'

'I can't.'

'Yes, you can. You especially. Look how many times you've astonished us already.'

'Have I?'

'Whatever we expect, you do something more. Over and over again.'

His words did the trick. Mave stood up straighter and responded with a small smile of her own.

Meanwhile, the band on stage were coming to the end of their performance. When they finished their final comic number, there was laughter and applause, but no call for an encore. As they ran in through the green curtain, Sholdo Felp hurried out. The audience buzzed with anticipation. Even before Sholdo made his announcement, everyone seemed to know that the Rowdies were the next act.

Reeth was peeking through the curtain, waiting for the exact moment. 'Now!' He whirled his arm. 'You're on!'

'Let's give them a show to remember,' said Ollifer.

As Reeth drew the curtain aside, they ran out onto a raised walkway, a line of wooden pallets leading to a central stage. The interior of the warehouse was a vast cavernous space, with a stone floor underfoot and iron girders overhead. The audience had been sitting cross-legged on coats and cushions, but now they jumped to their feet and cheered. The sound built up and up to a continuous roar.

The band gave them a show to remember. It was a triumph from beginning to end. The audience loved each and every song even before they heard it. They believed in the Rowdies more than the band believed in themselves.

It was insane and exhilarating, like being borne up on a tide. Wave after wave of affirmation lifted them higher and higher. Astor felt as if she could do *anything*. When they played Mave's love song, she reduced the backing to a single drum tap, very, very slow, and the audience stood as still as statues, drinking in the lyrics. On 'Do or Die', she came to the end and started up again, forcing the band to repeat the chorus for an even more thunderous climax.

The other band members were equally inspired. Ollifer walked out along the walkway, posturing and gesturing, addressing songs to particular individuals. Verrol also went out along the walkway, encouraging the crowd to join in the choruses. Mave added flourishes on her melodium and threw in an impromptu solo on one of her own compositions. Even the phlegmatic Purdy caught the mood; he advanced to the front of the stage, dropped to his knees and played two songs from a kneeling position.

The audience adored every minute of it. Astor looked out from behind her drums and saw a sea of faces radiating approval. They responded to every change of rhythm, swaying their shoulders, waving their arms and snapping their fingers. For the fastest, heaviest rhythms, they danced furiously and flung themselves about – as much as anyone could fling themselves about in such a press of bodies.

When the band finished their final number, the crowd absolutely refused to let them go. They had to play the two encores they'd prepared, then another two they hadn't. For the third, they did a speeded-up version of 'Where Nobody Goes'; for the fourth, they did a crazy mix of *all* the songs they'd played in the night. During the fourth, people began tossing cushions high in the air.

In the end, Mr Felp virtually had to force the band off the stage. 'No more!' he shouted to the crowd. 'That's it! That's all!'

Reeth came out along the walkway to shepherd them in. 'They're out of their heads!' he cried, surveying the crowd in disbelief.

'So are we,' cried Ollifer.

Once back in the triangular room behind the curtains, the band members looked at one another and burst out laughing. The crowd outside was still going wild, cheering and whooping and singing the words of their songs.

Mr Felp rejoined them. 'I don't know what to say,' he said, shaking his head. 'I'm speechless.'

'How did you get to be so good?' asked Reeth in wonder.

The whole band was as if bonded together in a single state of euphoria. When they started to speak, they all spoke at once.

'I couldn't believe it in "Muddy Boy Beat"—'

'I hit that note and just kept following it—'

'It was bouncing off the walls—'

'What about our fast version of—'

'How did it even manage to work?'

'And that loop in "Ghost of Love"—'

'I was making it up as we went along—'

'Remember the bit in "Break-out Time"—'

'That was you—'

'Mave too—'

'We were all waiting for that chord, and you kept holding it off—'

'I could hear it without playing it—'

'The audience almost stopped breathing—'

Mr Felp flapped his arms for attention. 'I'm going to find transport for you. You'll never get away if you try to walk.'

They listened and understood. The noise in the warehouse was as loud as ever, but now it had spread to the streets as well.

'They must be dancing out there,' murmured Mave.

'Wait till I come for you,' said Mr Felp, and disappeared through the side door.

Mave had an uncharacteristic look on her face, almost self-satisfied.

'Are you happy?' Verrol teased her.

She nodded. 'You?'

Ollifer jumped in first. '*Happy* isn't the word for it. This is better than happy.'

'You said it!' Astor draped an arm over his shoulder. '*Better than happy.* I like it!' In that moment, she could almost have kissed him.

Reeth seemed to share in the euphoria. Although he'd only been peering out through the curtains, he'd clearly lived every second of the performance.

'I almost died in "Be with Me Soon",' he told Astor, 'when you changed the rhythm halfway through. Why did you do that?'

'No idea.' Astor grinned. 'I just felt like a change.'

'I was praying you hadn't lost it altogether.'

'No,' Astor laughed. 'I came back when I was ready. Didn't you realise? Tonight was the night when nothing could go wrong.'

Just then, the side door opened, and two men swept in. One was tall, the other short, and both wore grey coats and grey caps.

'You're the Rowdies?' The tall one scanned around and seemed to be counting. 'Mr Felp said for you to come with us.'

'He's found transport?' asked Reeth.

'That's right. There's a carriage waiting outside.'

Purdy, Mave and Verrol gathered up their instruments. The short man stood by the open door and kept an eye on the street outside. The crowd was still making a noise, still singing and dancing, but they hadn't congregated around this particular door.

'Coast's clear,' said the man. 'Let's go.'

The carriage had pulled up right next to the door. Astor whistled. This was no ordinary carriage, but a magnificent equipage with black lacquered woodwork and elaborate gold trim.

'Mr Felp did us proud.' Verrol grinned.

The short man opened the carriage door, and a set of three steps unfolded automatically with a hiss of compressed air. The band members went up one after another.

'Don't push!' Astor protested to Reeth behind her.

'It's not me, it's—'

'In you go!' shouted the tall man behind Reeth.

Astor stumbled into the carriage and discovered that the seats inside were already taken. More men – and none of them Mr Felp. They jumped to their feet in the same moment the carriage door slammed shut.

Astor had no chance to react. Her arms were pinned behind her back, and a pad clamped down over her mouth and nose. A sickly-sweet smell . . .

She had time only to notice that the men wore uniforms in the blue-and-gold livery of the Swale household.

Then the sickly-sweet smell overcame her.

Astor woke to the sound of train wheels. *Clicketty-clack, clicketty-clack, clicketty-clack*: smooth and regular and soothing. But when she thought back over what had happened, she felt more inclined to panic.

She had been kidnapped by Swale-men! Tricked into one of the Swales' carriages, drugged with some sort of chemical! She had walked right into the embrace of her enemies.

Clicketty-clack, clicketty-clack, clicketty-clack, sang the train wheels.

She was lying on a bed on a silky-soft coverlet. She fumbled around in the dark and located a lamp behind her head, then the switch.

Light flooded the compartment. Astor blinked and took in wall-mirrors and wood panelling, a cream-coloured ceiling and burgundy-coloured curtains. This was a sleeping compartment furnished like a boudoir. Very strange. But she couldn't summon the strength to get up off the bed. Her body was still under the influence of the drug, and after a while her mind started to sink back too. Waves of drowsiness washed over her, and she fell into another long sleep.

When she awoke for the second time, the light was still on. She tried to sit up and almost fainted from the pounding in her head. She rested on the side of the bed until the dizziness went away. When she was sure she could keep her balance, she rose to her feet and crossed slowly to the door.

It was no surprise that the handle wouldn't turn. They had locked her in.

There was a curtain over the upper part of the door. She drew it aside and found herself looking through a pane of glass into a darkened corridor. The windows across the corridor were barred and closed with shutters of some kind.

She turned to consider the curtains on the opposite wall of her compartment. Presumably they covered a larger window that faced directly onto the world outside. She went across to inspect.

When she parted the curtains, she found this window also shuttered. The slats were made of steel, fixed solid and bolted to the window frame. They overlapped in such a way

222

as to leave only the tiniest upwards-angled cracks. Astor knelt and looked up, but saw nothing except darkness. So it was still night-time . . .

Her mind was fuzzy and refused to work on solutions. She stood in the middle of the compartment, chewing at her lower lip. They had sealed her in as if in a tomb.

At that moment, she heard a faint but unmistakable *rap-rap-rap*. She stared at the wood panelling under the mirrors. Someone in the next compartment was knocking on the wall.

'Who's there?'

She put her ear to the spot, raised her fist and rapped on the wood herself. A muffled voice came back.

'This is Verrol. Is that Astor?'

'Yes. I'm locked in.'

'Me too. Can you see outside?'

'No.'

'Nor me.'

'So the Swales got us after all.'

'Ye-es.' Verrol sounded puzzled. 'But why not take us back to Swale House? Why put us on a train? And why the whole band?'

'Are we all on the train, do you think?'

'Probably. In separate compartments.'

'Is there another compartment next to yours?'

'No. What about you?'

'I'll check. Wait a minute.'

Astor rose and crossed to the other side of her compartment. She rapped with her knuckles on the wall beside the bed.

No answer. She rapped again, as loud as she could.

'Yes?' It was Mave's voice, very faint.

'You'll have to shout,' Astor told her.

'What's happening?'

'It's the Swale-men who came after Verrol and me before. You remember? When Granny drove them away.'

'Yes. Because you'd found out about their plot. But why me?'

'I don't know.'

'Are they taking us to prison somewhere?'

'Perhaps.'

'Will they torture me to find out what I know?'

'Of course not.' Astor tried to sound confident. 'You only know the same as everyone else.'

She felt bad about having involved innocent people. She talked on soothingly a few minutes, then went back for further discussions with Verrol.

'It doesn't make sense,' he said, after she'd repeated her conversation with Mave. 'The whole of Granny's Gang knows about the plot, so the Swales can't keep it secret just by kidnapping the band.'

Astor thought about it. 'Do you remember the red-faced man with the dog? You wrapped the dog-leash round his throat?'

'Yes.'

'*He* said something about taking all five of us.'

'Mmm. Right.'

'What does it mean?'

'It's a mystery. Too many questions.'

'So what do we do?'

'Wait for the answers.'

'Wait? Do nothing?'

'What can we do?'

'Try to escape.'

'No, I think we should wait. Go back to sleep and wait.'

Astor felt there ought to be *something* to do – but her head was spinning, and she was still woozy from the drug. The idea of going back to sleep seemed suddenly very attractive.

She headed back to bed and climbed in under the coverlet, fully dressed. No sooner had she switched off the lamp than she fell into a deep, dreamless sleep.

The next time she awoke, she was roused by the sound of a door sliding open. A retainer in blue-and-gold livery stood leaning in at the doorway. Dim daylight filtered into the corridor and silhouetted him from behind.

'You'll need to get up now, Miss,' he said. 'Mr Bartizan and Mr Phillidas want to talk to you.'

50

Astor was escorted along the corridor, through a connecting passage and into the next carriage. The next carriage was a dining car: a long, open room of polished tables laid with placemats, silverware, glasses and neatly rolled napkins. The windows were shuttered, but daylight came in through the cracks, while glittering crystal fixtures shed artificial light from the ceiling.

Verrol, Mave, Ollifer, Purdy and Reeth were already seated at one of the tables. Servants hovered all around, but they were waiters rather than liveried retainers.

'Take a seat.' Reeth gestured with his one good arm.

He at least didn't appear particularly worried. Astor took a seat and followed his gaze to the other end of the carriage. All the Swale brothers were there, Lorrain as well as Bartizan and Phillidas.

In the next moment, they advanced towards the band. Bartizan was smiling genially, thumbs hooked in his waistcoat pockets. Lorrain stared at Astor as though his eyes would drop out of his head. Phillidas was his usual cadaverous self, expressionless behind dark glasses.

Six feet away, Bartizan brought the advance to a halt. 'Well, well, here we all are.' He nodded at Astor. 'You've changed a bit since we last saw you.'

He meant her hair, of course. And of course that was what Lorrain was staring at. Astor had almost stopped thinking about it, but the white must be plainly visible now.

She dismissed Lorrain from her mind and concentrated on Bartizan. 'So you hunted us down,' she snapped. 'What will you do with us now you've caught us?'

'I wouldn't say "hunted".' Bartizan seemed in a fine humour. 'We kept you under observation, naturally. We've been receiving regular reports about you and him and the band.'

His eyes flicked towards Verrol on the word *him*, but Verrol gave no hint of a response.

'Here's how it is,' Bartizan continued. 'A new situation. Let bygones be bygones. We want to think of you as allies rather than enemies.'

'Our interests march side by side,' said Phillidas.

'Hand in glove,' Bartizan agreed. 'You have information you could use to make trouble for us. But why would you want to? We can help you and you can help us.'

Astor struggled against a growing sense of unreality. 'Why did you drug us, then? Why have we been locked in?'

'An unfortunate short-term necessity.' Bartizan didn't bat an eyelid. 'We were afraid you wouldn't listen to our offer otherwise.'

'That's for sure,' Astor muttered.

'You see? You'd have run off before we could talk.'

Purdy spoke up. 'You're saying we're free to go now?'

'Of course, of course.' Bartizan was all benevolence. 'If our offer doesn't interest you.'

'Although you'd be advised to wait till we reach London Town,' Phillidas put in. 'You wouldn't want to jump from a speeding train.'

Was that a hint of a threat? Astor wondered. She didn't trust the Swales an inch, not after the way they'd treated her in the past.

'So we're travelling to London Town?' said Ollifer.

'Indeed we are.' Bartizan beamed. 'The capital of England, where you can make your fortune. After all, you're entrepreneurs too, in your own way. You've had the initiative to discover something new to sell.'

'And we're willing to buy,' added Phillidas.

'Swale Brothers Incorporated is always on the lookout for potential moneymaking ventures,' Bartizan went on. 'Especially in the current industrial downturn. We believe you've developed a very marketable commodity.'

Mave's elfin face was screwed up in perplexity. 'What are they talking about?' she asked.

'Gang music!' Reeth had worked it out long ago. 'The Rowdies playing gang music.'

'Exactly,' Bartizan confirmed. 'We've been hearing about this new music, and we think it has the potential to become enormously popular. But you'll need backing from people with contacts and influence. Like us.'

'You can realise our potential,' Reeth enthused.

'Starting with a performance at the Royal George Hall,' said Phillidas.

'The Royal George Hall?' Reeth whistled between his teeth. 'You can really set that up?'

'Power and money,' said Bartizan smugly. 'We can make anything happen once we have your agreement.' He spread his arms in an expansive gesture. 'Why don't you think about it over breakfast?'

He snapped his fingers, and a group of servants started forward from the other end of the carriage, wheeling trolleys laden with silver-domed dishes.

'We've brought your instruments along too,' said Lorrain. He had been standing a pace behind his brothers, but now spoke up for the first time.

Bartizan nodded, and snapped his fingers again. A second group came forward, bearing the melodium, brass guitar, clapper and pealer, and drum kit.

'So you'll be all ready for the Royal George Hall,' Lorrain told the band.

Astor noticed that he didn't quite look at her. Why would he? Of course, she was nothing to look at now . . .

Breakfast was a glorious feast of chicken soup, bacon omelette, ham and egg pie, stuffed tomatoes, smoked fish, potato fritters, pastries and cheese and treacle tart.

'This is the life,' said Ollifer between mouthfuls.

'I could take a lot of this,' agreed Reeth.

Astor hadn't realised how ravenous she was. She eyed Verrol across the table and saw him demolish plateful after plateful with cold efficiency. He hadn't said a thing while the Swales were making their offer, but he would have plenty to say now, she was sure.

The problem was that Purdy, Mave and Ollifer had no reason to hate Bartizan and Phillidas as she did. And Reeth hadn't even been present when Granny confronted the Swale-men with their dogs. Only she and Verrol knew what the Swales were really like.

Discussion on the offer began after the waiters had poured coffee. Verrol pushed away his dessert plate with a scowl.

'There's a trick to it,' he said.

Ollifer leaned back in his chair. 'What trick is that?'

'I don't know yet.'

'Seems all fair and square to me,' said Reeth. 'We do something for them, and they do something for us.'

'You don't know who you're dealing with,' Astor objected.

'Yes, plutocrats.' Reeth was heating up, talking faster and faster. 'I don't have to like them, I don't have to trust them. If they said they were doing this for our benefit, I'd run a mile. But it's a trade with a profit for them. I can believe in that.'

Astor turned to Verrol. 'You think they want something more out of us?'

Verrol shrugged. 'Something, yes.'

'More than just our silence about the coup?'

Reeth jumped in again. 'But that's a trade in our favour too! Don't you see? They can't afford to have us as enemies, so they must make the band a success!'

'Must and will.' Ollifer weighed in. 'They'd have all the connections to the wealthiest people. They could buy the Royal George Hall if they wanted. If we get *them* pushing behind us . . .'

'It's the big opportunity!' Reeth's excitement showed itself in the usual way as he sawed at the air with his arm. 'Turn this down, and there'll never be another. This is a once-in-a-lifetime chance. We have to seize it now. Believe me, I know what I'm talking about.'

For a moment, his intensity silenced all other discussion.

'You were a performer once, weren't you?' said Astor.

'Did you turn down your big opportunity?' asked Mave.

Reeth grimaced and shook his head. He gestured with his good arm towards his missing arm. 'This is what finished me. I played the double bass in a dance band. But after the accident . . . there's no such thing as a one-handed bass player.'

'What happened to your band?' asked Ollifer. 'Have I heard of them?'

'Oh, they weren't good enough to make it to the top.' Reeth pulled a wry face. '*I* wasn't good enough. I was never on your level.'

'But still . . .'

'I could've kept writing songs. I used to do that, and people said I had a knack for words. But my tunes were never quite strong enough.' He turned to Mave. 'Not like your tunes. I'd give my other arm to have what you've got. But I was only ever a small talent. Just talented enough to recognise real creativity when I see it.'

'You're our manager,' murmured Mave.

'Yes, that's all I ask. To be associated with people like you. To manage you and help you to the top. I'll never be on stage, but I can play a part behind the scenes. I can help create *you*.'

Astor had never thought much about Reeth's feelings before, but she felt sorry for him now. She still didn't want him to win Mave and Purdy over to his side, however. She flashed Verrol a look of warning . . . when Purdy spoke up first.

'London Town's the biggest city, isn't it?' he asked out of the blue.

'Yes, in the world,' Verrol agreed. 'Why?'

'And the Royal George Hall? Is it the biggest venue in London Town?'

Ollifer nodded. 'The biggest and most famous.'

'Well, then. Don't you remember Granny's last vision? "The biggest venue in the biggest city." That's where she saw us performing.'

'She said rows and rows of toffs,' Ollifer remembered. 'Dressed in their clothes and finery.'

'Like the plutocrats and their friends.' Purdy became more and more animated. 'This is what Granny foresaw. This is *it*!'

'Perhaps she didn't mean literally "the biggest",' Astor suggested without much hope.

Purdy fixed her with a glare. 'We made a promise when she was dying. We promised to make her vision come true. Now we have to keep our promise.'

And that was that; the discussion was over. Astor didn't like it, and she could see Verrol didn't like it either. But they could hardly argue against a deathbed promise.

'I'll go and tell the Swales our decision,' said Reeth in triumph.

52

After breakfast, there was nothing for Astor to do but go back to her own compartment. She was depressed about the band's new direction – and even more depressed when she examined her reflection in one of the wall-mirrors. Not only had the white in her short-cropped hair grown through another inch, but even her face had become less full and rounded, quite hollow under the cheek-bones. In her own eyes, she looked almost gaunt.

She lay on the bed, stared at the ceiling and listened to the rhythm of the carriage wheels. She wished she could fall asleep. Through the wall behind her bedhead, she could hear faint music. Mave was playing to herself on her melodium.

Time passed. Astor grew so bored with her own company that she got up and went out into the corridor. Verrol's compartment was one way, and Mave's was the other. She would have called on Verrol, but his door had been slid shut and the curtain drawn over the window. Whereas Mave's door was slightly ajar . . .

Mave was now singing as well as playing to herself. Her voice suited her personality, very soft and pure and quavery. Astor recognised 'Ghost of Love', the love song that the band had recently added to its repertoire. Three paces away, she paused to listen.

'Ghost words of love for you
You'll never hear
Ghost touches in the night
Still I'm not here

Ghost tears that fall for you
Dry on your skin
Ghost wishes want you so
Never let in.

I'm just a ghost of love
Verrol can't feel
Never be, never be, never be real.'

Astor could hardly believe it. 'Verrol can't feel'? Verrol? Mave had composed a love song to *Verrol*! And she'd disguised the name in the version she'd given to the band!

Astor didn't stop to think, just slid the door wide and strode into the compartment. Mave, sitting on the side of the bed, broke off and spun round, her dark-ringed eyes wide with surprise. She seemed very small and vulnerable.

'Verrol!' exclaimed Astor.

She didn't mean it as an accusation, but a guilty look came over Mave's face.

'That was private. You shouldn't have listened.'

'You're in love with him?'

Mave stared down at her melodium. 'Maybe it was just words made up for a song.'

'No, not for you. Your songs are real feelings. How long have you felt like this?'

Mave kept her eyes lowered and said nothing. Astor grew impatient with her silence, annoyed at her unhappiness.

'This is ridiculous. Breaking your heart in private. Don't be so pathetic. You have to *do* something.'

'I don't want to compete with you,' said Mave.

233

'Me? Why me?'

'You and him . . .'

'Don't talk nonsense. There's never been anything between me and him.' Astor paused and recalled. 'Okay, maybe there could've been in the past. But not now. It's gone. Finished. Impossible.'

Mave raised her eyes doubtfully. 'Anyway, I wouldn't have a hope with him.'

'Yes, you would. What makes him so special? He's only a man.'

'He's a prince.'

'A prince?'

'To me.'

'Huh. He was a servant when I met him. You ought to think more highly of yourself. You're beautiful in an unusual way, with a gentle, sweet personality.'

A wistful smile passed across Mave's face. 'I think he'd prefer someone not so gentle or sweet.'

'How do you know till you try? Surely you want to find out one way or the other? I'll find out for you.'

'No. Please don't.'

'But you have to know. If he's interested, good. If not, you can leave it behind and get on with your life. You can't keep breaking your heart forever.'

'Yes, I can,' Mave murmured.

Her lack of spirit was exasperating. 'I'll ask how he feels about you,' Astor told her. 'I won't let on how you feel about him.'

'I'd die if he knew,' said Mave. 'It's only a daydream.'

'I'll find out one way or the other,' Astor repeated. 'Right now.'

She swung out of the compartment. Her head whirled, and a confusion of feelings made a knot in her chest. She wasn't quite sure what she was doing herself. But, unlike Mave, she had to do *something*.

Verrol's door was still shut, the curtain still pulled across. Astor knocked once, then slid open the door without waiting for an answer. He was kneeling by the window on the other side of the compartment, a table knife in his hand. There were several similar knives around him on the floor.

'Yes, stolen property.' He grinned as he followed her gaze. 'I borrowed a few knives from the dining car after breakfast. I've been working on these shutters.'

Astor noted the worn-down condition of the knives on the floor, and the steel scrapings scattered around. He had been sawing off the bolts that fastened the shutters over the frame of the window.

'Almost done,' he said. 'I decided to improve the view. Close the door behind you.'

He went back to his sawing, while Astor slid the door shut. Asking him about Mave seemed to have become suddenly very difficult. The conversation was never going to run in the right direction while he was busy with his task.

'Right,' he said, as another bolt head popped off and rolled across the floor. 'It should come off now.'

He rose to his feet and gripped the shutters at the top and

bottom. The muscles stood out on his arms as he heaved and wrenched. Finally, with a loud, protesting creak, the metal sheared away, and the window was exposed.

Natural daylight filled the compartment. It was still a daylight filtered through smog, but with a more greenish tinge than the yellowish smog of Brummingham. Staring out, Astor could see roofs and chimneys and whole streets go past in a whoosh. Further in the distance were the faint silhouettes of spires and domes, the concentrated heart of the metropolis.

'London Town,' Verrol announced. 'We'll arrive in less than half an hour. Fenchurch Street Station, I expect.'

'I remember Fenchurch Street,' said Astor, as childhood memories came back to her. Fenchurch Street Rail Station and Clerkenwell Aerodock . . . the River Thames and the Great Bridge of London . . . Victory Monument and St James's Palace . . . the Imperial Credit Exchange and the Houses of Parliament. Most of all, she remembered the area between Holborn, where she had lived, and Covent Garden, where her father's orchestra had played.

'I wonder if it's all the same,' she said. 'I grew up in London Town.'

'You told me. So did I.'

His tone was so neutral that for a moment she didn't register what he'd said. Then it hit her.

'You? You grew up in London Town too?'

'Yes.'

'I told you, but you never told me?'

'I'm telling you now.'

The grin had left his face, and his eyes were fixed on hers. It was no slip of the tongue; he was fully aware of what he was saying. Astor forgot about Mave and the reason for her visit.

'You're going to confess your past, aren't you?'

'Yes.'

'Why the change of heart?'

'Because I can't stand not being able to talk to you. Things are wrong between us.'

'You've been holding back on me.'

'Not any more. My full name is Verrol Stark.'

Astor felt the blood drain from her face. Her mouth opened, but nothing came out.

'Yes, *those* Starks.' He nodded. 'The London crime family. The Starks and the Mauls.'

She sucked in air and began breathing again. Verrol was studying her reaction.

'I know how much you disapprove of criminals. That's what I was. That's why I didn't want to tell you. My father was Emer Stark, the head of the Stark family.'

Criminals! thought Astor, numb with shock and horror. *Criminals* was the very least of it. It was the Starks and Mauls who had killed her father. *Disapprove* didn't even approach her feelings about them.

'We ruled the roost when I was a kid,' Verrol went on. 'The Mauls had the north and west of London Town, and we had the south and east. Gambling, smuggling, protection, sly-grog shops – we controlled it all. My father had me picked out as a future leader ahead of my brothers. Then the feuding started.'

He paused. Astor didn't want to hear, yet she *had* to hear. 'Go on,' she said in a small, tight voice.

'I was twelve years old at the time. I can't even remember the cause. In the next two years, I lost my brothers, my cousins, my uncles, nieces and nephews. My father too, in the end. There was no stopping it. It was a matter of honour to do worse to the Mauls than they did to us. They slaughtered us, and we slaughtered them.'

'*You* killed people?'

'I killed my first man when I was thirteen. Another six before my fifteenth birthday.'

Astor didn't try to hide her shudder. 'You must have developed an early taste for it.'

He seemed about to protest, then shook his head gloomily. 'I was good at it. Very good. I gathered a group of cousins, all around my age, and we became the Starks' deadliest killing team. For a long time, the Mauls never realised – they thought we were too young to be a threat, and kept targeting the adults.'

He was no longer looking at Astor, but focused on a mid-air point somewhere between them.

'It was my team that killed the head of their gang, Towey Maul. We planned it ourselves. For two weeks we tracked his movements and set up hiding places. It had to be done with a concealed pistol that we passed from hand to hand. We achieved the ultimate stroke of revenge, but we brought a heap of trouble down on our heads. From then on, we were out in the open, and the Mauls were determined to get us. Especially me.'

'Why you?'

'I fired the shot that killed Towey. Two weeks later, my mother sent me off to stay with her relatives in the North of England. Plain, respectable people. It was supposed to keep me out of the way until things cooled down. That's what she told me, at least. I kept waiting and waiting to be called back. Instead, the relatives got me into service at Dorrin Estate, so the Mauls couldn't trace me through them, they said. They said the situation in London Town was worse than ever, and they were afraid for their own safety. They never said that my mother had been killed in a revenge attack.'

His voice had sunk to a dull monotone. When he spoke again, he seemed to drag himself back from a long way away.

'My mother had kept it a secret where she'd sent me, you see. Even a secret from my father. The Eden Street Massacre happened while I was at Dorrin Estate, and I never knew.'

'When the gangs wiped each other out.'

'It was suicide revenge. After my mother's death, my father called for volunteers, and the Starks gave their lives to destroy the Mauls. Forty-eight bodies, they counted on Eden Street. Every last member of our family, and almost all of theirs.'

'But not you.'

'I should've been there.'

Astor shook her head. He might have belonged to a different species, for all she could make sense of him. 'You feel bad because you didn't die with the rest of your family? Didn't you ever feel bad about killing people in cold blood?'

'Then or now?'

'When you shot Towey Maul, for instance.'

He shrugged. 'I don't know about cold blood. It was war, and the Mauls weren't innocents. We only killed people that were trying to kill us. Nobody else was involved.'

'Yes, they were.'

'What?'

It came out then in a hot, angry rush. '*You killed my father!*'

He stared at her blankly. 'I don't—'

'My father never hurt anyone in his life! We were just out for a walk! And your murdering gangs opened fire on each other!'

'He got hit by a stray shot?'

239

'Stray shot!' Astor spat out the phrase with hatred. 'You might just as well have come and aimed a pistol at his heart. He ended up just as dead.'

'When did it happen? I could've been at Dorrin Estate by then.'

'It's not who pulled the trigger! You're all responsible! Your whole mad, twisted way of thinking! You said it yourself! You said it before! "I was good at killing," you said!'

His face seemed to stiffen, and a hooded look came over his eyes. In that moment, he looked very much like a predator.

'I didn't kill Scarrow,' he said.

'Why not?' Astor grimaced. 'What's one more to a person like you?'

'I fought against it. I can control it.'

'It? What's *it*?'

'A cold, deadly feeling,' he said. 'Like the blade of a knife.'

'The killer instinct.'

'I can control it,' he repeated.

Astor turned away to stare through the window. The train line now ran below the level of the ground, and there was nothing to see except the occasional bridge flashing by overhead.

'So much for sharing secrets,' said Verrol bitterly. 'I told you my past. I never guessed you hadn't told me all of yours.'

'Don't try to turn it back on me. Just *don't*.'

'That's it, then. You'll always hate me from now on?'

Astor refused to answer or even look at him. For another minute, she continued to stare out at nothing in particular. Then she turned on her heel and walked out.

PART THREE

London Town

54

London Town was a frenzy, a madness, a wild whirl of busyness. As soon as the train pulled in to Fenchurch Street Station, there were whistles, bells, shouts and alarms. The vast booming hall was filled with a million echoing sounds. Blue-uniformed officials strode about with sternly preoccupied faces, barrow boys waved their arms and spruiked their wares, green-uniformed porters dashed in and out of the billowing steam.

A dozen Swale servants formed a protective wall around the band and escorted them through the crowd. They swung left, then right, then left again. Only Reeth seemed to know where they were going.

Astor goggled at luggage passing across on mid-air cables; at food dispensers where silver trays rotated endlessly behind glass panes; at the knives of a sausage machine that chopped a continuous length of hot sausage into sandwich-sized portions. Her head was still spinning with all the bustle when they emerged suddenly into the relative quiet of the street outside.

It was late in the afternoon, but so dark that the street lamps had been already lit, shedding a sickly glow in the gloom. A light drizzle drifted down through the air, and the pavements and roadways were black and glistening. Carriages stood waiting for passengers along by an elevated platform similar to the railway platforms inside.

Although Astor had grown up in London Town, she had never seen so many different kinds of carriage. There were

steam traction engines pulling trolley-cars, streamlined velocipedes, and basketwork rickshaws driven by clockwork and
coiled springs. The horsedrawn hansom cabs looked old-
fashioned by comparison.

Bartizan and Phillidas were nowhere to be seen, so Astor
turned to Reeth. 'Where now?'

'The Royal George Hall.'

'What? Straightaway?'

'You perform tonight.'

'But . . . that's impossible.'

'Not for the Swales. Power and money. What they want is
what they get. And they get it fast.'

He rubbed his hands together. He had obviously been
talking to the Swale brothers, and seemed to enjoy the associa-
tion with power and money.

The servants shepherded them into a trolley-car pulled by a
traction engine in the form of a horse. It had the usual boiler,
flywheel and firebox, but the front of the boiler was encased
in a shiny metal cast of a horse's head. Reeth and the band
sat on two front benches under the canopy, while the servants
occupied the benches behind.

The journey across London Town was an unreal phantasma-
goria. The traction engine rushed through the great shopping
streets of the West End sounding its steam-powered horn and
brushing aside rickshaws, bicycles, dog carts and all slower
vehicles. In spite of the drizzle, the pavements were thronged
with crowds. Bells jingled from overhead wires, red and yellow
gas jets flared from coiling brass pipes that framed the shopfronts. The shops themselves were like palaces, glittering with
reflections behind their huge display windows. Glass dominated everywhere – even glass statues on the street corners.

Astor had visited the West End on shopping expeditions when her father was alive, but it had changed almost beyond recognition. Now revolving fans were mounted on brackets above the pavements, presumably to blow away the worst of the smog. Other fans wafted warm, scented air from the interiors of the shops; smelling the exotic perfumes, Astor felt the allure. There were billboards on the kerbs, signs in the windows, posters on the lampposts, no inch of space left empty. It was all so bright, so colourful, and so impossibly much of it!

Even the sky was occupied. When Astor looked up, she saw great balloons looming above the streets, their surfaces covered in slogans and smiling, painted faces. As the balloons rolled slowly over and over, so too did the painted faces.

The sights looking down were equally strange. Every now and then, the roadway transformed into metal, and their trolley-car bumped and rattled over ten or twenty yards of continuous metal grating. When Astor peered down through the bars of the grating, she saw a whole further street below, running crosswise to their own. Another level of crowds and bustle, another level of gaslights and shopfronts – and their trolley-car passed over the top of it all!

Astor sat fascinated, twisting her neck in every direction. This mighty metropolis *felt* like the heart of an Empire. She remembered how her father had spoken of it as 'the city where dreams come true'. Would that happen for the Rowdies?

It seemed no time at all before they reached their destination, and the traction engine came to a stop in front of the curving facade of the Royal George Hall. Monumental piers rose up, pink marble against black-tiled walls, supporting a stupendous dome of green copper.

'Is that for *us*?' exclaimed Mave when they climbed out.

As the band gazed in awe, the Swale servants swooped and encircled them again. 'This way! This way!'

They walked halfway round the building until they arrived at an unmarked door. The Swale brothers were waiting for them there, along with a policeman on sentry duty. At a signal from Bartizan, the policeman opened the door, then stepped back. The Swales trooped in, followed by Reeth and the band, but not the escorting servants.

They went up a great many stairs, then passed along a corridor. The carpet was thick and soft like lush, green grass. At the far end were two men arguing in raised voices. One wore a bright plaid waistcoat, a bushy moustache and side-whiskers; the other was more sombre in a three-piece suit, lightened only by a silver chain and fob watch.

Coming closer, Astor realised there were other people involved in the argument as well. Faces looked out from an open door on the left of the corridor: scowling faces, anxious faces. The man in the plaid waistcoat gestured in their direction as if calling on them for support. He gestured a great deal, spreading his hands and waving his arms theatrically.

Bartizan strode forward. 'What's going on, Mellencott?'

The man in the three-piece suit turned to him with evident relief. 'Fosserby here says there's a problem. Your telegram arrived too late to cancel the Silver Rose Band, so they've turned up to perform. Now he says he has contractual obligations to them.'

The man called Fosserby swung towards Bartizan and Phillidas. 'I'd like to make the switch, but . . .' He made another theatrical gesture, conveying helplessness. 'I have a business to run, and they have a legal signed contract.'

'A business with *shareholders*,' Bartizan rumbled, like a storm cloud threatening to burst. '*Plutocrat* shareholders.'

Fosserby's helplessness turned to desperation. 'I'll do anything I can. Absolutely anything. Only I don't see . . .'

'What was their fee?' Phillidas demanded coldly.

'A hundred guineas,' answered Fosserby.

'We'll pay two hundred for them *not* to play.'

'You can't just barge in and take over,' said one of the faces in the doorway.

But the Swales intended to do just that. 'Three hundred,' said Phillidas.

'That's our final offer,' added Bartizan. 'Plain and simple. Take it or leave it.'

There was a shaking of heads in the doorway. For the first time, Astor noticed the trumpets and trombones in their hands.

'We need the exposure,' said one. 'This is important for us.'

Phillidas laughed his braying, humourless laugh. 'Your idea of importance isn't worth much. There'll be invited guests in the box seats from the fifty wealthiest families in the land. Potential backers for our band worth tens of billions of pounds. They've come to see if the Rowdies can live up to expectations. *That's* important.'

Fosserby lent his support to the Swales. 'Three hundred guineas. Think about it. As much in one night as you've earned in your whole careers.'

'It's not the money. We've never played in the Royal George Hall before.'

'Reject this offer, and you'll never play anywhere again,' snorted Bartizan.

'We'll lock you out of every venue in the city,' added Phillidas.

'They can do it too,' warned Fosserby.

Phillidas produced a pocketbook, slipped off the elastic and began writing out a bank draft on the spot.

'Use your heads,' Fosserby urged.

The members of the Silver Rose Band used their heads. As they talked among themselves in a quieter tone, Fosserby closed the door on them.

'That's settled, then.' With a sigh of relief, he turned to the Rowdies. 'Now I'll show you to your dressing rooms.'

 Back along the corridor, Fosserby threw open three doors in a row. Whatever his private feelings about the switch of bands, he gave Astor and the others a dazzling smile.

'We call these our Top of the Bill dressing rooms. Shall I send along our cosmetician and coiffeuse? Or do you prefer to do your own make-up for the stage?'

The band members looked at one another and almost burst out laughing. Up until now, their appearance on stage had been the same as their appearance every other day of their lives.

Ollifer took to the idea more seriously than the rest. 'Send them along, certainly.'

'Excellent.' Fosserby emphasised his departure with a flourish and a bow. 'You'll be called to go on in half an hour.'

The band divided up: Mave and Astor in the first dressing room, Verrol and Purdy in the second, and Ollifer in the third.

Reeth was about to head off when Astor called him back.

'Wait. What was that Phillidas said about living up to expectations?'

'Yes, and *potential* backers,' said Verrol. 'Are we on trial?'

'In a way.' Reeth ran his hand over his ponytail. 'The Swales want their fellow plutocrats on board too.'

'Why? They have enough money of their own, don't they?'

'The more the better.' Reeth scanned the circle of faces all frowning at him. 'Look, perhaps I should've told you, but I didn't want you to worry. The Swales view it as a trial, but you'll sail through it. Child's play for musicians like you.'

'We should've been told,' said Purdy.

'Okay, my mistake. It won't happen again.' Reeth was already backing away as the band members turned towards their respective dressing rooms.

The dressing room that Astor shared with Mave was like an Aladdin's cave. They gazed wide-eyed at the enormous mirror, the dresser, the rows of bottles and jars, the wigs and exotic costumes hanging on pegs and racks.

'How could anyone ever use all this stuff?' Mave gasped.

Astor had decided not to report her last conversation with Verrol, since she had nothing to report on his feelings for Mave anyway. As it turned out, Mave didn't ask. Instead, she wanted to talk about the switch of bands.

'I feel sorry for the Silver Rose Band, don't you? They were all set for their big chance, just like us. Then the Swales snatched it away from them.'

'Yes, and gave it to us,' Astor agreed. 'We've made enemies for life there.'

'Reeth wouldn't mind.'

'Why do you say that?'

'I heard him tell Ollifer once. You have to make enemies if you want to get to the top.'

Astor laughed. 'Not Ollifer. He wants everyone in the world to love him.'

The coiffeuse and cosmetician turned up a moment later, two doll-like women in their forties or fifties. They were obviously not impressed by the raw material they had to work with. Mave refused all make-up except a bright red lipstick that turned her mouth into a vivid gash. Astor allowed the coiffeuse to put curls in her hair, but combed them out afterwards. However, she accepted lipstick and rouge – 'or the audience won't see your features in the stage lights, dear.'

There was nothing much to do after that, so Astor and Mave went along to visit the others. They found everyone gathered in Ollifer's dressing room, not only Verrol and Purdy but the coiffeuse and cosmetician too. The make-up women were in their element with Ollifer, who more than made up for the rest of the band's indifference.

The conversation was general, which suited Astor. She didn't want to be seen avoiding Verrol, but she didn't want to talk one-on-one with him either. Then Reeth burst in with a worried expression on his face.

'I've been studying your audience,' he announced. 'I don't like the look of it.'

'What's wrong?' asked Ollifer. 'Empty seats?'

'No, the house is packed. It's the way they're dressed, all bow ties and jewellery and furs. Terribly posh and sophisticated.'

'Potential backers.' Purdy shrugged. 'You said it would be child's play.'

'Maybe I spoke too soon.' Reeth's expression grew even

more troubled. 'These people are different. They're not expecting gang music, that's for sure.'

'What are you saying?' Verrol asked.

'I'd hate for the band to fail, now that we've come so far.'

'So?'

'Perhaps you could tone down the gang-music side of it. Make it less raw, less confronting.'

'Gang music isn't a *side* of it,' said Mave. 'It's what we play.'

'You can play other ways too. Like that love song you do.' Reeth was almost pleading, his earlier confidence vanished completely. 'Just tone it down a bit, that's all I'm asking. Slower and smoother.'

Seeing Reeth's desperate look, a twinge of doubt entered Astor's mind too. Was it really possible they could fail?

At that moment there was a knock on the door, and Fosserby stuck his head into the dressing room. 'You're on in three minutes,' he said.

The audience was exactly as Reeth had described. In the front rows, the ladies wore necklaces, tiaras and elaborate hairdos, while the gentlemen wore black tailcoats, cummerbunds and starched white shirtfronts. Many of the women carried opera glasses, many of the men sported monocles.

Further back, the faces diminished to tiny pale spots rising up tier upon tier. The auditorium was vast, its domed ceiling spanned by arching girders and lace-like ironwork. Astor took in a general impression of gilded balconies and crystal chandeliers, but her mind went blank when confronted by such a multitude of people.

The other band members carried their instruments onto the stage; Astor's drums were set up ready at the back. Opera glasses and monocles flashed and angled towards them as they launched into their first song.

Immediately they discovered another problem. The acoustics in the auditorium were like nothing they'd ever encountered before. There was no echo or reverberation. It wasn't that the sounds didn't carry, but the air seemed to swallow them up. It was like playing in front of a wall of cotton wool.

The audience was like cotton wool too. They listened with polite attention and produced a smattering of polite applause at the end of the song.

Still, at least they're listening, thought Astor. *It's better than boos and catcalls.*

By the end of the third song, though, she would rather have had the boos and catcalls. At least there would have been some reaction. Instead, the level of polite applause at the end of each song was exactly the same as the one before. It was unearthly and unnerving. Nothing they did had any impact.

The band had made no decision about toning down their music, but unconsciously they followed Reeth's advice. Ollifer adopted a more mellow singing style; Purdy produced a softer guitar sound; Mave and Astor held themselves in check; Verrol abandoned his dancing. None of it made any difference. The audience appeared attentive but remained unengaged.

Unable to let themselves go, the band started to become self-conscious. Mave blew two notes out of tune on the fifth song. On the sixth song, Ollifer stumbled over his words. Then even the unflappable Purdy was late coming in for a solo. Astor held it together until the eighth song – when she committed the worst blunder of all.

The song was 'Down in the Channel', usually a big build-up number, slow but very powerful. By now, though, they had diluted most of the power out of their playing. Halfway through, Astor glanced to the side and saw Reeth standing behind the curtain, his face a picture of despair.

His dreams are slipping away, she thought. The Rowdies would lose their potential backers, the Swale brothers would drop them, they would never perform at a London venue again. Failure was no longer just a possibility but a certainty.

The thought twisted in her guts and distracted her from her drumming. She struck her main drum on the wrong beat, missed the next two beats, tried to recover and fell into the rhythm for a completely different song.

Her false rhythm threw them all off. There was a moment of discord, each instrument struggling to continue on its own way, jerking and pulling in contrary directions. Then everyone faltered to a stop. Absolute silence.

She looked up. The band members were staring at her in shock, in accusation. She felt that every pair of eyes in the entire auditorium was staring at her. She shook her head and wanted to cry.

But something in her wasn't made for crying. Something in her fought back. She'd had enough of playing for an audience that didn't want to listen. They didn't deserve the Rowdies. So much the worse for them!

'We play for ourselves!' she shouted to the band. '*For ourselves!*'

Mave got the idea. She swung to face Astor, turning her back on the audience.

'Yes!' cried Astor. 'All of you! Ignore them! We're going down *in flames!*'

She struck up the rhythm for 'Where Nobody Goes'. Verrol and Purdy also turned their backs on the audience. The insult had more impact than any other part of the performance so far. A hostile murmur ran round the auditorium, and several gentlemen started to rise from their seats. These were not the kind of people on whom anyone ever turned their backs.

Astor grinned. *They don't like it*, she thought, *and I don't like them. Good. Let's empty this whole auditorium.*

Verrol came in on cue, then Mave, then Purdy. There was no toning down the music now. They played it as it was meant to be played: loud and brutal and jagged. Olliffer alone still faced the audience, but he too went back to his true style of singing.

Playing only for pride and pleasure, they watched one another's moves and added to them, spurred one another to greater and greater heights. It was insane and perfect – the spontaneity of a practice session combined with the intensity of a stage performance. Shedding self-consciousness, they threw themselves into the music, and the music bore them up and swept them along. Gang music had never sounded so raw and savage.

At the end of 'Where Nobody Goes', in the moment before they launched into another song, Astor heard Olliffer shout, 'It's working!' She had no idea what he was talking about; all she knew was that he sang his heart out on the next song.

Verrol danced and whirled his clapper like a madman, Mave bobbed and Purdy did a kind of strut to the rhythm. There was

254

one particular riff that they latched on to and repeated over and over. They worked it and warped it, twisted it and teased it, more and more discordant every time.

We'll empty this auditorium, Astor exulted. *Drive them out, batter their eardrums, send them running.*

But when she looked out at the end of the song, nobody had left. The gentlemen who had risen from their seats were as if frozen in mid-motion. Astor couldn't read the expression in the audience's eyes, but she could see a great many mouths hanging open.

'I told you!' cried Ollifer. 'It's working!'

What was working? They certainly weren't driving out the audience as Astor intended. What did Ollifer think she intended?

During their next song, Astor had the strange sense that the acoustics had changed. The sounds seemed to be amplifying, bouncing off the ceiling, swelling and spreading. The band was no longer playing in a bubble of their own; or if they were, the bubble had expanded to include the entire auditorium.

Astor couldn't tell if the audience was angry or revolted or what – but in some way they were definitely stirred up. Incredibly, unthinkably, the mood had changed. By the end of the song, she had come up with another idea.

'Turn round and take them on,' she yelled at the band. 'Stare them in the eye.'

The band obeyed. After a moment of silence, a ripple of applause broke out. Not polite applause, but real clapping. The ripple grew and became a wave of enthusiasm. Verrol, Mave and Purdy looked at one another in disbelief.

Astor beat out a salvo on her drums, and the audience hushed. She dropped back to a steady tap with a single drumstick, letting the anticipation build. She pointed the other drumstick at Mave, who came in with a low, quavering wail, a sound to make the hairs stand up on the back of the neck. Sixteen beats further along, the whole band joined in at full volume like a dam bursting.

They gave it everything. Astor could hardly see as she shook her head from side to side and the sweat ran down over her eyes – but the whole audience seemed to shimmer to the beat. Elaborate hairdos swaying ... opera glasses discarded ... bejewelled arms fluttering up and down. She would never have guessed they had it in them.

She floated on a tremendous surge of satisfaction and relief. Her blunder had almost killed off the band – but her spirit had brought them back. The auditorium throbbed with life and energy.

She laughed aloud, wiped the sweat from her face and kept right on drumming, drumming, drumming ...

The show was over. For the Rowdies, it had been a night of impossible glory. They were still dazed by their success, and the music still swirled and pounded in their heads. The world all around was a blur of admiring eyes and lit-up faces. They had conquered the city.

They left the building by the same door they had entered. A crowd of people outside greeted their appearance with a hubbub of excitement. Smartly dressed young men flourished silver-topped canes and cheered enthusiastically. A ring of policemen held them in check as they tried to push forward.

'Oh, wow!' said Mave. It was as much as any of them had said in the last ten minutes.

They had to wait for their own transport to arrive. Meanwhile, the struggle between the crowd and the police ebbed and flowed. To Astor, the scene seemed weirdly remote even when the crowd advanced to within a few yards of her. She waved, and several young men tossed their top hats high in the air.

There were other admirers of even higher social standing. Beyond the crowd, a number of horsedrawn carriages had pulled up, open-topped barouches trimmed in gold and bedecked with plumes. When a footman pushed forward from one particular carriage, the police let him through. He stopped in front of Verrol, bowed, pressed an envelope into his hand, then turned back without uttering a word.

Verrol opened the envelope, and a scent of exotic perfume wafted to Astor's nostrils. She tried to catch a glimpse as he skimmed through the elegantly scrawled handwriting.

'That's an assignation note,' she said. 'Someone wants to make a rendezvous with you.'

She looked up just in time to observe the wave of a gloved hand from the lady in the carriage. Directed towards Verrol, of course.

'Just as I thought,' she sniffed.

That envelope was the first of three, and each time the police allowed the message-bearer to pass. Obviously the ladies who took an interest in Verrol had a great deal of power and influence. Observing them at a distance, Astor had no doubt they were beautiful, but could see only the richness of their clothes and the glitter of their jewellery.

Verrol only glanced through each note, shrugged and said nothing. He didn't throw them away, however, but tucked all three in his breeches pocket. Astor was disappointed in him.

She was thankful when their transport arrived: a convoy of velocipedes. They looked like boats on wheels, with pointed prows and sleek, streamlined sides. At the front, a driver and assistant propelled the vehicle by pedal power, while the driver used a tiller to steer the small front wheel. At the back, a folding leather hood enclosed the passenger compartment, which was just large enough for two.

Without exactly planning it, Astor ended up sharing a velocipede with Verrol. Perhaps it was time to have a one-on-one conversation with him anyway. For Mave's sake, at least . . .

She launched into the attack as soon as the vehicle moved off. 'I'd never have thought they were your type.'

'Who?' His blank look was infuriating. He was still in the cloud of euphoria that Astor had left behind.

'You know who. Those three fine ladies in their carriages. Isn't that against all your principles?'

'What principles? I didn't know you thought I had any.'

'You once said you're a better man now than in the past.'

'I'm surprised you remember.'

She couldn't see his face in the dim interior light, but she could picture the old sardonic expression coming back over it.

'What do you think of Mave?' she asked.

'What should I think?'

'I mean, do you find her attractive?'

He considered a while. 'Yes. In her own way, beautiful. Beautiful like a wild animal.'

It was exactly what Astor would have said herself. She was surprised that he'd seen what most men wouldn't have noticed.

'She's more your type than those fine ladies.'

'How do you know? Perhaps I find their type more attractive.'

'She's such a sweet, gentle thing.'

'Which makes her less my type. I'm the opposite of sweet and gentle, as we've established.'

'Complementaries can attract. It might not put her off.'

'It put you off.'

'Mave didn't have a father killed by murdering crime families.'

There was a long silence between them. *He has his guard up after that*, Astor thought. *Now he'll never reveal what he really thinks about Mave.*

In the end, though, it was Verrol who returned to the subject. 'She'd run a hundred miles if I made a move. I'd frighten her off.'

'You'd have to be very gentle and considerate, of course.'

'Even though I'm not?'

'I'm sure you can be whatever you want with women.'

'So that's what you'd do if you were me?'

'Yes. No. I don't know. Maybe she's the kind to sweep off her feet before she has time to think about it. I'm sure you can do that too. Most girls would enjoy being swept off their feet.'

'Are you speaking from experience?'

'Me? No, not girls like me. I meant girls like Mave. I come from a different sort of background. I was brought up with different expectations.'

'Proposals and offers of marriage? Formal engagements?'

Astor remembered her humiliation over the supposed engagement to Lorrain, which Verrol had witnessed. She hoped he couldn't see the reddening of her cheeks. 'I was taught to think of marriage in a different way. It's much simpler for you and Mave. You can just kiss her.'

'I can?'

'Take her in your arms and kiss her. Be passionate.'

'I don't have to tell her I love her?'

'She wouldn't believe you anyway. You convince her with a kiss.'

'You think she'd respond to that?'

'I know she would. Only if you really care for her, of course.'

'Otherwise . . .?'

'Otherwise it would be wrong and cruel.'

'Mmm. It would be like feeding an innocent to the wolves, wouldn't it?'

Astor could have hit him. Why would he never give a straight answer? She really wanted to know about his feelings for Mave, but he still hadn't told her. His ironic way of talking never gave anything away.

At that moment, there was a tap on the hood, a signal from the driver's assistant. Astor realised with surprise that the velocipede had pulled to a halt. A footman opened the door from outside.

58

They found themselves in a cobbled courtyard. The velocipedes carrying the rest of the band had already arrived, along with a great many other assorted vehicles. Astor surveyed the building that rose up around the courtyard, storey upon storey and row upon row of windows, disappearing into the darkness. It was very impressive . . . but why had they come round the back?

'Where are we?' she asked Verrol.

'No idea.' He shrugged. 'Reeth was in charge of the arrangements.'

Reeth stood nearby with Purdy, Mave and Ollifer. More vehicles were arriving all the time, horsedrawn or steam-powered, hired cabs or private coaches. Many of the coaches were quite magnificent, flying flags and displaying coats-of-arms. Some were even decorated in exotic animal fur, spotted, striped and tawny.

The passengers who stepped out were less eager to make a show of themselves. Heavily cloaked, they hurried across the courtyard with collars turned up to hide their faces.

'Why the secrecy?' Astor wondered aloud.

'Let's ask Reeth,' suggested Verrol.

But as they moved to join the others, Phillidas Swale emerged from a hired cab. He raised an arm and called out to the band, 'Follow me!'

Even by night, he wore his tinted glasses. He led them towards the same door where all the arrivals were going in – a tradesman's entrance flanked by two guards carrying lanterns.

'What is this place?' Astor asked, as she came up level with him.

'Norfolk Palace.' For once, Phillidas lowered his usual bray to a whisper. 'The Duchess of Norfolk married Jeremiah Higgis five years ago. One of ours.'

'Ours?'

'The entrepreneurs, of course. Industrialists, bankers, plutocrats.'

Inside the door, they passed along a corridor to a foyer – and suddenly entered a different world. Instead of darkness and secrecy, here was a scene of light and colour, bustle and chatter. The guests were revealed in all their expensive finery as they shed their cloaks and passed them across to an army of footmen.

Listening to the chatter, Astor picked up many regional accents, from the North Country, Scotland, the Midlands and more. All visitors to London Town? The Rowdies hardly fitted in with the finery, yet several guests nodded and smiled at them. Phillidas led them up a grand staircase, past bronze and marble busts on pedestals.

At the top was a reception room overflowing with people. Here the chatter was twice as loud. Phillidas pushed forward, and the band followed him across the room. Heavy plush curtains had been drawn over every window.

There were refreshments for the guests, but not served by any ordinary servants. Instead, clockwork mannequins moved slowly around on rails laid over the carpet. They had painted faces, painted jackets and shirts, and their fixed wooden arms held out trays of drinks or platters of daintily cut sandwiches.

Astor bumped into one of them when she stopped suddenly in the middle of the room. There in the crowd was the very same man whom she and Verrol had observed through the back of the fireplace. Ephraim Chard, with heavy jowls and slicked-back hair! What was he doing here?

The mannequin servant whose path she had blocked clicked over with tiny forward movements, rocking impotently back and forth. She stepped away from his rail and continued after the rest of the band. She was still wondering about Ephraim Chard when a voice boomed out ahead, 'Ah, they've arrived!'

262

That voice could only belong to Bartizan Swale. He was waiting for them at the far end of the room. He swung and spoke to people on his left, people on his right. 'Form a line. Children, out of the way now.'

By 'children' he meant the Swale children, Blanquette, Prester and Widdy. Astor saw her old enemies as they moved aside; they saw her too, and grinned and waved.

Phillidas came up to stand between Bartizan and Lorrain. The youngest Swale brother looked as impossibly handsome as ever. Astor sensed rather than saw his gesture, indicating a space for her, but she ignored it. Instead, Ollifer took up position next to Lorrain, with the other band members further along. Astor was on the very end of the line.

Ting! Ting!

As the sharp sound of a spoon on glass hushed the chatter, an old lady in a blue silk gown stepped forward. The Duchess of Norfolk, Astor guessed.

'If I may have your attention, please. Thank you for your attendance at this very special meeting. Our plans are almost complete, and the last pieces of the puzzle have fallen into place. Those of you who were at the Royal George Hall tonight saw for yourselves the extraordinary audience reaction to the Rowdies band. Theirs is a music to inflame the heart and stir the blood.'

She fluttered a hand to indicate the band members, and waited for the buzz of approval to die down.

'As you know, the militias are the key to our success. However, the militiamen are simple ex-soldiers, and political argument and rational thought can influence them only so far. We need something to influence them on a more basic, physical level. That is exactly what this band can do.'

Verrol stood next to Astor in the line, and she heard his low, angry mutter. 'I knew there was a trick. It was never just about making money from us.'

'Their rhythms will set our ex-soldiers marching,' the old lady went on. 'With the right words, their songs will arouse passion and rage and feelings of injustice. One piece of the puzzle in place. And now, let me hand you over to the Right Honourable Mr Ephraim Chard, opposition leader in Parliament and head of our Progress Party.'

Ephraim Chard stepped forward to address the crowd. 'The time has come,' he announced in a deep, ringing tone. 'The hour of decision is at hand. The Progress Party can count on thirty-seven votes in the Commons, as against forty-nine for the Rural Party. The rest are waverers, all forty-two of them. They vote with Hassock now, but a show of force will soon change their minds. We're in the best position we've ever been in, and as good as we can hope for.'

The plutocrats began to applaud, but Chard raised a hand for silence.

'A new session of Parliament begins on November the sixteenth. On that day, King George comes to the House to make a speech and declare Parliament open. A show of force then will not only cow the waverers but also persuade the King to a change of heart. No need for a separate march on St James's Palace. No delay, no time for anyone to interfere. We'll be in power before they wake up to what's happening. November the sixteenth is the perfect date for our coup.'

This time there was no holding back the applause. Astor whispered to Verrol behind her hand. 'What's the date today?'

'November the seventh.'

So close, thought Astor. It was hardly more than a week away. Such valuable information, if she could have passed it on to someone like her stepfather . . .

Chard let the applause run for several minutes, then raised his hand once more. 'King George has been led astray by pernicious influences. When the Progress Party takes power, we shall immediately set about building a better Britain. We shall generate demand, get the wheels of industry turning and return to full productivity. Make this country profitable by making your factories profitable. And how do we do that?'

The answer came simultaneously from a hundred throats. 'War!'

Chard nodded. 'War the destroyer and war the creator. By destroying old goods, we create the need for new goods. Why would the army need new bullets and shells when it's not firing the old ones? Why would they order new uniforms when the old ones have no bullet holes in them? Only the Progress Party understands the simple iron law of economic growth, that we produce to replace what's been destroyed – and nothing destroys more quickly or effectively than a war. Our first act as a new government will be a general declaration of war.'

Astor sensed the tension in Verrol standing beside her. She didn't need to look to know that his fists were clenched and his eyes were hard and staring.

'However, I'm a politician and you're entrepreneurs,' Chard continued. 'We're not officers or military men ourselves.' A faint titter of amusement passed through the crowd. 'It's not our role to do the actual fighting. I'm glad to say that the Swale brothers have solved the problem for us. Allow me to introduce Mr Bartizan Swale.'

Bartizan planted his feet apart, and his voice filled the room. 'I'm a plain-spoken man, as anyone will tell you, so I won't beat about the bush. Our great venture requires a figurehead who commands respect among the military and the militias. My brother Phillidas and I have secured the services of one of Britain's greatest war heroes. A man who commanded all the allied forces at the Battle of Bratislava, yet still led from the front and was seriously wounded. The ideal symbol of patriotism, with the kind of courage that military types admire. Friends, colleagues and fellow entrepreneurs, I give you our new figurehead – Marshal Dorrin.'

Astor wasn't the only one who gasped, but she was certainly the loudest. She leaned forward and looked along to the opposite end of the line, where Bartizan was pointing. A man had stepped forward, gazing straight ahead like a soldier on parade. He was dressed in full uniform, with multiple rows of medals on his chest. Her stepfather!

'My only wish is to do my duty—' he began.

'Thank you, Marshal.' Bartizan cut him off short, showing less respect than he expected the 'military types' to show. 'And now a toast.'

Astor was still looking along the line as Bartizan raised his glass. She could see her mother too, just visible beyond the Marshal. Had Mrs Dorrin even realised her daughter was present?

All around the room, glasses were raised in the toast.

'To the next war!' bellowed Bartizan. 'The greatest and longest war ever!'

A hundred voices echoed the final phrase. 'Greatest and longest war ever!'

59 The speeches ended with the toast, and the crowd divided into a great many groups eagerly discussing the latest developments. The individual band members were immediately besieged by well-wishers, so that they could hardly talk among themselves. Astor wanted to go and speak to her mother, but she was approached by Blanquette, Prester and Widdy.

'We saw you drumming,' said Prester.

'We were in the Royal George Hall,' Blanquette explained.

'You were amazing,' said Prester.

'Betht muthic!' lisped Widdy.

'We were wondering if we could help,' said Blanquette. 'Play something on stage along with the band.'

'We love your music so much,' Prester added.

'Some extra little sounds,' said Blanquette. 'Only where you wanted, of course.'

Widdy made wild drumming motions with his hands.

Astor could hardly believe them. The last time she'd had anything to do with the Swale children, they'd been looking forward to shaving her head and seeing her locked up. Now they were her devoted fans, who only wanted to imitate her! But she didn't forgive or forget *that* quickly.

'No.' She shook her head. 'Not possible.'

Widdy pouted childishly. 'Why not?'

'You're on our side now,' Blanquette pointed out. 'You help us and we help you.'

That was more like the old Blanquette. But Astor felt sure Bartizan and Phillidas wouldn't back up their

267

children's demands, not if it meant losing the band's co-operation.

'No,' she repeated. 'We don't have time to work on incorporating new sounds.'

Blanquette tried another angle. 'What does the rest of the band say?'

Mave was within earshot, and Blanquette drew her attention. Mave's response was the same as Astor's.

'Impossible.' She shook her head, and pulled Astor aside for a private conversation. For a moment, they managed to escape from the well-wishers.

'What did she mean?' Mave's voice was a fierce whisper. '"The right words"?'

'Who?' Astor struggled to think back.

'The old lady. She said our songs would do all these things with "the right words".'

'Mmm.' Astor remembered the Duchess's phrase, and now wondered about it for the first time.

'We have to find out,' Mave insisted. 'We have to ask her.'

'Where is she?'

'Let's search.'

Astor agreed – for her own reasons. She could search for her mother as they both searched for the Duchess.

For a while, they meandered through the crowd, pretending not to notice people who wanted to talk to them. Everywhere they overheard conversations going on among the plutocrats.

'Long overdue.'

'I haven't turned a profit in two years.'

'Three years for me.'

'We're the ones who generate the wealth.'

'I'd just built a munitions factory when they declared peace.'

'This nonsensical government.'

'They don't think about the economy.'

Astor grimaced. In spite of their riches, the plutocrats felt themselves very hard done by.

They still hadn't found the Duchess when Mrs Dorrin appeared suddenly out of the crowd. She looked flustered and pink in the face as she hurried up.

'There you are, dear! So many things to talk about. But later – we're leaving now. Come and visit me.' She thrust a folded piece of paper into her daughter's hand. 'Please, dear. This is where we're staying, at the Marshal's London residence.'

And then she was gone. Astor was left with her mouth hanging open. She unfolded the note and read:

14, Walnut Tree Walk, Lambeth

It was a revelation that her stepfather even owned a London residence.

Meanwhile, Mave had moved on a little, still scanning the crowd. Now she came back for Astor. 'I've seen Bartizan and Phillidas. Let's ask them instead.'

Astor followed her to a group that included Lorrain as well as Bartizan and Phillidas, talking with a very plump lady and a man with a face like a spaniel. The man broke off in mid-sentence.

'Ah, our musicians!' he said. 'The inspiration for our militias!'

Mave fronted up to Bartizan. 'What did she mean about our songs having to have "the right words"?'

'The Duchess of Norfolk,' Astor explained.

'Well, that's a direct question,' Bartizan boomed. 'You'll need to make some changes, of course.'

'What changes?' Mave seemed to have lost her usual shyness.

'Nothing you can't easily do,' said Lorrain.

'What?'

Phillidas clicked his tongue. 'New words for marching songs. We don't want dancing songs or songs about love. New words about bravery and nationhood and the struggle for victory.'

'You mean . . .' Mave was aghast.

Astor finished the sentence for her. 'You mean *all* the words?'

'It's a trade-off,' said Bartizan. 'We can make you into the biggest band ever. But we need a small contribution from you first.'

'*Small!*' Mave spluttered.

'Of course it's small,' Bartizan huffed. 'The music's still your own.'

'Although the music would be better if you could insert a few military drum rhythms,' said Phillidas. 'Along with your usual rhythms.'

'It's only for November the sixteenth.' Lorrain spoke up. 'After that, you can go back to playing the way you like.'

'Exactly.' Bartizan nodded. 'Nothing to it. The pair of you can explain it to the rest of the band.'

Astor and Mave exchanged glances. It was true, they couldn't just speak for themselves; the whole band would have to make the decision. Obviously the Swales and the plutocrats weren't going to change *their* minds.

'And now, I'm sure you're all very tired.' Bartizan's fleshy lips parted in a smile. 'Time to show you to your accommodation upstairs.'

'I'll show them,' Lorrain volunteered.

'Yes, do that,' said Bartizan.

 Five minutes later, the Rowdies and their manager were going up in a steam elevator, accompanied by Lorrain and a number of servants. It was the largest, grandest elevator in which Astor had ever travelled, with walls of quilted satin.

Lorrain addressed the band in general, but singled Astor out with his eyes. 'Your accommodation is on the roof garden, right at the top. My brothers and I are two floors below you. We're all guests of the Duchess of Norfolk.'

At the top was a small pavilion of metal and glass. Lorrain led the band across to a doorway barred by a turnstile. He unlocked the turnstile, and they passed through, clack by clack, out onto the roof in the moonlight. The servants stayed back inside the pavilion.

It was an unearthly scene. The sky had cleared, and cool white brilliance poured down on a forest of fronds and ferns and foliage. The roof garden was a botanic display of exotic vegetation – made even more exotic by the moonlight. Bleached of colour, every shape was as if cut out of paper: stark black or glittering silver.

Overhead was a panorama of a different kind. A dozen families of airships hovered high above, three or four or five

271

cigar-shapes tied together nose to tail. They looked strangely delicate against the wide open sky, held as if suspended and motionless by the moon.

'What's that?' Verrol demanded.

He wasn't pointing at something in the sky, but at something much closer. Astor focused and saw a fine mesh of lines running just above the foliage, enclosing the entire roof garden.

'That?' Lorrain seemed surprised. 'Only nets for keeping the birds off.'

'Looks like a cage to me,' said Verrol. 'For keeping people in.'

Lorrain didn't respond to the hostility in his tone. 'No, no. You're free to come and go as you choose. Just summon one of the servants at the turnstile, and they'll escort you.'

And keep an eye on us at the same time, thought Astor.

Lorrain led the band along a path of gravel chips. For all their jungle-like appearance, the clusters of vegetation were carefully labelled and seemed to have been planted to a plan. Astor inhaled a symphony of smells: fruits and flowers, grass and resin. They passed several glasshouses set back from the path and approached a larger octagonal stone building.

'You can practise as loud as you like here, and nobody will be disturbed,' Lorrain told them. 'The perfect place for you.'

They entered the stone building under an arching trellis of vines. The interior was like a hunting lodge, with rugs and furs on the floor, tapestries on the walls, and a ceiling painted as a blue sky with clouds and cherubs. Around the central living area were eight curtained recesses.

Lorrain went up to one particular recess and drew aside the curtain to reveal a chamber furnished with bed, bedside table and candelabra.

'Your individual bedchambers,' he announced, and turned to Astor with a smile. 'This should be yours.'

'Why me?'

'Because it's the most luxurious.'

'So?'

'You're the leader of the band, aren't you?'

Astor shook her head, while Reeth took it upon himself to explain. 'Everyone's equal in the Rowdies.'

'Oh.' Lorrain gave Astor a sideways look from under his eyelashes. 'Well, because you're the most beautiful, then.'

Astor thought she must have misheard. From Verrol, it would have been ironic, but Lorrain wasn't the ironic type. 'What did you say?'

His eyes skittered away, and he blushed with embarrassment. 'You played so beautifully tonight,' he mumbled. 'I thought you were the leader because you gave orders to everyone else. That's what I was trying to say.' He faltered his way to a stop.

Verrol jumped in sharply. 'One time she gives the orders, other times somebody else does. You wouldn't understand.'

Astor frowned. She didn't know why Lorrain was being so complimentary, but he didn't deserve such rudeness.

'Thank you.' She smiled at him as though Verrol hadn't interrupted.

An answering smile appeared on Lorrain's face. 'I don't always agree with my brothers,' he said. 'But I'm sure you can do it. You can do anything.'

He made a farewell bow, then left without another word.

'Can do what?' asked Purdy.

Everyone looked at Astor, who shrugged. 'We talked with Bartizan and Phillidas. Mave and me. There's more to what we have to do for the plutocrats. More to the trade-off.'

'What?' Reeth demanded.

'You didn't know?' Astor eyed him closely and decided his surprise was genuine. She turned to the other band members. 'We have to have a discussion about the future of the Rowdies.'

'Isn't it all mapped out?' asked Reeth.

'No,' Verrol snapped.

'You haven't heard everything yet,' said Mave. 'Neither of you.'

'I think it should wait until morning,' said Astor. 'When we're fresh. This is too big to decide when we're tired and irritable.'

She aimed the last word at Verrol, whose scowl deepened.

Mave nodded agreement. 'After a good night's sleep,' she said.

Verrol gestured towards the curtain that Lorrain had drawn aside. 'All yours, then,' he told Astor.

And since someone had to sleep in the most luxurious bedchamber, Astor did just that.

 In the middle of the night, it began to rain. It was still raining when they got up in the morning, drumming on the roof and gushing from gutters. They sat round a table in the central living area and began the discussion that had been postponed the night before.

When Astor and Mave explained about the changes to their songs required for 16 November, Verrol uttered a derisive laugh. 'Marching songs! Military rhythms!'

'They'll insist on new words,' said Astor. 'Inserting new rhythms is more negotiable.'

Ollifer shrugged. 'If we do one, we may as well do the other.'

The battle-lines in the discussion were soon established. Ollifer and Reeth were perfectly happy to make changes; Verrol and Mave were opposed; while Purdy would go with the general opinion. Astor hated the idea of inserting new rhythms and sympathised with Mave's objection to new words, but still wanted to mediate and hold the band together.

'The words are meant to go with the tunes,' Mave maintained. 'Inseparable.'

'Okay, that's how you feel about *your* songs,' said Ollifer. 'But you wouldn't have a problem with the others?'

'Yes, I would. Someone made up those words for those tunes. You have to respect that.'

Reeth brushed aside all obstacles with a sweep of his arm. 'Isn't this a little bit precious? We can't afford to indulge in personal preferences right now.'

Mave refused to retreat. 'It's a matter of musical integrity.'

'We have to make *some* compromises.' Reeth wouldn't retreat either. 'Everyone does. That's how you get to the top.'

'I see it as a challenge,' said Ollifer portentously. 'Do we have the versatility? Can we adapt? I think we can.'

'Why should we?' Mave shook her head. 'They don't have the right.'

'It's only for one day,' said Reeth. 'If we do this for the plutocrats now, we'll have them in our debt forever.'

Mave glowered at him. 'If we let them push us around this time, they'll always control us. Another time they'll expect other changes.'

'If we refuse them this time, there won't be another time.' Reeth appealed to the band in general. 'You should let me worry about things like this. I am your manager, after all.'

Verrol weighed in. 'Things like what?'

'Negotiations. Planning. Practicalities. You focus on your stage performance, I focus on the big picture. I look after the band's overall career.'

'You think that's a big picture?' Verrol's tone was scoffing, but his body was taut with suppressed anger. 'I'll tell you a bigger picture. A bigger picture is the intended coup on November the sixteenth, and the plutocrats launching the greatest, longest war in human history. Perhaps you forgot about that?'

There was a moment of silence until Ollifer spoke up. 'I won't be fighting. If other people want to fight, let them.'

'Who do you count as "other people"?'

Ollifer shrugged. 'Militiamen, for example. Anyone who volunteers.'

'Oh, this won't be a volunteer war.' Verrol's voice was dangerously quiet. 'This will be a conscription war. Press-gangs will go round seizing people off the streets, out of the slums, forcing them into the army. Poor people, working people. But never the plutocrats.'

His mouth twisted in a bitter sneer. Astor knew his views on war from their conversations at Swale House; he'd been serious then, but he was passionate now.

'You heard the way they talked last night,' he went on. 'They want to make their factories profitable again. Destroying old goods in order to create a demand for new goods to replace them. They don't care if a few people die in the process. A few thousand people. A few hundreds of thousands. A few millions.

You heard what Chard said about bullet holes in uniforms.'

Astor did remember that. When Chard had spoken of bullet holes as a reason for replacing old uniforms, he'd totally failed to mention the person inside the uniform.

'I'm a voice, not a political thinker,' said Ollifer.

Reeth nodded. 'We're not responsible for the state of the world.'

Even Purdy agreed. 'I just play my guitar. I don't want to get involved in politics.'

'You already are!' Verrol brought his fist crashing down on the table. 'You're on the same side as the warmongers!'

Reeth sniffed. 'I don't see it like that.'

'You don't *want* to see. If our music helps this coup succeed, the new government will declare war, and millions will die. What could be clearer than that?'

'It's not our responsibility,' said Reeth. 'We only provide the music.'

Verrol sprang to his feet and paced back and forth, fuming. 'The plutocrats are right about our music. It can make people feel before they think. It stirs the blood and senses, it has the power to make people do things. Do you understand what I'm saying?'

He stopped pacing and faced the group around the table. 'It's a power that can be used for good or used for evil. It's our responsibility to use it for good. We choose. We can create feelings of joy and warmth, or we can create feelings of rage and revenge. It's up to us.'

Reeth shook his head. 'Who's to say what's good or evil? The plutocrats believe one thing, you believe another. Who am I to decide?'

Verrol's lip curled. 'We know about you, Reeth. You're so

desperate for success, you'll use any excuse. You want us to make your dreams come true.'

'And Granny's dreams,' murmured Purdy.

Verrol continued to address Reeth. 'It's not our job to compensate for the failures in your life.'

Reeth winced under that. Even Astor felt it was unnecessarily cruel. She tried to smooth over the situation. 'I'm sure he didn't mean it the way it sounded.'

Verrol shot her an angry glare that said, yes, he did mean it exactly the way it sounded.

'Whose side are *you* on?' Mave asked her.

Astor was looking to find common ground without coming out too obviously on anyone's side. The band members had disagreed often enough in the past – why couldn't they talk it through now? But this was a deeper division than any before.

So the argument went round and round, the same claims and counter-claims were endlessly rehashed, and the differences became more and more entrenched. Purdy seemed to be inclining to Reeth and Ollifer's point of view. In the end, they couldn't even agree on how to reach a decision.

'A simple majority,' said Reeth. 'It has to be.'

'A majority of *band members*,' Mave put in sharply.

'I'm your manager. I'm supposed to be part of the team.'

'It has to be by consensus,' said Verrol. 'Anyone has the right of veto.'

'No!' Reeth, Ollifer and Purdy all objected to that – but did their majority objection override Verrol's veto?

'We should've worked this out long ago,' said Mave.

'Who'd ever have thought it would come to taking a vote?' Astor lamented.

Reeth tried one final appeal. 'I can't believe you'd let a tiny thing like this stand in your way. You'll miss your chance and regret it for the rest of your lives. Decide now, and you can have it all.'

He was frantic to resolve the deadlock in favour of their plutocrat backers. But Mave looked away, and Verrol shook his head. The gathering broke up without coming to a decision.

Astor retired to her chamber, drew the curtain and stretched out on the bed. She didn't want military rhythms in her drumming repertoire, but she was confused about everything else. She needed time to work out her feelings.

The fact was, she'd *loved* the triumph of winning over that stuffed-shirt audience in the Royal George Hall, and she'd *loved* the glow of adulation surrounding her afterwards. Even from Blanquette, Prester and Widdy! When the Rowdies played gang music, it was like waving a magic wand; they could make impossible things happen. She was sure the Royal George Hall was just a beginning.

But it might be their ending too. She remembered how Bartizan and Phillidas had threatened the Silver Rose Band: *We'll lock you out of every venue in the city.* Presumably the same could happen to the Rowdies. They'd be forced to slink back to Brummingham with their tails between their legs – and even there the Swales could make it hard for them.

It was easier for Mave and Verrol. Having an audience hardly mattered to Mave, and Verrol was happy to live in the moment without long-term goals. She'd told him once that he lacked ambition; now she understood his reasons for being the way he was. Still, the truth remained that he didn't care so much about the band's level of success.

Whereas she cared almost as much as Reeth. She'd made a decision, back when her hair turned white, to make the Rowdies her whole purpose in life. Now that she'd tasted real success, London success, she didn't ever want to give it up. She couldn't bear the thought of only playing for the gangs in Slumtown.

On the other hand, she understood what Verrol was saying about war. Reeth might pretend there were alternative possible opinions, but there weren't. The death of millions of people was an evil thing, plain and simple. She'd seen the real motives behind it too, not dressed up in fine phrases about loyalty, duty and patriotism. She didn't want to contribute to starting a war.

She was also aware that she'd surprised Verrol by trying to mediate from a middle position. He'd expected her support, and he'd been disappointed not to have her backing him up like Mave. Of course, Mave had her own motives for being on his side . . .

By the end of an hour, she was as confused as ever. She rose from her bed and came back out into the main living area. Reeth and Ollifer sat together talking in low voices, while Purdy strummed on his brass guitar. Since when did Purdy have his guitar up here?

Then she spotted her own drum kit stacked by the door. 'Ah, they brought us our instruments.'

Reeth looked up. 'Yes, for the band to practise.'

Astor knew what Reeth wanted them to practise. She shrugged and went to sit by herself at the table. There was no sign of Verrol or Mave.

She surveyed the bedchamber curtains. Mave's curtain was open, her chamber empty. Verrol's curtain was closed and drawn all the way across.

A sudden shocking image jumped into her mind – of Verrol and Mave behind the curtain *kissing*. Her heart skipped a beat. Was it possible? Where else could they be? The image was as vivid as if she'd actually seen it.

She remembered her advice to Verrol: *sweep her off her feet before she has time to think about it.* Why on earth had she said that? And: *take her in your arms and kiss her.* Heavens, she'd even told him to *be passionate!*

She stared at the curtain, willing it to give up its secrets. Of course, Verrol and Mave had established a new sympathetic connection in this morning's quarrel. Astor's imagination ran riot. She scanned the others in the room, Ollifer, Reeth and Purdy. Didn't they know? Or didn't they care? But it was wrong, wrong, wrong! Verrol was a predator, Mave was so vulnerable . . .

Then her gaze lit on her drum kit again. If the servants had brought up their instruments, did that mean it had stopped raining? She strained her ears for even the lightest patter on the roof overhead. Nothing! In which case . . .

She strode across the room and flung open the door. Heavy clouds hung in the sky, but there was no rain falling. So Verrol and Mave didn't *have* to be in his chamber at all. They might have gone out into the garden.

She walked out herself, for a stroll that was also a search. Almost at once, she found Verrol leaning back against a wall at the side of the building. He was busy doing something with several lengths of cord.

'What's that?' she asked.

'I'm plaiting a rope.' His tone wasn't exactly friendly.

'Why?'

'So I can get down from here when I want.'

'Down to the ground?'

He uttered what might have been an affirmative grunt. Astor guessed that he too disliked the idea of an escort of servants. 'Where did you get those cords?'

He jerked a thumb towards the trellis of vines that arched over the lodge entrance. Crisscross cords supported the vines – except where Verrol had cut them away.

'It'll take days to make a long enough rope,' she said.

He didn't bother to reply. He had hardly raised his eyes from his task throughout the conversation.

'Have you seen Mave?' she asked.

Another jerk of the thumb directed her attention to a faint sound from another part of the garden. It was the unmistakable music of the melodium. Mave had obviously come out to play by herself.

Astor decided to let both of them be.

The weather continued rainy, on and off, and the divisions in the Rowdies continued unresolved. They didn't quarrel openly, but there was constant friction, sniping and suspicion. Indoors or outdoors, they sat alone or talked in their separate groups: Verrol with Mave, Ollifer with Reeth, and – for lack of alternative – Astor with Purdy. Purdy suggested a band practice once, but the others shook their heads. What was the point?

Astor couldn't believe it had all fallen apart so fast. It was as though the divisions in the band had long been simmering under the surface. Apparently, they had never had anything in common except the music.

Reeth and Ollifer were now as thick as thieves, always conferring together. At other times, Reeth conferred with the plutocrats, descending from the roof garden with an escort of servants. He was keeping the Swales up to date with the band's deliberations, he said.

In fact, the band was as far from a decision as ever. One evening, Reeth made an announcement with a hint of a threat.

'Only seven days left. The plutocrats already have alternative plans to fall back on. The Rowdies aren't indispensable, you know.'

He refused to say what the other plans were. Instead, he made a further announcement the following morning. 'I've been writing new lyrics for some of the band's songs, so they'll be ready when you make your decision. Otherwise we'll run out of time.'

'Except it won't be the decision you want,' growled Verrol.

'It's sheer hackwork,' Reeth continued as though Verrol hadn't spoken. '*Victory* and *valour* and stuff. All for a single day's performance. I don't think any real songwriter would want to do it.'

He looked at Mave, who immediately looked away. He faced the general silence with an imperious smile. 'But that's what I'm here for, isn't it? To take those kinds of burden off your shoulders.'

From that time on, Astor often saw Ollifer with a sheet of paper in his hand, moving his lips as he recited to himself. No doubt he was already learning Reeth's revised lyrics.

She soon ran out of topics to chat about with Purdy, who was never much of a conversationalist. She would have loved to talk with Verrol in the old way, but that seemed impossible. He gave the impression they could only be friends if she joined up with Mave in his faction.

Astor's worries about Verrol and Mave had faded. She watched them out of the corner of her eye, and she was sure they weren't lovers. When Verrol started to disappear for long periods, she noted that Mave was rarely absent at the same time. It wasn't hard to work out what he was doing.

She took a walk round the edge of the roof garden and discovered what she'd been expecting: Verrol's handmade rope tied onto the trunk of a particularly sturdy tree. She traced the rope five paces to the side of the roof, and there was a hole cut in the netting. The rope went through the hole and down over the edge.

Astor dropped to her hands and knees, and stuck her head out through the netting for a better look. The rope descended thirty or forty feet before the London smog swallowed it up. She could make out the outlines of elevated bridges and cables, and the glow of multi-coloured lights buried deep in the murk. But she could only guess how far the rope went down – probably another hundred feet to the ground.

Between the clouds above and the smog below, it was a deeply depressing scene. Astor wondered vaguely where Verrol had gone, and why he kept going and returning. Then it hit her.

Those three fine ladies in their carriages!

There could be no other explanation. Who else did he have to visit? She had seen the assignation notes they sent him, she had seen him stow the notes in his breeches pocket. Was he visiting one of them or two of them or all three of them?

She felt sick to her stomach. He was a traitor to his own principles. Or perhaps the ladies had rich plutocrat husbands, and this was his idea of revenge? But that didn't make it better, that made it twice as bad!

And to think she'd suspected him with Mave. Sweet, innocent Mave! Suddenly she remembered what he'd said in the velocipede – that the three fine ladies were more his type than Mave. His very words!

Oh, she despised his type and their type. They were all cold and immoral and heartless! The sick feeling in her stomach turned into a dark, smouldering anger.

 Next day, everything continued as before. Verrol disappeared down his rope again; Reeth went off to talk with the Swales; Mave played her melodium; Purdy strummed on his guitar; and Ollifer wandered around silently reciting the new song lyrics. Astor remained angry, but she was also very bored. When the rain stopped, she decided to set up her drums and practise outside.

She found a secluded spot between two clumps of rhododendron bushes. Before long, she was pounding away at full volume, as if she was on stage again at the Royal George Hall. She began experimenting with a kind of double backbeat that didn't belong in any of the band's existing songs.

Lost in her own world, she didn't notice Reeth's presence at first. He stepped forward into full view only when she paused in her drumming. Presumably he had just returned from discussions with the Swales.

'Sorry,' he said. 'I didn't mean to interrupt. It's a treat to hear you playing again. What were you doing there?'

'Experimenting.'

'Mave ought to hear it. She could come up with a great song to that rhythm.'

Astor nodded, remembering his experience as a band musician. Of course, he knew all about rhythms.

'That youngest Swale brother was right about you,' he laughed. 'Didn't he say you can do anything?'

It was the longest conversation they'd had since the quarrel. Astor accepted the compliment, and tossed off another burst of drumming with a tricky crossover rhythm.

'Improvising again,' said Reeth when she finished. 'You've never done that on stage either.'

'No.'

'Because I was wondering. Are military rhythms hard to do?'

Astor frowned. 'Military rhythms?'

'I know you don't like them. But that's not because they're difficult, is it?'

''Course not.'

'Even though they're so different to what you normally play?'

'Easiest thing in the world,' said Astor, and struck up a rat-tat-tat marching rhythm.

'I suppose.' Reeth seemed unconvinced. 'But that sounds like a very simple one.'

'They're all simple. I can make them up as I go.'

She launched into a new marching rhythm, swapped into another, then another, then another. She concluded with a long drum roll.

Reeth grinned. 'You *can* do it. I should never have doubted you.'

There was something about his grin that Astor didn't like. He wasn't looking at her but past her, over her shoulder. She spun round – and found herself staring straight at Verrol.

'That's what we need for November the sixteenth,' said Reeth.

Verrol appeared shocked . . . hurt . . . crushed . . . angry . . . Astor didn't know *what* his expression was. She had never seen his face so bare and defenceless. He must have come back up his rope, heard the military rhythms, and approached from the other side of the bushes.

Astor couldn't speak. He thought she had joined Reeth's faction, that was obvious. He didn't actually hiss the word *traitor*, but he didn't need to.

Then a new voice called out. 'What's all this? Marching rhythms?' It was Ollifer striding up from another direction.

'I was only demonstrating,' said Astor. The excuse was for Verrol, but it sounded lame even to her own ears.

Verrol ignored her and turned to Reeth. 'It won't do you any good,' he snarled. 'I still veto our role in the coup.'

Reeth seemed very pleased with himself. 'You insist on your right to a veto?'

Ollifer objected. 'We never agreed on that.'

'No, no, it's not a problem. Let him do what he wants.' The smile never left Reeth's face. 'When he's out of the band.'

There was a long silence. Astor struggled to digest those last words. *Out of the band?*

A moment later, Mave and Purdy also appeared. Everyone seemed to sense that something critical was happening.

Reeth explained it to them in the coolest of tones. 'We're

discussing the size of the band. I've thought for a long time that five of you are too many. I'm suggesting that Verrol here should drop out.'

Mave's eyes grew even rounder and larger than usual. 'Do you want to drop out?' she asked Verrol.

'No. He wants to get rid of me.'

'Well, if any band member chooses to go their own way . . .' murmured Ollifer. He had already adjusted to the idea.

'I'm with Verrol,' said Mave. 'If he doesn't fit in, then nor do I.'

Reeth had an answer for everything. 'It's not so much fitting in. The rest of you are necessary to the sound of the band. He isn't.'

Astor found her voice. 'Why not?'

'Think about it. I know he's been with you since the band was formed. But seriously, what contribution does he make?'

Astor thought about it. 'He's our dancer.'

'Yes, and a very good dancer.' Reeth spoke the word with a hint of disdain. 'But musically, what contribution? Take away his clapper and pealer – what do you lose? The important percussion comes from your drums. He adds nothing much to that.'

Verrol turned on Reeth with a dangerous glint in his eye. 'And how much do you add? If I'm not necessary to the band, what about you?'

'I have a different role. You're the disposable one.'

'No, *you're* disposable.' Verrol blazed up in anger. 'In fact, I'll dispose of you right now. Off the side of this building.'

He advanced on Reeth like a wolf on its prey. Reeth gritted his teeth and crouched in a fighting stance. Even if he'd had two good arms, he wouldn't have stood a chance. There were cries from everyone around, Astor's loudest of all. She knew what Verrol was capable of.

Verrol reached forward with both hands – then seemed to have second thoughts. He stopped, dropped his arms and glared at Reeth from half a pace away. Suddenly, he turned his back and walked off.

Reeth was shaking, but he was no coward. 'I would've fought him,' he muttered. 'I won't give in to threats.'

'That's right,' Ollifer agreed. 'If he can't hear criticism without losing his temper . . .'

Mave watched Verrol go, but didn't try to follow. She appeared upset and uncomfortable over the scene that had just taken place. Astor felt exactly the same.

At that moment, the rain started to fall again. First a few large drops, then more and more, buffeting the leaves of the rhododendron bushes.

Astor picked up her tin basin and brass gong, while the others collected kegs, pans and pots for her. With a minimum of fuss, they carried the whole drum kit back under shelter.

There was no going back once Reeth had said it. The possibility of dropping Verrol was out in the open, and tensions within the band went up another notch. Verrol did himself no favours by his long periods of absence, while Reeth pushed his arguments with Purdy, Mave and Astor. Astor couldn't tell whether he won over any of the others, but she turned a deaf ear herself.

The trouble was, he was basically right. Leaving aside Verrol's dancing, the clapper and pealer added little to the band's sound. Astor wouldn't hear it from Reeth, but she admitted it in her own thoughts. Verrol brought out the best in the rest of them, and his dancing was an inspiration – but his importance to the band had lessened as their success had grown.

Meanwhile, she found it impossible to talk to him. He was bristling and surly with everyone else; with her, he wouldn't even exchange words. She might have made more of an effort to explain how she'd been tricked into playing military rhythms if he hadn't kept going off to visit his fine ladies. She was still displeased and disappointed over his behaviour.

One time, she drew Mave aside for a private conversation about him. Mave wasn't particularly eager to talk, but Astor *had* to open her mind to someone. She practically dragged Mave into her bedchamber, and made her sit on the side of the bed.

'I'm sorry it didn't work out with Verrol,' she said.

'What?' Mave looked up, then down again. 'Oh, that. I never expected it to. Did you ask him?'

'Sort of.'

'And he said he wasn't interested in me?'

'He has other interests.' Since Mave didn't ask the obvious question, Astor had to supply the answer herself. 'Do you remember waiting outside the Royal George Hall? Did you see when three messengers come up to him with envelopes?'

'Maybe. I think so.'

'I saw what was inside. Assignation notes. Three fine ladies arranging rendezvous with him. He never threw those notes away. And now . . .'

She snorted and swung her arms. Mave seemed unperturbed.

'Don't you understand?' Astor had to struggle not to shout. 'That's where he goes when he goes down his rope. He's off with them!'

'All of them?'

'How should I know? One at least. Probably two. Most likely three. It's not as if he *feels* anything for them. They get what they want, and he gets what he wants. Revenge is probably part of it for him.'

Mave shook her head, not comprehending. Astor rushed on without stopping to explain.

'Can you believe him? Rich, powerful women! Dolled-up beauties! Perfume and powder! That's *his* type!'

'Better to be his friend, then,' said Mave. 'I think he and I are friends.'

Astor was amazed by her calm acceptance. 'Aren't you shocked and repelled? Aren't you ashamed for him?'

'I can see *you* are.'

'On your behalf. How could he prefer that kind of woman to someone like you?'

'I told you he was only a daydream for me.'

'A daydream you're breaking your heart over.'

Mave gave a tiny shrug. 'I don't mind. I never expected love to make me happy.'

Astor frowned at her. She'd always known Mave was strange, but this was beyond strange.

'I've written another three songs,' Mave went on with a wistful smile. 'One about him, and two about feelings that come from him.'

'I don't get it.'

'No, nobody would. It's like . . . I need my unhappiness. I use it, I transform it. It's what I write my songs out of.'

'But . . . wouldn't you rather be happy?'

'No, I'd rather be creative. I know it's stupid, but that's the way I am.'

Astor studied her features: the small, sad mouth, the pointed elfin chin and the huge, round eyes. It was true, it was almost impossible to imagine Mave happy. She just wasn't made for it.

'Not stupid,' said Astor. 'But I'd rather be me. I go for what I want.'

Mave was studying her too. 'Yes, when you find out what it is you want.'

Astor found Mave's direct gaze oddly disconcerting. She looked away.

'Hmm, well, I don't know if the band will ever get to play your latest songs, the way things are going.'

Mave stood up to leave. 'That's all right,' she said. 'I can play them for myself.'

 Something was stirring on the streets of London Town. It might have been the movement of countless feet or the conversation of countless voices – nothing clearly distinguishable, just a low murmur of activity. But it was a murmur that hadn't been there before.

Reeth kept making threats about the plutocrats' alternative plan. Four days, three days, two days away from 16 November, and still the band hadn't reached a decision. Astor had committed her future to the Rowdies, and now she saw it all slipping away. But in spite of her disappointment with Verrol, she couldn't wish him out of the band. It would never be the same without him.

On the morning of 15 November, the rain came down in bucketfuls. Other band members stayed in their bedchambers; only Astor and Purdy sat in the living area, and they weren't talking. If there was a knock on the door, they didn't hear it. The first they knew was when the door swung open, and a cold, damp gust blew in.

'Shut that—' Astor snapped, before she saw who it was. 'Oh, sorry. Come in.'

It was Lorrain Swale. The wind had tousled his hair and brought colour to his cheeks, heightening the appeal of his perfect features. He looked at Astor and cleared his throat.

'Er-hum. The Swales need to talk to you.'

'Just me?' She stared boldly back at him.

'Yes.' He gestured towards the door. 'I've brought umbrellas for both of us.'

Astor was happy to escape the tedious atmosphere of the lodge. She followed Lorrain outside, where two servants waited with enormous, steel-strutted umbrellas. One of them walked beside her and sheltered her from the rain.

The umbrellas were needed only for the short distance to the pavilion. Once under cover again, Lorrain left the servants behind and escorted her himself. They descended by the stairs rather than the steam elevator.

Two floors below the roof garden, Lorrain turned to her with an odd look in his large, dark eyes. 'I bent the truth a little,' he said. 'I'm the only Swale that needs to talk to you.'

He appeared flushed, even beyond the effect of the wind.

With anyone else, she might have suspected his intentions, but instinct told her that Lorrain was too much of a gentleman.

In fact, he led her not to a room but along a corridor to a bay window.

'Please, take a seat,' he said.

Cushioned seating had been built into the window, curving round inside the glass. Astor did as he asked. It was strangely pleasant to sit snug and warm and dry while the rain sluiced down the outside of the windowpanes.

Lorrain didn't sit. 'I brought you here . . .' he began, then broke off.

He tried again. 'I thought this would be a suitable place . . .'

Again he couldn't finish. He loosened his necktie and ran a finger round inside the collar.

'I've been thinking about it for days. I . . .'

He seemed to have a question to ask. Astor would have helped him out if she could have guessed what it was. He uttered a strangled sort of groan, and dropped down on one knee.

'Will you marry me?' he said.

Astor gawped at him. 'Did you just say what I think you said?'

'Yes. Marry me. Be my wife. Please.'

She had an urge to giggle like a fool, and another urge to jump up and run. But the soulful look in his eyes kept her fixed in place.

'But that's . . . I mean . . . it doesn't make sense.'

'It does to me. I think I've loved you ever since I first saw you.'

'Oh? So why didn't you do something about it? You had your chance three months ago.'

'I couldn't.'

'I came to Swale House thinking we were going to be engaged. I wouldn't have minded a proposal of marriage then.'

'I know, I know. I felt so bad. But you were only there as a governess. My brothers would never have allowed it.'

'Haven't you got a mind of your own?'

'You don't understand. My brothers have absolute control of the family finances. They make all the decisions. Except they can't decide my feelings.'

'Your feelings? Well, *I* had no idea about your supposed feelings. Perhaps you should have given me some tiny clue?'

'Not "supposed". Don't say that. I admit I'm not very good at showing how I feel. I'm too inhibited and conventional, too nervous. I keep things bottled up. But please believe that my feelings are real.'

His eyes seemed to grow even larger, with a kind of soft melancholy.

'Okay, I believe you,' Astor conceded.

'And not completely bottled up,' he went on. 'Do you remember when you played the piano in the schoolroom? You were like an angel making music. My heart almost melted away. You must have seen that.'

'Maybe.'

'And I was always looking at you, so many other times. I couldn't keep my eyes off you.'

'Plenty of men used to *look* at me,' said Astor. 'Looking's cheap.'

He sighed, and lowered himself from one knee onto both knees. 'I know I don't deserve you. I'm not a strong personality. I think too much before I act, and I always seem to miss the moment. I can offer you a life of wealth and luxury, but I know I'm not much in myself. It's true. I'm not bold or brave or witty or vivacious – there are a hundred negative things to say about me. But I'm not a bad person, and I've never deliberately hurt anybody. The one promise I can make is that if you marry me, you'll be loved and cared for all the rest of your life.'

It was the longest speech Astor had ever heard him make, and she didn't doubt his sincerity. But sincere feelings didn't necessarily translate into deeds.

'So you'd want to marry me even if your brothers cut you off without a penny?'

'That doesn't have to happen now. I would never ask you to marry me if I couldn't support you. It wouldn't be right or proper. But you're not a governess any more.'

'I'm not a plutocrat's daughter either.'

'No, but you're a huge success. A famous performer. My brothers don't care about music, but they love success.'

'You won't have to fight for me, then?'

Lorrain wasn't sensitive to irony. 'Oh, it'll be difficult. They'd probably still prefer a plutocrat's daughter. I *will* fight for you, though. It'll be difficult but not impossible. They've changed their attitude enough for me to do the rest.'

'That's good.' Astor raised an eyebrow. 'Unfortunately, I've changed too. Look at me.'

A look of distress came over his face. 'What?'

'Look closer.' She reached up and touched her hair.

'It's turning white.'

'You noticed?'

'Of course I did.'

'But do you realise it'll get worse and worse? It'll keep growing through until I'm totally white. I'll look like an old woman.'

'You'll be as beautiful as ever to me.'

296

'Are you serious?'

'You'll be stunning when your hair's totally white. Nothing like an old woman.'

She looked into his eyes and saw he meant it. He might be mad or blind, but he really believed she would be stunning with totally white hair.

'Well,' was all she could find to say. She bathed in his admiring gaze.

'You still haven't given me an answer,' he prompted, after a period of silence.

'I need to think. Have you said anything to your brothers yet?'

'Not yet. But I'll *make* them agree. I won't let you go again.'

Astor had to smile. 'You sound very determined.'

'You'll have to get your parents' approval too.'

'*If* I accept your proposal. I haven't said yes or no. I need more time.'

'As long as you like.'

'And please.' She gestured as she spoke. 'Don't stay there on your knees.'

He rose and stood upright. 'Shall I escort you back to the roof?'

'No, I'm comfortable here. I'll stay and think about your proposal.'

'Of course. May I ask one favour?'

She didn't understand until he reached for her hand. She grinned at his tentative, hopeful look. 'You want to kiss my hand?'

'Please.'

'Even though we're not married? Not even engaged?'

'May I?'

'You may.'

He lifted her hand to his lips and planted a soft kiss on the backs of her fingers. Then he turned and left – though not before Astor glimpsed a hot red blush spreading over his cheeks.

Astor's head was spinning. She'd managed to talk sensibly for the last five minutes – at least she thought she had – but as soon as Lorrain was gone, the sheer improbability of it burst in on her again. He wanted to marry her after all!

It was like reading a story about herself – a story with the happiest of endings. Her old dream had come true in the end, and for the moment she just wanted to enjoy it.

She curled up a little more warmly on the cushioned window seat. The rain still slid down the outside of the glass, while she was safe and snug inside. She replayed the scene that had just taken place over and over in her mind, with more satisfaction every time.

I made it happen, she thought. *I did it.* Bartizan and Phillidas had belittled her, her stepfather had discarded her, everyone had humiliated her. What a slap in the face for them all if she accepted Lorrain's proposal!

She pictured an interview with her stepfather . . . when she would visit his Lambeth residence and summon him to hear some important news. Then she would tell him of Lorrain's proposal and request his formal consent. How his face would fall! How he would hate it! Because it wouldn't really be a request at all. If Bartizan and Phillidas backed Lorrain, it would be as good as a command. She had seen enough at the Duchess of Norfolk's reception to know that the plutocrats' figurehead was little more than their puppet.

She moved on to imagine a grand wedding scene . . . a church wedding, of course, perhaps in St Paul's Cathedral. Marshal Dorrin would be forced to act as father of the bride and give her away – well, he'd be happy about the giving away part, at any rate. And Lorrain would be there at her side with his beautiful eyes, his raven-black hair and perfect features . . . she couldn't go past how extraordinarily handsome he was. There wasn't a girl in all of England who wouldn't be mad with envy.

And he considered *her* beautiful. Even when the white entirely replaced the copper in her hair, he thought she'd be stunning. *Stunning* rather than *pretty*? She'd given up on pretty – she was sure nobody could be *pretty* with brilliantly white hair. But perhaps she could be attractive in a different way? Lorrain's words and the admiration in his eyes had brought back a sense of her own appearance that she'd almost forgotten.

She remembered passing several wall-mirrors on the way to the bay window – and in the end she just *had* to look. She rose and retraced her steps along the corridor as far as the nearest mirror.

No wonder Lorrain had noticed the white! When she gazed at her reflection, the white jumped right out at her. She was amazed at how fast it had grown through. With the thinner shape of her face and her more prominent cheekbones, she would hardly have recognised herself.

She half-closed her eyes and imagined the effect when her

hair was all white. Was that *stunning*? For better or worse, it was undeniably striking . . .

'Excuse me, Miss. Would you be wanting to go back yet?'

She spun round and discovered a servant hovering respectfully a few yards away. Where had he come from? Had he been keeping a watch on her all this time?

She shrugged. 'Yes, all right.'

The illusion of privacy had gone; better to find a quiet spot on the roof. She followed the servant up the stairs and back to the pavilion. However, she shook her head when another servant offered to accompany her across the garden with an umbrella. The rain had nearly stopped anyway.

A quiet spot . . . she walked halfway down the path towards the lodge then swung aside for one of the glasshouses. This one contained potted palms and cacti of every shape and size imaginable. She went in, found herself an empty wooden tub, turned it over and sat down.

This time she tried to think seriously about Lorrain's proposal. A hundred calculations ran round inside her head. On the plus side, he was a kind and gentle person. He had said he'd never deliberately hurt anyone, and she had no doubt he really would love and care for her.

On the negative side, he was weak . . . but at least he recognised the fact. His brothers pushed him around, but they wouldn't dominate him so easily when she was his wife. And he would surely have a claim on the family assets if he asserted his legal rights.

She went back to the plus side. Lorrain could provide her with a life of comfort and security, and one part of her longed for a little more of both. It was what she had grown up with as a child, a calm and civilised existence. As Lorrain's wife, of course, the comforts would be a thousand times more luxurious.

On the other hand, there was the band. What might she be sacrificing there? Were the Rowdies going anywhere, or had they already reached the end of the road?

Her calculations became more and more tangled, and still she was no further forward. The idea of marrying Lorrain remained strangely cut off from reality. Most of all, she couldn't get a grip on her feelings for him. Could she actually love him? Would it be the right sort of love? When she tried to examine her own heart, somehow it kept slipping away from her.

If only she had someone with whom to talk things over. Ollifer and Reeth weren't suitable, Purdy was no expert on feelings, and there hadn't been much empathy in Astor's last conversation with Mave. Verrol, of course, was impossible. She needed an outside perspective, someone who wasn't caught up in the band and its factions. Perhaps her mother . . .

A voice calling her name broke in on her thoughts. 'Astor! Astor! *Astor!*'

'Here,' she replied.

A moment later, Mave stuck her head in at the glass-house door. 'I've been looking for you everywhere. Reeth has summoned a meeting. He says it's decision time for the Rowdies.'

They were gathered round the table in the living area of the lodge: Reeth, Ollifer, Purdy and Verrol. The arguments were already in full swing by the time Astor and Mave joined the group. Astor sat and listened and tried to catch up.

Reeth insisted that this was the band's last chance before the plutocrats adopted their alternative plan. Otherwise, the arguments were all the same. Verrol refused to bend to the plutocrats' demands, and Reeth and Ollifer wanted him dropped from the band.

Reeth was trying to break down Mave's support for Verrol. He punctuated every assertion with a flourish of his arm. 'I know you're not interested in the politics, only the music. I wouldn't presume to alter any of your songs. My new words are garbage anyway. I've used eight old tunes, and all the band has to do is play them over and over.'

Mave pursed her lips and said nothing. Reeth redoubled his efforts.

'It's not as though anyone will be paying attention to us while they're marching and shouting. They'll be too busy doing their political stuff. Then, afterwards, everything goes back to the way it was.'

'Including *him*?' Mave indicated Verrol. 'Can he come back into the band afterwards too?'

Reeth sucked his lips. 'I was thinking of the music.'

'I wouldn't want to come back,' said Verrol. 'Not to a band that's sold its soul.'

'You see?' Reeth broadened his appeal to include Astor. 'Won't compromise, won't negotiate. He's impossible.'

Astor had heard it all before. She lost concentration, and her mind drifted back to the scene in the bay window. Lorrain stammering out his proposal . . . confessing his hidden love . . . admiring the whiteness of her hair . . .

'Where do *you* stand?'

She blinked and came back to the present. Reeth had just asked her a direct question.

'What? Marching songs for the militias? Or dropping Verrol from the band?'

'Both. Either. This *is* important, you know.'

If they agreed about nothing else, they agreed about that. Verrol's disapproving stare matched Reeth's disapproving frown.

'What would you say if I told you Lorrain Swale had asked me to marry him?'

The words were out before she'd made up her mind to utter them. Jaws dropped all around the table. Verrol looked as though he'd been poleaxed from behind.

Mave was first to find her voice. 'Would you have to leave the band if you got married?'

'What about Bartizan and Phillidas?' asked Purdy. 'Will they agree to it?'

'You *can't* leave the band!' Reeth thumped the table in triumph. 'You'll have to do what they want now!'

Astor shrugged. 'I don't know what it might mean. I haven't said yes yet.'

'But you will,' Ollifer suggested.

'I'm thinking about it.'

There was a violent crash as Verrol sprang to his feet and hurled his chair across the room. 'Thinking about it? *Thinking* about it?'

Astor stiffened at his aggressive tone. Ollifer answered on her behalf. 'Of course she's thinking about it.'

Verrol's mouth twisted in a savage sneer. 'So the humiliation doesn't matter any more? All forgotten? All forgiven?'

'What humiliation?' asked Mave.

Verrol's eyes remained fixed upon Astor's. 'He turned his back on her. She thought they were getting engaged three months ago, but he wasn't interested.'

'He was interested,' Astor retorted. 'His brothers would have prevented it then.'

'You mean, he does whatever they tell him? What a lover! What a hero!'

'He's gentle and sensitive. You wouldn't understand.'

'Oh, I understand. Big, wet, lapdog eyes.'

'He's very handsome.'

'And very rich. Money makes everything all right, does it?'

'At least he's not a killer.' Astor broke eye contact and swung to address the others. 'Do you know who this man is? Verrol Stark, the son of Emer Stark. From the London crime family. He told me himself he's killed at least six people.'

'That's enough!' Verrol hissed.

'Enough? I haven't even started. You don't have the right to judge *anyone*.'

'I know he doesn't love you, that's all.'

'What would a killer know about love?'

'He doesn't have it in him. He just wants a trophy to decorate his mantelpiece.'

'That's a lie!'

'It's the truth.' He leaned forward across the table and grabbed her suddenly by the wrist. 'Not real love.'

'Let go of me!'

His only response was to tighten his grip and pull her closer. His eyes burned into hers. 'You fool!'

Astor struggled to break free. He seemed hardly aware of how much he was hurting her.

'He loves me for what I am. He always has. His feelings for me have never changed.'

304

'So? Do you think mine have?'

The pain made her gasp. She swung her other hand and struck him hard across the face.

He dropped her wrist and drew back in surprise. He lifted a hand to his cheek, where a red welt was spreading on the skin.

'Listen,' he began. 'I'm trying to tell you—'

'I don't want to hear. You just showed your real nature.' She held up her wrist, which still tingled with pain. 'You were vicious then and you're vicious now.'

'Not the sort of person we want in the band,' put in Reeth.

Verrol was simmering. He looked as though he might have thrown another chair if there had been one within reach.

'Don't do this,' he said to Astor.

'Perhaps we should get back to business,' Ollifer proposed. 'We still have to vote on the size of the band.'

'Good idea.' Reeth glanced at Verrol. 'Now we have some notion who we're dealing with.'

Astor surveyed the band members and saw no hope for Verrol. Mave looked shocked and startled, Purdy had his brows drawn down. It was easy to guess how the vote would go now.

For herself, she didn't care. Verrol's fate was his own fault. She was sick of the lot of them.

Without another word, she jumped up from her chair and marched off to her bedchamber. But not to her bed. She was looking for the folded piece of paper she'd left on her bedside table, the note from her mother with the address of Marshal Dorrin's London residence.

There it was:

14, Walnut Tree Walk, Lambeth

She marched back out into the living area. The scene was unchanged: Verrol still standing, the others still sitting.

305

'We're going to take a vote,' Reeth told her with a very smug smile on his face.

'Not me,' said Astor. 'I'm off to see my mother. I may just ask my stepfather for his consent to my marriage.' She turned to Verrol. 'I'll borrow your rope to climb down, if you don't mind.'

She defied him to say otherwise. He remained silent and motionless, with clenched fists and hanging head.

'Good, then.' She headed for the door. 'You can all decide whatever you like.'

The rain had stopped, but the rope was wet and slippery. She descended like a mountaineer, walking backwards down the wall, hand over hand. The smog grew thicker as she descended, and the light grew dimmer.

By the time she touched ground, her palms were raw and her arms were aching. She hurried to put a safe distance between herself and Norfolk Palace. At the first intersection, she paused and took stock. There were sounds all around in the smog: raucous male voices, bursts of singing and drunken mirth. She had the address . . . but who to ask for directions?

She advanced cautiously. As she'd suspected, the male voices belonged to a company of militiamen. They occupied the entire width of the street, sitting or sprawling on outspread groundsheets. Something was cooking on a spit over an impromptu fire in the middle of the road. They waved bottles of ale in their hands as they laughed and talked.

Astor didn't intend to ask *them* for directions. By the sound of their accents, they weren't London locals anyway. She was about to turn and try elsewhere when she noticed two policemen in high domed helmets. They were standing in the shadows, no doubt keeping a watch on the revellers. Much more suitable!

They weren't helpful or friendly, though. When Astor asked the way to Walnut Tree Walk, they became instantly suspicious.

'Walnut Tree Walk? What's your business there?'

'What's your business *here?*'

'Where did you come from?'

'This isn't your sort of area.'

Astor backed away. 'Doesn't matter,' she muttered, and headed for the nearest side street.

She thought they might follow, but they didn't. As she turned into the side street, she almost bumped into a small boy flattened against the wall. Astor had the impression he'd been watching the policemen watching the militiamen.

'Want to go to Walnut Tree Walk, do yer?' he asked in a throaty whisper.

'Yes. You've got sharp ears.'

'Sharp ears, quick eyes, smart fingers – that's me. I can take yer there.'

He wore a beanie pulled down low and a threadbare jacket with the collar turned up high. Snub nose, freckles, wide mouth and front teeth missing . . . He reminded Astor of the Slumtown kids in Brummingham.

'I can't pay.'

'Yeah, I saw yer weren't carryin' a purse.' His tone suggested that if she'd been carrying a purse, he would have already snitched it. 'You can owe me. This way.'

307

He sped off down the side street, moving with exaggerated stealth. Astor had to jog to keep up.

'Dugard Lane,' he called back over his shoulder as they turned a corner. Then, at the next intersection, 'Renfrew Road'. A little later, he announced 'Gilbert Road' and 'Wincott Street'.

Although they went by a quiet route, Astor heard the sounds of more militiamen in the main streets. One time she glimpsed a large company drawn up as if on parade while their leader addressed them.

Finally they came out from the back streets and onto a main street themselves. The boy checked in both directions.

'Kennington Road, all clear,' he said, and pointed. 'Walnut Tree Walk fifty yards on the left. You're on yer own now.'

'Thank you. What's your name?'

'Smidgie.' He tapped a finger against the side of his nose. 'But that's secret information. Keep it to yourself.'

'You must live round here to know the streets so well.'

'Nah. I'm from the Battersea slums. I make it my business to know things.'

'You belong in a slum gang?'

'In London Town, we call ourselves street gangs. Street kids and street gangs. I'm in the Piepickers.'

'What do you know about these militiamen?'

'Some of 'em have been here a week. They come marchin' in from out of town. It's buildin' up to a big showdown.'

Astor understood the nature of the showdown. 'Tomorrow. They're taking part in a coup against the government.'

'I know that too.' Smidgie tapped the side of his nose again. 'But mum's the word, eh?'

Astor wondered at his knowledge – but only for a moment. Then she hurried out into Kennington Road and along to Walnut Tree Walk.

Walnut Tree Walk proved to be a street of expensive-looking houses half hidden by the trees along the pavement. Astor checked out the numbers on the front doors. Number 14 was a dignified house of three storeys, with white stonework framing every window.

She mounted the steps and tugged on the bellpull. A dull resonance sounded somewhere deep within.

The man who came to the door was no ordinary servant but an upright soldierly figure resplendent in full military uniform. No doubt he had served under the Marshal in some of the great battles of the Fifty Years War.

'I've come to see Mrs Dorrin,' she said.

The man stood back to allow her entry, and she advanced into the lobby. It was as big as a hall, with an immensely high beamed ceiling. Wooden staircases ascended to the upper floors, flags draped the walls, and the floor was tiled in a pattern of black and white squares. It wasn't showy, but it was undeniably grand.

'Please wait here, Miss. I'll fetch Mrs Dorrin.'

Astor was left alone in the foyer. The place smelled airless and enclosed, as though the leadlight windows hadn't been opened in a very long time.

She wondered what was happening back on the roof garden. With Verrol ejected, would the rest of the band start practising the new versions of their songs with Reeth's new words? Or would they wait for their drummer to return?

Mrs Dorrin appeared at the top of the staircase on the first level. She uttered a cry of delight and came hurrying down.

She was dressed in primrose, with the usual bows and frills and flounces. Everything about her seemed to bounce up and down as she negotiated the steps.

'Astor, my dear! You came!' she exclaimed. 'I thought – I hoped—'

Astor cut short her flustering with a hug. Her mother smelled of perfume and felt warm and rounded under all the frills. At the end of the hug, they both spoke up in the same moment.

'I wanted to tell you—' Astor began.

'I'm so sorry for what happened—' said her mother.

They stopped speaking in the same moment too. Astor understood that her mother wanted to apologise over the engagement that wasn't an engagement. But no apology could excuse what had happened . . . and Astor discovered that, strangely enough, she didn't care anyway. It all belonged in a different time and place, and even her resentment had been somehow left behind.

'Mother.' She took hold of Mrs Dorrin's hands and looked into her face. 'Lorrain Swale has asked me to marry him.'

'But . . . what . . . when . . . I thought . . .?'

'This time it's true. He proposed today.'

There was a long silence. Astor expected to be showered with congratulations. Of course her mother would be overjoyed at this happy ending; of course she would push her daughter into marrying Lorrain.

Perhaps I came here in order to be pushed, thought Astor.

But the response wasn't what she expected. Mrs Dorrin let out a small 'Oh!' of amazement. Then an anxious look crept over her face. 'But do you really love him, dear?'

Astor was taken aback. 'I don't know.'

'Tell me what he said. Tell me everything.'

Before Astor could speak, a voice called out from an upper floor. 'Mrs Dorrin? Mrs Dorrin? Where are you?'

Astor's mother pursed her lips. 'Your stepfather,' she said, unnecessarily. 'Let's find another room. Somewhere more private.'

70

The room they found was very private: a trophy room that was more like a lumber-room. There were no windows, and the only light came in through the door, which they left ajar. Stuffed heads of animals projected from the walls, grotesque silhouettes of horns and snouts and antlers. Fusty smells of hide and fur filled the air.

Astor told her mother about Lorrain's visit to the roof garden and the scene in the bay window, the things he'd said and the way he went down on his knee to propose. 'I think he's genuine,' she concluded. 'I'm sure he's genuine. He's a good person.'

'And very good-looking.' Mrs Dorrin still seemed thought-ful rather than enthusiastic.

'Isn't it everything you always wanted for me?' Astor chal-lenged.

Her mother's reply was another question. 'You've decided to accept him, then?'

'No. I haven't decided anything yet. But I thought you'd be pleased.'

'If you love him. Do you?'

Astor didn't appreciate the interrogation. This wasn't like her mother at all. 'Why shouldn't I love him?'

'That's not an answer, dear.'

'Well, how do you tell?'

'You'll know it if you feel it.'

Astor shook her head. 'I'm still getting used to the idea that *he* loves *me*. Love can grow gradually, can't it? I don't believe you have to fall in love all at once.'

'Not all at once, I suppose. But it has to start with a spark.'

'What sort of spark?' Astor studied her mother's face in the dim light. There was a stillness about her quite unlike her usual fluttering. Astor's resentment changed to curiosity. 'What was it like for you? How did it feel when you fell in love with my father?'

'Ah, that was a long time ago.'

'But you remember?'

'Oh, every detail. It was at a music recital. Chamber music in a private drawing room. I was in the front row, and he was one of the five musicians.'

Her voice had gone very quiet and soft. She paused, but Astor knew better than to interrupt.

'There was something about him, you see. I think it was the way he gave himself so completely to his violin. All the musicians were absorbed and concentrating, but nobody so much as him. His fingers pressing on the strings, his bow sliding back and forth, bringing out the notes. It was just beautiful to watch. I stared and stared at him. I wanted – I don't know what I wanted.'

Astor was moved. She'd always taken her mother's romanticism with a big pinch of salt, but she'd never heard *this* before.

And now . . . an oddly mischievous sort of smile played over her mother's lips.

'I stared at him so hard he must have felt it. He looked up, our eyes met, and he dropped his bow.' An irrepressible giggle slipped out. 'He actually dropped his bow in the middle of the recital!'

'Oh. You broke his concentration.'

'And wrecked the entire performance. He got into awful trouble over it. But that was the only time. Afterwards, I was his greatest strength and support. Just to see him absorbed in his music . . . I loved that about him. He called me his muse—'

'*I heard that!*'

The door flung open and crashed back against the wall. Marshal Dorrin stood outlined against the light. His voice was shaking, his whole body was shaking – with anger.

'You're talking about *him*, aren't you?'

Astor answered for both of them. 'Do you mean Lorrain Swale?'

Her cool tone only infuriated him further, until he could hardly bring out his sentences. 'You know who I mean. *Him!* Don't play that game with me! Don't you dare! I'm not a fool!'

'You were listening at the door,' said Astor's mother quietly.

'I'm your husband! I have a right to know what goes on under my own roof!'

Astor looked from her stepfather to her mother and back again. Where had this fury come from? It was obviously an old story between the two of them. Her mother looked embarrassed, as though over something ugly and unseemly.

'Not now,' she murmured. 'Astor has some news . . .'

Her words didn't even begin to penetrate.

'It's still him!' the Marshal ranted on. 'Always him! Why did you take a second husband if you can't stop thinking about the first? Why didn't you tell me? I should've been told! You should've come right out and said you could never love me!'

'But I do,' said Astor's mother. 'My second love.'

'It's not as much. It's not the same.'

'It's not the same, no. I can't say whether it's as much. One can love different men in different ways.'

'*Phah!*' The Marshal snorted like a cannon going off. 'Women's excuses. Women's trickery! Shuffling the truth! You don't know what loyalty is!'

'I've never looked at another man since I married you.'

'No, but in your memory . . .'

'How do you know what's in my memory?'

'*He* is! Every minute of every day!'

'That's not true.'

'Prove it!'

Astor's mother spread her hands. 'I can't. Of course I can't.'

Astor wished she were somewhere else. She understood why her mother was so embarrassed. It was like someone exposing a gaping wound in public.

She stepped forward in front of her mother and tried to break the thread of the Marshal's monomania.

'I came to give you some news,' she told him. 'Something important that concerns you.'

He did break off, but only to glare at her. Then the accusations came pouring out.

'You came here to talk about him. That's why *you* came. His daughter. His living memory. Doing what you always did. I know what used to go on between the two of you.'

Astor caught a faint shrug of the shoulders from her mother. So this was an old story too? Astor could hardly believe it – yet her stepfather confirmed it with every raging word.

'You thought I didn't know, but I did. Mother and daughter working together. Talking lovingly about him. Talking against *me*. This time I've caught you at it.'

Astor stopped listening; she was busy with the illumination unfolding inside her head. She'd always wondered why her stepfather disliked her, why nothing she did could ever please him. Now she realised it wasn't personal – he didn't even see her as a person. For him, she was no more than the living memory of her father. In the fantasy he'd created, she *had* to be cast as his enemy.

So obvious, yet she'd never guessed! He'd always appeared so controlled and unemotional, while all the while this seething mass of jealousy had been bubbling away underneath. With the intensity of hatred she saw in him now, it was amazing he hadn't thrown her out of his house years ago. In this part of his life, he was a kind of madman.

On and on he ranted. Astor was only half aware of the same phrases and accusations endlessly repeated. She paid attention, though, when he came forward into the room and gripped her mother by the arm. His tone changed suddenly from angry to plaintive.

'I don't want any of this, Mrs Dorrin.' He spoke as though Astor wasn't there. 'I don't like these thoughts in my mind. Tomorrow I have to act as a soldier and a leader. I need to forget this mess and muddle. Come away now.'

He wheeled around, and wheeled his wife around with him. She had no choice but to accompany him step for step. Holding her tight by his side, he marched from the trophy room.

He still hadn't finished, however. Once outside, he slammed the door and plunged the room into total darkness. A moment later, Astor heard a key turn in the lock.

Astor went to the door and turned the handle. Useless, of course. She shook and rattled the door, but it was made of solid oak. Nothing less than a battering ram could have forced it open.

However, the darkness wasn't quite total after all. Her eyes made the most of the thin thread of light coming in under the door. She stared round the room until she could distinguish the projecting shapes of animal heads and several box-like shapes in the corners.

Imprisoned by her stepfather . . . yet she didn't hate him. She'd hated him when he abandoned her to the life of a governess, when she'd still seen him as a war hero and an authority figure. Now he was a smaller, sadder person altogether. She no longer respected him enough to hate.

She went across to investigate the boxes. They were covered with rugs of fur and animal hide. Underneath, she found brass-bound chests – all of them padlocked.

She gathered a few rugs, and made a nest for herself. Leaning back against the wall with a sheepskin pulled up over her knees, she reflected on her current situation.

There was no question now of asking her stepfather for his consent to her marriage with Lorrain Swale. That wasn't a problem, because she didn't want to marry Lorrain anyway.

Her mother was right. The triumph of such a marriage attracted her, but she could never really love Lorrain. There would never be a spark between *them* like the one between her mother and father.

Rejecting Lorrain, of course, she also rejected comfort and security and the lifestyle of her dreams. But were those still her dreams? She was a different person to the girl who'd arrived at Swale House expecting to get engaged three months ago.

When she thought back over the last three months, they hadn't been exactly pleasant. Grief as well as glory, terror as well as elation, bad times as well as good. No, not *pleasant*, but very, very exciting! The thrill of her escape from Swale House . . . the adrenalin rush of performing for a hostile audience . . . the heart-stopping confrontation with Scarrow and his pistol . . . She *liked* the intensity of surviving on the edge! Her new life was better than the old dreams!

And even for the band, did she really want an easy route to the top? The Swales' power and money could guarantee them instant success – but how much more challenging to struggle for it on their own! How much more exciting!

Another thought hovered on the threshold of her consciousness, but she pushed it away. Suddenly restless, she threw off the sheepskin, jumped to her feet and went across to give the door another rattle. This time she tried to make as much noise as possible.

'Let me out! Let me *out*!' she yelled until she was hoarse.

On the other side of the door there was only silence. The servants must have been given orders to ignore her.

She returned to her nest by the wall and snuggled down under the sheepskin again. She had the impression that the stuffed animal heads were leering at her.

The thought that had been hovering came a little closer . . . and closer. She could no longer put it off. It was a thought about her new life . . . about the thrills and excitement . . . and the person who was somehow at the centre of all those things. A man who was the opposite of Lorrain in every respect.

She let his image float before her mind's eye. Tall, lean and rangy . . . with that sardonic, mocking face . . . that lazy, loping gait . . . that underlying taut muscularity. Unpredictable and dangerous, a spring pressed back and ready to explode.

Verrol.

It struck her like a kick in the stomach. She had fallen in love with Verrol!

She only had to think it to know it was true. The most unsuitable person in the world! The very last person she would have wanted to fall for! It was absolutely impossible and absolutely undeniable.

And it had been true for a very long time.

She burst out laughing. What a moment to make the biggest discovery of her life! She laughed and laughed till the tears rolled down her cheeks.

The only witnesses were the stuffed animal heads. Her mother had had her moment during a public music recital – but *hers* was by herself in a darkened room, locked up like a prisoner. Verrol wasn't even here for it!

All she had were her memories. And she didn't have to go very far back before she found one that was particularly significant. Just an hour ago . . . in the instant before she'd slapped him . . .

Do you think mine have?

She'd been too angry to take it in at the time. She'd been shouting at him, insisting on Lorrain's love, telling him that

318

Lorrain's feelings towards her had never changed since he'd first set eyes on her. And Verrol had said, 'Do you think mine have?'

It was a declaration of love! Without tenderness or courtesy, but as plain as if he'd gone down on his knee. A furious, frustrated declaration of love . . . and she'd nearly missed it!

She wiped the tears of laughter from her face. Of course there would be complications – like the quarrel, the band, the three fine ladies. But for the present, it all seemed wonderfully simple. She'd worked one thing out at last, and every other problem would have to fall into place around it.

She rolled over under the sheepskin and curled up with a warm glow of satisfaction. Later she fell asleep, still smiling to herself.

The sound of a key in the lock awoke her. Astor twisted over as the door swung open, and saw her mother standing in the doorway.

'It's all right, dear. Your stepfather has gone off now.'

Astor stretched and sat up. 'So now it's okay to let me out?'

Mrs Dorrin didn't respond to the sarcasm. 'No, there'll be trouble later. But he can't stop me doing it.'

Although she couldn't see her mother's expression, Astor sensed an air of resignation. 'Why do you put up with his madness?'

'Madness? I suppose that's one word for it. He can't help himself. He's obsessed.'

'Since when?'

'It's been growing. Perhaps because of his age. Perhaps something happened when he was wounded in the war.'

'What? It wasn't a head wound, was it? I thought it was his chest?'

'Yes, his chest. That's not what I meant.' Mrs Dorrin took a backward step. 'Come out into the light.'

Astor rose and went to join her mother in the corridor. The daylight was pale and grey, but dazzling to Astor's eyes.

Her mother put a hand on her arm. 'He really was a war hero, dear. I've talked to men he used to command, and they worshipped him. Still do. He was a very brave man, absolutely fearless. And a great general. It was his decisive action that won the Battle of Bratislava.'

'When he got himself wounded, too.'

'Yes. He was shuffled off to administrative duties afterwards, until he recovered. He was still there when the war ended three years later. He never fought again, more's the pity.'

Astor shrugged. 'At least it kept him alive.'

'But it wasn't his sort of life, dear. He was no good at administration. He needed to be up and doing, making decisions in the thick of battle, not stuck behind a desk. Then, after the war, he made the mistake of retiring altogether. And married me, which was the worst mistake of all.'

'Because of *him*. Not because of *you*.'

Astor's mother nodded. 'I'm not disagreeing, dear. I don't expect you to excuse him. I just hope you might understand why *I* can. He used to be a very admirable man.'

'"Used to be"!'

'Even at the time I married him. He was noble and honourable and straightforward. You'd hardly have noticed this one tiny thing eating away at him. This insecurity.'

'But it grew.'

'Yes. I don't even know what began it, some little occasion when he realised I was thinking about your father. I wasn't pining, just remembering. Of course I remembered your father now and then.'

'Of course. There'd be something wrong with you if you didn't.'

'But you see, he had no experience of relationships. He knew I'd been married before, but I don't think he really understood what that meant. A few months into our marriage, he started to become jealous.'

'You should have told me.'

'Perhaps. But then we *would* have been conspiring together, wouldn't we?' Astor's mother shook her head and moved on. 'The trouble was, he had too much time on his hands after he retired. Too much time for brooding. Your stepfather's not a naturally imaginative man – quite the opposite. But when it comes to me and your father, you wouldn't believe the wild fantasies he invents. He knows nothing about women, and he's terrified of what he doesn't know.'

Astor snorted. 'What happened to his bravery?'

'I suppose there's one sort of courage you need for fighting wars and another sort of courage you need for love. You saw him. Just a mass of fears and obsessions.'

'Towards me too.'

'I'm afraid so. You're your father's daughter. And he was fearful of you because he thought you might see through to his weakness. He's ashamed of being jealous even though he can't stop himself. If you saw through to it, you'd condemn him for it.'

'I *do* condemn him for it.'

'I know. The young aren't very kind.'

'He doesn't deserve kindness.'

Somewhere along the corridor, a grandfather clock began chiming out the hour. Astor waited for it to finish . . . and suddenly realised how many strokes it was sounding.

She turned to her mother as the echoes from the final stroke died away. 'What's the time?'

'Twelve o'clock.'

'How did I sleep so long? It's the day of the coup!'

'Yes, that's where your stepfather's gone.'

'When did he leave?'

'A whole hour ago. I had to wait to be sure.'

'It must be happening right now! I have to go!' Astor strode off down the corridor towards the lobby.

Her mother scurried to keep up. 'I heard they plan to reach the Houses of Parliament at one o'clock. He's their figure-head, though I don't know why.'

'He's an old fool is why. The plutocrats are making use of him. They despise him.'

They passed through the lobby, where the servant in military uniform sat on a stool by the door. Astor ignored him and opened the door by herself.

Her mother was still talking, a little breathlessly now. 'That's what I thought. He'd never have stooped to it before. Now he's trying to regain respect . . . play the war hero . . . be the man he once was . . .'

The last words were uttered from the top of the steps as Astor swung away along the pavement.

73

Astor hurried back the way she had come. There were no sounds of militiamen anywhere around now. A rising breeze blew scraps of litter along the empty streets.

She had no time to think about her stepfather or his role in the coup. One single sentence stayed in her mind from all her mother had said: *there's one sort of courage you need for fighting wars and another sort of courage you need for love.* Astor was determined to have the courage for love – and for one man in particular.

Remembering street names, she found her way back to Norfolk Palace without any wrong turns. She was almost there when the eerie calm was broken by a rumble of rolling wheels: the sound of a great many vehicles driving off. Keeping to the shadows, she continued round to the side of the palace, where the rope was.

Climbing up the rope was going to be far harder than climbing down. She gritted her teeth, took a grip . . . and wondered at the vibration of the rope in her hands. Then she realised that someone was already climbing down.

Several storeys above was a dark figure descending in the murk. It was human in its arms and legs, but also with an odd kind of lumpishness. Astor waited.

A minute later, the figure resolved into Purdy, and the lumpishness resolved into the shape of his brass guitar, strapped over his back. The rope lashed from side to side as he came down the last ten feet. Astor let him touch ground before she spoke up.

'What's happening?'

Purdy spun round as if shot. '*You!* We were waiting for you.'

'Where are you off to?'

'We're going to stop a war.'

She gaped at him. 'Uh?'

'Verrol asked us to wait till the last minute. Hoping we could get you to join us.'

'Where is Verrol?'

'Gone on ahead to organise the London street gangs.'

Astor felt as if she'd wandered into someone else's conversation. 'I don't understand any of this.'

'It's the day of the plutocrats' coup,' Purdy explained. 'Did you forget?'

'Of course not. But what's your role? Why you?'

A voice floated down out of the murk. 'We're helping Verrol now.'

Astor looked up and saw another figure on the rope. This time it was Mave. She descended awkwardly with the melodium dangling and bouncing against her hip.

'I thought . . .' Astor turned back to Purdy. 'When I left . . . I thought you were going to vote Verrol out of the band.'

Purdy grinned. 'No way. He's a Stark.'

'You don't mind that he . . .?'

'It was a feud of honour. Kill or be killed.'

Astor had almost forgotten Purdy's strange attitude to the Mauls and Starks. In his eyes they were like legendary heroes.

When Mave touched down, she was grinning too. 'Reeth and Ollifer wanted us to vote Verrol out of the band,' she explained. 'We voted them out instead!'

'Three against two,' Purdy added. 'Mave and me and Verrol. Reeth turned really nasty about it. We haven't seen either of them since.'

Astor was still struggling to adjust. 'So the band's kept its dancer and lost its singer. But what are *you* doing now?'

'We've been politicised,' said Mave with a laugh.

'The London street gangs want to drive out the militias,' said Purdy. 'Verrol's been talking to them. Last night, he brought three gang leaders up on the roof to talk to us. It's all been planned. Stop the coup and stop the war.'

Astor was surprised. She remembered how Granny had hardly cared about the coup. Were the London gangs different, or had something changed?

Before she could ask, Purdy snapped his fingers. 'Enough talking. Will you come with us?'

Astor nodded.

'Let's go, then,' said Purdy, and set off running.

Mave, though, had one more thing to say to Astor. 'Do you see how wrong you were?'

'What?'

'About Verrol and those ladies. You thought he was going off to meet them. When all the time he was going off—'

'To talk with the street gangs!' Astor finished the sentence first.

'Come *on*!' cried Purdy, looking back over his shoulder, about to turn the corner into the next street.

Astor and Mave took off after him. When they reached the corner, he was still forty yards ahead.

'Where are we going?' Astor asked.

Mave answered in short puffs of breath. 'Across the river. Short cut with boats. Gathering in Westminster Gardens.'

Purdy led the way into a broad, curving avenue, then turned sharp right into a long alley. At the end of the alley, they emerged suddenly into a sloping street with high stone kerbs that ran down towards the River Thames.

Mave gestured ahead. 'Nearly there.'

The view between the buildings opened out as they approached. The surface of the river was brown as mud, with a kind of oily sheen. Wisps of mist curled over it – but less smog than Astor had seen in a long while. The breeze over the water must have blown much of it away.

The sky was clearer too. The sun appeared as a pale round blur of yellow, ringed by two yellow haloes. The outer halo extended over half the sky.

As they came closer again, a distinctive marine smell came to Astor's nostrils, a smell of fish and kelp and tar. Now she could see the quay that stretched all along the south bank of the river. Hundreds of boats were casting off and heading out across the water: dinghies and skiffs and small boats of every kind. There were also a few larger barges with paddle-wheels at the back and rotors on top. The rotors whirled round under the force of steam jets issuing from their tips, driving the paddle-wheels by a series of gears and chains.

It was a scene of busy yet organised activity. Everyone involved seemed to know exactly what they were doing. Oars dipped and plunged, voices yelled orders, passengers stepped into boats or waited in lines. Whereas the rowers and crews were all adults, most of the passengers appeared younger. They wore the raggedy clothes and moved with the quick, darting movements of slum kids.

Purdy had stopped at the top of the steps leading down to the quay, surveying the scene.

'Where's Verrol?' asked Astor, as she and Mave ran up.

Purdy pointed, and Astor saw him at once. Tall and lean and unmistakable, he stood at the other end of the quay calling boats up one by one. She wanted to shout out to him, but he was too far away.

326

'Hurry,' said Purdy, and started down the steps. 'Before all the boats are gone.'

Already, the lines of waiting passengers were coming to an end. One particularly large barge took on board the entire remaining queue that Verrol was supervising. Astor bit back her disappointment when she saw him jump across onto the deck himself.

Perhaps it's for the best, she told herself. *Our moment will come later.*

 By the time Astor, Mave and Purdy took their places in a dinghy, Verrol's barge was halfway across the Thames. Other boats bobbed around them, but they were at the tail end of the flotilla. The majority of the street-kid army had already disembarked on the north bank.

Purdy sat in the prow, while Astor and Mave occupied the stern. Their rower sat amidships, a solidly built woman with arms like tree trunks.

'So you're not getting married to Lorrain Swale,' said Mave.

'No.' Astor looked at her curiously. 'How do you know?'

'Because it's Verrol you want.'

Astor pulled a wry face. Was she really so obvious?

'You worked it out quicker than I did,' she said.

They fell silent for a while. Astor looked out across the water and listened to the waves slapping under the sides of the dinghy. There were several artificial islands moored in the Thames, with canvas changing booths, diving platforms, and masses of red, white and blue bunting.

'Did you hear what he said yesterday?' she asked at last.

'When?'

'Just before I hit him across the face. I think I heard him say, "Do you think mine have?" Meaning that his feelings for me have never changed.'

'I heard it too. Meaning that he's always been in love with you.'

'So I can't resist him and he can't resist me!' Astor exulted.

'Congratulations.'

Astor remembered Mave's love song to Verrol and realised how hurtful her words might be. 'I'm sorry. I didn't intend to . . . But you did say he was only a daydream for you.'

'I wasn't being sarcastic. Congratulations. He's the one you want.'

'Yes, he is. He *is*!' Astor couldn't help herself – she was too elated to worry about Mave's feelings for long. 'I wish I could write songs like you. I'd write the most passionate love song ever written. Burning like flames of fire.'

'That's a song I could never write. All *my* love songs are sad. You're more of a happy person.'

'I will be.' Astor laughed and clenched her fists. 'I'll make sure of it!'

There was no stone quay on the north bank of the river, only a series of floating wooden wharves. As the dinghy nosed in, Purdy stood in the prow and looped the painter round an iron bollard.

'Westminster Gardens,' their rower announced, speaking for the first time in the whole journey.

The gardens were at the top of a grassy slope. Astor, Mave and Purdy climbed the slope and came to a strip of densely planted trees and evergreen shrubs. On the other side of the vegetation was a park – and the throb and murmur of a vast crowd of people.

The street kids had climbed the trees and hidden in the shrubs, quietly surveying the crowd. Astor, Mave and Purdy crept forward from cover to cover until they found an untenanted shrub, a perfect observation post. They burrowed into it, parted the leaves and looked out.

It was an intimidating sight. Several thousand militiamen had assembled in their companies, filling the park from side to side. They displayed regimental flags, wore patched-up versions of military uniform, and carried either rifles or pieces of wood carved and painted to resemble rifles.

Purdy pointed. 'Look there!'

Astor looked and saw a line of vehicles drawn up in the street that bordered the park. There were traditional coaches and carriages, low-slung velocipedes, and steam-powered charabancs with tall, shiny funnels. Some were decorated with exotic animal fur, and Astor knew at once to whom they belonged.

'Plutocrats,' she muttered.

Then a buzz of anticipation drew her attention to two floats set up in the middle of the crowd. They were like high mobile stages, cloth-covered and cordoned with brass poles and ropes at the top. A number of figures had just mounted the steps and were taking up position on the left-hand float.

Bartizan and Phillidas Swale stood side by side, with Lorrain a little further back and the Duchess of Norfolk a little to the front. A uniformed officer held up an enormous megaphone for the Duchess to speak into.

'Soldiers! Fellow countrymen!' she began. 'Defenders of our land! Today you are needed as never before! Britain must be defended – from itself! Defended from a peace that destroys us like a cancer!'

Her words were stirring but her voice was thin and weak, even through the megaphone. Her distinctive aristocratic accent didn't help either. When she spoke of making Britain strong again and achieving the goals abandoned at the end of the Fifty Years War, there were a few yells of approval from the crowd, but no great surge of enthusiasm.

Astor soon stopped listening and focused on Lorrain instead. Did he still hope to marry her? She watched how he fidgeted and shuffled and looked awkward beside his brothers. His whole body language announced that he didn't want to be there on the float – yet he *was* there, nonetheless. He had given in to his brothers' wishes, as he always would. How could she ever have considered his proposal? Even if he gave in to *her* wishes, she didn't want a man she could just order around.

The Duchess concluded her speech to a smattering of applause, then introduced 'the great patriot and industrialist, Mr Bartizan Swale'. Bartizan stepped forward and seized the mouthpiece of the megaphone with both hands. Clearly he meant business.

'Yes, patriot and industrialist!' he bellowed. 'I take pride in those words! I'm a plain-spoken man, and I stand here today to make you a promise. When we topple this Hassock government and start the next great war, each and every one of you that wants a job will have one. That's a promise!'

It was like a match to kindling. The militiamen roared their support and acclamation. This was what they had come to hear.

'You made the sacrifices in the last war,' Bartizan went on. 'You did your bit for your country. Until the pacifists of the Rural Party manipulated their way into power! Gained the ear of King George! Declared peace! They're the ones who betrayed you! Those pacifists over there!'

He swung an arm, and the crowd turned their heads in the same direction. Astor couldn't see where he was pointing, but she knew the Houses of Parliament were close by.

'So this is my promise – *our* promise, endorsed by every industrialist and factory-owner in the country. As soon as we can start up our factories again, you'll have the first choice of jobs. Comfortable, well-paid jobs! If you want to go off and fight overseas, of course you'll be the officers in charge. But you don't have to go off and fight. You've already proved your patriotism. Now it's time for you to receive the rewards.'

The roar of the crowd grew louder and louder. Bartizan planted his feet further apart and hooked a thumb in his waistcoat pocket. 'Time for you to receive the rewards,' he repeated. 'And time for other people to make the sacrifices. The beggars, the thieves, the parasites in the slums! The young scum who infest our towns and cities! They're the ones we'll sweep up off the streets. Clean them out of this country and send them all overseas! Let them face the bullets! *They'll* be the foot-soldiers in the next great war!'

The militiamen broke into a mighty cheer. It seemed they were almost as eager to see others suffer as to receive rewards themselves. Astor began to understand why the London street gangs had become so determined to stop the coup.

She turned to Mave and Purdy, standing beside her in the shrub. 'Did you know about this?'

'Only since last night,' answered Mave.

'Verrol and the gang leaders expected it,' said Purdy. 'They explained it to us.'

Meanwhile, Bartizan was bellowing at the top of his voice to be heard above the din. 'King George is at the Houses of Parliament right now! He needs to listen to your views! He needs to hear what you want! War or peace?'

'War! War! War!' The response was a chant that spread from one side of the park and swelled to an ear-splitting volume. '*War! War! War! WAR! WAR! WAR!*'

'Then let's march!' thundered Bartizan.

Phillidas, who had played no part until now, strode to the side of the float and clapped his hands. It was a signal to a whole group of people who had come up on top of the second float. Astor gasped as she recognised Ollifer and Reeth . . . and not only Ollifer and Reeth but the Silver Rose Band . . . and not only the Silver Rose Band but the Swale children, Blanquette, Prester and Widdy!

Astor heard a hiss of indrawn breath from Mave. 'They're replacing us! This is the alternative plan!'

It made sense. The members of the Silver Rose Band had brought their instruments with them: two trumpets, a trombone and a drum kit. Widdy carried a rattle as big as his head, Prester a tambourine and Blanquette a pair of cymbals. But Astor had eyes only for the changed colour of Blanquette's hair. The girl had dyed it pure white in imitation of the white growing through in Astor's hair!

She wants to be like me, thought Astor in amazement. *She wants to be me!*

Then Phillidas shouted, 'Now! March!'

Blanquette clashed her cymbals, Prester shook his tambourine, and the Silver Rose Band launched into a marching song.

'*To the Houses of Parliament!*' boomed Bartizan through the megaphone.

Company by company, the militiamen wheeled and marched off towards the street that led to the Houses of Parliament. The floats moved too, hooked up to traction engines, gliding on hidden wheels. The band continued to play as they rolled along. With so many brass instruments, they didn't sound at all like the Rowdies, yet they were playing the familiar tune of 'Hair Hang Down'.

Astor was hardly aware of the disturbance behind her in the shrub, or the urgent exchange of words. But she turned when Purdy jogged her elbow.

'Come on!' he cried. 'We're going to the Houses of Parliament. A different way round the back.'

 The different way was along the grassy slope by the river's edge. Once again, Astor, Mave and Purdy found themselves at the tail end of the street-kid army. Hundreds of raggedy figures flitted ahead: dirty, unkempt, wearing odds and ends of clothing. Apart from the lack of metal jewellery and the coloured armbands they wore over their sleeves, they looked much like the inhabitants of Slumtown in Brummingham. The odds and ends of clothing included bowler hats, braces, mittens, clogs and brass-buckled belts.

The grass came to an end at a stone wall, where a grand brick building looked out over the Thames. The street kids vaulted over the wall, streamed across a terrace and arrived at a pavement with cast-iron lampposts. On the other side of the road stood the Houses of Parliament.

Astor looked to the right as she crossed the road, and saw the militiamen crossing the very same road two hundred yards away. They were marching to the rhythm of the replacement band, heading for the front of the Parliament building. They seemed not to notice the parallel army of street kids heading for the back. Astor could hear Ollifer singing at the top of his voice – Reeth's new martial lyrics, of course.

High spiked railings surrounded the riverside gardens behind the Houses of Parliament. The street kids had already bent the bars apart in several places. Astor squeezed sideways through a gap; Mave and Purdy had to unstrap their instruments before they could pass through behind her.

They came out among flowerbeds and manicured lawns, miniature hedges and ornamental ponds. It would have been a peaceful setting but for the street kids swarming all over it. Astor, Mave and Purdy joined the throng that was gathering between two projecting wings at the back of the building.

The building itself was three storeys high, with stone buttresses, stone carvings and pointed stone arches. Castle-like battlements topped the walls, and the roof above was a brilliant, burnished gold. Everything about the architecture spoke of pomp and majesty. On the bottom floor, the doors were French windows with panes of glass all the way down to the ground.

'What's happening here?' Astor asked the kids in front of her. 'Are there guards blocking the way?'

'Nah, they're all on the other side.'

'That's where we should be too,' said Purdy.

'When we're ready. Shush and listen.'

Everyone fell silent as a tall, rangy figure took up position before the glass doors. It seemed that Verrol was in charge of this particular operation. Other gang leaders stood beside him, nodding silent support as he addressed the horde.

'Listen up. The militias and plutocrats aim to get what they want by a show of force, so we have to make a better show. We *out-demonstrate* them. A few of you have pistols, but whatever you do, don't use them. They have many more guns than us. If it turns into a shooting match, we're finished.'

Astor surveyed the kids around her, and for the first time noticed the range of weapons they carried: sticks, chains, iron bars, blades, even an old cutlass. She didn't see any pistols, though.

'We out-demonstrate them with more noise, more aggression, more determination,' Verrol went on. 'We have to throw them off balance, make them lose heart. They have their band to inspire them – but we have the original Rowdies. These are our other weapons!' He fished in his jacket pocket and brought out the clapper and pealer. 'Our band will swamp their band!' His gaze searched the throng. 'Band members, step forward, please!'

Of course, he expected Mave and Purdy to be there, but he didn't know about Astor. His voice had radiated confidence when he said, 'Our band will swamp their band,' but he couldn't hide the undertone of anxiety when he asked the band members to step forward.

Then his gaze found Astor in the throng, and his face lit up. Though it might not have been obvious to anyone else, she saw how the stress dropped from him. When he grinned, it wasn't one of his usual sardonic grins, but simple relief and delight. As she made her way forward behind Purdy and Mave, he whirled his clapper and pealer in the air.

'The Rowdies!' Purdy responded, and raised his guitar in a triumphant flourish.

Verrol couldn't take his eyes off Astor. He returned the clapper and pealer to one jacket pocket and produced her drumsticks from another.

'I brought them from the roof garden,' he said, holding them out to her. 'I never gave up hope.'

She quirked an eyebrow as she took them from him. 'Pity you couldn't bring my drums as well.'

'You'll find substitutes.' He was still grinning. 'Friends again?'

Astor shook her head. 'No.'

She could have laughed aloud at the sudden alarm that dashed the grin from his face. *Much, much more than friends*, she thought.

'Tell you afterwards,' she said.

Looking into her eyes, he must have found something to restore his hope. He turned to the street kids and raised an arm. 'Okay! Let's out-demonstrate them! Let's go!'

There was a sound of breaking glass, followed by a cheer as the doors swung open. The street-kid army surged into the ground floor room of the Parliament building.

It was a wide space of green carpet and dark polished wood, with relatively little furniture. Oil paintings hung on every wall, portraits of notable past MPs and ministers. A staircase curved up to a higher floor, blocked off by a barrier and a sign that said

SESSION IN PROGRESS

Astor scanned around for substitute drums. Immediately her gaze fell upon two great bronze urns that stood on either side of the staircase. Perfect as drums – once emptied of the potplants growing in them. She seized one and up-ended it, scattering soil and potplant all over the carpet.

336

Mave caught onto the idea and did the same for the other urn. 'I'll carry this for you!' she cried.

Then Purdy discovered a drum of a different kind. It was an umbrella stand, a hollow cylinder of wood inlaid with copper. He tossed out the umbrellas and brought it across as a third item for the drum kit.

Meanwhile, the front of the street-kid army had advanced to the opposite side of the building. The French windows here were identical to the ones they'd just entered. For a moment they crowded behind the glass, until Verrol gave the command.

'*Now!*' he yelled.

More sounds of breaking glass, another forward surge, and the horde poured out through the open doors. Astor, Mave and Purdy were carried along in the rear of the flood.

Out in the open, the anti-government demonstration was already in full swing. Astor would have clapped her hands over her ears if her hands had been free. The noise was deafening and the scene was like a madhouse.

The forecourt of the Houses of Parliament was a level expanse of cobblestones. It was enclosed by high spiked railings similar to those that surrounded the gardens at the back. A line of Parliamentary guards stood inside the railings with rifles raised – about forty of them, ceremonially dressed in braided red coats, plumed helmets and very white breeches.

Outside the railings, the militiamen massed in their

thousands. Their roaring and chanting was a constant barrage of sound. The ones at the front gripped and shook the railings; the ones further back brandished their rifles in the air – or rifle-shaped pieces of wood.

The roaring and chanting kept time with the music of the Silver Rose Band, coming from their float behind the railings. Reeth capered around encouraging the musicians like a conductor, while Ollifer accompanied his singing with operatic gestures directed towards the Houses of Parliament. The Swale brothers and the officer with the megaphone still stood on the other float, which was drawn up nearby. The Duchess had apparently climbed down.

Meanwhile, the street kids had halted behind the line of guards, unsure of their next move. The cacophony of sound seemed to have stunned them.

Astor leaned across to Purdy and yelled in his ear. 'Where do we set up the drums?'

'Where's Verrol?' Purdy mouthed back.

At that moment, the Silver Rose Band reached the end of a militarised version of 'Break-out Time'. Up on the band's float, Reeth signalled for silence. Gradually the roaring and chanting fell away, and all eyes turned to the other float.

An upright figure with a mane of silvery hair was mounting to the platform. Marshal Dorrin's hour had come. Bartizan, Phillidas and Lorrain stepped aside as he advanced to the cordon at the front. He was dressed for the part in full military uniform, with rows of ribbons and medals displayed across his chest.

A spontaneous burst of cheering and applause erupted from the ex-soldiers all around. The hero of the Battle of Bratislava had lost none of his glamour in their eyes. A few of them raised rifles and fired shots into the air.

The Marshal raised an authoritative hand. 'No shooting!' he ordered. He repeated the order when the officer with the megaphone swung the mouthpiece towards him. 'No shooting. This is a peaceful demonstration. Stand at ease.'

Then Phillidas came forward to hand him a scroll of paper. Marshal Dorrin unfurled it, cleared his throat and began.

'Your Majesty, we have four demands to lay before you.'

Astor whirled to look where the Marshal was looking. Above her head was a balcony that projected from the second storey of the Parliament building. She couldn't see who stood there from her position underneath – but presumably King George himself had come out to face the crowd.

'Four demands or, um, points of principle,' the Marshal continued. He read from the scroll. '*Point number one. An end to unemployment. Start the factories working again. Justice for those who served. Punish the parasites.*'

There was a hubbub of excited chatter from the balcony above.

'What nonsense is this?'

'They don't have the right!'

'Why are we even listening?'

'The Parliament votes on policy!'

Obviously the King wasn't the only one who had come out to face the crowd. By the reaction, Astor guessed that members of the governing Rural Party were also up there.

'*Point number two,*' the Marshal continued. '*The King must dismiss Norbus Hassock and appoint a new Prime Minister. Out with Hassock and in with Ephraim Chard.*'

The militiamen cheered. 'Out with Hassock!'

'Dismiss him!'

'Down with the PM!'

'Bring in the other one!'

They hardly seemed to know the name of 'the other one'. Marshal Dorrin read on.

'*Point number three. A new cabinet. Dismiss Dottering and appoint Shanks as Minister of Defence. Dismiss Averill and appoint Stigwell to Foreign Affairs. Dismiss Borsted and appoint Tumbley as Home Secretary.*'

The chatter on the balcony turned into outrage and alarm.

'The Progress Party's behind this!'

'They're trying to take control!'

'They don't have the numbers in the House!'

But other voices shouted back.

'Yes, we do!'

'We can form a majority!'

'Your time is over! You've had your chance!'

The last shout reminded Astor of the ringing tones of Ephraim Chard. It seemed that Opposition MPs from the Progress Party had come out on the balcony too.

'*Point number four.*' Amplified by the megaphone, the Marshal's voice overrode all others. '*The King must tear up the Peace of Brussels and declare war on either France and Prussia or Russia and Austria.*'

The quarrel overhead intensified. The Progress Party went at it hammer and tongs with the Rural Party.

'You want to start another Fifty Years War!'

'What's wrong with war?'

'We're still the government!'

'We have the support of the people!'

'Only ex-soldiers!'

'The best of the people!'

In the middle of the uproar, Mave suddenly pointed. 'There's Verrol. He's calling us over.'

340

'Let's go!' cried Astor.

They pushed forward through the street-kid army. Verrol stood at the very front, just behind the line of Parliamentary guards.

'Here?' Astor demanded.

He brought out his clapper and pealer. 'Yes, this'll do.'

Astor put down her bronze urn on the cobblestones. Mave and Purdy arranged the other two makeshift drums alongside, then readied their own instruments.

But suddenly the King himself began speaking from the balcony. Astor glanced back and saw a single figure in red robes among the black-suited MPs. Flowing red robes, white ermine collar and cuffs, the royal crown on his head . . . King George was in formal regalia for the opening of Parliament. He had remained aloof from the quarrelling so far; now he addressed himself exclusively to Marshal Dorrin.

'I hope you can explain this behaviour, Marshal.' He sounded a little peeved and a little pompous. 'The King is sole Commander-in-Chief of the British armed forces, or had you forgotten? There will be no war until I declare it.'

Marshal Dorrin had been standing at attention, but now he became even more stiff and straight. 'We know that, Your Majesty. We only offer you advice. Better advice than the Rural Party has been giving you.'

'When I say Commander-in-Chief, Marshal, I mean your Commander-in-Chief. You may be retired, but you still owe me your loyalty. And I tell you, we have seen enough young lives lost in senseless war. I need no one's advice to make up my mind about *that*. Peace is—'

'Long live the King!' Reeth broke in on King George mid-sentence, yelling at the top of his voice. 'Music!'

The Silver Rose Band struck up a new song to the tune of 'Be with Me Soon'. Reeth pushed Ollifer to the front of their float. 'Sing!'

Ollifer sang.

> *'Soldiers of Britain,*
> *Faithful and true!*
> *Fight the King's enemies,*
> *March to war soon!'*

'No!' cried King George. 'That's not what I—'

'Louder!' ordered Reeth, and the Silver Rose Band drowned the King out with a further level of volume.

> *'Fight for our Monarchy!*
> *Fight for our Law!*
> *Be with me by my side*
> *Marching to war!'*

The militiamen stamped their feet in time to the rhythm and pressed forward against the railings. The Parliamentary guards began to back away, pace by pace.

'Stand fast!' Verrol shouted.

But the guards shook their heads.

'Look at those railings.'

'They're going to give way.'

'It's not like our rifles are loaded.'

The militiamen were now deliberately shaking the railings, which bent over at an alarming angle. Ollifer's soaring voice seemed to inspire them to greater and greater efforts.

Astor prodded Verrol with the end of her drumstick. 'Let's play!'

But it was too late. Fifty yards of railing collapsed under the weight of bodies pressing forward. Astor sensed rather than saw the Parliamentary guards turn tail and flee.

'Run, lads!'

'Save yourselves!'

With Verrol, Mave and Purdy, she stood behind her drums as a great tide of militiamen trampled over the railings and swept down towards them.

It was a mob charge, but they had military discipline too. Shoulder to shoulder they ran, holding their rifles like lances before them. The genuine rifles were tipped with bayonets, the wooden replicas were tipped with knives. Astor, Verrol, Purdy and Mave had nothing except their musical instruments.

Astor watched her death rushing towards her. They had no time to retreat. Then Mave shouted something – Astor didn't catch the words, but she saw Mave was facing the other way round. She swung round herself . . . and there was the street-kid army rushing to save them!

It was the strangest sight. The street kids had taken down oil paintings from the ground floor walls of the Parliament building and carried them now as shields. The advancing portraits looked like an advancing line of be-robed and bewhiskered old gentlemen.

Baffled by this unexpected counterattack, the militiamen slowed down. The street kids whooped and accelerated. The two lines met with a clash just in front of the Rowdies. Astor saw bayonets and knives stab into the paintings, chewing through canvas and wood. Few of the blades penetrated far enough to endanger the kids behind. Before the militiamen could withdraw their weapons for a second thrust, the street kids pushed. Around Astor, Verrol, Purdy and Mave, they pushed so hard they forced their opponents back ten paces.

The militiamen pushed too. It turned into a kind of stalemate, giving ground in one place or losing ground in another, half a yard forward or back. Although the street kids were quick and clever, the militiamen had superior weight and numbers – and the psychological advantage of the Silver Rose Band spurring them on. But the Rowdies could do something about that.

'Play!' cried Astor. '"Made for Love"!'

She seized her drumsticks and launched into the opening bars. The bronze urns gave off a strange, deep resonance, the upturned umbrella stand had a satisfyingly sharp snap. The overall sound grew more familiar when Verrol joined in, then Purdy and Mave. The one thing missing was a singer. Ollifer's powerful voice was working against them, on an opposing song and a contrary rhythm.

'Come on!' Astor shouted. 'More power!'

With pounding drumsticks, she extracted maximum volume from the urns and umbrella stand. 'Made for Love' was still one of their most driving songs, and it was starting to have an effect. The nearest kids pushed forward with new determination and advanced another half yard. Although the Rowdies' music was no louder than the Silver Rose Band's, it was much closer to where the action was.

But the balance was about to change. Astor groaned when

she saw Reeth and Prester mounting the steps at the back of their float. They must have left to cross to the other float, because now they returned bearing the huge cone of the megaphone. Clearly they planned to amplify Ollifer's already sonorous voice!

> *'Raise the flag and fight the fight!*
> *British soldiers, British might!'*

With Reeth supporting the megaphone on his shoulder, Ollifer sang out far and wide. The militiamen took fresh heart and drove the street kids back over the half yard they'd recently gained.

A singer, thought Astor. *We have to have a singer.*

'You!' she yelled at Verrol. 'You sing!'

'What?'

'Be our singer! Use your voice!'

'But—'

'Just make it loud!'

Verrol started to sing the words of 'Made for Love', tentatively at first, then more and more forcefully. He could hold a note and he certainly had the volume; it was the husky, rasping quality of his singing that was so odd. But the oddity didn't matter right now.

Again the balance tilted. For those close by, Verrol's voice matched Ollifer's for volume. What's more, Astor, Purdy, Mave and Verrol were better musicians than the Silver Rose Band, and 'Made for Love' had a stronger rhythm.

Astor could see the street kids nodding their heads in time to the beat. Some of them joined in the chorus line.

'Made for, made for, made for *love!'*

The song came to an end with a final repeated chorus – and as it happened, the Silver Rose Band's song came to an end at the very same time. In the pause that followed, Bartizan Swale pointed to the Rowdies and bellowed an order. 'Soldiers! Silence that other band!'

The militiamen might not have taken the order from him alone, but they listened when Marshal Dorrin repeated it. 'Yes, silence that other band. Engage and pin enemy centre. Enfilading column to the left. Cut them out of the line.'

The military language meant nothing to Astor. She watched companies of troops march across and mass opposite the Rowdies, like a sea with swirling currents. The part of the front that faced them was now more densely packed than anywhere else, a dozen soldiers deep.

'Rifle butts and bayonets only,' the Marshal commanded. 'No shooting. We don't fire on civilians.'

Company leaders barked out orders, and soldiers pressed forward in an organised advance directed specifically against the Rowdies. Meanwhile, the Silver Rose Band struck up another song from the Rowdies' repertoire. It was the tune of 'Down in the Channel', but with a modified rhythm and completely different words.

Astor jumped to a new possibility. 'Play the same song in the real version!' she shouted.

She beat out the original rhythm on her drums while Verrol roared and rasped out the original words. He had obviously memorised the lyrics to all the band's songs.

The soldiers advancing towards the Rowdies made a gain of three yards before the street kids dug their toes in the cracks between the cobbles, bent lower and leaned their shoulders into their makeshift shields. Some of them cried out as knives and bayonets found their flesh. But they held the line, and the advance ground to a halt.

Astor felt as if she was pushing back too, infusing energy into the kids' resistance. She redoubled her efforts, and so did Verrol, Purdy and Mave. Three verses into the song, their efforts paid off. Ollifer stumbled over his words!

Mave flashed Astor a grin, Purdy swung his guitar in triumph. Verrol just sang louder than ever – and Ollifer stumbled again.

It was exactly as Astor had hoped. Ollifer had sung the original words to the original rhythm hundreds of times, whereas he had learned Reeth's new words only over the last few days. When the real version got into his head, he couldn't drive it out.

He struggled . . . and the Silver Rose Band struggled with him. They had scarcely practised with Ollifer beforehand, and it showed. As for Blanquette's cymbals and Prester's tambourine, they were more of a distraction than a help, while Widdy's rattle missed two beats out of three. The harder they all tried, the more ragged they became.

Astor willed them to failure. *Get it wrong, get it wrong, get it wrong!* With the real version of 'Down in the Channel' winning out, the militiamen were surely losing impetus.

Except they weren't. Suddenly a hand looped round her neck, clamped onto her chin and yanked her head backwards. Another arm appeared on the other side, tattooed, with an elastic bandage over the wrist. There was a smell of sweat and bad breath, and the touch of cold metal at her throat.

She couldn't move her head, but she could swivel her eyes – just far enough to glimpse the face that leered over her shoulder.

347

'Yes, it's me. Did my wrist in, didn't yer?' he hissed.

It was the militiaman from the railway carriage. Scarrow.

Scarrow wasn't alone. Behind her, Astor glimpsed a dozen more militiamen hurrying forward. They must have penetrated the street kids' line in some other place, then run around at the back. This was the true point of the attack; the push from the front had been merely a diversion.

Her warning cry was cut short as the hand tightened over her chin and reduced her voice to a gurgle. 'Look ou – *ergh!*'

Verrol, Mave and Purdy broke off, spun around – but it was already too late. Scarrow's attack team came up on either side and encircled the whole band. They were armed with bare bayonets, the blades without the rifles.

Verrol looked ready to spring, but Scarrow pressed his blade against Astor's throat.

'Back off!' he snarled.

Verrol stayed where he was. Astor felt the sting of the blade drawn lightly across her throat.

'*Back off!*'

Verrol backed off a step, and so did Mave and Purdy. The street kids glanced over their shoulders and saw what was happening, but they were locked in their own struggle. Their shields were the only bulwark that stopped the main mass of soldiers flooding forward.

Verrol's hands clenched and unclenched as his eyes held Scarrow's. 'Let her go.'

Scarrow sneered. '*Let her go?* Is that the best you can do?'

'I'm warning you.'

'Well, well. I'm shaking in my shoes. Pity you don't have a gun on me this time.' Scarrow spat out a blob of spittle that landed on the front of Verrol's jacket. 'Take her drumsticks,' he ordered the nearest militiaman.

Astor couldn't use her arms with the blade at her throat, but she still had hold of her drumsticks – until the militiaman wrested them from her. He looked inquiringly at Scarrow.

'Break them.'

Unable to snap them in his hands, the man broke them over his knee.

'Now smash her drums.'

Other militiamen knocked over the two bronze urns and the umbrella stand. They couldn't do much damage to the urns, but they kicked a great hole in the umbrella stand.

Scarrow nodded with satisfaction. 'Now you,' he told Verrol. 'Clapper and pealer. At my feet.'

Verrol stepped forward, holding out his clapper and pealer.

'At my feet. Kneel and lay them at my feet.'

Verrol's mouth was a thin, tight line, his eyes unreadable. He knelt and placed the clapper and pealer by Scarrow's feet.

'Stay where you are,' Scarrow ordered, and kicked out suddenly at Verrol's face. Verrol swayed to the side and avoided the blow. Still he remained kneeling.

'You gutless coward.' Scarrow pulled back on Astor's head and made a menacing gesture with his blade. 'What are you?'

'A gutless coward,' Verrol repeated in a quiet, flat voice.

Astor couldn't stand it. 'You're the gutless one, Scarrow. He can't do anything while you're threatening me.'

'More than a threat, girlie.'

'You kill me and he'll kill you. You wouldn't stand a chance against him, one on one. You don't know what he can do.'

'Nothing much, by the time I finish with him.'

'You're a fool, Scarrow. You're not the killer. *He* is. It's what he used to do.'

Scarrow said nothing, and Astor wondered what was passing through his mind. Verrol hadn't moved a muscle, but he had that coiled-spring look. How quickly could he strike? Could he do it before Scarrow slashed the blade across her throat?

'Don't bring out the killer in him,' she advised. 'Let me go, walk away, and nothing will happen. He doesn't *want* to kill you.'

Scarrow only laughed. 'No, he wants to be a gutless coward. I reckon I'll need to kill you first to put a bit of fight into him.'

As his hand closed over her mouth and nose, something exploded in Astor's mind: fury, defiance, a crazy recklessness. She twisted her mouth to the side and cried, 'Do it, then! Try it and find out what—'

It was so fast that even Astor couldn't see what happened – and she'd been expecting it. In the first moment, Scarrow dropped as if chopped off at the knees, and the edge of his blade, instead of slicing sideways, scraped harmlessly over her collarbones. In the second moment, his direction was reversed, and he shot violently upwards. He flew through the air, crashed into one of the militiamen, and tumbled to the ground.

In the third moment, Verrol was on his feet beside Astor. 'You okay?'

'Not a scratch.'

'That was insane. Why did you—?'

He was interrupted by an animal-like growl from Scarrow, who was getting slowly back on his feet. The militia leader had

350

lost his bayonet, which lay nearby on the cobbles. Blood pulsed from his nose and trickled over his chin.

'You'll die for that.' He spat out a tooth and turned to the surrounding militiamen. 'Grab him, lads. All together. Beat him to a pulp. Just leave me the final blow.'

The men came forward with out-thrust bayonets. They seemed more cautious than their leader, circling this way and that, each waiting for someone else to move first.

'Stick him!' roared Scarrow. 'Make him bleed!'

Quick as a whip, Verrol reached out for the nearest soldier, twisted his wrist and caught the bayonet as it fell from his grasp. Then he pivoted, struck another soldier in the face with the hilt and kicked a third soldier's legs out from under him. A fourth soldier took a slash to his arm that made him drop his blade; a fifth lunged forward only to find himself whirling away in the opposite direction.

Compared to Verrol's dancing poise, his opponents seemed off-balance, comically clumsy. He struck another in the solar plexus, swung two more together so that their heads clashed with a tremendous *crack!* In a matter of seconds there was no one left to fight. The militiamen who remained on their feet retreated to a safe distance.

Verrol turned to Scarrow. 'Now, just you and me.' Verrol's voice remained calm and level, though he was breathing in short, sharp breaths. 'To the death?'

But Scarrow had seen enough. His eyes were wide and his rage had evaporated.

'No.' He started to back away. 'Not a fair fight.'

Verrol lifted the soldier's bayonet he still held in his hand. 'You mean this?' He pointed to Scarrow's bayonet. 'There's yours. Take it.'

Scarrow made no move towards the bayonet. Astor stepped forward, picked it up and held it out, hilt first, towards him. He shook his head.

'You prefer to fight hand-to-hand?' Verrol inquired in the same level tone.

'I don't want to fight.' Scarrow appealed to Astor. 'You said I could walk away. Tell him to let me go.'

'That was before,' Astor answered.

When Verrol took a step towards him, Scarrow's courage failed completely. He scrambled away and tried to run. Astor darted forward and tripped him up by the heels. He lay face down on the ground, actually sobbing with fear.

Verrol came forward carrying one of the bronze urns. 'Ask him to sit up.' He grinned.

Astor guessed his plan. 'Sit up, you. Nice and straight.'

She had to prod and kick the militia leader into position. In the end, he sat up straight with his arms at his sides. He offered no resistance as Verrol dropped the urn down over his head and shoulders.

'Perfect fit!' Astor laughed. She used the sole of her foot to push him over on his side. He was helpless in the urn, arms trapped and head enclosed. Another push sent him rolling away across the cobbles. The other militiamen in his team watched from a distance, showing no inclination to come to their leader's aid.

Astor didn't stay laughing for long, however. That urn had been one of her drums . . . and her umbrella-stand drum had been smashed, her drumsticks broken. Even in defeat, Scarrow's team had achieved their mission of silencing the band.

She surveyed the state of the fighting in general. It wasn't going well for the street kids, who were being forced back all along the line. Ollifer was still singing Reeth's warlike lyrics, while the Silver Rose Band was still pounding out military rhythms.

Up on the balcony, the quarrel had now become an all-in brawl. MPs wrestled and threw punches at one another – including Ephraim Chard. The Leader of the Opposition looked very different with his hair awry and his collar ripped off.

There was a new development in the other direction too. The street behind the floats was now filled with vehicles: the coaches, charabancs and velocipedes of the plutocrats. Like vultures flocking to a feast, they had followed along after the main march to observe the triumph of their coup.

Mave and Purdy came up to discuss the situation. Mave had collected the broken drumsticks, which she displayed with a rueful grimace. 'We can't play without your drums.'

'The Rowdies are nothing without rhythm,' Purdy agreed.

Astor exchanged glances with Verrol. His shrug was an admission that he'd run out of ideas. Astor bit her lip. She had one possible solution, even though it was the height of desperation . . .

'Know what I'm thinking?' she said.

'What?'

'We don't have a drum kit, but someone else does.'

They followed the line of her gaze to the Silver Rose Band on their float.

Purdy whistled. 'Capture *their* drum kit?'

Verrol seemed doubtful. 'We'd have to break through the lines and attack from behind.'

'Yes, and take over their float.' Astor snapped her fingers. 'You get the megaphone to sing through.'

Verrol thought about it, and a smile came over his face. 'Right. What are we waiting for?'

The militia companies pushing against the wall of shields were more numerous in some places than others. Astor, Verrol, Mave and Purdy ran across the forecourt until they found a point where the opposing line was only a single soldier deep. Then Astor had another inspired idea.

'We'll soften them up with missiles!' she cried. 'Cobblestones!'

Astor and Verrol used the bayonets they'd acquired, while Mave and Purdy helped with their fingertips. They dug into the cracks between cobbles and prised up the individual stones. Once the first one was lifted out, the next ones were easier to work loose. Everyone scooped up as many as they could carry.

Then they began the bombardment. From a position behind the street kids, they hurled stone after stone. Soldiers staggered and cried out as the missiles struck home. Some clutched at their heads, streaming blood; a few slumped wordlessly to the ground.

'Now!' Astor ran up to combine with the street kids in the shield wall. 'Pack together!'

She wrapped her arms round two of the kids' waists, bent low, put her shoulders against their backs, and pushed. Verrol and Purdy formed up with their shoulders against *her* back, and Mave completed the scrum at the rear. As a single mass, they bent low and pushed forward together.

The combined weight of bodies bore the street kids forward at the front. The militiamen were slow to react, half of them still nursing injuries from the cobblestones. Suddenly the opposing line broke, the kids cheered in triumph, and the Rowdies burst through to the other side.

'Keep going!' Astor ordered, as she straightened and broke up the scrum. The kids wheeled aside, and the band members continued on ahead.

Still in the lead, Astor didn't head directly for the float, but towards the street behind. 'More cover this way,' she puffed to Verrol, as he caught her up and ran alongside.

No one tried to intercept them. They jumped the flattened railings between the forecourt and street, and plunged in among plutocrats' vehicles. Horses stamped and snuffled, steam engines dripped water and hissed with escaping steam. The plutocrats obviously didn't want to show their faces because every window of every vehicle was covered over with blinds or curtains.

Astor and Verrol ran along between the rows of vehicles, crouching and ducking low. Mave and Purdy were right behind them. There were a few gruff barks of 'Hey!' and 'Hoy!' and 'Where you going?' from drivers who sat muffled up in their greatcoats. They weren't really interested, however; it wasn't *their* battle.

Astor ran until she came level with Ollifer's singing and the Silver Rose Band, then swung to approach from behind. The float rose seven feet above the ground, and a set of steps led up to the platform from the back. The Silver Rose Band played on with no suspicion that their musical enemies were preparing to attack. Astor and Verrol mounted the steps side by side.

Four steps up, they paused to survey the people on the

platform. At the back was the drummer, seated on a stool behind his drum kit; further forward, the two trumpeters and trombonist; then the three Swale children; then Ollifer at the front. Reeth stood on the edge of the stage holding up the megaphone into which Ollifer sang.

Astor pointed at the drummer, and Verrol nodded. Stealthy as ghosts, they came up onto the platform behind their first target. The drummer was lost in his own world of sound and rhythm – until Verrol pulled the stool out from under him and swept him off the back of the stage.

He was too surprised even to cry out. As he fell backwards, Astor snatched the drumsticks from his hands.

The musicians on stage turned to look as their rhythm backing dried up. Astor flashed them a smile and beat out a rat-tat-tat rhythm on the drums. A real gang-music rhythm, played as it should be played.

Meanwhile, Mave and Purdy had also climbed up on top of the float. Purdy advanced on one musician who had swung round with a trombone still raised to his lips. When Purdy seized the horn of the instrument and pushed, the trombonist was forced to back-pedal one step, then another, then another. On the third step, he fell off the edge of the platform.

The trumpeters didn't wait to be treated the same way. They lowered their trumpets, ran for the steps and climbed down of their own free will.

Reeth glared in protest. 'You can't do this! You *can't*!' It was like a complaint against the universe.

'Seems you made another bad career move,' said Verrol.

'Backed the wrong side,' said Mave.

'Failed again,' said Purdy.

'Now you'll never get to the top,' said Astor.

They advanced across the platform, all four of them. Verrol hefted his bayonet lightly from hand to hand.

'*Waa-aa-aa-aah!*' Widdy burst out in a wail and charged full pelt at Astor.

She caught and deflected his lowered head, swinging him away to the side. He continued his charge until he ran right off the float. He was still wailing as he dropped.

Reeth, Ollifer, Blanquette and Prester were corralled in a corner at the front. Reeth carried the megaphone, Blanquette her cymbals, and Prester his tambourine.

'Jump or be pushed,' said Verrol.

For one second, Reeth seemed about to attack them. Then something in Verrol's look made him think better of it.

'Devil take you all,' he snarled. 'Devil take *everything!*'

He dropped the megaphone, turned and jumped. With an air of resignation, Ollifer did the same. Blanquette and Prester stayed teetering on the edge.

'I'm not made for jumping!' Blanquette appealed, spreading her hands.

'Surprise yourself.' Verrol encouraged her with a tiny prick from the point of his bayonet.

Blanquette shuddered, retreated to a final toehold, then gave up. With a groan, she stepped off into empty air and went sailing down. There was a clash of cymbals as she hit the ground.

'Now you,' Verrol told Prester.

'Wait.' Astor caught him by the arm. 'Who's going to hold up the megaphone?'

Prester looked from face to face. 'Me?' he suggested with a hopeful smirk.

Verrol sucked at his lips, then nodded. 'Okay. Pick it up.'

Prester whooped and flung away his tambourine. 'I never liked that stupid thing anyway!'

He seemed happy just to be allowed to stay on stage. He picked up the megaphone and balanced it on his shoulder, as Reeth had done. The mouthpiece was exactly the right height for Verrol to sing into.

But they never launched into their first song. Astor never even made it back to her drums. They froze where they stood – when they saw the number of rifles trained on them from below.

'Shoot them like dogs!' roared the thunderous voice of Bartizan Swale.

Astor looked at Verrol in helpless dismay. Because there had been no shooting so far, they hadn't reckoned with this particular danger. Now dozens of soldiers had turned away from the battle to take aim at the new musicians who'd conquered the float. The Rowdies were exposed and visible on all sides.

'Shoot to kill!' Bartizan thundered again.

'I said no shooting,' barked Marshal Dorrin.

Astor looked across and saw her stepfather and the three Swale brothers on the other float, thirty yards away. The Marshal was scowling and clearly annoyed about having his orders countermanded. Bartizan was fuming, his face so red it was almost purple. But there was one thing Bartizan hadn't taken into account.

'That's your son on that float,' Lorrain warned.

'Shoot to—' Bartizan began again, then stopped.

'Not *me*!' Prester pleaded. 'I don't want to die!'

'Get down from there!' Bartizan roared at him.

But Prester seemed confused and hypnotised by the rifles pointing in his direction. Astor felt sorry for him.

'You'd better go,' she said. 'Jump down now.'

Still he didn't move. Bartizan uttered a sort of strangled sound like an apoplectic bull.

Then Phillidas spoke up in his high, mechanical voice. 'You heard the order, soldiers! Shoot! Only not at the boy!'

The militiamen had their fingers on their triggers, but they didn't open fire. It wasn't so easy to avoid hitting Prester when he stood at the front of the band.

'Go on! Shoot!' Phillidas's voice went up another pitch. Of course, Prester wasn't *his* son.

'*Stop!*' Marshal Dorrin's voice was less piercing than Phillidas's, but it had the authentic ring of military authority. 'This army has only one commander. I give the orders here.'

Phillidas turned on him. 'Then tell them to shoot, you old fool.'

Marshal Dorrin shook his head. 'Lower your weapons, soldiers. A soldier does not fire on unarmed civilians.'

Some rifle barrels dropped, others remained raised. The militiamen were clearly trying to make up their minds.

Phillidas threw himself at the Marshal with a scream of frustration. His tinted glasses were askew on his nose, his bony face was working with passion. He punched out with both fists in a flailing, windmilling sort of attack. Lorrain caught onto his coat-tails in a vain attempt to hold him back.

The Marshal was at a disadvantage in age and height, but he had more experience of fighting. He stepped in between Phillidas's punches and delivered a short arm jab to the midriff.

Phillidas doubled up and let out a *whoof* of air like a deflating balloon. As he staggered back, the Marshal addressed the militiamen again.

'Lower your weapons, soldiers. That's an order.'

This time every rifle barrel went down – and stayed down. The Marshal turned and caught Astor's eye.

She was never quite sure about the meaning of his expression. Was there a hint of shame in it? If so, was he sorry for the way he'd treated her? Or was he simply sorry for becoming a puppet of the plutocrats? Of all possible meanings in that expression, only one was unmistakable – a gleam of recovered pride.

He swung back to the militiamen. 'Soldiers,' he announced. 'We have presented our petition to the King. This demonstration is now over.'

He stood stiffly to attention and raised his gaze to the balcony of the Houses of Parliament. Astor had no doubt that his gaze was focused on the red-robed figure of King George. He clicked his heels and saluted.

The King mouthed something in reply, but Astor couldn't make out the words.

Marshal Dorrin repeated his salute, then performed a smart about-turn. He didn't look at his stepdaughter again, not so much as a glance. The Swale brothers were already on their way to the back of the float, the sagging figure of Phillidas supported by Bartizan and Lorrain. The Marshal marched after them and hurried them down the steps. In the next moment the platform was empty.

Astor snapped her fingers and headed for her new drums. 'Gang-music time!' she shouted. 'Let's blast them out!'

The demonstration didn't end just because Marshal Dorrin said it was over, but the aggressive edge went out of it. The militiamen had been ordered not to shoot at the Rowdies, and they didn't attack in any other way either. For a while they continued to push against the street kids' shields, but many of them lost interest and drifted away from the battle-lines.

The leaders on the plutocrats' side had already left the scene, and it wasn't long before King George departed from the balcony. The MPs stopped fighting, dusted themselves down and followed him back into the Parliament building. Ephraim Chard was the last to leave, with his jacket in shreds and a dismal look on his face.

Astor soon got the hang of her new drum kit. She had a bass drum, a kettledrum, snare drums, side drums and chimes. Although the sounds weren't as interesting as her old pots and pans, they were a great deal louder, and volume was the important thing now. She pounded out the infectious gang-music rhythms, and soon the street kids weren't the only ones nodding their heads in time to the beat.

After a while, the Parliamentary guards with their plumed helmets and white breeches re-emerged and formed up as a second line of defence behind the street kids. They had recovered their courage now that no defence was actually needed.

A little later, the plutocrats' vehicles began to head off. Responding to orders from within, the drivers cracked their whips, or pulled on their levers and cranked up their engines. Every window remained covered; no doubt the plutocrats were more than ever eager to keep their faces hidden. The street kids cheered and hollered to see them go. It was the final confirmation – the anti-war forces had won a complete victory.

Astor began to relax and enjoy herself. She experimented with new effects on her new drums, inserting extra riffs and cross-rhythms. The other band members took their cue from her and threw in their own bits of invention. Soon they were all bouncing off one another and playing as well as they had ever done.

The biggest difference was Verrol's voice. Amplified through the megaphone, it reached out to every corner of the forecourt. Between verses, Verrol danced around with his clapper and pealer, while Prester stayed holding up the huge cone on his shoulder. The boy obviously considered himself part of the band, tapping his foot and joining in on the choruses.

Astor listened through a dozen songs before the realisation crept up on her, that Verrol's voice no longer sounded odd. In fact, it was absolutely *right* for gang music! The more she listened the more she liked it. Liked it – loved it! How could she ever have made fun of it? That husky rasp and the distortion of the megaphone made a perfect combination!

By the end of half an hour, the battle-lines had ceased to exist. Some of the militiamen wandered away, but most stayed on to listen to the music. As they clustered around for a closer look at the musicians, the band's float began to feel like a protected island amid a sea of milling bodies.

Meanwhile the street kids launched into an all-out dancing party, whirling madly around in groups and circles. They drew the guards into the dancing, and even some of the militiamen. Weapons, shields and plumed helmets lay scattered everywhere over the ground.

By the end of an hour, the band had almost run through their entire repertoire. The only remaining number was their especially slow one, Mave's love song. Verrol sang the words as Ollifer had always sung them, with no reference to his own name. Astor glanced towards Mave and had to look away in a hurry before she burst out laughing. He had no idea he was singing about himself!

She couldn't resist; she mouthed the lyrics silently with his name included.

> *'I'm just a ghost of love*
> *Verrol can't feel*
> *Ever be, ever be, ever be real.'*

And then it happened. Suddenly, for no reason at all, Verrol dropped both clapper and pealer. As they hit the platform with a double clunk, he spun round as if he'd been stung – to meet Astor's eyes staring at him.

She burst out laughing uncontrollably. He grimaced and raised his eyebrows . . . but of course she couldn't explain about her mother in the recital and her father dropping his bow.

'Tell you later!' she called out.

He broke into a grin – not his familiar sardonic grin, but almost boyish. She drummed a more emphatic rhythm and drove him back to sing the next verse.

Oh yes, there would be so many things to tell him later!

At the end of the love song, the band started on their repertoire all over again. They were enjoying themselves too much to stop. As night approached, a lamplighter rode up on his bicycle and began lighting gas lamps along the street. Still the Rowdies played on and on. They were inexhaustible.

EPILOGUE

———◆·◆———

Ten days later, Astor, Verrol, Purdy and Mave stood talking with Prime Minister Hassock in the ground-floor room of the Houses of Parliament. The green carpet had been cleaned up, the bronze urns were back in position, and many of the portraits had been re-hung on the walls. Two Parliamentary guards with rifles were stationed at the bottom of the staircase, resplendent in their plumes and braided red coats.

'Such an honour for you, and so very well deserved,' Hassock told the band members. 'There were some suggestions of an Imperial Service Order, but I wouldn't stand for that. Nothing less than an OBE, I said.'

Naturally he was grateful; he would have lost his prime ministership but for the Rowdies. Yet Astor didn't like the hee-haw sound of his voice or the way his smile switched on and off. He smelled of cigars and gentlemen's clubs, and his multiple chins and the size of his paunch spoke of years of good living.

'Today is your day,' he went on. 'The King is in your debt, my party is in your debt, all true-blue Englishmen are in your debt. Thanks to you, we have preserved the traditions of our constitution and the dignity of our monarchy.'

'Oh?' Verrol raised an ironic eyebrow. 'Is that what we did?'

Astor looked beyond Hassock to where the last few MPs

were ascending the staircase. They were all dressed for the ceremony in high collars, cummerbunds and tails. They smiled in the direction of the band as they hurried up to the chamber. Astor trusted their smiles as little as she trusted Hassock's.

'So what's happened to the plutocrats?' she asked.

'Ah, yes, them.' Hassock nodded. 'The ringleaders who haven't fled overseas are under house arrest. We aim to make some examples of them.'

Astor frowned. 'How many?'

'About fifteen. We can't pursue them all or the national economy would come to a halt. Disappointing, I know, but we have to be realistic.'

'What about the Swales?'

'The Swales fled overseas. The whole family, as I understand. Their assets will be confiscated and sold off.'

'To other plutocrats, of course,' said Verrol flatly.

Hassock shrugged and said nothing.

'What about my stepfather?' Astor asked.

'He's back on his estate. The King accepted that he was misled, rather than a ringleader himself. He won't be charged with any crime. That was your petition, wasn't it?'

'Yes.'

'Of course, he's still publicly disgraced.'

Astor felt sorry for her mother, who would share in that disgrace. Would her stepfather become even more paranoid when everyone turned against him? Or would he learn to appreciate the wife who stood by him? Astor hardly expected him to appreciate the stepdaughter who'd saved him from worse punishment.

'What about the kids in the slums?' asked Mave. 'What will you do for them?'

'Ah, indeed, that's a tricky one.' Hassock's smile flashed on and off. 'Naturally the honours bestowed upon you reflect on them all. You could consider yourselves their representatives.'

'I'm sure they'll be very happy to be reflected on,' said Verrol drily. 'But I think the question was, what will you do to improve the condition of their lives? How will you put food in their bellies and roofs over their heads?'

'Mmm, if only it was so simple. We all want to see improvements, of course. But it'll take a long time. We can only make a start.'

'What start are you making?'

Prime Minister Hassock gazed in various directions as though hoping the question would go away. When it didn't, he sighed and stroked his multiple chins. 'There *is* a problem, I'm afraid. By rising up against the coup, the street gangs saved my government and the dignity of the monarchy. That was a very good result. But the rising up in itself was *not* good.'

Astor shook her head. 'How do you mean?'

'Well, we don't want them to get into the habit of rising up, do we? We can't have them marching and demonstrating every time they're not happy about something. If we act immediately to improve conditions in the slums, it'll look as though we're rewarding their behaviour. We can't have them getting *that* impression.'

'So you won't even make a start?'

'Oh, eventually, eventually. We'll have to work out what's best for them. It'll need a great deal of thinking and planning.'

Astor turned aside. The way Hassock talked, it was as though they all belonged in some higher elite looking down on the gangs from far above. But the Rowdies came from the slums, just like the London street kids.

There were no more MPs going up the staircase now; instead an official in dark, old-fashioned clothing came down. He wore a massive chain of office round his neck and carried an ebony staff in one hand.

He cleared his throat and bowed towards Hassock. 'Errhem. Everyone has taken their seat, Prime Minister. The King awaits your presence.'

'Very good.' Hassock was already backing away as he addressed his last words to the band members. 'Black Rod here will assist you through the ceremony. Congratulations. Such an honour and so very well deserved.'

He hurried away up the staircase as the officer came forward to stand before them.

'Usher of the Black Rod,' he introduced himself. 'It will be my pleasure to escort you to the chamber and present you to His Majesty, King George the Fourth.'

It didn't look like a pleasure. His mouth drew down at the corners, and his whole face wore a pained expression, as though his breeches were too tight for comfort.

'I shall conduct you into the chamber on these two fingers,' he continued, raising his right hand and extending his middle and index fingers. 'Take a firm grip, one finger each, without wrenching. Stay on the carpet as I lead you forward to the King. When you come before His Majesty, bow low, then kneel.'

'Why only two fingers?' Astor asked. 'There are four of us.'

Black Rod went on with his instructions as though he hadn't heard. 'Comport yourselves with dignity and reverence at all times. No slouching, if you please. And none of your grinning or swaggering. Remember, you're not on the streets here. You're taking part in a solemn, traditional ceremony.'

Astor saw Verrol's lip curl, though he said nothing. She repeated her question in a sharper tone. 'Why only two fingers when there are four of us?'

Black Rod condescended to give a reply. 'Two candidates at a time is the form of this particular ceremony.'

Purdy spoke up. 'But we're all in it together. This is an OBE for the Rowdies.'

'It is *not*.' The contempt was unmistakable now. 'There are four separate OBEs to be awarded to four separate individuals for services to King and country. Nothing to do with any Rowdies.'

'We're a team,' Purdy persisted. 'That's how gang music works.'

'I have no idea how *gang music* works.' Black Rod appeared to have difficulty saying the words. His mouth twisted with distaste before he could manage to get them out. 'For whatever reason His Majesty saw fit to make these awards, they are certainly not for services to music.'

'Perhaps he really likes gang music,' said Verrol provocatively.

Black Rod drew himself up, tilted back his head and answered in his grandest manner. 'I can assure you that His Majesty would not even understand the meaning of the term.'

At that moment, a bell rang from the top of the staircase, and a voice called out, 'Let the candidates approach!'

Black Rod's features froze over and became an expressionless mask. In silence, he extended his middle and index fingers towards the two band members on his right: Mave and Purdy.

Mave pulled a face, and Purdy pretended to choose between fingers with an *eeny-meeny-miny-mo*. Still, they each took a finger.

Black Rod bowed, then turned and led them to the staircase. The guards stood to attention and shouldered arms as they went past.

Astor and Verrol watched them go up the stairs. Mave gave a tiny wave just before she vanished from view.

'Our turn next,' said Verrol – and Astor heard the hint of a question in his tone.

'Penny for your thoughts?' she suggested.

'I'm wondering how long we've got.'

'Before . . .?'

'Before Black Rod comes back to collect us.'

'We could just slip off first?'

Verrol grinned a wolfish grin. 'Do you really want an OBE?'

Astor shook her head. 'We already have one in the family.'

'I don't like these people.'

'They despise us. They're as bad as the other lot.'

'Nearly. The other lot wanted to declare war, and we had to stop that. But I'm not on either side.'

'Nor me. Because we're on the street kids' side.'

'The slum side.'

'The gang-music side.'

They looked at one another and laughed.

'So, shall we?'

'Let's.'

They strolled as if casually towards the glass doors at the back. But not casually enough to escape attention. The two guards dropped their statue-like poses and came after them.

'Stop!'

'Where are you going?'

The glass doors had not yet been repaired from when the street kids had broken in. With a rush of footsteps, the guards bustled forward to block the way. They held their rifles crosswise in front of the particular door that Astor was about to open.

'You can't do this!'

Astor gripped the rifle barrels and lifted them out of the way. 'I think we can.'

The guards spluttered with indignation as she turned the handle and opened the door.

'But they're expecting you!'

'You *have* to go to the ceremony!'

Astor stepped outside, and Verrol went with her. A light-filled haze hung over the sky, and the riverside gardens were vivid with colour. Scents of grass and flowers wafted on the breeze.

She wrapped her arm round his waist; he wrapped his arm round hers. Side by side, they walked off between miniature hedges, manicured lawns, flowerbeds and ornamental ponds.

The guards remained in the doorway, shaking their heads in disbelief.

'How *could* they?'

'Turning down an *OBE*!'

'They must be mad.'

'They can't get out anyway.'

But they could. The bars of the railings were still bent out of shape where the street kids had forced them apart. Astor and Verrol slipped through a gap and onto the street outside. Hansom cabs rattled past, as did a streamlined velocipede and a couple of basketwork rickshaws.

They paused just long enough to circle arms round each other's waists again. Then they turned to the right and sauntered off, disappearing in the direction of the river.

On writing **Song of the Slums**

Song of the Slums grew out of my own career as a musician, though not out of my own success, which was minimal. No long-term success anyway – but there were enough small moments along the way for me to imagine what it *might* be like.

Unlike Astor, I never played the drums, let alone the harp. Looking back now, I was at my best as a songwriter, middling as a singer, and rubbish as a guitarist. But I didn't have to be good to experience the joy of losing myself in a rhythm, bouncing off other musicians and interacting with an audience. I swear there's no higher, wilder, more wonderful feeling in the world.

So *Song of the Slums* is the musical career I never had combined with the rock 'n roll revolution the 19th century never had. Alternative-19th-century fantasy is the genre I've always gravitated towards – call it steampunk, call it gaslight romance. I'm fascinated by the atmosphere and the society, the bustles and top hats, the fogs and factories, the refined manners and hidden poverty . . . all intensified through the transforming power of fantasy.

The inspiration for this particular story goes back to the time when I was planning *Worldshaker* and googled 'steampunk images'. It was a revelation to see the steampunk guitars people have made – I mean, real playable electric guitars with brass gadgetry and copper gizmos, pipes and wires and cogs and wheels. Amazing! Those images planted an idea that eventually brought my two great loves together: the old love of playing music on stage and the new love of writing steampunk fiction.

Except . . . I should probably say 'gaslight romance' now, since invented steam-age machines retreat to the background in this novel, while the alternative Victorian setting and romance move to the fore . . .

Richard Harland, 2013

Acknowledgements

My deepest thanks go out to all the many people who saw this story through from dream to draft to finished book:

to Erica Wagner and Sarah Brenan, for believing in something different and bringing out the very best in it;

to Cathy Larsen for a stunning cover (and Katie and Tibby for turning into Astor and Verrol);

to Angela, Liz, Lara, Jyy-Wei and the whole team at Allen & Unwin who make the wheels go round;

to Selwa Anthony, my wonderful agent;

to Margo Lanagan, Rowena Cory Daniells, Tansy Raynor Roberts, Dirk Flinthart and Maxine MacArthur – the ROR gang, who critiqued the first draft at our Tasmanian retreat;

to Aileen, as always, my first best reader (my first best everything . . .);

not forgetting all the wonderful steampunk artificers around the world whose amazing steam-powered guitars and re-imagined musical instruments were the original inspiration for *Song of the Slums*.

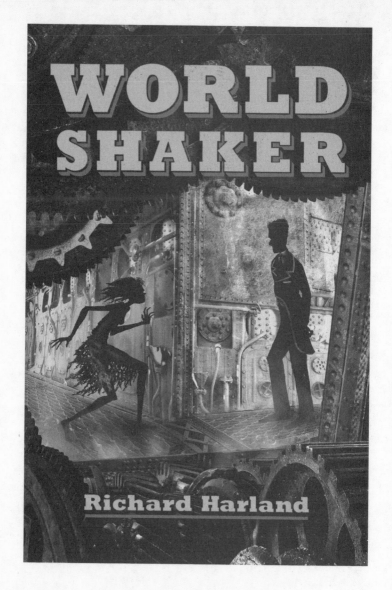

WORLD SHAKER

SHAKER

Richard Harland

'a page-turning, pulse-pounding read'
Kirkus Reviews

FROM THE CREATOR OF THE BESTSELLING *WORLDSHAKER*

LIBERATOR

Richard Harland

'Even better than the first volume (*Worldshaker*),
if that's possible!'
Revue des Livres pour Enfants

About the Author

Before achieving his dream of becoming a full-time writer, Richard Harland spent several years playing folk and rock music around Sydney, then several more years as a university lecturer. His steampunk novels, *Worldshaker* and *Liberator*, were published in Australia, US, UK, France, Germany and Brazil; *Song of the Slums* is set in an earlier period of the same imaginary 19th century world. Richard's fiction has collected six Aurealis Awards, and in 2012 he travelled to Paris to receive the prestigious Tam Tam Je Bouquine award for *Worldshaker*.

Richard lives near Wollongong, south of Sydney, between golden beaches and green escarpment. To learn more about him, visit **www.richardharland.net**

Richard has also created a website of tips on writing fantasy, SF and of course steampunk. It's 145 pages long and packed with information, at **www.writingtips.com.au**